Body Rush

Books by Anne Rainey

"Ruby's Awakening" in *Yes, Master*

Naked Games

Pleasure Bound

So Sensitive

Body Rush

"Cherry on Top" in *Some Like It Rough*

Body Rush

ANNE RAINEY

APHRODISIA

KENSINGTON PUBLISHING CORP.
www.kensingtonbooks.com

APHRODISIA BOOKS are published by

Kensington Publishing Corp.
119 West 40th Street
New York, NY 10018

All Kensington titles, imprints, and distributed lines are available at special quantity discounts for bulk purchases for sales promotion, premiums, fund-raising, and educational or institutional use.

Special book excerpts or customized printings can also be created to fit specific needs. For details, write or phone the office of the Kensington Special Sales Manager: Kensington Publishing Corp., 119 West 40th Street, New York, NY 10018. Attn. Special Sales Department. Phone: 1-800-221-2647.

Aphrodisia and the A logo Reg. U.S. Pat. & TM Off.

ISBN-13: 978-0-7582-9104-2
ISBN-10: 0-7582-9104-3

First Kensington Trade Paperback Printing: June 2010

10 9 8 7 6 5 4 3 2

Printed in the United States of America

For Lacy Danes and Teri Pray. I cannot thank you ladies enough for answering my many questions about the club scene. I hope I do you both proud!

Thanks to my very patient husband. You let me badger you nonstop with computer questions and didn't complain once. I love you with all my heart.

A special thank you to my mom. For all those times I got lost in my stories and forgot to call. You're the most understanding mother in the world. IOU a day of book shopping, as well as decadent lunch at Brios!

And of course, my beta readers. Thank you for the time, the emails, the feedback, the encouragement, and especially the friendship. I'd be a mess without you!

Contents

Prologue

The loud music hit her the instant she stepped through the doors. Lydia loved it. Going to Charlie's, her favorite hangout, after work on Friday night always helped her forget about the lawyers she worked for. There were three of them and they were all exasperating. Working at a law firm sucked in ways that most people couldn't grasp. Her only escape from the stress came when she met up with her two best friends, Roni and Jeanette. They'd known each other since grade school. While everyone else had moved on and forgotten about their school pals, the three of them had stayed in touch. Sometimes she thought they were closer now than ever. Maturity maybe. Who knew the reason, all Lydia knew for sure was that she'd be lost without them.

As she moved through the crowded room, Lydia felt someone's hand on her ass. She turned and glared at the man sitting with a group of men, all grinning like idiots. The hateful look she tossed his way must have worked because he pulled his hand back and started to scope out his next victim. Lydia spotted her friends sitting at a high round table at the back of the bar. Roni waved her over. Lydia smiled and headed toward her.

As she reached them she noticed her favorite drink, a fuzzy navel, ready and waiting. Roni moved to another chair, giving her the one on the end. "Why is it men think it's cute to grab a woman's ass? Do they really think it's going to get them laid?" Lydia shouted in an attempt to be heard over the noise. She slid onto the chair and grabbed her drink, wondering if she'd look like an alcoholic if she downed half the glass in one gulp.

"I'll never understand why men do half the things they do," Roni tossed back with an angry edge to her voice. "Trying to figure them out is a waste of time."

Jeanette leaned close and said, "There is one particular guy I wouldn't mind grabbing my ass. The only problem is I don't think he even knows I exist."

Lydia and Roni both moved closer, their attention rapt. Lydia spoke up first. "Are you still hot for that motorcycle dude coming into your café?"

Jeanette's gaze filled with unbridled lust. "If you saw him, you'd be drooling too. I'm telling you, he's the yummiest thing I've seen yet."

"You've lusted after this guy for what, a year?" Roni asked.

Jeanette laughed. "It feels that way sometimes, but it's only been about six months."

Lydia took a sip of her drink. Already she could feel herself relaxing, as if the last several days were a distant blur. She looked across the table at Roni and shook her head. She still couldn't picture her sharp-tongued friend as a psychologist. On a good day she was hard to get along with. On the other hand, Jeanette's job seemed to fit her to a T. Owning a quant little coffee shop seemed the perfect choice for her introverted friend.

"If you don't ask him out, someone else will," Lydia taunted, hoping to push her friend into making a move.

Jeanette bit her lip. "I'm so damn shy around him. He comes in with this black leather jacket and tight, faded jeans and I just want to jump him. All that dark hair and those dark eyes." She sighed. "Every time I see him I think, this is it. I'm going to ask him out. Or at least find out if he has a damned girlfriend. But I just get all tongue-tied. Like I'm in high school again." She clenched her fist around the longneck bottle of light beer she'd ordered. "It's frustrating as hell."

Roni piped up with her usual bit of sensitive logic. "He rides a motorcycle, he's gorgeous as hell and he comes to your shop every morning. Get a clue, girl; he wants to fuck you!"

Jeanette rolled her eyes. "What makes you think he wants me at all? He comes for the coffee, not the owner."

"Bullshit. He comes because you're hot and he wants to lay you across the counter. He could get coffee anywhere. Hell, he probably doesn't even live near your shop."

Lydia could see her friend's spirits perking up. "You really think so?" Jeanette asked.

Roni laughed and swallowed the last of her sex on the beach before waving the waitress over and ordering another. After the waitress had hurried off to fill their order, Roni said, "He's just watching you squirm a little. Enjoying the way you blush and stammer. It's a game. He's wondering how long you can hold out."

Jeanette started to peel the label off the beer. "I've never asked a guy out before. Usually they ask me. I'm not shy exactly, but I am a little old fashioned, I guess."

Lydia spoke up this time. "I think Roni's right. It's a new world these days. Men like it when a woman is sure of herself. You should definitely ask him out."

Jeanette's eyes grew round. "This coming from the shyest one of all?"

Lydia shrugged. "I've been doing some thinking. It's time we livened up our lives a little, don't you think?"

Roni narrowed her gaze, as if suspicious all of a sudden. "In what way?"

"I don't know," Lydia admitted as she looked down at her

half-empty drink. "It's just that we come here every Friday and nothing is ever any different. We work all week, date boring men and then come here to bitch about it. I'm getting sick of it. I'm ready for a change."

"*You* might date boring men, but that doesn't mean we all do."

Lydia knew that tone. Roni always got her back up when someone pointed out that she wasn't perfect. "Oh, really? What about that guy you went out with last weekend? You said he took you to the opera and you wanted to sleep through the whole thing it was so boring."

Roni slumped. "Men always think they're going to impress me by bringing me to some expensive restaurant or some fancy theater. Or they go the opposite route and attempt to please me by playing on my kinkier side. Just once I'd like to go out with a real man. Someone who isn't trying to impress."

"See? That's exactly what I mean. We all have these secret desires, but we don't act on them." Lydia looked at Jeanette, who'd remained silent throughout the exchange. "Just once wouldn't you like to toss caution to the wind and do something . . . wicked?"

Jeanette sat back in her chair and crossed her arms over her chest. "Yes, I would. I can't tell you how many times I've wanted to strip naked and just offer myself to Mr. Motorcycle Man. But how can I possibly do that when I don't know a thing about him? These days it pays to err on the side of caution."

Lydia nodded. "I agree we should be cautious, but that doesn't mean we can't, just this once, do something completely out of character." When Roni and Jeanette both started talking at once, Lydia held up her hand. "Hear me out. If you don't like my idea, then we'll forget I ever mentioned it. Agreed?" Both women looked at each other before giving her the floor. "Roni is ready to get down and dirty with an honest, blue-collar kind of guy. Jeanette, you're so hot for Motorcycle Man I can practically see steam coming off you. I have my own little fantasy in mind too. I say we make a bet to see who can make their fantasy come true first."

Roni snorted. "Are you serious? We're going to bet to see who can get laid faster?"

"Not just laid, dork. The bet is to see who can make their fantasy become reality."

Jeanette gasped. "I cannot believe you're suggesting this. I can see Roni suggesting something like this, she's half crazy, but you? I've never even seen you loosen the top button of your blouse, yet you're sitting there proposing we make our wildest fantasies come to life?"

Lydia's face heated. Jeanette was right. It was insane to think she could actually make her own fantasy a reality. If her friends had half a clue what she wanted to do, they'd commit her to a sanitarium. She was about to call the whole thing off when Roni spoke up

"What's the winner get?"

Jeanette's gaze swung to Roni. Lydia couldn't speak.

"You're actually considering this ludicrous bet?" Jeanette squeaked.

Roni grinned. "Why the hell not? It sounds like fun. And Lydia's right, our lives are boring as shit. While I admit I do have some pretty wild sex, there's still something missing. I want more, damn it."

Lydia wished she could be more like Roni. She took life by the horns. All Lydia could ever control was her cat, Socrates. "I haven't thought that far. What *should* the winner get? While we're at it, what does the loser have to do?"

Jeanette held up her hand. "Wait, I'm already confused. How does one lose?"

"By not making your fantasy real," Roni answered.

"So in order to win, I need to ask Mr. Motorcycle Man out?"

"Not just ask him out, but you have to do the very thing you've been dreaming of," Lydia said, already wondering what she'd gotten herself into.

"I've had a lot of dreams about that man."

"Make one of them happen and you're safe from losing," Roni said as she finished off her second sex on the beach.

Lydia took a deep breath and went for broke. "So, back to the question. What does the winner get and what does the loser have to do?"

"The winner gets to have her fantasy come to life, obviously," Roni chimed in. "The loser . . . buys the rest a round of drinks?"

"No, that's not incentive enough," Jeanette said, as if she were beginning to warm up to the idea. "The loser has to . . . strip naked and walk down main street."

Lydia shook her head. "Illegal. It can't be against the law."

"Then the loser has to clean my car," Roni tossed out.

Lydia and Jeanette both shuddered. "That's cruel and unusual punishment, Roni," Lydia said. "Damn."

Roni rubbed her hands together. "But it's legal and it's incentive enough to get you two busy."

"What makes you so sure you're going to win?" Jeanette shot right back, her back stiffening in pride.

Roni winked. "Because I never lose, honey."

Lydia sucked down the last of her fuzzy navel, then ordered another. "Okay, now for the next part of this wager. We each have to reveal our fantasy."

Jeanette shrugged. "Mine's already been revealed. I want to have wild and crazy sex with Mr. Motorcycle Man."

Roni frowned. "I want a man who wants me for me. A man who isn't out to impress."

Both women looked at Lydia. "I want to have sex with a stranger, no strings, no names, just sex." *Or maybe with two,* she thought, but she wasn't ready to admit that.

Jeanette's jaw dropped and Roni's eyes filled with awe. "Damn, I've never admired you more than I do right now," Roni mused.

Jeanette laughed and soon they were all cracking up. Deep down Lydia shook like a teenager on prom night. *What the hell did I just get myself into?*

Secret Desires

1

"Good morning, Mr. Gentry," Lydia said as Dane Gentry of the Gentry, Anderson & Dailey Law Firm strode through the door, a scowl marring his handsome face.

A grunt seemed to sum up what he thought of her chipper greeting. One thing Lydia had learned over the two years since coming to work for Dane, the man hated mornings. "Coffee's on your desk and here's your schedule for the day." She handed him the printout. If it were possible, his frown deepened as he looked her over.

"What time did you get here?"

She pushed her glasses higher on her nose and said, "Uh, five, Mr. Gentry. I had a few things to catch up on."

He rubbed his jaw. "Do I pay you overtime?"

Lydia was so confused by his question she just sat there, staring at him as if he'd lost his mind.

"Lydia, answer the question. It wasn't that hard."

"No, sir, you don't. I'm salary."

"Then it makes no sense to work overtime, now does it?"

"I suppose not, but I needed to finish up some research."

Dane shook his head. "You work too much."

Lydia was beginning to feel a spark of anger. She liked her job, but there were days when working for three lawyers really was a joke. "Are you complaining about my performance, Mr. Gentry?"

He frowned. "Of course not, but you put in way too many hours."

"Someone had to finish the research. I don't have a magic wand here . . . sir," she said, allowing a hint of sarcasm to seep into her voice.

Her boss leaned across the desk, coming way too close for comfort, and whispered, "You have a very smart mouth, Lydia. One of these days it'll get you into trouble."

Lydia tamped down the urge to move her chair closer, to inhale his clean masculine scent. She'd always had a weakness for Dane. He was so tall and broad shouldered. His messy dark hair with the little curl at the collar always made her want to reach out and play with it. Deep brown eyes watched her with an intensity that had her feeling as if someone had jacked up the temperature. It was no wonder he had so many female clients. She thought of his statement and answered, "There are times when I find my quick wit to be rather helpful, Mr. Gentry."

"Dane," he gritted out. "Will you ever call me Dane?"

"I see no reason to, no." This was an old argument between them. She stood on formalities and it drove him crazy, which was partly why she did it, of course.

"I can make it mandatory."

She laughed. "That can't be legal."

"Who gives a damn if it's legal or not?"

She was about to remind him that he was a lawyer when another voice intruded. "Is he giving you a hard way to go, sugar?"

Dane straightened and turned around. Lydia peered around Dane's massive body to see Mac Anderson striding through the door, a bagel in one hand and his briefcase in the other. Lydia went back to work mode. "Good morning, Mr. Anderson. Your schedule," she explained as she handed it over. "Don't forget you said you'd have lunch with your mom today at one."

Mac grinned and looked at Dane. "Think she'll ever call us by our first name?"

Dane snorted and crossed his arms over his chest. "Unlikely."

Mac was Dane's polar opposite. He walked around with a perpetual grin and everyone was a friend. In fact, she wasn't sure she'd ever seen the man grumpy. With his sandy blond hair and pale blue eyes, he looked more like a laidback surfer than a lawyer. His easy charm was merely a veneer though. He was every bit as sharp as Dane and just as cunning in the courtroom.

"This subject has been beaten into the ground," she replied as she pretended an interest in the e-mail she'd been going through. "You both might as well get used to the fact that I'm never going to call you by your first names. It's not professional and that's the end of it."

"Mouthy, isn't she?" Mac noted.

Out of the corner of her eye she saw Dane frown, again. "Someone needs to teach *Ms. Burke* a lesson, if you ask me."

"Someone has a meeting in half an hour and shouldn't be wasting time chatting."

"She has a point," another voice chimed in. They all three looked at the door to the office just as Trent Dailey marched through it, his movements precise, his expression serious. Lydia straightened in her chair. Trent had a way of making people check themselves. He wasn't exactly a drill sergeant, but she secretly thought he would have made an exemplary one if he ever chose to change professions. Ever the serious one, with his amber eyes, neatly trimmed black hair and powerful build, Trent rarely cracked a smile, and he always did everything with efficiency. She often felt like a slacker around him, and for a workaholic like her, that was saying something.

"If you two can find it in you to break away from the charming Ms. Burke, I have something I need to discuss with you."

Mac looked back at her and winked. "He's at it already. Look out, sugar, you could be next."

Dane didn't say another word, just growled something about coffee and stomped into his office, Trent and Mac hot on his heels.

The phone rang and she had the feeling her day was about to turn chaotic. "I just love Mondays," she mumbled, before picking it up.

Lydia had started the day with a smile, but that was well before Dane turned her world upside down. There wasn't a moment's peace. The minute she finished one task, she'd end up having fifty more dumped on her desk. And it was only noon!

"Lydia, I need you to get Gordon Michelson on the phone," Dane said. "I want to set up a meeting right away concerning his personal injury case."

"Yes, Mr. Gentry," she replied, barely containing a groan. As she closed the document she'd been working on for Mac and searched through her list of contacts for Michelson's phone number, Dane popped his head out of his office once more. "Lydia, did you do that research for the Wilson case?"

"It's not quite finished. I'll have it to you by the end of the day, sir."

"That's fine. By the way, don't forget to interview that potential client, Sam MacKenzie."

Lydia had finally reached the end of her rope. "Okay, you know what? This is too much for one person. I get a few things done and you drop a hundred more on me. I'm not a robot!"

She grabbed her purse and started for the door, aware she'd attracted the attention of her fellow coworkers. Dane was quick to intercept her. She tried to move around him, but he only grabbed her arm, halting her forward progress.

"Where are you going?"

"I need a break," she gritted out.

"I'm sorry. Don't quit, please."

She put her hand on her hip and glared up at him. "Well, of course I'm not quitting! But I am taking the rest of the afternoon off. You can get along without me that long, can't you?"

Dane leaned down and whispered into her ear, "If you don't come back tomorrow I'll come looking for you, sweetheart. I won't let you get away from me so easily."

Lydia shuddered at the sensual tone. All the time she'd worked for Dane, he'd never used that dark, mysterious tone on her. Or endearments for that matter. He wasn't like Mac, where every woman he met was either sugar or darlin', an influence of his Texas upbringing. Dane had just crossed a line, and despite warning bells going off inside her head, his wicked threat tantalized her.

As he released her arm and stepped to the side to let her pass, Lydia watched his lips tilt to one side. He was flirting with her and she was woefully unequipped to handle a man like Dane Gentry.

Lydia forced her feet to move, her entire body suddenly too warm for comfort. As she left the office building, she could swear all three men stared at her, and she had a sneaking suspicion it wasn't professional concern they had on their minds.

As soon as the office door closed, Dane let out a breath. Jesus, that was close. He'd been a heartbeat away from kissing her. That would be the wrong thing to do. Way wrong. But if that was the case, then why did he feel as if he'd lost a golden opportunity? What would she have done if he'd closed that little distance? Damn, Lydia Burke had been a fire in his blood for too long already. If he didn't do something about his fascination with her, he was going to lose it.

As he'd watched her get all authoritative and demanding,

he'd been tempted to push her to her knees and force her to submit. There was a chemistry between them. Hell, there'd always been a spark. Though he had a feeling she liked to pretend it wasn't there, Dane knew the truth. Lust, craving, obsession; whatever the label it didn't matter. It wasn't going away, not until they did something about it.

"Shit, that was close," Mac groaned. "I thought she was leaving you for good this time."

"She won't leave," Dane stated. "She knows I'd find her and bring her back."

"We've got another problem," Trent grumbled as he motioned them into his office. After he closed the door, he said, "Clyde just put in his two weeks' notice and we need to replace him."

As Dane glanced at Trent across the room, the throbbing in Dane's head gained momentum. Trent referred to the manager at Kinks, the bondage and submission club they owned. "Damn, he was the best we had so far. No one stepped out of line as long as Clyde was around," Mac said.

Dane moved toward Trent's desk and sat on the edge. "What happened?"

Trent pushed his fingers through his hair in agitation. "Hell, he always did say it wouldn't be a permanent thing for him," Trent explained. "He's getting married and his fiancée wants him to concentrate full time on the landscaping business they've set up. Being our manager wasn't really part of his five-year plan."

Dane crossed his legs at the ankles. "I met the fiancée once. She's such a damned prude, I'm surprised Clyde lasted this long."

Trent's eyes widened. "She came into Kinks?"

"No, she picked him up at the door one night; his car was in the shop. She took one look at me and went pale as a damn sheet." His lips twitched. "I think it was my leather dom hood that did it."

Mac laughed. "It's wrong for us to find amusement in that."

Dane laughed, though it felt hollow. The rest of his day would be shit because Lydia wasn't there. He never quite understood his fascination with her, which was one reason he'd kept his distance. He didn't like going into a relationship blind.

"Back to the problem at hand," Trent insisted. "We need to replace Clyde. I asked him if he knew anyone he could recommend. Of course, he didn't; that would've been too fucking easy. I thought maybe we could bump Ralph up. He's been there the longest and knows the ropes. We put him on as manager and replace his spot on the floor. It's bound to be easier to find someone to replace him, rather than taking the time to train someone new to take Clyde's position, agreed?"

Dane and Mac both nodded. Dane was the first to speak. "Fine by me."

Trent moved toward his office. "Done then. We can take care of it tonight."

Dane suddenly felt exhausted. "Did either of you think it'd be this much work to run that damned club?"

Mac arched a brow at him. "Having second thoughts?"

Dane shrugged and sat back. They'd taken over the running of the club a little over a year ago, after the previous owner had found out he had cancer. They'd grown close to Leo, so when he confided in them that he wanted the club to go to someone he knew and trusted, someone who would take care of it, they'd stepped in and made it happen. The place now made them a hefty profit. It was never about the money though, not for any of them. It was their home away from home. The only place they could truly be free to explore the darker nature of their souls. The three of them had gone to college together. It had been there that they'd discovered they shared a common passion for the kinkier side of sex. When the club had practically been dropped into their laps, it'd seemed perfect. But Dane hadn't counted on how much work was involved. Trent liked having a club to run, Mac just plain enjoyed sex, but he'd been drawn to the dom role. Still, being a club dom was fast losing its appeal.

"I don't know. I think I'm getting worn down from burning the candle at both ends."

Trent moved toward Lydia's chair and sat down. "I've been feeling the same way, but now that it's turning a profit we can start thinking of hiring more help."

Mac's usual grin was replaced by a scowl. "That could be tricky as hell, considering what we do during the day. We have to protect our interests."

"That's why we have the employees sign a confidentiality agreement and it's also why we never go out to the floor without our hoods." Trent reminded him.

The members of the club thought they wore the hoods for effect; never allowing anyone to see their faces lent to the dark mystery. The truth wasn't nearly as enticing. Dane knew the legal end was secure, but society didn't always care about laws and regulations. In the end, the general population would still view the club as a place that catered to sexual deviants. "Can you imagine if someone found out we run a BDSM club? We'd be finished as lawyers."

"It's not illegal, Dane," Trent growled. "You make it sound like we're drug lords or pimps."

"Our clients wouldn't give a damn about legalities, Trent, and you know it. They'd find a new law firm quicker than any of us could blink."

"You're forgetting one important factor here, buddy," Mac said, a mischievous gleam lighting his eyes.

"What?"

"Some of our clients are also members at Kinks. They want their privacy protected just as much as we do."

Dane nodded. "No shit. And they're way more connected than we are. We give them a place to play in safety. They'll damn near kill to keep that little privilege."

"Besides, it's not like anyone at Kinks is beyond reproach," Trent said. "I've yet to see a single goody-goody come near the place."

Trent's words brought Dane back to his talk with Lydia that morning. "Speaking of goody-goody. I'm about fed up with Lydia's constant refusal to call me by my first name. The woman's been my paralegal for two years."

"It'll never happen," Trent said, his voice resigned. "I don't know why you even bother. Lydia is way too professional. In her mind it's inappropriate. End of story."

"Damn, can you imagine her coming into Kinks?"

Mac's question tore straight through him. Hell yeah, Dane could imagine it. He'd done so a hundred different times, usually while he jacked off. "She'd faint dead away," he mused.

"There's just something sexy about that librarian getup she wears though," Trent added. "It makes me want to tear it off her and see what she keeps hidden."

"Paradise," Mac assured them. "I can feel it in my bones. That woman is built."

"Then I'm not the only one who's fantasized about my delectable paralegal?" Dane asked. Trent and Mac both shook their heads. Somehow that made Dane feel better, like less of a debaucher of virgins. "If she ever does venture into our lair, she'll be in for one helluva ride."

They all three grunted in agreement.

2

Lydia slammed her car door before pulling her cell phone out of her purse. She dialed with shaking fingers. Roni answered on the second ring.

"Hello?"

"I'm heading to lunch, do you have plans?" Lydia asked, her mind still reeling from the look on Dane's rugged face. It was the expression of a man bent on seduction, but why had it been directed at her?

"Nope, I was just heading for some fast food."

"Ah-ha!" Lydia cried. "I've saved you from a heart attack."

Roni laughed. "Most likely. Where do you want to meet?"

"How about Alejandro's?" Lydia asked, referring to one of their favorite Mexican restaurants.

Lydia heard Roni sigh. "You're determined to kill my diet, aren't you?"

"You don't need to diet; your body is perfect." Lydia secretly wished she looked as good as Roni. It seemed the older they got, the better Roni looked. It wasn't fair.

"Fine, but if my pants are tight tomorrow, I'm blaming you."

Lydia pushed the key in the ignition and started the car. "Deal, meet you there."

They hung up and Lydia sat there another few seconds to let herself calm down. *Why do I always let Dane do this to me?* She needed a vacation or she really would lose her mind.

As she put the car in gear and headed out of the parking lot, she recalled the day Dane had hired her. She'd been nervous as hell and she'd spilled coffee down the front of her tan skirt. Dane had handed her some tissues, a kind smile tilting his sexy lips. Trent had frowned at her as if she'd spilled the coffee on him instead of her. Mac had simply winked. Flustered and near tears she excused herself and nearly bolted for the restroom. When she'd finally managed to face Dane again, he'd offered her the job and told her she could start right away. She'd always wondered why he'd bothered to hire her. She'd been a total klutz, completely unprofessional, and yet he'd taken her under his wing.

She hadn't worked in a legal office before, so the first few weeks had been murder on both of them. She'd made a mess of everything, from accidently deleting documents to overlapping meetings. If anyone had deserved to be fired, she had.

Lydia rounded a corner as she pondered the big question: Why had he kept her on? She hadn't been the most qualified, not by a long shot. She wasn't even all that attractive, so it wasn't for the eye candy. As she pulled into the parking lot of Alejandro's restaurant and found a space, her mind glommed on to that look on Dane's face. She might not have known what she was doing two years ago, but she knew exactly what she was doing now, just as she knew that look. It said seduction. Her body warmed as she imagined being the object of Dane's lust. There wasn't a doubt in her mind he'd be something else in bed. She'd witnessed him when he was attracted to a woman. The few times he'd let his dates meet him at the office Lydia had glimpsed a rougher, more primitive side to her boss. What would it be like if all that sexual aggression was focused on her?

Lydia shook the thought away. That road led to disaster. Clearly it'd been too long since she'd had sex. Daydreaming about Dane wasn't what he was paying her for. He would never mix business with pleasure anyway so there really wasn't any reason to let her imagination go hog wild. Right?

A tap on her window yanked her from her thoughts. Roni stood outside her car giving her a what's up look and motioning for her to hurry up. Lydia turned off her engine, grabbed her keys and purse and hurried out of the car. "Sorry, my mind seems to be somewhere else today."

"I gathered," Roni mused as they walked together into the restaurant.

Lydia's stomach rumbled as the aroma of burritos and salsa hit her nose. They were led to a comfortable booth near the back, away from everyone else. They gave the hostess their drink order and settled in. After the woman left, Roni looked across the table and asked, "Want to talk about it?"

"Dane is making me insane," Lydia gritted out. "I feel like I never have a chance to catch my breath and it's making me want to make a break for it."

Roni crossed her arms, a stern look settling over her features. "Did you tell him he needed to give you more time off? You have a high-stress job, Lydia. You'll burn out at this rate."

Heat flooded her cheeks as she started to pick at her paper placemat. "Not exactly. I sort of stormed out."

Roni's eyes went round. "You didn't!"

For the first time in hours Lydia felt her muscles relax. "Actually, I did. And he even begged me not to quit."

Roni grinned. "Wow, I'm impressed."

"Don't be. I told him I wasn't quitting." Lydia's shoulders slumped. "I have the hardest time standing up to him."

"You always have the hardest time standing up to people. You're a pushover. A sweet pushover, but still a pushover."

Their waiter came and left two bowls of salsa and a basket of chips before glancing up at Roni. He licked his lips and stared, then dropped his order pad. He leaned down and picked it up, his face red when he stood back up again. As he stammered out a welcome, Roni grinned. *Ah, the goddess strikes again,* Lydia thought. It had been a joke between her and Jeanette that only Roni had the ability to make men of all ages stammer and drool. After Roni ordered her usual fajitas, he finally realized there were two people at the table. Lydia ordered two enchiladas and sour cream and shook her head as she watched him stride off. "You do realize that with you around, I'm pretty much invisible, right?"

"If you'd let me help you with your wardrobe a little, that wouldn't happen. I told you before you're a babe, you just like to hide it."

Her anger rose. "I dress like a professional. My job requires it."

"You hide," she simply stated. "You still think like that little Catholic girl your mother raised. It's not a sin to look attractive, Lydia, despite what your mother used to harp about."

Lydia wanted to rail at Roni, but considering she was dead-on accurate, it would be a waste of time. Her mother had wielded her rosary like a whip. She'd tried to beat it into her that ladies should be seen and not heard, to honor thy mother and father, obey thy husband. Lydia had always felt like a huge disappointment because she'd never quite measured up. After her parents' divorce, Lydia had gone to live with her dad, and she'd felt like an even bigger disappointment. It didn't seem to matter that her mom had never really wanted her. After her father had died from a heart attack, Lydia had never heard from her mother again.

"Don't," Roni warned, as if reading her thoughts. "I'm sorry

I brought it up. But I do wish you'd loosen up a little. It's okay to let loose, honey."

Their food arrived and Lydia just shook her head. "I should be eating lighter. I always eat when I'm upset, which seems to happen a lot lately."

"We all eat when we're upset. Besides, your metabolism doesn't seem fazed."

They both went silent as they ate; the waiter came back three times to ask Roni if she needed anything. Lydia didn't even bother to point out that she'd run out of diet pop two visits ago.

As she finished off the second enchilada an image of her mother binging on chips and cookies sprang to mind. Lydia dropped her fork. It hit the side of the plate with a clang and fell to the floor. She didn't bother to pick it up, she was too numb to move. "Oh, God, I've turned into my mom."

Roni choked on her pop. Several seconds later, she squeaked out, "You've done what?"

"Look at me, Roni, really look. My mother used to eat when she was upset. She used to dress in clothes every bit as conservative as mine, and do you know the last time I had sex?"

"Uh, no," she said, a note of concern in her voice.

"It was with that dork, Philippe. He was so lame I couldn't wait to get him out of my apartment. How pathetic is that?"

"That guy really was a dork. I hated that nasally laugh, and the way he used to go on and on about himself made me want to hit him."

"See what I mean?" Lydia's voice rose a notch as her hysteria grew. "Maybe half the reason I'm so stressed at work is because my personal life has gone down the toilet. I'm a younger version of my bible-thumping mom."

Roni rolled her eyes and reached across the table to grab her hand. "That's a load of crap and you know it. You are not your mother. Maybe you need to loosen up a little, but that doesn't mean there's anything wrong with you, Lydia."

"But what if—"

"No what ifs. I'm a psychologist remember? I say there isn't a damn thing wrong with you."

"You're my friend; you have to tell me that," Lydia bit out.

"You're letting that boss of yours make you crazy. Just chill, I have a plan."

Lydia sighed in relief and sat back. "Thank God. I really need a plan right now."

Roni bit her lip, as if unsure how to proceed. Lydia had never seen Roni unsure. It was more than a little disconcerting. "Do you remember me telling you about that club I go to sometimes called Kinks?"

"Yeah, but what does a fitness club have to with anything?"

Roni blushed. Right there in the middle of Alejandro's restaurant, Roni Smart actually turned red. If Lydia hadn't seen it she never would have believed it was possible for Roni to feel embarrassment. Suddenly Lydia wasn't so sure she wanted to hear any more of Roni's plan.

"It's not a fitness club."

Confused, Lydia asked, "What is it then?"

"It's a BDSM club."

The acronym meant nothing to her. "Huh?"

"Bondage and submission." Lydia was still confused so Roni explained further. "You know, masters and submissives, whips and masks."

Roni was into kinky sex games? How could she not have known about that? They'd been closer than friends for years. Hell, they were practically sisters. Roni was watching her, worry pulling at her brow. Lydia wasn't sure what to say. "Oh, uh. Wow."

"It's not so strange," Roni grumbled. "Don't look so horrified, damn it."

"I didn't say it was strange. Just . . . shocking. I never knew you liked that sort of thing."

"Yeah, well, we aren't sleeping together, so how could you know?"

Lydia's lips twitched. "Okay, you got me there. But, what does any of this have to do with me?"

"I'd like to bring you there, as a guest."

Lydia knew she couldn't have heard right. "Can you say that again?"

"You and me at Kinks Friday night. Is that clear enough for you?"

"Yep, that pretty much clears it up." Lydia looked around the restaurant, wondering if anyone could read lips.

Roni blinked several times before asking, "Then you'll go?"

Lydia's gaze shot to hers. "Not on your life."

"So you don't trust me, is that it? You think I'd take you someplace depraved, teaming with pervs?"

"Of course not, it's just that—"

Roni pushed her plate away and sat back. "Be honest, Lydia, you think it's weird."

Lydia didn't want to hurt her friend, but she wasn't about to be led into something she had no experience with either. "Uh, sort of, yeah."

"Come with me Friday night. Let me show you how wrong you are."

"What makes you think I'd ever say yes to this? I'm not into that sort of thing, Roni. I'm not judging you, but it's not my scene."

"I'm not saying I know your sexual preferences, but I do know you need something to shake you out of this lull you're in." Roni looked her over, then said, "Besides, you might just surprise yourself."

Lydia shook her head. "Do I have to do anything? Like have sex or something?"

Roni laughed. "Don't be ridiculous. It's not like that. There's just music and a lot of people enjoying a common passion. I won't lie to you, it can be shocking at first because you'll see people doing various sexual things. But all you need to do is stick with me, observe and who knows, maybe you'll meet someone."

"Various sexual things?""

Roni bobbed her eyebrows. "Yeah, it's sort of hot to watch."

"I can't believe I'm actually considering this. What do I even wear?"

Roni cocked her head to the side. "I think I have something that would fit you. A sexy skirt. We need to show off your assets a little."

Her clothes were her shield and she wasn't comfortable losing it. "I'm really not sure about this, Roni."

"Your fantasy was to have sex with a stranger. This is a good opportunity to make that fantasy a reality."

"But bondage and submission? That's a little out of my comfort zone. Hell, that's a lot out of my comfort zone."

"How do you know if you've never tried it?" Lydia still hesitated, which prompted Roni to plead her case a little more. "Let me ask you this then: When you sleep with a man, do you prefer he take the lead or do you like to take the lead?"

That one was easy; she'd always preferred the man to run the show. "I like it when he leads."

Roni nodded. "I thought as much, though I do think you have a bit of a dominatrix in you too."

Lydia couldn't begin to wrap her mind around that little tidbit so she didn't even try. "Your point is?"

"Can you really tell me you aren't intrigued by the idea of meeting some gorgeous stranger and having him dominate you? Don't you think it'd be just a little exciting to explore that forbidden side of your nature?"

Lydia imagined meeting some tall, dark-haired man. Someone who knew how to please a woman, who knew how to wring every last drop of pleasure out of an orgasm. It wasn't a bad image. And for some reason it vaguely resembled Dane. Damn, she needed to get that man out of her mind. "Yes, it's intriguing," she blurted out.

Roni's face lit with excitement. "Then come with me. Who knows, maybe we'll both get to fulfill our fantasies and then we'll win the bet."

Lydia frowned. "Is this cheating? Should we tell Jeanette?"

The waiter came with their checks. Roni winked at him and he sauntered off practically whistling. "It's not cheating," Roni replied. "Stop worrying."

Lydia couldn't believe what she'd just agree to. Had she lost her mind completely?

Roni stood and grabbed her purse from the seat beside her. Lydia followed suit. As they left the restaurant, Roni turned to her and said, "No second guessing this. It'll be fine, you'll see."

"Friday nights I usually watch all my shows that I've recorded throughout the week."

"Quit making lame excuses. Come over to my place early so we can get you ready."

Lydia laughed. "Uh, we're so not the same size, Roni."

Roni hugged her, then stepped back. "Don't be such a pest. Just come over and I'll take care of the rest."

"Fine, but Roni?"

"Yeah?"

"I'm only going for the drinks and music, and maybe because I'm a little curious, but that's it."

"We'll see," she replied, then walked away, waving at Lydia over her shoulder.

3

Lydia still couldn't believe she'd agreed to go to a bondage and submission club. What had she been thinking? Roni had always been good at talking her into things, but this time Lydia could very well be in over her head.

After Roni wiggled an agreement out of her to go with her on Friday night, Lydia had gone back to her apartment, intent on sticking to her plan to take the rest of the day off. The responsible thing would've been to go back to work. Dane could be looking for her replacement even now. As she sipped her diet cola and stroked her spoiled cat, Socrates, her mind conjured up the image of Dane just before she'd stomped out. His sensual smile and the heat in his gaze could melt a glacier, but why had it been directed at her? The doorbell rang, disrupting her thoughts. Lydia was only too grateful for the interruption. If she kept thinking about Dane Gentry she'd surely go insane.

She moved Socrates to the cushion next to her, smiling when the sleepy animal let out a disgruntled growl. "I'll give you a treat later," Lydia promised, before heading toward the door. As she opened it, her heart nearly stopped beating.

"Mr. Gentry," Lydia cried, "what are you doing here?"

"Dane," he gritted out. "Will you ever call me Dane?"

Lydia almost smiled at his disgruntled tone. "Probably not."

He pointed behind her. "Care to let me in?"

She should tell him to go away—the last thing she needed was his powerful presence destroying her control and invading her personal space—but a naughty voice in her head urged her to take a chance. She stepped aside. "Please, come in."

Thanks," he murmured as he moved around her, his hard body brushing against her curves. God, the man was deliciously muscular. Just that simple touch and she could feel the strength beneath his black slacks and white dress shirt.

Electricity arced between them and Lydia had to force herself to keep it cool, casual. He'd most likely come to see if she really was planning to return to work. His visit had nothing whatsoever to do with lusty cravings.

"Can I get you a drink?" Lydia asked, as she watched him move about her living room. She tried to pry her eyes away from his firm ass, but she wasn't very successful. She was only human after all. "I-I have cola and iced-tea or I can make a pot of coffee, if you prefer." Damn, she was babbling.

"Nothing for me, but thanks," he said as he looked at her bookshelves, then his attention caught on the pictures hanging on one wall. There was only one predivorce family photo, the rest were pictures of herself with her best friends Jeanette and Roni.

"Is this your mom and dad?"

She really didn't want to discuss her parents. "Yes."

"You have your dad's eyes."

"Thanks."

His gaze went over her body before he replied. "You resemble your mom, but to tell the truth, you're prettier."

She didn't know what to say to that, so she stayed silent. As he moved closer, her body temperature spiked. "Why only the one picture of your parents?"

"My dad died six years ago, he had a heart attack. My mother and I don't speak."

"I'm sorry." He shoved his hands in his pockets. "I'm not terribly close with either of my parents. They're both workaholics. I don't think having a child was part of their plan. I learned long ago to stay out of their way."

Her heart went out to him. She, better than anyone, understood the need for a parent's love. "My dad and I were close; he was very loving. Mom always had a rather depressing outlook on life though. I never quite lived up to her expectations."

His gaze held a wealth of emotion as he stared down at her. "Her loss."

Lydia shrugged. "Surely you didn't come here to talk about my parents."

A muscle in his jaw twitched. "No, I wanted to know if you were serious about coming back to work."

"Yes. I'm sorry for storming out the way I did. I'm just feeling stressed."

"It's my fault." He reached out and stroked her cheek. Lydia had to bite her lip to keep herself from leaning into his touch. "You work too hard, Lydia."

"It's a high-stress job." She cleared her suddenly dry throat. "More vacation time would be helpful."

"I agree. I'm sorry for not thinking of it sooner," he murmured.

"Is that all you wanted, Mr. Gentry?"

"No," he whispered as his fingers continued to caress her cheek. Lydia had never felt so turned on by a mere touch. "I wanted to ask you something. And I want you to be honest with me."

"I'm always honest with you," she said, unable to contain the desire coursing through her.

"Are you attracted to me, Lydia?"

Lydia put her hand against his chest in attempt to push him away. He didn't budge and she suddenly became pleasantly distracted by the hard body beneath her fingers. "You're my boss," she squeaked. "This isn't appropriate."

When he dropped his hand and stepped back, giving her distance, Lydia knew she should be grateful he wasn't going to push her, but she already missed the connection.

"I know," he growled. "I shouldn't even be here. Staying away didn't seem like a good idea either though. I've tried that and it hasn't worked out so well."

Lydia recognized his disgruntled tone, but she couldn't allow him to breach her defenses. It would be way too easy to lose herself in a man like Dane. "I don't know what you want from me."

He shoved his fingers through his hair, a scowl marring his handsome features. "I want to know the truth. I want to know that I'm not the only one fighting an attraction here."

Lydia looked down at the floor and took a deep breath, then let it out slowly. She should tell him to leave. Keep things professional. She should never let him see how vulnerable she could be to him. "Please," she groaned.

He stepped forward and cupped her chin, forcing her to look at him. "I'm not going to push for more just because you admit you're attracted to me, sweetheart. Just put me out of my misery. I'm begging here."

The sincerity in his chocolate brown gaze tore at the last threads of her defenses. "I call you Mr. Gentry because it reminds me that you're my boss and I shouldn't let my feelings get in the way of work," she admitted.

Dane smiled and leaned down, placing a gentle kiss to her forehead. "And how's that working for you?"

"Not well," she muttered as she pushed her glasses higher on her nose.

He chuckled. "It doesn't seem to matter how hard I try, Lydia, I still can't seem to stop thinking about you."

Lydia couldn't believe her ears. Surely she was dreaming. "You think about me?"

He dropped his hand and stepped backward. "If I told you I've fantasized about you, would it shock you?"

It was too good to be true. In fact, she wondered if he was playing her. Men didn't fantasize about dowdy women. They fantasized about women like Roni. "You've always dated women that were model perfect. I'm not even close."

He tilted his head to one side. "You think because you dress conservatively that men can't possibly be attracted to you?"

Lydia let her silence speak for her. She had a mirror; she knew what she looked like.

Dane shook his head, his thumb stroking her lower lip. "You don't know how wrong you are. You're the whole package, Lydia. An intelligent, honest, pretty, kind woman who has me in knots every single time I see her. One of these days I'm going to show you how desirable you are, inch by inch, then we'll see."

Oh, God, she'd never survive it.

"Until then, there's this . . ." his voice trailed off as he leaned close and touched his lips to hers. It was soft, undemanding, and Lydia melted. He slipped an arm around her middle and pulled her in close before he slid his tongue along the seam of her lips. She sighed and gave him entrance. Dane delved inside, tasting her as if starved. She wrapped her arms around his neck and let out a moan as he worked her into a fever pitch. When he pushed his hips forward, Lydia felt the rigid length of his cock. Her body ached for him to fill her, driving them both over the edge of pleasure.

Little by little he pulled his mouth free, but he kept his strong arm tight around her waist. His brown gaze was nearly black as he murmured, "You taste sweeter than I imagined, baby."

Lydia shuddered, already aching for more. "We shouldn't—"

He placed two fingers against her lips. "Shh, it was just a kiss."

Lydia's cheeks heated. "Of course."

"I want you to think about us together. Will you do that for me, baby?"

She let out a nervous laugh. "After a kiss like that? I don't think I have a choice," she whispered.

He dropped his arm and stepped back. "Ah, but that was just the beginning. A mere teaser. I'm going to make you beg, baby, and it's going to be so fucking sweet too." He moved toward the door and opened it, then turned. "And no more Mr. Gentry either."

Lydia watched him close the door behind him. She could barely catch her breath as she collapsed onto the couch, her blood rushing through her veins. "What just happened?" she murmured as she touched her lips, not surprised to find them still warm from his scorching touch. Beg? Hell, she wasn't far from it now and all because of a kiss. What would it be like if they actually made it the bedroom?

Nope, she'd never survive it.

Lydia had made it through the rest of the week without begging Dane for another of his delicious kisses, which was a miracle. Each time he looked at her, she could feel his lips all over again. His wicked smiles told her he knew exactly what she was thinking too. He'd called her at home Thursday night, but she'd been too much the coward to pick up the phone. When he'd seen her the next morning, she'd known the challenge in his gaze was meant for her alone. He wouldn't let her pretend the kiss had never taken place. Part of her was thrilled, but part of her still worried where it would all lead.

Now it was ten minutes after eight Friday night and she stood horrified in Roni's penthouse apartment bedroom staring into the dresser mirror. "This can't be legal." She turned and stared at her ass. "This skirt is way too tight, short and . . . leathery. Also, I can see my nipples through this shirt."

"You look hot. Quit bitching."

Lydia pushed her glasses up her nose and said, "I look like a prostitute. A near-sighted prostitute at that."

Roni stopped adjusting her black corset. "Are you saying my clothes are slutty?"

"I'm saying on you they look sexy, on me they look abnormal."

Roni looked at her from head to toe. "I was going to suggest you take your hair down, but I think it actually looks better up. This place has a 'no costume, no entry' rule. And you have this strange librarian fetish look going on with the glasses and the bun. I didn't see it before, but combined with that leather skirt and that sheer top, you're going to be the hit of the ball."

Lydia wasn't sure why she'd agreed to wear the pink chiffon blouse. It had an elastic neckline and cuffs, with a hem that fell below the waist. The black bra and waist cincher made it look deliciously sexy . . . for the bedroom. Wearing it inside a club for others to see had her knees knocking together. The fishnet stockings seemed to bring the outfit together. As she looked at her body, she had a strange feeling that she was really staring at her evil twin.

"You know, you could have told me about the costume rule," Lydia admonished. "I would've been better prepared."

"You would've made an excuse and backed out, you mean."

It sucked when your friends knew you so well. "Probably."

Roni took a bottle of red wine from the dresser and poured them each a glass. Lydia picked up her glass before Roni could bother to hand it to her. As she sipped it, Roni finished dressing. She really shouldn't be surprised that Roni had such erotic clothing, but seeing her best friend dressed in a tight-fitting black latex catsuit and knee-high boots was a little shocking.

With her blond hair pulled into a tight, high ponytail, Roni exuded confidence and sex appeal. The men at the club must drool every time she walks through the doors. She didn't resemble Roni the psychologist at all. All she needed was a leather whip and a man on his knees begging to please her and her look would be complete.

"You ready?" Roni asked, her tone one of concern.

Lydia's nerves were shot, but she nodded anyway.

Roni grabbed her hand and pulled her out of the bedroom. As they picked up their purses, Roni looked her over one more time and shook her head. "I can't believe it's really you. Damn, girl, you're hot! You're going to drive the doms crazy, honey, trust me."

Lydia wrapped her arms around her waist. "I'm not sure I want to drive anyone crazy," she said, her voice rising as hysteria began to set in. "I'm not even sure why I let you talk me into this."

Roni opened the door to her apartment and ushered her through it. As she turned the lock and started down the hall, she said, "Because you need this and we both know it. And because you trust me not to get you into anything you can't handle."

When she put it like that, there really wasn't anything more to be said. As they arrived at the elevator, the doors opened and a man stepped out. His gaze roamed over Roni first, then Lydia. Her face heated as he lingered on her chest. When their eyes met, he smiled. Lydia wanted to sink into the carpet and disappear. Roni tugged her onto the elevator. As the doors shut she noticed the man hadn't moved, and just before the doors shut, he winked.

Lydia covered her face and groaned.

Roni laughed. "You'd better get used to it; that's going to happen a lot over the course of the evening."

"Get used to it?" Lydia cried. "I'm ready to make a break for it here!"

Roni tsked. "Don't be a chicken shit."

That had her standing straighter. "I'm not a chicken shit; I'm an introvert. There's a difference."

The elevator dinged, indicating they'd arrived at their floor. As the doors opened, Lydia held her breath, worried they'd run into another man. This time there were no gawkers, just the silence of the lobby.

Roni stepped out, then stopped when she realized she was alone. Lydia couldn't seem to get her feet to move. As the doors started to close, Roni slammed her hand against the opening. "Not a chicken shit, huh?"

Lydia gritted her teeth against the need to tell her friend to stick it where the sun doesn't shine and stepped out of the elevator. Roni removed her hand and said. "Now was that so hard?"

"Kiss my ass," Lydia shot right back.

"FYI, that's not something you're going to want to say at Kinks."

They both burst out laughing as they made their way to the parking garage. Lydia relaxed a fraction when she slipped inside Roni's black Corolla.

Roni started the car and turned toward her. "Ready?"

"As I'll ever be."

Roni's face lit with excitement. "Let's go play."

4

It wasn't at all what Lydia expected. After she'd read through the rules and regulations, which were quite detailed, and signed on the dotted line, Roni had escorted her to the Great Room, which consisted of a large comfortable sitting area and several high round tables and stools along the outer edge of the room. Lydia tried not to gawk, but really, who wouldn't? She noticed several couples kissing and touching, and it aroused her in a way she never expected.

Her body heated instantly when she noticed a man sliding the handle of a whip up a woman's thigh until it disappeared beneath her skirt. The woman flung her head back, her eyes closed as if in rapture. Lydia could imagine the leather handle sliding inside the woman's pussy, or maybe her ass—and the thought made her tingle. When he pushed the whip deeper the woman's mouth dropped open as if on a scream. Lydia's pussy grew damp as she imagined the feel of the leather parting her swollen lips and sinking deep. She quickly looked away when the man spotted her watching.

A pair of blond women seated on the floor next to an overstuffed chair caught her attention. They each had a leather collar around their necks with a metal ring in the front, which attached to a leash. The man holding the pair of leashes was a large African American dressed from head to toe in black leather. He gazed down at both women with affection and said something to one of them, who immediately started to lick the other woman's nipple through the sheer blouse she wore. The man petted her and continued to carry on a conversation with another man seated across from him. He had his own submissive seated on the floor between his thighs. Lydia's jaw nearly dropped when she spied the woman's fingers wrapped around his exposed cock. She slowly stroked him, teasing the head with her thumb, fondling it as if she were in a room alone instead of in a room full of people.

Lydia felt as if she were on sensory overload. Her nipples tingled and her pussy had already soaked clear through her panties. As she let her gaze sweep the room, she noticed several men watching her, lust in their eyes. Suddenly, Lydia was grateful for the low lighting. It gave her just enough courage to keep from bolting out the door. She stayed close to Roni as they reached one of the round tables along the edge of the room. Roni pulled one of the stools out and sat down. When Lydia started to do the same she realized just how tricky an endeavor it would prove to be, considering the tight skirt allowed no room for movement. It took all her concentration just to get in the chair without exposing herself to one and all.

Roni pointed upward and Lydia's gaze followed until she spotted another level. "What's up there?"

"That's what's known as the Upper Dungeon. That's one of the areas where members can play."

"Dungeon? That sounds so . . . medieval."

Roni nodded. "It sort of is, I guess. There are suspension racks, bondage tables, even a spanking bench. Would you like to go up and see it?"

Lydia shook her head, her heart pounding too fast. "I think I'm good right here."

Roni looked over her shoulder, her eyes widening. "We've attracted the attention of the owners it seems."

Lydia swiveled around and watched in awe as three large men with leather hoods walked toward her. They all wore jeans and black T-shirts with the words GET YOUR KINK ON in bold white letters across the chest. The half-hoods the three men wore effectively concealed their identity but kept the lower half of their face visible. They were well over six feet and had just enough muscle to make a woman pant. The man on the left had midnight black hair and amber eyes that seemed to see clear to her soul. The one in the middle had sandy blond hair and a flirty half smile, while the man on the right had chocolate brown hair that curled at the ends. For some strange reason he looked familiar. As if she'd seen that curl before. They all three looked intimidating as hell.

"Clyde tells me you have a guest this evening. Care to introduce me?" The deep timbre traveled the length of her spine as the man with the chocolate brown hair spoke to Roni.

"Lydia, this is Apollo, Zeus and Poseidon," Roni answered, as she gestured to each man in turn. "They own Kinks."

Lydia quirked her brow and stared at the one called Apollo. There was something about that brown hair and those mesmerizing eyes. She'd seen him before, she would swear to it. "The names of Gods?"

"The nicknames are necessary to preserve our privacy," Apollo explained. "What brings you to Kinks, Lydia? Are you new to the scene?"

"Very new."

"Can I give you a tour of the place then? It might make you feel better if you know what we're all about."

Lydia looked at Roni. She nodded. Lydia started to step off the stool, but Apollo was quicker. He wrapped his hands around her waist and lifted her in the air, then set her on her feet, directly in front of him. This close she could smell his woodsy scent. "Uh, thanks."

He started walking and she tried to stay in step beside him, but it wasn't easy with his long strides. He slowed his pace and one side of his lips kicked up as he looked over at her. "That skirt doesn't allow much room, does it?"

She laughed. "No, it really doesn't."

When he held out his elbow, Lydia stopped walking and stared at it, unsure what to do. His brown eyes seemed to be daring her. He leaned down and whispered, "Afraid I bite?"

"Around here, yeah," she muttered.

Apollo laughed and she heard a few snickers coming from behind her. She turned, frowning at the two men. "Do you two intend to follow?"

The black-haired Poseidon shrugged. "What can I say, we like to watch."

Lydia rolled her eyes and looked at the other man, who had yet to speak, he merely grinned at her. "You two are in for a boring night then, because I'm not all that exciting."

Apollo asked, "If that's the case, then why are you here?"

"I let my friend talk me into it." Lydia pointed toward herself. "I've been having second thoughts since I put on this outfit."

Apollo looked her over, his gaze resting on her breasts for several seconds. "You have a beautiful body, Lydia."

Lydia's face heated. "Thank you."

"If you dress like this all the time you must hear compliments like that quite often. In fact, I'm surprised you aren't here with a man."

Lydia barely contained a snort. "Well, I'm not seeing anyone at the moment, and I can assure you this is not how I normally dress."

"I see," he said, then held out his arm once more.

This time Lydia slipped her arm through his. His expression turned darker, more wicked, as if she'd just accepted an invite to his bed. She tried to force herself to breathe normally, concentrating on not tripping and making a fool of herself. As they reached a staircase, he let her go ahead of him. Lydia grasped the railing and carefully made her way up to the second level, trying not to think about the three men following behind her, possibly seeing up her skirt. When she reached the upstairs landing, Apollo was right there, taking her arm again. "In this place it's always a good idea to be with someone," he explained. "Or at least appear that you are. A beautiful woman alone attracts a lot of attention."

"I'm not beautiful," she corrected him. "Please don't let the sexy clothes fool you. I'm a slightly round and horribly nearsighted paralegal. That's the real me."

Apollo touched the edge of her frames with his finger, tracing them as he murmured, "The glasses and the way you wear your hair, it's like something out of an adult fetish film. You look like a naughty librarian and it's damn sexy, Lydia. Didn't you know that?"

"N-no, I didn't know that." Lydia couldn't move, could only stand there while Apollo touched her frames. When his finger stroked over the skin of her cheek she shuddered.

"Is your boss a man?"

"Uh, yes. Actually, three men."

"I bet they've noticed. I bet they've even fantasized about you."

Lydia shook her head, unable to catch her breath. "No, they'd never see me that way." Well, it was just a little lie.

"Don't be so sure," he said as he dropped his finger. "Turn around."

Lydia obeyed, there wasn't any other choice. They stood in front of a doorway to another room. A woman was spread out on a table, her ankles and wrists bound as a man dribbled hot wax down her belly. She moaned and writhed, much to the man's delight. Another man lay over a bench, his bare ass in the air as a woman in an outfit much like Roni's black catsuit wielded a wooden paddle like a pro. She swatted him and the man begged for more. Lydia's clit throbbed as she imagined what it must feel like.

"Have you ever been spanked, Lydia?"

She swiveled around on her heel. "Certainly not."

All three men stood close, only a few feet away, their gazes locked on hers. Apollo closed the gap between them and leaned down until their lips were but a breath away from each other. "You shouldn't mock what you've never tried," he chastised, then he pressed his lips to hers, gentle and teasing. At the first contact, Lydia went rigid, unsure if she should push him away and demand an apology or pull him in closer. When his hand cupped the back of her head and she heard him emit a low growl, she gave in and melted against his hard body. She wrapped her arms around his neck and angled her head for a deeper kiss. His tongue came out and swept over the seam before biting gently down on her plump lower lip.

"Open those sweet lips, baby, let me in," he softly ordered.

Lydia sighed and Apollo sank his tongue deep, licking and tasting, playing with her tongue. He rained kisses over both her cheeks before drifting lower and teasing the side of her neck. Lydia knew she should stop him, push him away and go back to Roni. When he skimmed his tongue up and down her flesh, directly over her vein, it was all she could do to keep from coming right then and there. He bit down and her pussy pulsed and swelled with need. Her hands moved lower until she clutched at his shoulders, fingernails biting into flesh and muscle. She closed her eyes and gave herself over to the moment. His mouth moved lower, skimming over the tops of her breasts. When he kissed each nipple through her clothes, her legs shook with anticipation.

"Come with us," he growled. "Let us show you pleasure."

Us, he'd said. Lydia pulled back, breathing as if she'd run a marathon. "Oh God, what am I doing? I-I should get back to Roni."

"Lydia, look over the railing," Apollo demanded.

Lydia looked down at the Great Room below, easily spotting Roni's blonde ponytail. Lydia couldn't believe what she was witnessing. Roni stood in a corner of the room with a kneeling man's face pressed against her latex-covered crotch. Roni petted the massive man's bald head as he ground his face against her harder.

"As you can see, she's quite happily engaged at the moment. Come with us, Lydia, we won't hurt you, you have my word."

Lydia looked up at Apollo, then over at the other two men, who'd stayed silent and watchful throughout the exchange. She could still taste the intoxicating flavor of Apollo's kiss. "Why me?"

A glimmer of sexual heat lit Apollo's eyes as he lowered his head toward her ear. "Because we've always had a fondness for naughty librarians."

And just like that, she caved.

5

"An attached apartment?" Lydia asked as she was led into a room on the third floor. Apollo flipped a switch by the door and light flooded the room. The interior had been decorated in sleek, modern furniture. A black leather couch and loveseat sat in the center. A long oak bar ran along one wall. Along another wall sat a strange black padded bench with metal rings all along the sides. She had no idea what that was for. A forty-two-inch high-definition, flat-panel television sat on a shelf imbedded into the wall above the bench.

Apollo shrugged. Poseidon and Zeus moved to the bar and took out a couple of glasses, then poured some amber-colored liquid in each of them.

"While it's interesting to watch the others downstairs," Apollo answered, "we prefer our privacy."

"Do you bring women up here often?" For some reason the thought made her angry. She didn't want to imagine the tall, dark-haired man in front of her entertaining other women in this room.

He walked a few feet and picked up a remote control from a shelf. "Do you really want to know?"

"Not really," Lydia admitted as he pushed a button and the lights dimmed. Another button had soft music filling the air. Not at all like the hard pumping bass from downstairs, this music was soulful and seductive.

Poseidon and Zeus leaned against the bar, their gazes on her. Lydia pulled her purse off her shoulder and took out her cell phone. "I need to call Roni. I don't want her to worry."

Apollo nodded. "Of course, we'll give you some privacy."

Lydia dialed Roni's number as the three hooded men went through a doorway into another room. She couldn't stop herself from wondering what was through that doorway. A bedroom or something more? As she remembered the dungeon from downstairs, Lydia shook her head. "Scratch that, I don't want to know."

Roni picked up on the second ring. "Where are you?"

She sounded worried and for some reason it calmed Lydia a little. "I'm fine. I'm still with the owners."

"They want you," Roni stated. "I could see it in their expressions. Be careful, they're all three dominants and they know what they're doing, whereas you're a newbie."

"I know. I think Apollo must run the show though, because the other two follow his lead."

"That doesn't surprise me. I've seen him in action. He's something else. Are you sure you know what you're doing?"

Lydia slumped against the door. "To tell you the truth, I have no idea what I'm doing. I should probably just leave now."

"It's your choice," Roni said, her tone softening. "Say the word and I'll come and get you. I don't care if they do kick both our asses out."

Lydia straightened, alarmed at the thought of never seeing Apollo again. Never experiencing another of his scorching kisses. "This might be a huge mistake, but I think I want to stay."

"I had a feeling you'd say that." She paused then added, "Okay, but they damn well better use condoms. And make sure they understand that no means no."

Lydia barely contained a chuckle. "Yes, Mom."

"Don't be a smartass. You're a babe and they're like three big hungry wolves. I'll be worrying all night so call me the minute you're out of there."

"I'll be fine, Roni, really," Lydia soothed. "Besides for some reason I trust them. I can't explain it, but it's almost like I know them."

The line went quiet a moment, before Roni said, "That is strange, considering no one has ever seen them with their hoods off, and to my knowledge no one knows their real names either."

Lydia heard them shuffling around in the other room so she finished her call. "I'll call you and give you all the dirty details."

"It's that or I call 911 and come searching for you."

As they hung up, Apollo came to the doorway, fists clenched at his side. He didn't speak, simply lifted one hand and crooked his finger at her. Lydia dropped her phone back into her purse and stepped away from the safety of the door. The closer she came to the imposing man, the faster her heart beat. By the time she'd reached him, she thought it'd beat right out of her chest.

His hand came up and cupped the back of her head. "You have nothing to fear, baby. No one will hurt you, I promise."

Lydia reached up and touched the bottom curve of the hood, wishing he'd remove it. At once Apollo's hand covered hers and she frowned. "Why the secrecy, Apollo?"

"It's my choice. Just as it was your choice to come here tonight. You wanted something when you ventured into Kinks. What was it, Lydia?"

"The truth?"

"Please," he growled.

"I-I wanted to have sex with a stranger." *I cannot believe I just said that.*

His gaze darkened. "I see. Is this a fantasy of yours?"

"Yes."

"I would be pleased to make your fantasy come true, Lydia. The three of us can give you a night you'll never forget. All you have to do is say yes."

She let him pull her hand down for a kiss. His tongue swirled around the center of her palm and her clit throbbed. Lydia imagined that talented tongue licking her to orgasm. Suddenly she felt another pair of hands on her, caressing her back and bottom. Lydia leaned her head back and saw that Poseidon had slipped up behind her. Zeus stood next to her, watchful and quiet.

Lydia looked back up at Apollo and murmured, "Yes."

Apollo's expression changed to that of a hungry lion. In the next breath he had her off the floor and cradled against his chest. He took her into the adjoining room, and placed her gently in the center of a large bed covered in a red satin comforter. Lydia sat up and held her hand in the air just as Apollo started to come down on top of her.

"Wait, I'd like to freshen up a bit." Okay, so she was stalling, but when a woman is faced with three large, gorgeous men about to make her every desire a reality, she's allowed a little time to collect her thoughts.

Apollo planted a hand beside her hip and growled, "You aren't contemplating escape are you?"

Lydia laughed, feeling herself relax a margin. "I'm not going anywhere."

He held out his hand, she took it and allowed him to help her from the bed. He pointed to a corner of the room. "Through there. You'll find everything you need."

"Thank you."

Lydia made it to the bathroom without tripping over her own feet. Amazing, considering her jangling nerves. After she flipped on the light and closed the door, Lydia collapsed against it. "I am in so damn deep."

Mac, known as Zeus to the members of Kinks, glared at Dane. "Fuck, what the hell are we doing here, Dane?"

"I wish I knew. I've clearly lost my mind." Dane knew he never should have given Lydia the tour, but the instant he'd spotted her sitting at that table his cock had stood at attention. Lydia had come into his territory and he'd be damned if he'd let her go now.

Mac whipped around and said, "Trent, talk some damned sense into him, will you?"

"He's Poseidon and I'm Apollo," Dane admonished. "Remember the rule. Even up here we use the nicknames."

Mac pushed his fingers through his hair. "Fine then. What the hell were you thinking inviting Lydia here, *Apollo*? What if she recognizes one of us? We're so screwed."

"Could either of you have walked away from her?" Dane asked, knowing the answer. They'd all three been captivated by Lydia's presence at the club. Dane's paralegal was taking a walk on the wild side and he'd be damned if she did it with anyone other than the three of them.

Mac came closer, nearly nose to nose. "My dick is hard enough to pound dents out of a damn pickup truck, but if she realizes who she's with it'll humiliate her. Are you willing to lose her forever?"

Dane had already thought of that, but his libido wasn't listening to reason at the moment. "She hasn't figured it out yet and she won't." Christ, he hoped that was true. "We keep the masks on and watch our voices. Especially you, Zeus; that Texas accent is a dead giveaway."

Mac rolled his eyes. "Yeah, I already figured that out, genius, but what happens after? We go to work on Monday and it's business as usual?"

This time it was Trent's turn to speak. "If this is our only chance to have Lydia beneath us, then we take it. She came *here*, we didn't lure her. And I'd rather it be us than some other asshole. The other doms would've seen her for the little lamb she is and pounced." Trent looked pointedly at Mac. "If you're having second thoughts, then leave. We won't stop you."

"I'm not having second thoughts, Poseidon. But I don't want this thing to blow up in our faces either. This is Lydia we're talking about, goddammit. She's too sweet to screw with and you both know it."

"I would die rather than hurt Lydia," Dane muttered. Just the thought had his gut knotting up. "But I can't let her walk away, not now. I can't explain it, all I know is she stays. We can figure the rest out later."

The door to the bathroom opened and Lydia stepped out. They all three fell silent as they watched her move toward them, her steps slow and a little unsure. The closer she came the harder Dane's blood pounded through his veins. When she was directly in front of him, a shy smile curving her lips, he knew the truth. He could never have let her walk away.

He reached a hand out and cupped her cheek. "You're beautiful."

She looked down at the floor. "I'm really not, but thank you anyway."

Dane couldn't believe she was so unaware of her own appeal. It was true she didn't have the ideal hourglass figure and her facial features weren't picture perfect either, but Dane had always found perfection boring. Lydia was anything but boring. Her nose was a little crooked and her glasses were outdated, and her curves were just lush enough to give a man something to hold on to. She had a freshness that appealed to him. She was nothing like the jaded women he'd too often dated. Lydia's intelligence and strong will were extremely sexy. The thought of her submitting to him had his cock swelling painfully. He wanted to see her come apart in his arms. Before the night was over she'd be relinquishing her control and giving in to him.

"You know we're doms, don't you?" Dane asked, needing her to understand what the three of them would demand of her.

"Yes," she tentatively replied, "but I've never done anything like this, Apollo. I've never—"

"You aren't trained as a sub, I know," Dane inserted. "We aren't going to expect more from you than you can give."

She squinted as if suspicious. "What *do* you expect?"

"Only that you trust us to give you pleasure." When she still looked wary, he said, "We don't find it necessary to tie our women up and order them to call us master every time we have sex. It's something we enjoy, yes, but not the only thing. Trust me, Lydia." He took her by the waist and backed up until he reached the bed. He sat down and pulled her between his wide-spread thighs. Dropping his hands away, he ordered, "Take off your shirt for me, baby."

Dane's heart sped up as he watched her shaking fingers pull at the ties of the waist cincher. In his peripheral vision, he saw Mac and Trent move behind Lydia, close but not touching. As she loosened the black garment and pulled it down her hips, Dane knew a kind of hunger he'd never known before. He'd wanted Lydia for too long. Craved her. Now that he was so close to finally burying his cock inside her tight little cunt it was torture to wait, to take it slow. Lydia deserved his control though, not some fast fuck that would leave her unsatisfied.

She took off her glasses and placed them on the bedside table before taking hold of the hem on the sheer pink blouse. Dane had the urge to grasp the material and rip it off her. It was just a damn good thing patience had been the first thing he'd learned as a dom. He'd become adept at waiting, drawing out the pleasure. When the delicate fabric lifted, revealing a slightly rounded belly and black satin bra, Dane groaned. She tossed the blouse aside. Dane didn't give a shit where it landed; his entire concentration was on her breasts. The tempting mounds were more than the bra could contain, sweet swells of flesh spilled over the tops of the curved cups. Lydia bit her lip and took the front closure between her fingers, then popped it open. Her round creamy tits filled his vision. Dane wrapped his hands around her back and pulled her forward. He covered one puffy pink nipple with his mouth and sucked. Sweet ambrosia filled his mouth.

"Oh God," Lydia cried.

Dane let his tongue circle her areola, then pulled as much of her flesh into his mouth as he could. Slim fingers wrapped around his head, holding him tight against her body. He lifted only long enough to nip at the tempting tip. She moaned and pressed more fully against him. Dane caught himself and pulled back. "Take off the rest of it, baby. Show me that pretty body."

Her wet nipple glistened in the low light and he could swear he smelled the heat of her pussy. He couldn't wait to go down on her, suck at her little bud and sip her honey. When her fingers went to the zipper at the back of her skirt, Dane held his breath. Her gaze never strayed from his as she slid the zipper down. Mac and Trent stood behind her, their gazes devouring the lush curves she exposed. When she pushed her skirt down her hips, Dane sucked in a breath at the panties she slowly revealed. Black satin with little red hearts. "Damn, that's hot," he growled.

"Fucking beautiful," Trent replied.

Lydia covered her face with her hands and mumbled something he couldn't understand. Dane reached up and pulled her fingers away and placed a kiss in each palm before entwining his fingers with hers. She was shaking like a leaf. "Don't be embarrassed, baby."

Lydia shook her head. "I don't know why I thought I could do this. I'm not a wild, impetuous person. Friday nights are usually spent with my DVR."

"I won't allow you to feel shame," Dane stated, hoping to get her beyond her own insecurities.

"I'm not ashamed."

"Yes, you are. You think it makes you a bad person, being here with the three of us. Be honest, no lies."

Lydia sighed. "I usually have sex with the lights off and I've never engaged in anything even remotely this adventurous."

Dane grinned at her word choice. "Engaged?" She frowned and tried to pull her hand away, but he wouldn't let her. "Sometimes it's good to let yourself just feel, Lydia. There's nothing wrong with what we're doing. We're consenting adults here."

"Yes, all four of us," she ground out.

Trent and Mac both chuckled. Lydia winced. Dane dropped her hands and patted his lap instead. "Come here, baby." Lydia eyed his crotch, her mouth dropping open when she spied the erection pushing against his fly. "It's not a snake. Come here." He put more command into the words this time and Lydia obeyed, causing Dane to realize that Lydia needed that little commanding tone in order to get her over her initial shyness.

As she sat down, Dane had to bite back a curse. He needed to be out of the jeans. He desperately wanted to feel Lydia skin to skin. "Take your hair down. Let me see it."

Lydia reached up and took several pins out of the bun, then shook her head. Soft brown curls fell down her back and shoulders. "Damn, that's a lot of hair."

"The bun keeps it out of my way while I work," she explained.

"The bun is kinky as hell, but this is beautiful." He gripped a handful, brought it to his face and inhaled. Coconuts, yum. "Very sexy."

"Thank you," she softly whispered.

He wrapped an arm around the back of her and looked up at Trent and Mac. In perfect unison, they moved closer. Trent dropped to his knees and pressed a kiss to Lydia's thighs, while Mac stroked her hair. As Trent's mouth traveled closer to her black-satin-covered pussy, Lydia pressed her legs tighter together. Dane knew she was nervous, but he could also see the arousal that forced her to stay put. As Trent's lips came into contact with her panties, Lydia jumped.

"Shh, it's okay. Let him touch you, baby."

"Apollo, I . . ." her words trailed off as Trent's tongue licked her clit through the material. Son of a bitch, Dane had never been so jealous. He wanted his lips and tongue there. They'd shared women before, plenty of times, but he'd never gotten territorial. As he watched Trent spread Lydia's thighs apart and lick again, Dane wanted to yank him backward; putting distance between them seemed suddenly imperative. Dane contained the urge, but barely. When he looked up at Mac, Dane could see a gleam of amusement pass over his expression. He'd punch the ass later for that little smirk. As Mac reached down and pinched Lydia's nipple with his index finger and thumb, Dane snarled. The sounds coming from between Lydia's sweet lips was enough incentive for Dane to let the games continue.

While Dane smoothed his palm over her back, Mac slowly went to his knees. Dane watched Lydia's eyes flutter shut. She leaned back and opened herself completely. It was like watching a flower bloom.

"Such a sweet little pussy," Trent murmured as he continued to tease her through her panties.

Mac cupped one round tit and squeezed before dipping his head and biting the hard tip. Dane's cock throbbed as Lydia moaned and writhed atop his thighs. "Take her panties off, Poseidon. Let's see our pretty little submissive."

Trent lifted his head and grinned. Lydia's eyelids fluttered open as Trent grasped at the edges of her panties and yanked, ripping the fragile material in two. Lydia gasped at the savagery of it. Dane's mind was covered in a haze of lust as he looked at Lydia's neatly trimmed curls glistening with the moisture of her arousal.

"So pretty, baby," Dane whispered. "The prettiest cunt in the world."

Trent placed his thumbs on the puffy lips and opened her. "Mmm, a juicy little peach." He leaned down and licked her slit, then pushed his tongue deep. Lydia threw her head back and cried out. Mac continued playing with her nipples, suckling one, then biting the other. As Dane held Lydia still, it was anyone's guess which one of them would come first, Lydia or him. Watching her fly apart in his arms had his balls aching.

Dane licked his middle finger and reached between Lydia's thighs, sliding inside her wet heat. He'd barely breached her opening when her hips bucked wildly. As he pushed in all the way her cries grew louder, her legs widening to give him better access.

"So fucking tight. I'm going to love having my cock here, baby," Dane murmured.

"Please . . . oh, God," Lydia moaned as she threw her head from side to side. She wrapped her legs around Trent's head and squeezed, trapping Dane's finger inside her slippery cunt. Trent hummed his approval and clutched her hips, holding her still for his assault. All at once, Lydia shouted and thrust her pussy into Trent's face. Her orgasm seemed to go on and on, it made Dane wonder when she'd last been with a man.

Several seconds went by before she collapsed backward, trusting Dane to hold her up. Mac and Trent both sat back on their heels and waited for their cue. Dane stood, cuddling Lydia close to his chest, then he turned and placed her in the center of the bed. Her eyes opened just as Trent and Mac both stood on either side of him. Without another word they undressed. When the last of their clothes were strewn across the floor, Lydia licked her lips, her gaze zeroing in on first his cock, then Trent's and Mac's.

"On your knees, sub," Dane ordered.

Lydia rose slowly to her knees, a hint of fear in her eyes. Dane took his cock in his own fist and stroked it twice before he swiped a finger over the drop of moisture on the bulbous head. He held out his finger and murmured, "Be a good girl and crawl to me."

Dane was surprised as hell when she obeyed without question. She took hold of his hand and brought his finger to her mouth and sucked the digit clean. When she looked up at him, a naughty grin curving her lips, Dane knew he would crave that look for all time.

6

Lydia was in another world. That was the only way to explain how she could even consider letting three men pleasure her at once. Up until that moment the wildest thing she'd ever done was let her high school sweetheart make out with her during a football game. She'd felt guilty afterward and had prayed for two days straight.

This time Lydia only wanted to feel. She didn't want to think about what would happen after. As Apollo held his cock in his fist, Lydia's thoughts scattered. It was so close, within touching distance. She craved the flavor of him. She couldn't explain why, but she felt as if she'd hungered for him forever.

"You can taste it, Lydia."

Lydia didn't speak as she stared at Apollo's hard flesh. She licked her lips and moved forward another inch, then let her tongue shyly swirl over the swollen crest. Lydia heard Apollo's deep rumbling voice praising her, urging her on. Lydia opened wide and wrapped her lips around his flesh. She could only manage the first few inches, he was wider and longer than any man she'd known. Suddenly a large, calloused hand was petting her spine and traveling toward her buttocks. Lydia moaned and sucked another inch of hard flesh into her mouth.

"Such a pretty mouth, baby," Apollo ground out as he wrapped his fingers in her hair. "Just a little more now. Let me feel that throat tighten around my dick."

Lydia pulled back, releasing his flesh entirely and glanced up at him. The dark eyes and black leather hood made him appear fearsome. Panic swamped her as Lydia realized just how vulnerable she was with three such powerful males, all immensely turned on.

"No," Apollo bit out. "Don't go there, Lydia. We won't hurt you. This is about pleasure, only pleasure."

Lydia watched as Poseidon moved onto the bed, a bottle of oil in his hands. She didn't even know he'd retrieved it. She turned her head, wary of his intentions. He only smiled and popped the top before pouring some of the fragrant liquid into his palms. As he touched her upturned bottom, Lydia jumped.

"Shh, it's okay, sweet girl," Poseidon soothed, his voice barely a whisper. "It's just a massage."

Apollo cupped her chin and forced her to look at him. "Didn't it feel good with my finger in that hot little pussy, while Poseidon teased your clit?"

Lydia's face heated at the reminder of just how good it had felt to let herself go so completely. To let them take over, strumming her body like an instrument.

"Imagine how good it's going to feel when we fill you with our cocks, baby. Spreading you open, pushing you into another realm where there's nothing but sweet satisfaction."

Lydia's blood ran hot as a series of X-rated images fired into her brain. Still on her knees, she reached up and grasped Apollo's hard-on and stroked.

"Christ, yeah, just like that. Touch me, Lydia. Own that dick."

Barriers fell away as Apollo's words flitted through her. Once more she sank her mouth onto his flesh, this time sucking half his length deep. Apollo cursed and wrapped a lock of her hair around his fist. He didn't pull her onto him, just held her firm, the slight sting to her scalp lent to the eroticism of the moment. Out of the corner of her eye she watched Zeus step forward, his fist wrapped tight around his own cock as he moved up beside Apollo. Lydia licked and suckled Apollo's thick crest, then released him and moved over to Zeus. She licked the pearl of moisture at his tip and Zeus groaned. He didn't speak a word, merely dropped his hand and let her play. A sense of feminine power came over her as she realized how much pleasure she could bring the three men. Lydia lowered her mouth over Zeus's cock, enjoying the differences between the two men. Apollo was larger around, but Zeus was a little longer. Both men were bigger than any she'd ever been with. As Lydia reached over and cupped Apollo's balls, she felt Poseidon's hands smoothing over her ass. He kneaded the tight muscles of each cheek before drifting his fingers higher over her lower back. Lydia moaned and sucked Zeus harder, hollowing her cheeks and bringing him to the back of her throat. Soon she felt Apollo's hand in her hair, pulling her backward, forcing her to release Zeus. She looked over at Apollo as she took his hard length into her mouth.

"Fuck, baby, you're so damn hot. You like this, don't you? Sucking the both of us, making us crazy with that tongue."

Lydia hummed as Apollo wrapped his hands around her face and began to fuck her mouth. First with slow easy strokes, then harder. The forceful action had her body vibrating. Poseidon's fingers travelled down to her hips, then ventured between the round globes of her ass. Lydia started to tense as a finger circled her anus, but as Apollo drove his cock clear to her throat, Lydia forgot her uneasiness and allowed herself to be taken into that other realm Apollo had promised her.

Zeus placed one knee on the bed, then brought his cock to

her cheek, rubbing the head over her soft skin. She felt surrounded by them, thoroughly entrenched in their wicked world.

"You're a very naughty girl, aren't you, Lydia?" Apollo asked, his voice rough with arousal.

Lydia could only moan as Apollo moved his hips back and forth, sliding his dick over her ravenous tongue. Lydia braced herself on the mattress as she looked over at Zeus. He smiled down at her, then gently slapped her cheek with his cock. It shouldn't have been a turn on, but Lydia's pussy flooded with her juices and she badly wanted him to do it again.

"Mmm, she likes that, Zeus," Poseidon murmured as he continued to tease her tight pucker with his oiled finger. Another hand found its way between her thighs and suddenly there were two fingers sinking inside her hot cunt. "So tight and hot. You're going to drive us all crazy with this sweet little body, aren't you, Lydia?"

Zeus slapped her cheek again and again with his erection, each slap drawing more moisture to her pussy and causing her clit to swell and throb.

Lydia took Apollo's cock farther down her throat, until he was balls deep inside her mouth. Suddenly he pulled away. "Enough," he commanded.

As if of one mind, Poseidon pulled his fingers free and moved away, while Zeus stepped backward.

Lydia glanced up. Witnessing the dark arousal on Zeus and Apollo's faces had her own body coiled as tight as a spring. "You need to come again, don't you?" Apollo asked, as he stroked her lower lip with his thumb. "This time we'll be buried inside of you when you do."

"Come here, sweet girl," Poseidon growled from his position behind her. She looked over her shoulder to see him lying on his back on the bed, his legs spread. His cock jutted away from his body, the veins pulsing with vitality. Lydia turned around and before she could lose her nerve, straddled his thighs.

Within seconds he had her spread out on top of him, his mouth covering hers. She couldn't think, couldn't move. Poseidon's lips were different from Apollo's, softer, fuller. They were pressed to hers, his tongue in her mouth, playing and teasing with the flesh of her bottom lip. She melted against his hard strength. As his powerful arms came around her shoulders, holding her tight, Lydia sighed and surrendered to him. His tongue scoured her mouth, taking immediate possession of her, sucking at her tongue.

Another pair of large, masculine hands moved down her back to cup her ass. A sharp swat had her yelping and scrambling to get away. Poseidon held her still, his voice soft and soothing against her ear. "Shh, it's okay."

She frowned down at him. "Someone just hit me. It's definitely not okay!" She heard a chuckle and whipped around. "It's not funny," she ground out between clenched teeth as she glared at Apollo.

"Don't be so skittish, baby. A spanking can be damned pleasurable."

Apollo's gravelly voice shouldn't have been so damn sexy, but as she lay there trapped in Poseidon's arms and surrounded by three muscular male bodies, she couldn't quite bring herself to stay angry with him. "Then let me swat your ass," she muttered, hoping to sound indignant. Judging by the twin grins on Apollo and Zeus's faces she'd failed miserably.

"Spank a dom?" Apollo asked, his voice teasing. "I don't think so, little Lydia. You're the sub, remember?"

Poseidon reached up and grabbed a handful of her hair, forcing her to look at him. His tender gaze relaxed her a measure. "I think you need to let us please you, sweet girl." This time when his lips covered hers, they weren't gentle. In fact, he all but demanded entrance. Lydia obeyed. In her soul she knew she'd do nearly anything for these three men. The notion sent a bolt of fear licking through her. No one should wield that much power.

Out of the corner of her eye she saw Zeus and Apollo climbing onto the bed. Apollo moved in behind her, while Zeus knelt on his knees beside her head. Poseidon licked her lips one more time before pulling back.

Somewhere along the way Apollo must have used the massage oil and she'd been too far gone to even realize it because his warm oiled hands started to rove over her hips, his electrifying touch leaving her skin tingling. He spread her open and stroked her anus with his slick index finger. "Such a pretty ass, baby. So damn tight. I definitely think it needs a good fucking."

"Oh, God," Lydia moaned as she felt him wiggle his finger inside her puckered opening.

Apollo grunted. "Jesus, baby, you're going to milk me dry when I get my dick in there."

Poseidon reached over and grabbed a pack of condoms from the bedside table, then handed one to Apollo. She felt Apollo press a kiss to the base of her spine before lifting away from her. Lydia watched as Poseidon ripped the foil packet with his teeth, then handed it to her. "Put it on me, sweetheart."

Lydia took the condom and leaned back. She'd never been the one to put the condom on before so it took more than a few tries before she finally had it right. As she glanced up at Poseidon, and then Zeus, she was shocked to see them staring at her with affection. This was about sex, she reminded herself. Her heart had nothing to do with it. But as Zeus reached up and stroked her lips with his finger, she couldn't help but feel this night was as unique for them as it was for her. They may not have deep feelings for her, but it would definitely be a night to remember.

Dane couldn't pull his eyes away from Lydia's ass. He'd had anal sex with women before. Each time had been a satisfying experience, but none of those women had been Lydia. He'd fantasized about that heart-shaped ass of hers. He'd always known she'd be as tight as a fucking fist, but he'd never realized how deeply it would affect him. She was a virgin there. He knew it in his bones. No man had ever touched her that deep, that intimately. Something unfurled inside his chest as he became aware of how much she trusted him. His mind stuttered to a halt as he realized the truth. It wasn't Dane she was submitting to, but Apollo. How could a man possibly be jealous of himself? It was inconceivable.

As he reached up and clutched her hip, Lydia shuddered. Trent lay sprawled out beneath her, and Mac knelt beside them, stroking his cock, patiently awaiting Dane's command. It was rare for a dom to take orders from another dom. The three of them had realized back in college that they actually enjoyed the exchange of power. Sometimes Trent was in command, other times it was Mac. This time it'd been his turn. When they'd spotted Lydia, Dane wanted to thank fate for being on his side. She'd happened into his territory on the same night that he'd been the one in command.

Dane opened the bottle of oil and poured more into the palm of his hands. He smoothed his palms together, warming the fragrant liquid, before he touched Lydia's satiny skin. She moaned as he gently massaged her, readying her for the invasion of his cock. Untouched territory. The thought tore a growl from his chest.

He smoothed his fingertips over her lower back. "You're so delicate, baby, but I won't hurt you. You trust me, don't you?"

"Mmm, that feels so incredible, Apollo. You are one talented man."

His chest swelled with pride at her words, but the joy was short lived as he heard her call him Apollo. He wanted to hear his real name whisper past her plump lips. He let his fingers drift over the small indentations above her bottom as he murmured, "You are being a very good little sub, Lydia. Shall I reward you?"

"Please, don't tease," she moaned.

Dane let his slick fingers dip between her ass cheeks and slid one digit up and down her anus. Over and over again, making certain she was completely slick with the sweetly scented oil before he wiggled it into the tight pucker a bare inch. Her startled intake of breath at the tiny invasion reminded him that she was new to anal sex. He forced his raging libido down, hoping to build the pleasure slowly.

"Look at Zeus, baby." When she turned her head and looked at the other man, Dane murmured, "He's waiting for you to take him to heaven."

Dane watched as Lydia reached out and wrapped her small fingers around Mac's cock. Dane liked to watch—it never failed to turn him on. Watching Lydia slide her palm up and down Mac's dick had Dane's balls drawing up tight. Trent wrapped his hands around Lydia's tits and pressed them together. He nuzzled her cleavage before nipping one hard bud with his teeth. Lydia arched her body and cried out.

Mac groaned and moved closer. "Suck it, darlin'," he ordered.

Dane's heart nearly stopped as he heard Mac's Texas accent. Lydia merely closed her eyes and opened wide, letting Mac slip his cock between her lips.

"Will you beg for us, sub?" Trent asked. Lydia whimpered and sucked on Mac harder. Dane slipped two fingers deep, stretching her little ass wider, the need to fill her with his cock instead of his fingers beginning to ride him hard.

Her body, once so pliant, now seemed strung tight. The little purring sounds she made nearly did him in. Dane leaned down, covering her body with his own, sandwiching her between himself and Trent and whispered, "Admit you're mine, baby, tell me now before I fuck this tight little ass."

Lydia released Mac's dick and cried out, "Oh, God, this is so insane."

"Say it, little Lydia."

Lydia shook her head, denying him the small reward.

He grinned. "For now. You'll get away with that for now, baby." He pulled his finger free and poured more oil onto his fingers, then spread it around. "When my cock slides in this sexy little butt it'll feel so incredible. You're going to feel every pulse, every thrust." He slid three fingers into her this time, spreading her open, willing her muscles to relax. She writhed beneath him and he had to hold her hip to keep her from hurting herself.

"Spread your legs a little more," he ordered. When she complied, his entire body shot out of control. He could see everything. Her heart-shaped ass, the pink pucker of her anus and her wet, swollen cunt. She was completely on display.

"It feels forbidden, doesn't it?" Trent asked. She replied with a jerky nod as she buried her face into his chest. "You're a treat, Lydia. A rare treat."

She lifted her head and started to speak, but Dane slid his fingers in another inch and all that came out was a whimper. Now Dane was buried clear to his knuckles inside Lydia's ass.

"There are several sensitive nerve endings around your anus. When my dick fills you it's going to feel so damn good. When Poseidon buries himself deep and Zeus fills that mouth with cock, you'll truly be our little submissive then, Lydia."

"Yes, Apollo. Please, just fuck me, please!"

Just what he wanted to hear. "I want to make sure you're ready for me." He pulled his fingers free and added a fourth, then pushed inside, stretching her, pushing her beyond her own comfort zone. He made every attempt to go slow, allowing her body to adjust to the invasion. She moaned and spread her legs farther, pushing backward against his hand, as if needing more.

"Mmm, that's it, sub," he murmured, "now." Dane's body was on fire and his dick was aching for release.

He reached for the bottle of oil once more and poured a

small amount over his sheathed erection. Trent petted her hair and stroked her back, while Mac leaned down and took her lips with his own. Gently, Dane separated the round globes of Lydia's backside and touched the head of his cock to her entrance. Alert to any sign of pain, he pushed the head inside, just barely breaching the tight outer ring of muscle. It was such sweet torture to hold back from thrusting deep. Fucking her hard and fast, the way his body so desperately craved. But for Lydia he'd walk through the fires of hell if it meant hearing her screams of pleasure.

7

"Oh, God, it's too much! I can't," Lydia cried out, all but ready to leap from the bed. The feel of Apollo's cock inside her ass, stretching her, it wasn't at all like the pleasure she'd felt when it'd been his fingers there. She planted her hands on either side of Poseidon and started to push herself off his body.

Apollo quickly pulled out and smoothed a hand over her hips. "We're going to take this slow, baby," he soothed. "There's no rush."

"I don't think I can do this," she moaned as frustration began to rise up.

Poseidon kissed the side of her neck and slid his arms around her, pulling her gently back down against his chest. "Of course you can, sweet girl," he murmured, "but you need to relax for Apollo. You're tense and scared; that's normal the first time. But we won't hurt you. We want only pleasure for you."

Apollo leaned down and kissed a fiery path down her spine, lingering at the base. His lips had her forgetting the flash of panic. As he licked her overheated skin, Lydia felt herself relaxing by slow degrees. "That's it, baby," Apollo whispered against her hip where he nipped her, sending a jolt of excitement clear to her womb. "Let us take you there slowly. No rush, no pain."

Suddenly Zeus moved in closer. The instant his cock came into view, she turned her head and licked him from base to tip. He petted her hair and lifted his dick away from her. She frowned, then watched as he cupped his balls, a wicked grin on his face. She knew what he wanted and her mouth began to water as she anticipated the flavor of those soft orbs.

As Apollo continued to kiss and massage her tense muscles, Lydia opened her mouth and let Zeus pull her head toward his scrotum. The instant her tongue tasted his musky male essence, Lydia groaned and wrapped her lips around the smooth flesh. She stuffed as much of him into her mouth as she could before sucking, hard. Zeus cursed and gripped a handful of her hair and held her against his body, as if loath to let her go.

"Lick him, sub," Apollo ordered.

Lydia released him and swept her tongue back and forth over the underside of his balls, teasing the sensitive skin that led to his anus. Zeus groaned and threw his head back. Lydia continued the sweet torture, relishing the pleasure her tongue created.

"So fucking hot, sweet girl," Poseidon stated, his voice low and rough. "You are a treasure."

"Our pretty treasure," Apollo agreed as he slid his cock over and around her anus. Lydia tensed, knowing what was coming and afraid all over again. The feel of Poseidon's hard dick against her pussy had her clit throbbing as lust swept through her. It blocked out all else. Lydia spread her legs wider, giving them better access to her body, surrendering to them completely.

"That's it, open for us, Lydia," Apollo murmured, the head of his cock slipping inside her ass at the same time that Trent's cock pushed inside her pussy. "Give us what we want."

Suddenly Lydia's fears vanished and all she could do was lie there and feel as the two powerful men slowly filled her. Her eyelids drifted shut as she let herself be taken away, but when she felt strong fingers in her hair she opened them again and saw Zeus staring down at her, a smile of approval lighting his light blue eyes. No words were spoken as Lydia leaned over and took him into her mouth. Her tongue flattened and she took his engorged cock deep, hitting the back of her throat, before releasing him and performing the act all over again. Soon, he was taking over as he cupped her chin in one hand, while the other held the back of her head. As he slowly began to move his hips back and forth, Lydia could only watch in fascination as his expression changed, became more intense, almost savage. As his movements gained momentum, Poseidon and Apollo began a slow, torturous rhythm inside her ass and pussy. With every part of her filled, her body began the slow climb to rapture. Apollo growled her name and slammed his hips against her ass, embedding his cock deeper still. Poseidon's thrusts became more forceful as he began to fuck her pussy with fast furious strokes.

"Christ, Lydia, you're the tightest fist. So goddamn hot I'm about to burst into flames."

Apollo's erotic words pushed her into another world and she began moving her own hips, taking over the rhythm. "That's it, fuck us good, sweet girl. Show us what you like," Poseidon urged.

Zeus slid his cock all the way out of her mouth, then wrapped his fist around it and smacked first one cheek then the other with the engorged flesh. Lydia whimpered, her pussy clenching and aching for release. Poseidon groaned her name and slammed his hips upward, pushing her beyond her own comfort zone. Apollo slid his cock all the way to the very edge, then pushed in again, dragging a moan from between her lips. Zeus slid two fingers into her mouth and Lydia automatically closed around them, suckling and teasing with her tongue. He hummed his approval and murmured, "You're a hungry little sub, aren't you? You want a mouthful of come?"

"Yes, please," she begged, nearly insane with the need for release.

"Tell me how bad you want it, darlin'."

A haze of lust washed over her. "I need it, Zeus. I need you to fill me. I want you fucking my mouth. I crave the taste of your come so bad, please stop teasing me," Lydia cried out, astounded at her own untamed behavior.

"Damn, you," Zeus grumbled. "You're so fucking sexy I just want to keep you forever." He held his cock up for her and said, "Take what you want, sugar. Anything you want, it's yours."

"Zeus," Apollo growled, as if in warning.

There was something there, Lydia thought, something she should be aware of, but as her lips closed over Zeus's cock and tasted his salty precome, Lydia forgot about the vague suspicion. Zeus's gaze darkened as he pushed his cock deeper, fucking her throat. When Poseidon grabbed her ass and pulled her down for another hard thrust, Apollo seemed to lose control. He pushed his cock deep and swatted her ass at the same time. She yelped but didn't release Zeus. Another swat and the sensitive skin on her ass started to tingle.

"Christ, baby, your ass is so fucking good and tight," Apollo said, as he swatted her again. "It belongs to me," he vowed as his palm landed over and over with increased force each time as he fucked her from behind. Poseidon's hips shot upward, hard. Lydia felt her herself flying apart as white-hot electricity shot through her from head to toe. Again his palm landed against her flesh, as both men fucked her harder, faster. Zeus took hold of her face as he drove his cock in and out of her mouth. He went clear to her throat until she gagged, then he pulled back and started all over again. As Apollo smacked her once more, she shot over the edge. The force of her orgasm thundered through her bloodstream until all she could do was ride out the storm. Her pussy bathed Poseidon's cock and she screamed around Zeus's cock filling her mouth. Apollo slammed his hips against her one more time and shouted out his own climax. Poseidon quickly followed as he gripped her ass and held her still, his release fueling another series of ripples from her pussy.

Zeus was out of control, his balls slapping her chin when suddenly he gripped her hair and shot his hot come all over her tongue and down her throat. Lydia swallowed the creamy heat, then swirled her tongue over the tip of his cock, licking at the last few drops, before she pulled back and collapsed on top of Poseidon. She had a vague notion of Apollo pulling free, while Poseidon petted her back and hair a moment before she fell into an exhausted slumber.

"Fuck me," Trent groaned.

"Yeah, my sentiments exactly," Mac muttered. "Damn, it's only been a few minutes and already I want her again."

Dane stood silent by the door, Mac and Trent on either side of him. The three of them had pulled on their jeans, but none of them wanted to stop watching the alluring Lydia Burke as she slept peacefully in their bed. Right after she'd fallen asleep, Dane had seen to the task of taking a washcloth to her. He'd take extra care to be gentle so as not to disturb her, but through it all she'd stayed asleep, only grumbling a few times. After he covered her up, she'd turned on her side and succumbed to exhaustion. He quirked his lips as she started to snore. Damn, that was adorable.

"What are we going to do?" Mac asked, his voice low to keep from waking Lydia. "When she wakes up and goes home, it's what? Business as usual?"

Dane motioned them into the other room. He closed the door behind them and turned to Mac. "No. I can't let her go now," he admitted. There was no way he could ever let her go. She'd slipped in under his defenses somewhere along the line and now she belonged to him. It was as simple as that.

"Then you must have a plan," Mac growled, "because I'm fucking clueless as to how you can possibly think this will work out."

"I don't have a plan. I'm just as confused as you. But can you truly say you're ready to let her walk away? To some other man's bed?" Mac and Trent both glared at him. "Yeah, that's what I figured. So, instead of bitching, help me figure this thing out."

"We could be honest," Trent inserted quietly as he stared down at the floor. "Tell her who we are."

"That'll go over well," Mac muttered. "We'll just whip off our masks and yell 'Hey, Lydia, guess who'?"

Trent shot him an icy glare. "Your smartass remarks are going to land you on your ass."

Dane held up his hand as Mac was about to dig himself in deeper. "There's no other way. We have to tell her the truth."

"Tell me the truth about what?"

All three of them spun around as the small, feminine voice floated over to them. Lydia stood by the bedroom door, the red blanket wrapped around her body like a protective shield. Her long brown hair was a mess of curls cascading down past her shoulders. He loved her hair. He still couldn't believe she was able to get all of it into such a small, unassuming bun.

"It's nothing, sweet girl," Trent said, as he strode across the room. He took her in his arms and kissed the top of her head. Dane watched the tender display, shocked to see Trent acting so affectionate. He was usually the first one ready to leave after sex.

Dane drew up next to them. "Did we wake you?"

"No. I just . . . I need to leave."

Dane's gaze shot to Trent's and they both knew the truth. Letting her leave would spell the end. She would never come back to Kinks. She'd had her walk on the wild side and now she was ready to go back to her sedate life. Dane wanted to howl at the moon. He'd never felt so helpless, so lost. He wanted to keep her in the room, never let her out of his sight. Reality was far different than his fantasy world though.

"We'll drive you," Dane offered.

She shook her head and stepped back, hitching the blanket higher. "That's okay. I'll call a cab."

Mac stepped in and said, "We don't mind driving you."

Dane wanted to kick Mac's ass for speaking up. If she recognized his accent they'd be dead in the water. Luckily she didn't seem to notice. "In your leather hoods?" she asked, her lips curving up at the corners.

Trent patted her on the ass. "She has a point." He moved toward the phone sitting on the bar. "I'll call the cab while you dress."

Dane wanted to protest. It couldn't be over. No way was this the end. He contented himself with the fact that he'd see her at work Monday. He'd have the rest of the weekend to come up with a plan. As she stepped back into the bedroom, Dane had the urge to go after her. To tie her to the bed and keep her. He could make her beg for him all over again. Show her how good life would be with him. He shook himself out of his reverie. Shit, he was like a kid with a new toy. One he didn't want to share!

"She's done a number on you," Mac said from his position next to the bar.

Dane didn't want to explore his feelings too deeply. "She's done a number on all of us, Zeus."

He sighed. "Yeah."

Trent hung up the phone and came toward them, hands

shoved into the front pocket of his jeans. "The cab will be here in forty minutes. We'll escort her down."

Dane pushed his fingers into his hair as impotent anger began to ride him. "This is crazy. There's got to be a way to break it to her gently."

"I have a suggestion," Mac injected.

Dane took in Mac's tense expression. He knew that look. Mac was feeling Lydia just as intensely, he was just better at hiding it behind a bunch of smartass remarks. "I'll listen to anything at this point," Dane said, hoping for a miracle.

"We give her the weekend to recoup," Mac offered. "Monday we'll sit her down and explain things to her as gently as possible. We'll tell her it wasn't planned, but that we care about her. It's that or we don't tell her at all and risk never having her again."

None of them had to say it aloud. Losing her for good simply wasn't an option. "Agreed," Dane and Trent said in unison.

"I'm ready."

Dane glanced over his shoulder. His heart nearly stopped beating at the sight of her. The pink blouse and skirt were designed to drive men to their knees. Coupled with the glasses and the demure bun, it was a lethal combination.

Dane strode across the room. "Just let us get our shirts on and we'll walk you down. I don't want you alone in the club."

"Thank you."

Christ, she was being so polite one would think they'd had a nice chat over tea, rather than wild and crazy sex. She was back to being Lydia Burke the paralegal, he realized. Already Dane missed the wanton who'd come apart in their arms.

Dressed now, Trent, Mac and Dane walked her out. Together they escorted her through the thinning crowd and put her in the cab. No more was said as she looked up at them, a shy smile on her face as she closed the car door. When it pulled away from the curb, they all three let out a disgusted sigh.

"It's going to be a long fucking weekend," Trent ground out.

Dane couldn't speak past the lump in his throat. As he watched the cab disappear around a corner, he had a horrible feeling he'd just let something precious slip through his fingers. Monday couldn't come soon enough.

8

Lydia looked at her reflection in the mirror. "No one can tell," she assured herself. No one could possibly know how she'd spent her Friday night. It was now Monday morning and she was supposed to go to work and be professional. Life goes on. Hell, she'd already spent the weekend punishing herself over the stupidity of her actions. She'd prayed for forgiveness. She'd even gone to confession. Nothing helped and she had a sneaking suspicion it was because she'd liked it and wasn't truly sorry. She'd enjoyed Apollo, Poseidon and Zeus. They'd given her something special, a chance to let loose and pretend she wasn't the good Catholic girl for once in her life.

After she'd gotten home Friday night, or rather Saturday morning, Lydia had called Roni to let her know she was home safe. Roni had pumped her for information but she'd kept the details vague. She didn't want to share the pleasure with anyone else. She wanted to keep the memories close. Roni had called her again Saturday afternoon wanting to take her shopping. Jeanette had even tried to coax her out of the house by mentioning the grand opening of Manic Stacks, a new used bookstore in town. Lydia had denied them both. She knew they'd worry, but Lydia had wanted to wallow in her own misery. She'd even tossed around the idea of getting a permanent membership to Kinks in the hopes of seeing the men again. She'd quickly nixed that plan when she realized she just wasn't adventurous enough for more than one night of passion. It had happened and now it was over. She should be thinking about work, not three gorgeous men in leather hoods who had the power to make a woman melt.

She covered her face in her hands and groaned. "Oh, God, three men at once." What had she been thinking? It was a foolish thing to do. She could have been raped and murdered. But that argument wasn't getting her anywhere because deep down she'd trusted them or she never would have given them the time of day. Lydia still felt there was something familiar about the men. It had nagged at her all weekend. That little curl in Apollo's hair. That slight accent of Zeus's. Poseidon's intense eyes. Who were they really? Why the secrecy? She glanced at her watch and sighed. "I'm late. On top of everything else, I'm freaking late!"

Ensuring that her glasses were on straight and the bun was in place, Lydia left the bathroom and grabbed her car keys. As she opened the door to her apartment another thought struck. "Well, at least I didn't lose the bet," she mumbled. Her shoulders slumped as she locked the door behind her. Somehow the bet didn't seem so important anymore. All she could think about was how any one man would ever be able to measure up to Apollo, Poseidon and Zeus. Her future was looking bleaker by the second.

Her cell phone rang just as Lydia reached her car. She grabbed it out of her purse and answered as she slid in behind the wheel. "Hello?"

"You're late."

At the sound of Dane's gruff voice, Lydia slammed her car

door shut and threw her purse on the passenger seat. "I'm aware of that. I'm on my way."

"You're always here well before eight, it's now eight thirty. Is something wrong?"

Nothing that couldn't be fixed by three deliciously power-ful men in hoods. Her face heated at the errant thought. "No, I'm just getting a late start. Sorry, it won't happen again."

"It's fine, take your time," he said, his voice softening. "I was worried."

Her lips quirked. "Afraid I wasn't coming back, huh?"

"You'd have every right to quit, Lydia. No one would blame you." He paused. "When you get in, come to my office so we can discuss a raise and more vacation time."

Great, now she felt guilty for acting so surly. After all, it wasn't his fault she'd made a mess of her personal life. "Thank you, Mr. Gentry. That sounds great."

"I don't want to lose you, Lydia. And it's Dane, remember?"

He sounded far too serious and even apologetic. She didn't know what to make of either. "You won't lose me . . . Dane. I'm happy with my job. It's just been stressful trying to fill too many shoes."

"Understood. I'll see you soon then."

"Yes, soon."

After they hung up, Lydia stared at the phone. "I need a va-cation," she mumbled as she put the key in the ignition. "Hawaii would do nicely." As she pulled out of the parking space she imagined a Hawaiian vacation, complete with three hooded strangers to see to her every desire. "Crap, I'm so going to hell."

Lydia couldn't seem to move, could barely take a breath, as she stared at two dozen red roses in a beautiful crystal vase, a big red bow tied around the gorgeous bouquet. They'd been delivered right after she, Dane, Trent and Mac had gone to lunch. She'd never received flowers before so she hadn't even considered that they might be for her.

Damn, someone had sent her flowers. She was afraid to go anywhere near them or the card sticking out of the top. Finally, after five minutes of staring at the fragrant red petals, Lydia pushed back her chair and stood. She plucked the card out of the center and read it.

Sweet Lydia,
Thank you for a memorable evening. We hope to see you again soon.
Your admirers,
Apollo, Poseidon and Zeus

She collapsed into her chair and read the card again. "Oh. My. God." She groaned and quickly tucked the card into her purse before picking up the phone.

"Hey, chicka," Roni answered in a chipper voice, "what's up?"

"They sent me flowers," Lydia muttered.

"Who?"

Lydia slapped a hand against her forehead. "Who do you think?"

Silence hit her.

"Roni?"

"Uh, yeah. Wow. You must have made an impression on them. What did the card say?"

"That they hope to see me again soon. Are they insane or what? And how did they even know where I work?"

"The form you filled out at Kinks, remember? And why insane? You enjoyed yourself, didn't you?"

Lydia was ready to scream. "I'd forgotten about the form. Yes, I enjoyed myself, but that's not the point here."

"Then what is the point?"

How could such an educated woman be so dense? It was inconceivable. "I had sex with three men, three hot, mouthwatering men, Roni. But it was only supposed to be one night. Sex with a stranger, remember?"

"And you don't want a repeat performance?"

"What I want and what I should do is not the same thing. I shouldn't even accept the flowers. I should be putting the whole thing behind me and praying I don't go to hell."

"Listen to me, Lydia, really listen," she ordered, her tone firm. "You're upset because you did accept the flowers and you do want a repeat performance. Here's the clincher. You are not going to hell just because you had a good time at Kinks and are now considering doing it again."

Lydia ignored Roni's argument. She couldn't allow herself to go down that oh so tempting road. She needed to forget about Friday night, period. "What if Dane and them ask about the flowers? What am I supposed to say?"

"Hell, tell them the truth. Say they're from an admirer."

Roni's simple answer made her wish she could reach out and strangle her. "I guess that could work."

"Of course it could work." Lydia heard voices in the background. "I need to go, but call me tonight."

"Sure. Talk to you later." Lydia hung up the phone and looked at the flowers again. They wanted to see her again? Her heart did a little flip as she imagined making love to Apollo, this time without the mask hindering her view. She'd enjoyed the three of them, but it'd been Apollo's touch that had stayed with her, haunting her dreams. She'd been secretly afraid the night had meant nothing to him. After all, while it was unique for her to spend the night with three men, it was obvious he and the other two men were a little more experienced. Come to think of it, maybe the flowers were a standard thing for them. They probably sent flowers every time they spent the night with a woman. She sighed. Here she was imagining them pining away for her when the truth was much uglier. She'd just been another notch on their bedpost most likely.

Lydia grabbed a file from her desk and forced herself back into work mode. It was her one saving grace, keeping her mind busy kept her from going crazy.

As she entered Dane's office and tossed the file onto his perpetually messy desk, a paper fluttered to the floor. She bent to retrieve it when a word at the top caught her attention. Kinks. Lydia took hold of the paper with shaky fingers. She quickly scanned it and realized it was an electric bill and it was on Dane's desk. As if she'd conjured them, Dane, Trent and Mac walked in. She looked at each man in turn, then looked back at the paper in her hand. "No," she breathed out, "it can't be, it simply can't be."

"Lydia?"

Her gaze shot to Dane's hair. That curl. Oh, God, she should have recognized that curl of his. He was Apollo. It was so clear now. She looked over at Trent and recognized the blue eyes as Poseidon's. She didn't even have to look at Mac to know he was Zeus. She should have picked up on the accent. She would have probably had they not kept her in a perpetual state of arousal, which had continued throughout the weekend.

She held up the paper, her body trembling as the truth sank in. "You really should learn to clean your desk, *Apollo.*"

Dane stepped forward, concern etched into his features. "We can explain, baby."

"Don't even try it." Lydia wadded the bill into a ball and threw it at him. It hit him in the chest then fell to the floor. Dane's gaze trapped hers. She started for the door, her legs shaking so badly she thought she might fall at any moment. As Dane stepped into her path, she stiffened, determined to get out of there before she broke down. She'd be damned if she'd let them see her cry. "Move, now." Her voice quivered as misery engulfed her.

Dane's jaw hardened. "Not when you're so upset. You aren't driving in this condition."

Trent moved up beside Dane, his eyes imploring. "It's not like you're imagining. We didn't set out to trick you, Lydia. It wasn't like that, I swear it."

She couldn't hear their explanations or she really would lose it. "Let me go!" she shouted, her nerves shot.

"I'm sorry," Dane muttered, his soft tone nearly tearing her apart.

He stepped out of her way and she fled the room, barely remembering to grab her purse as she reached her desk. When she saw the flowers sitting on the edge, tears filled her eyes, blurring her vision. She tripped over her own feet but kept her balance. It took her three tries to get the door open. She heard someone calling her name, but it didn't stop her haphazard flight from the office building. As she reached her car, opened the door and threw herself inside, a floodgate opened. Her world crumbling down around her, Lydia remembered her mother preaching to her about the road to hell. Was this her punishment? Was this the penalty for enjoying their touch?

9

"Son of a bitch!" Dane shouted. He turned and put his fist through the wall. There'd be pain later, he knew, for now all he could see was Lydia's ashen face and shaking fingers as she'd held that bill up for him to see. What had he done?

"Mac, follow her home," Trent ordered. "Make sure she makes it there safe."

"Yeah," Mac muttered. He shot Dane an angry glare before leaving the office.

Dane bent and picked up the wadded-up bill. "She'll never forgive us. Never."

Trent went to the desk and pulled out a drawer. He took out two glasses and poured a shot of whiskey in each, then handed one to him. Dane grabbed it and downed the fiery liquid in one gulp. Trent followed suit. He poured them each another shot. "She's hurting right now. We need to give her time."

Dane pointed to the door. "Did you see her face? She's completely crushed, Trent!"

"I saw her, but I have a question for you."

"What?" he gritted out as he sat down and looked at the paper in his fist. Christ, he deserved to be shot for what he'd done to her.

"Do you love her?"

Dane's gaze shot to Trent's. "What?"

Trent crossed his arms over his chest and stared down at him. "You heard me."

"We all care about Lydia. She's been a part of our lives for two years. The other night with her has us all panting after her like little lost dogs." Even as the words fell out of his mouth, he knew they were lies. His feelings for Lydia went deeper than lust. He'd always known that if he ever had her beneath him, he wouldn't want to let her go. Sharing something so personal with Trent wasn't an option though.

"Mac and I care about Lydia, that's true. We've even fancied the idea of having her again. But for you, it's different. You love her, don't you?"

Dane suddenly felt like cinder blocks were sitting on his damned shoulders. He didn't want to talk about his feelings for Lydia. He damn sure didn't want Trent and Mac fantasizing about her either. If another man touched her now, he'd cut their damn hands off. Would she ever forgive him? The thought of hurting her tore at his gut. "My feelings are none of your damn business. All that matters is fixing this. I hurt her. I deserve to be drawn and quartered."

Trent shook his head. "We all participated. It's not your burden alone." He downed the second shot and put the glass back on the desk. "Give her some time. Let her think on it."

Yeah, let her think about what a shit he was, great plan. "And then what?" Dane growled.

Trent smiled. "And then you beg her forgiveness and you do it on your knees."

"You think that's really going to work? This isn't like forgetting to buy her a gift for her birthday!" Dane could still see the pain in her eyes. That look would haunt him forever. "This can't be washed away with an apology."

"No, it can't. But she's a reasonable woman. And she has a heart of gold. And unless I'm way off, I think she cares about you. I think she has for a while now."

Dane recalled the day he'd gone to her apartment, the soft kiss they'd shared. The way she'd melted against him as she'd admitted to being attracted to him. That had been before Kinks. "It won't matter. She won't forgive me for this."

"She looks at you differently than she does Mac and me. She always has. Besides, do you really think she didn't have a clue who she was with the other night? She's worked for us for two years. If you ask me, Lydia had at least some idea. She might not have been conscious of it, but deep down she knew who she was moaning and writhing for. I'd bet money on it."

Could it be? Had she suspected and still gone through with it? It seemed too much to hope for. "I don't know, Trent. That sounds like we're trying to assuage our consciences to me."

He shrugged. "We'll see. Give her a few days then go talk to her. Explain what happened. Make her listen to you. See how she reacts."

Dane hated the idea of waiting. He wanted to go to her now. He needed to talk to her, to tell her it wasn't some damned stunt. They hadn't been trying to play with her feelings. Dane had wanted her so badly he'd let himself believe it would all work out. He'd been an ass.

"And if she doesn't forgive me?" Dane said, admitting the unthinkable.

"Then tie her to the bed and make love to her until she does."

"You're a damned Neanderthal." Even so, Dane thought Trent's idea had merit. If all else fails he'd kidnap her and show her how good they could be together. Just the two of them. He could spend hours loving her.

If she didn't shoot him first.

His cell phone rang and Dane grabbed it, hoping it was Lydia. "Lydia?"

"No, it's Mac. She's home safe." Mac paused, then added, "She's really upset, Dane. I'm worried about her. She shouldn't be alone."

"Are you outside her apartment now?"

"Yeah."

She wouldn't want to see any of them, but maybe Dane could reach one of the friends she always went to lunch with. "I'll take care of it."

Mac sighed. "This sucks. We really screwed up this time."

Dane couldn't have said it better. "I'll fix it," he vowed. *Please, God, let me fix it.*

Lydia had cried herself dry. The only other time she'd done that was when her father had died. Her entire body ached and like a bad movie, the image of that electric bill fluttering to the floor kept zipping through her mind. She still had a hard time reconciling the three men she'd made love to with the three lawyers who made her life crazy. How blind can one person be? Now that she knew the truth it seemed so obvious. She'd been a fool. And they'd played her like a fiddle too. They must have had a good laugh afterward. The thought had her throwing the tissue box across the room. "Assholes," she ground out. Suddenly the doorbell rang and Lydia jumped.

"Go away!"

"Lydia, it's us, open up."

What were Roni and Jeanette doing there? "I'm not up for the company right now, Roni," Lydia called back.

"Don't make me use my key."

Lydia had given Roni a key to her apartment when she'd gone on vacation one year. She'd needed someone to look after her plants. She tried to muster up some irritation at being forced into letting them in, but Lydia knew she'd only wallow in self-pity if left to her own devices. She got up from the couch and strode to the door. When Lydia flung it open to find Roni and Jeanette both staring at her with worry, a bag of groceries in Roni's hands, Lydia's anger boiled over.

"Dane called you, didn't he?"

Roni frowned. "He called. He was worried and didn't want you to be alone."

Lydia crossed her arms over her chest and stared at her two best friends. "Did he tell you what he did? Did he share that little tidbit with you as well?"

Roni pushed her way inside and went straight to the kitchen. Jeanette pulled her in for a hug. All the starch went right out of her. And here she'd actually thought she was all cried out. Go figure. She pulled out of Jeanette's arms and went back to the couch. Socrates jumped onto her lap and purred, then curled into a ball and fell asleep.

"He told Roni what happened," Jeanette said. "Roni called me. I'm sorry, sweetie."

Lydia shrugged and started stroking Socrates. "I shouldn't have gone with them. It's partly my fault."

"What do you mean?"

"They didn't exactly drag me to their apartment above Kinks kicking and screaming. I went willingly. If I hadn't, they never would've had the chance to pull this stupid stunt."

"So now you think you're being punished for spending time with the three of them?"

Lydia bit her lip and looked down at the black ball of fur in her lap. "Maybe. I feel like I'm getting what I deserve here, ya know?"

Roni came back into the room carrying three black cherry coolers. "Please don't tell me you're blaming yourself for this, because that'll just piss me off." She handed Lydia and Jeannette a cooler then sat in the chair across from them. "There's also chocolate chip ice cream in the freezer. I figured we might need it later."

Lydia unscrewed the cap and took a long drink before replying. "You have to admit it's pretty ironic. I spend a wild night with three men and what happens? They turn out to be the men I work for! I can't help but feel like I'm being punished for my transgressions."

"That's a load of crap. You're still letting your mother get to you." Roni placed her cooler on the coffee table and leaned forward. "I want you to know that I talked to Dane at length. I'd love to castrate the ass. What he and those other two idiots did was wrong, no question. But after he explained, I came to the conclusion that it wasn't truly his intention to hurt you. I think he saw a chance to finally be with you and he jumped at it. Does that make it right? Hell no, but it does explain his actions a bit better. Also, try to remember that he didn't lure you to Kinks, Lydia. You went willingly. You wanted to spend the night with a stranger, remember?"

"Yes, but they weren't strangers, were they? They should have said so when I explained my reason for being there to begin with."

Roni's eyes widened. "You told them about the bet?"

"Not exactly. Apollo, er, Dane wanted to know why I was there. I told him I'd fantasized about having sex with a stranger. I was honest. He wasn't."

"Maybe he was just trying to give you what you wanted," Jeanette said. "You know, letting you believe they were strangers."

"I don't know. Maybe," Lydia grumbled. "Still, he should've told me."

"Yeah, he should have." Roni sighed. "I'm sorry, hon."

Now Lydia felt bad. "It wasn't all their fault. I shouldn't have been there to start with. I shouldn't have—"

"Stop flogging yourself," Roni ordered. "Your mother used her beliefs to twist you up inside and that's where a lot of this self-recrimination is coming from. Stop trying to be the daughter she always wanted and start being your own person. She moved on with her life and left you behind, Lydia. You didn't leave her."

Lydia knew in her heart, Roni spoke the truth. "You're right. It's just . . . I've never felt so much pleasure. My lord, sex has never been like that for me. Never. Even now I can't seem to stop thinking about it. Dane was so gentle, but forceful too. How messed up is it that I can't stop thinking about him? I should hate him for what he did, but instead I want him again. What sort of woman am I?"

"Normal. Tell me this. Since it was that good, then what's the real reason for the tears? Is it because you're starting to fall for Dane?"

Lydia shrugged. Roni had it right; Lydia was falling for him. She suspected she'd started falling the minute she'd interviewed for the position as his paralegal.

Roni's lips quirked. "I've noticed you've not mentioned how great it was with Mac or Trent."

"They're all great lovers, but I guess it's Dane's deceit that's left me feeling so betrayed." Lydia took another drink of her cooler and looked over at Jeanette. "I really hate when she goes into psychology mode on me."

Jeanette laughed. "Don't we all."

Roni flipped her hair behind her back and smiled. "It's all part of my charm."

"You aren't nearly as charming as you'd like people to think,

Roni," Jeanette said. "Remember that time you spit on Jimmy Linedecker in third grade?"

"That little dweeb kept pulling my ponytail. He deserved worse."

They all three laughed. After several Jimmy stories and a few more coolers, Lydia looked at the two women and tears sprang to her eyes. "I don't know what I'd do without you guys. Thanks for coming over. I really needed the company."

Jeanette patted her knee and Roni waved a hand in the air. "You'd do the same for us, honey."

It was true. They'd always looked out for each other. Jeanette and Roni were the sisters she'd never had. Lydia moved Socrates onto Jeanette's lap and stood. She planted her hands on her hips. "Okay, who wants ice cream?"

They passed the rest of the evening finishing off a half-gallon of ice cream and a bag of cheesy chips while they watched a horror movie marathon on cable. At three in the morning, she'd had to usher them out the door. They'd only agreed to leave because she'd sworn she was okay.

It wasn't until she slipped into bed with the lights off, finally alone with her thoughts, that Lydia realized Roni had been right. She'd been hurt because she cared. It hadn't just been sex for her. It'd been much more. And for some crazy reason she wasn't nearly as upset with Mac or Trent. It was the thought of Dane betraying her that had shards of glass cutting at her heart.

He'd starred in so many of her fantasies. She'd always wondered what it'd be like if he were to ever see her as a desirable woman, rather than an uptight paralegal. Well, she'd gotten her wish. Unfortunately all she'd been to him was a good time, a novelty. He felt bad, sure, now that she knew the truth. He was concerned and wanted to make it right, but not because she meant something to him.

She would have to quit, find a new job. Oh, she could have eventually faced Mac and Trent, could've even forgiven them.

But she could never look at Dane and know how good it felt to be held by him, to be touched by him, to know his kisses, how perfect their bodies fit together. Leaving was the only sane thing to do now that she knew her heart was involved. Besides, he would be glad she left. It would save them all from further embarrassment.

10

Dane tried to focus on the e-mail, but after reading the same subject line four times, he gave up. It was no use pretending an interest in work. All he could think about was Lydia. The devastation on her face as she'd sprinted out of his office kept running through his mind. She'd have every right to hate him, to never speak to him again, but the very idea made him want to howl in rage.

It'd been two days. Two damn days of not seeing her bright smile, not teasing her until she blushed. Not hearing that hated *Mr. Gentry* pass through her pouty lips. He'd tried calling her. He'd even gone to her apartment. She refused his every attempt to make it right. He was at his wit's end.

"Hey," Mac said as he poked his head into his office. "I hate to bother you, but I was wondering if you'd decided on what to do about Lydia."

Since Lydia hadn't returned to work things were going to hell around the office. He hadn't realized how efficiently she'd handled her job. Without her around, the past couple of days had turned chaotic. He felt like a total shit for taking her for granted.

Dane dragged his fingers through his hair and groaned. "I'm not hiring anyone else. Lydia is still my paralegal."

After Mac was seated in a chair across from him, he handed Dane a resume, then sat back. "At least hire a temporary replacement."

Dane pretended to scan the woman's qualifications, but he really didn't give a damn. He didn't want to work with anyone but Lydia. He handed the paper back to Mac. "I'll think about it."

He nodded. "You're getting behind. You can't do your job and Lydia's both."

Like he needed the reminder. "Yeah," Dane grumbled.

"She still won't speak to you?"

"Hell no. She won't answer my calls and she refused to see me last night when I stopped over at her apartment."

"She's always been a stubborn one," Mac reflected, scratching his chin.

Dane couldn't agree more. Hell, Lydia's willfulness had been half the appeal. She wouldn't bow to just any man, and giving up control wouldn't be an easy thing for her either. He'd ached to watch her submit to him, but thinking back to that night he wasn't sure who had actually run the show. He was pretty sure she'd turned him inside out with her whispered pleas and tantalizing body. Christ he missed her. It was insane to need someone as badly as he needed Lydia. He should leave her alone. Let her get on with her life, but even the thought burned like acid.

His fax machine started up and Mac quirked a brow. "You expecting something?"

"No, I'm not." A sense of foreboding skated down Dane's spine as he rolled his chair backward and grabbed the paper from the tray. He scanned it quickly, then shot out of his chair. "Son of a bitch!"

Mac stiffened. "What is it?"

Dane threw the paper on his desk, then reached in his left drawer and took out his wallet and keys. "I'll be back."

Dane saw Mac lean forward and grab the paper before he cursed and got to his feet. "Don't go to her like this, man. You're too worked up. You're liable to alienate her more."

Dane clenched his fist around his keys as he glared at Mac. "Alienate her more? She faxed me her resignation! Enough's enough. She can damn well face me. I've let her hide long enough."

He didn't wait around for Mac's reply. Dane stormed out of the office, his muscles coiled tight. All the blood in his body seemed to head south as he imagined paddling Lydia's sweet ass for even considering leaving him so easily. Better yet, he'd tie her pretty wrists first, then spank her. After her flesh had turned a nice shade of pink, he'd fuck her until neither of them could stand.

Dane knew he'd restrained his true nature when he'd coaxed her into giving her passion free rein. This time, he'd show her exactly what a dom does to a defiant sub.

Lydia had groomed Socrates until the chubby cat had gotten annoyed enough to scamper off to her bed in the laundry room. She'd reorganized her kitchen cupboards, steam cleaned her carpet and she'd even alphabetized her bookshelf. It was useless. All the busy work in the world couldn't erase the fear spiraling through her.

She'd gone to an office supply store and faxed in her resignation. It'd been a huge step in the right direction, or so she tried to convince herself. She'd tried not to wonder about Dane's reaction. Would he miss her at all? With her luck he already had her replacement picked out. Then again, what did she care? She wanted to move on, hadn't that been her plan? Forget about that incredible night at Kinks and look for a new job. One that didn't involve three handsome lawyers who had a penchant for wearing leather hoods. Her doorbell rang and Lydia dashed across the room, only too happy for the interruption. As she peeked through the peephole, she sucked in a breath and jumped back.

"I know you're in there, Lydia. Open up or I'll break the door down."

Dane's deep voice had the power to make her body vibrate with need. It wasn't fair that a voice could be so sinful, so enthralling. "I thought I made it clear I don't want to see you," she shouted back.

"I don't give a damn what you want. Open the door."

Lydia crossed her arms and called out, "No!"

"Don't push me. You know I'll do it."

She chewed her lower lip, her heart at war with her brain. She knew what she should do: keep the door locked and wait for him to give up and leave. Her soul seemed to ache for him though. In fact, her damned fickle heart was leaping with joy at the idea of seeing him. In the end, there really wasn't a choice. Dane was too hardheaded. She'd seen how he could get in the courtroom. If he said he would break the door down, then that's exactly what he intended to do.

She sighed and stepped forward, then flipped the deadbolt. The instant she turned the knob Dane pushed the door wide and forced his way inside. He slammed it shut behind him and Lydia instinctively stepped backward, the dangerous look on his face turning her blood to molten lava. Oh, God, now he resembled the masterful Apollo. The gleam of sexual awareness in his dark eyes and the sensual tilt to his lips were reminders of how easily he could turn her into a begging wanton. His wrinkled white dress shirt stretched over a muscular chest and taut abs, and the black slacks couldn't begin to hide an erection like Dane's. Her mouth watered.

He dropped his briefcase on the floor next to the door and said, "Did you really think you could quit?" He moved closer, his steps slow, purposeful. "Just fax me a damned piece of paper and I'd be forced to let you walk away from me?"

"You don't have a choice." Lydia swallowed the lump in her throat and moved around the chair. Putting furniture between them seemed like a smart idea. "I quit, end of story."

"The hell it is," he growled as he stopped and crossed his arms over his chest. "I've given you space, Lydia, but it's time we talk."

"There's nothing to say."

He pointedly glanced at the chair and quirked a brow. "Afraid, little Lydia?"

Afraid of her own ability to keep her hands off him, yeah. "You don't scare me, Dane. You'd never hurt me."

"Then quit acting so skittish and come here."

She stuck her nose in the air and kept her position. "I'm fine right here. Say what you want and leave. I have things to do."

A muscle in his jaw jumped. "Like look for another job?"

She shrugged, as if his presence was a nuisance. "That's only one of the things on my to-do list."

"You aren't leaving, so forget it. And I'm about tired of you acting like I raped you the other night. You enjoyed us, damn it. I know you did."

Her face heated at the reminder of just how much she had enjoyed their attentions. "I never said you raped me."

His face softened a fraction. "It was wrong not to tell you who we were, baby. I hurt you and I'll have to live with that for the rest of my life. But I can't bear to think of you leaving me. The thought of never seeing your pretty smile again has my gut in knots."

Pain shot through her. "Why, Dane? Why did you go through with it? I deserved better, don't you think?"

Dane moved and it took every ounce of willpower she possessed to keep from running. He stepped around the chair, his movements slow, as if afraid of spooking her if he came at her too fast. When he was within inches, Lydia inhaled, taking in his masculine scent. God, she missed him. It wasn't fair that he smelled so good, looked so delicious, while she resembled something out of a horror movie. It seemed to emphasize how far out of her own league she'd ventured.

"There are no excuses for my actions. I know that, baby." He touched her cheek and Lydia very nearly leaned into him. She held firm, but barely. "So help me I didn't do it to hurt you. It wasn't some damned stunt to make a fool of you either. I saw you sitting at that table with Roni and my brain closed down. All I could think about was getting you in my bed. I would've done anything to make that happen."

"Including pretending to be someone else," she reminded him, still angry at his betrayal even though his nearness was causing her anger to slowly melt away.

He grimaced. "If I had it to do over again, I would tell you. As God is my witness, I would tell you before I ever brought you to that apartment." He stroked her lower lip and Lydia groaned. "You have to be honest with me too, sweetheart. Would you have gone with me? Knowing it was me, would you have let me have you?"

Lydia grabbed his wrist and forced him to move his hand away. He did, but his reluctance was etched into the hard planes of his face. "I don't know. I honestly don't know what I would've done."

"Why did you come to Kinks?"

Lydia knew that question would come eventually, but she still wasn't prepared to tell him the reason behind her presence at the club. "I told you. Sex with a stranger."

"Can you honestly stand here and say you didn't have some idea who Apollo really was?"

Lydia shook her head, unwilling to go down that road. "I didn't know and you didn't tell me. You should have told me."

"I think you had some idea, Lydia. You just don't want to admit it, not even to yourself."

"It doesn't matter now. It happened. We move on."

"The hell we do. Damn it, Lydia. Can't you see I care about you? I've never been so jealous of anyone the way I was jealous of Apollo."

She frowned, confused since he in fact was Apollo. "That's crazy."

"I know. It makes no sense, but hearing you call that name when I took you from behind about killed me."

Immediately the image of him sliding inside her, while Trent lay beneath her, filled her mind. Her pussy flooded with liquid heat. "Don't, Dane," she whispered, her voice husky with arousal. "I don't want to talk about it."

He stepped closer, filling her senses with his powerful presence. "Why? Because it turns you on?"

Lydia didn't dare tell him the truth. Everything about him and that night turned her on. "No," she lied.

Dane smiled and cupped her face in his palms. "Sweet Lydia, don't you know I can tell when you're lying?" His gaze moved south, stopping on her breasts. "Your nipples are rock hard through that thin little T-shirt and I'll bet your pussy is wet too, isn't it, baby?"

"Dane, please..." Her voice trialed off. She wasn't even sure what she was pleading for, to be released or to be swept into his arms.

He dipped his head and covered her lips with his. Lydia moaned and wrapped her arms around his neck. He was so tender, so warm. She'd been so cold for the past two days and suddenly a raging inferno blazed inside her. As his tongue coasted over her lips, she let out a sigh and parted for him. He took his time, dipping between her lips and tasting her as if he had all the time in the world. She wrapped her arms around his neck and pulled him in deeper, edgy all at once for everything. She didn't care about his deception, she didn't want to worry about her future. She just wanted to feel his rough hands on her breasts, his cock filling her, driving out the sadness.

He groaned. Suddenly his warm palm lay flat against her bare flesh beneath her shirt, inching upward until the caress of his thumb on her aching nipple had her body vibrating with need. Lydia whimpered and Dane lifted his head, his gaze holding hers captive. "If you don't want this, say it now, Lydia," he ordered, his voice a rumble of sound in the room. "Push me away and I'll go. I'll leave you alone. It'll kill me, but for you I'll do it."

He was giving her a chance to stop, to hold on to her dignity, but at what cost to her heart? Did she dare give him another chance?

"You won't regret it, baby," he murmured as if reading her mind. "I'd rather be skinned alive than cause you pain."

"I-I want you, Dane," Lydia admitted, "but we haven't resolved anything. I'm still angry and hurt over what you did."

"It hurts because you care about me," he said softly. "Admit that much at least."

"I told you already that I was attracted to you, but it doesn't matter now."

"It's more than physical," he ground out. "Why are you holding back? Why deny your feelings?"

"I can't do this," she cried. "Please, Dane."

He held her firm, refusing to let her retreat. "Can't do what? Help me understand why I'm not worth a second chance?"

Anger rose up and for the first time Lydia didn't hold back. "You want the truth? Fine. I'm the one not worthy!" She jerked out of his arms and pointed to the family photo on the wall. "I wasn't good enough for my own mother, Dane, why the hell would I be good enough for anyone else?"

"You can't really believe that. You're the sweetest, most lovable woman I've ever met." His expression softened and Lydia felt the first tear trail down her cheek. He swiped it away with his thumb and murmured, "You've had me going in circles for two years, baby. Your mother had something precious, but she was too blind to realize it."

She turned away from him, too scared to hope, but when her gaze caught on her mother's image, everything seemed to fall into place. She wasn't like her mother, maybe she never had been. Dane stepped in front of her and she saw the emotion flickering in his warm brown eyes. "You're right," Lydia whispered. "I do deserve to be loved."

He wrapped his arms around her and held her tight. "Let me love you, Lydia. I know I haven't earned a second chance, but so help me, you won't regret it."

Lydia buried her face in his white dress shirt, barely able to contain the emotions flowing through her. She wanted him with a desperation that bordered on pain. It couldn't be natural to want a man the way she wanted Dane.

He pushed his hips forward and Lydia felt the heavy weight of his cock pressing into her belly. "Damn, baby, I can't think for needing you. The past few days have been pure hell. Put us both out of our miseries, I'm begging you."

Lydia leaned her head back, surprised when she witnessed a hint of vulnerability in Dane's expression. Could he be as scared as she? "What is this for you, Dane?"

His thumb feathered back and forth over her nipple and Lydia had to contain a whimper. "You're the woman I look forward to seeing each morning, Lydia. The same woman who had me practically salivating with her prim little outfits and intelligent wit. The truth? You've been in my life for two years and I'm just now getting around to telling you how I really feel. I've wanted you, but I was too much the coward to step up and do something about it. You're different than any woman I've ever known. Sweeter, more defiant, and such a contradiction you've had my head spinning ever since you took me and those other two dumbasses to heaven."

It was too much. She was slowly drowning and she knew it. She tried to look away, but strong fingers cupped her chin and coaxed her gaze back to his. "The instant you took off those clothes at Kinks you became mine, Lydia. It may have been Apollo, Poseidon and Zeus you gave your body to, but I'm the man you'll scream for from now on." With his other hand massaging her breast, Dane whispered, "Do I stay?"

This was it. Her chance to back out. Instinctively Lydia knew he wouldn't hold it against her if she asked him to leave. Could she live the rest of her life without his touches? Without knowing what it would be like to make love to Dane without the other two men there? No masks, no fake names? It was beyond tempting.

Yes, she did need him. Dane was the only man who had ever managed to entice her inner vixen, that daring woman she'd been at Kinks. It could be the biggest mistake of her life, but letting him leave without having him filling her, chasing away the cold, was a much more depressing scenario.

"Stay, please," she answered as new determination filled her with strength.

11

Dane's heart soared as those two words passed her lips. He wasted no time, sweeping her into his arms and striding down the hall. "Bedroom?"

She wrapped her arms around his neck and nuzzled his shirt. "First door on the right."

God, she felt good in his arms. He'd ached for her. For days his body had been cold from the inside out, as if only she had the power to warm him. When he stepped into her bedroom, his gaze swept the room, taking in the king-sized bed with the white comforter and canopy. The walls were painted a pale peach and the curtains on the window had a little seashell pattern. Dane noticed a large painting of a tropical beach behind the headboard and a big seashell-shaped area rug on the floor. There were plants all over, all of them looked well loved. He didn't know what he expected. Her living room with the soft, mauve couch and chair had been more along what he'd imagined Lydia's apartment to look like. White walls and comfortable-looking furniture, but nothing that really hinted at the naughty minx he'd witnessed at his club. This little oasis was definitely a nice surprise. It told Dane a lot about the woman she attempted to keep hidden. "Your bedroom is pretty," he murmured as he placed her on top of the white bedspread.

She scooted to the edge, letting her legs dangle over the side. "I've never been to the ocean, but I've always wanted to go."

He had a feeling there were a lot of things his sweet Lydia had never done, and he couldn't wait to introduce her to every decadent one of them. "I'll take you to Cancun," he promised as he took off her glasses and placed them on the table next to the bed. "We can eat lobster and make love on the beach. Would you like that, baby?"

"Dane." Her whispered voice held a warning and Dane didn't want to hear it. He leaned down and covered her lips with his own, stealing any further protests. She tasted like summer, soft and warm and inviting. He could drown in Lydia's kisses. She clutched onto his shoulders, digging her little nails into his flesh through the cotton shirt. As she moaned, Dane took the kiss deeper, drawing her backward on the bed and covering her with his body. Her tongue came out, shyly exploring, and Dane opened, sucking it into his mouth. Lydia groaned and arched against him, her breasts flattening against his chest, driving out all sane thought. It wasn't easy for him to lose control. He took pride in maintaining control in the bedroom, but Lydia went to his head quicker than whiskey.

He pulled back and muttered, "Clothes."

Immediately Lydia grabbed the hem of her shirt and tugged it upward. He started unbuttoning his dress shirt, watching as she exposed herself for him, one slow inch at a time. He knew she wasn't intentionally trying to be seductive, but watching the pink T-shirt reveal her sexy slightly curved belly, caused Dane's blood to pump hard and hot through his veins. As she exposed her breasts to his view, a haze of lust washed over him, driving out all else. He yanked, popping several buttons down the front of his shirt, and tossed it away. She stilled after her shirt hit the floor and bit her lip. Her plump breasts were a thing of beauty. Full, round and creamy, with little berry tips that he wanted to nibble on for hours. He ached to tie her breasts and spank them until they were a pretty shade of pink, then he'd fill her hot little pussy and drive them both over the edge.

Dane started to loosen his black leather belt, then stopped and waited to see if Lydia would continue her little striptease. Her gaze ate him up and, if he didn't miss his guess, she was also holding her breath.

"Breathe, baby." She flushed and let out a shuddering breath, her pretty tits jiggling. With her long dark hair spread out on the pillow beneath her, Dane thought she was the most adorable thing he'd ever seen. "Finish it, Lydia."

Her fingers shook as she untied the front of her sweatpants. Dane felt a trickle of sweat run between his shoulder blades. After he pulled his belt free and laid it on the bed, he quickly finished undressing. With slow precise movements, Lydia slid her sweats down her thighs, revealing a pair of sheer red panties. He could easily see her dark curls. Dane inhaled, smelling her wet heat. Christ, he wanted to taste her. It had driven him crazy watching Trent lick at her sweet honey.

Dane clutched Lydia's waist and slid her farther onto the bed, then straddled her. With his hands at either side of her head, caging her in, he growled, "The other night you weren't made to submit. This time I want to give you a taste of what it means to be dominated. Do you trust me, Lydia?"

She closed her eyes and whispered, "Yes."

Dane wrapped a hand around her throat and gently squeezed. Her eyes popped open and both of her hands flew to his, intent on dragging his fingers away from her vulnerable neck. "Trust, Lydia. Drop your hands." Lydia stared for long seconds but finally relented. He smiled down at her and released her. "Good girl." Dane leaned down and licked a spot just behind her ear, then let his tongue travel downward, tasting a potent mix of cinnamon and woman.

"Dane."

Hearing her huskily whisper his name made his cock achingly hard. He took his journey farther south until he reached the swell of her breast. "Cup it for me," he ordered. When she didn't obey, Dane leaned back and wrapped his fingers around it, then smacked the hard tip.

She jumped. "Dane!"

"Next time do as I say. I won't repeat the commands, Lydia. You do everything I say without question. Understood?"

She frowned up at him, that tempting defiant streak ever present. He spanked her breast again, this time a little harder. "I asked a question, sub."

"Yes." Her voice wasn't quite steady when she muttered, "I understand."

He smiled, his heart swelling. He could become addicted to Lydia's special blend of defiance and submission. It was what every dom craved. A strong, independent woman outside the bedroom, but a sweet little submissive between the sheets.

"Does your nipple hurt, Lydia? And be honest with me."

She glowered at him. "Not exactly."

She was clearly confused by her own reaction. "What does it feel like to have this pretty tit spanked?" He squeezed, drawing another moan from between her lips. "Does that little sting make your clit throb, baby?"

"You're driving me crazy, Dane," she tossed back.

He chuckled. "Good, then I'm not alone here." He dipped his head and licked the hard bud, easing the slight sting, before sucking it into his mouth. He flicked it with his tongue and Lydia whimpered, digging her fingers into his hair, clutching his scalp. He continued teasing and nipping before he moved to the other swollen nipple and lavished it with the same avid attention.

He traveled kisses down her ribcage to her belly before dipping his tongue into the little indentation there. She writhed beneath him and Dane let a low growl loose. He lifted his head and stared at the arousal in her eyes, the pretty flush of her cheeks. "You're beautiful, Lydia. Such a lovely submissive, and all mine."

"Dane, please," she pleaded. "I need you so badly."

He cupped her mound through the panties. They were drenched with her passion. "Shh, I know. But let me take my time. I need to savor this sweet body."

"Maybe it would be better to rush, then savor later."

Dane chuckled. God she was addicting. "No, sub." He used the term on purpose, bringing them back to the game. "Quickies aren't my thing. Relax and let me play with my pussy."

Dane reached down and caressed her tiny bud through her panties. She moaned but stayed still. He stared at the red panties and knew a sense of possessiveness he'd never before felt. If any other man saw her like this, he'd rip his head off. It wasn't an entirely comfortable notion, considering how many times he, Mac and Trent had shared women. He knew in his gut there would be no repeat performance for them, not now that his heart had become involved.

He licked a fiery path over the lace and watched her twist and thrash beneath him. He gripped her hip. "Open these silky thighs for me, baby." Lydia obeyed without question this time—already she was becoming accustomed to his commands. He slid his index finger beneath the elastic leg band and pushed it out of his way. He inhaled the delicious scent of her arousal as he stared at the swollen clitoris and delicate slit. Dane stroked a finger between her pussy lips and had to hold her down to keep her from bucking him clear off the bed. He loved her uninhibited response to his touch. Slowly, Dane dipped his head between her thighs and tasted her sweet pearl.

"Yes!"

Delving his middle finger into her hot opening, he let his tongue slide over her swollen clit. Her moans turned to harsh cries. "Mmm, so fucking responsive. You drive me crazy, Lydia." Every whimper, every time his name passed through her lips, it drove him higher and higher. He clenched his jaw against the need to slide his cock deep, to fuck her so hard she could never leave him again. He pushed a second finger deep and had to bite back a curse as the delicious squeeze of her vaginal muscles tightened around him. She was going to kill him when he entered her, but he'd die happy.

He'd been hungry since that night at Kinks, and only Lydia could satisfy his appetite now. He pulled his fingers free and heard Lydia whimper and beg for him to come back. Instead he turned around so he faced her patch of dark curls. The position put his cock in line with her clever mouth. He rose over her, used his thumbs to open her wet cunt and licked. Her body arched and she screamed his name. It was the sweetest sound he'd ever heard.

Dane lifted his head and gazed down at her. "Lick my cock, sub. Fill that hot little mouth."

She turned on her side, facing him. Dane watched as she placed a teasing series of kisses over his balls and up the underside of his cock. "Fuck, that's a good girl. Play with me, baby."

As she reached the swollen tip, Dane stiffened. She opened wide and sucked him deep. She pulled all the way back, before doing it all over again, his cock touching the back of her throat. Her delicate fingers wrapped around the base and she moaned, the vibration traveling over his dick like a thousand little fingers.

Dane pushed his hips against her face and fucked her mouth the way he liked. "That's it, suck it for me," he commanded, and watched her eyes drift closed as she accepted his loving.

He put his arm around her hips and fondled her ass as he slipped his tongue into her honeyed opening. She whimpered and Dane suddenly wanted more. He pushed his middle finger inside her rounded backside, remembering how tight she'd held him when he fucked her ass. It'd been such sweet torture. He wanted her there again soon, but first he had a need to see her flying apart. This time for him alone. He licked her clit and fucked her tight ass with his finger. Lydia arched her back and undulated against his mouth. Maintaining a measure of control had never been so damn hard.

Together, they luxuriated in each other's bodies. Dane pumped her ass while he licked and nibbled on her swollen nub. The combination had Lydia pushing against his face. He nuzzled and sank his tongue deep as his finger fucked her ass harder, faster. Soon she released his cock and shouted his name as spasms wracked her body.

12

Lydia was a boneless mass. She'd never come so hard in her life. Not even the night at Kinks could compare to having Dane all to herself.

He turned around on the bed and came over the top of her, aligning their lower halves so his cock nestled between her thighs. "Mmm, you feel so damn good," Dane murmured. "Tell me you're on the pill, Lydia. Tell me now before I lose control."

Lydia nodded. The thought of having him without any barriers sent a fresh wave of heat crashing through her. "I'm on the pill."

"Thank God," he groaned. Dane pressed forward, the head of his cock pushing between the folds of her pussy. "I wanted this, my cock filling your sweet pussy instead of Trent's. I'll never share you again. Never again."

He sounded jealous, and he spoke as if they had a future together. The thought filled her heart with joy. When he pushed in another inch, spreading her open, her mind fragmented.

"Dane," she moaned. His name came out as a plea and he dipped his head and nipped the side of her neck. The delicious sting zipped straight to her clit.

"Put your hands above your head, sub," he whispered into her ear, "wrists together."

Lydia quickly obeyed, trusting Dane to bring her nothing but sweet, hot pleasure.

One large hand wrapped around her wrists, while his powerful body pinned her down. He lifted his head, his gaze sweeping over her body and he hummed his approval. "You're lovely like this. I want you tied down. Could you handle that? Do you trust me that much, sub?"

She did trust him, but the very thought sent a trickle of fear down her spine. He had too much power over her and she could so easily become lost in him.

"I have no right to ask, but give me a chance here, sweetheart. I won't hurt you."

Her eyes must have conveyed her assent. Good thing too, because she couldn't seem to speak past the lump in her throat. Dane kissed her forehead, then pulled out of her. He left the bed and she started to bring her arms down, but Dane was quicker. He grasped both of her hands and kept them pinned to the mattress above her head.

"I didn't give you permission to move. Stay still or I'll spank you. Understood?"

The thought of defying him on purpose was almost too tempting. She'd enjoyed his spanking before and she almost craved the sting now.

Dane chuckled and shook his head. "You are such a little tease, baby. I have so many things to teach you. It's going to be a pleasure." He lifted his hands, trusting her to obey him. "Now, be a good girl and stay still while I get a few things."

When he left the room, Lydia wondered what he could be up to. Within seconds he reappeared, his briefcase in hand. She frowned. "Dane?"

He winked and set the case on the bed. "I stopped off at the store before I came here." He fiddled with the lock and the catch sprang free. He opened the case, but Lydia couldn't quite see what he was doing. When he held up a pair of handcuffs, Lydia's mouth dropped open. He placed them on the bed, then took out a tube of lubricant and a small, purple object. Lydia had no idea what it could be. It had a flared base and slender neck. The rounded, slightly teardrop-shaped tip widened into a bulb that had Lydia's suspicions rising.

Dane put the items on the bed, then picked up the handcuffs and came back down on top of her. She shuddered as his warm, muscular chest pressed against her hard nipples. "You look scared, baby. Don't be."

He opened the handcuffs, placed the cold steel on her left wrist and clamped it shut, before doing the same to the other. Lydia wiggled her wrists and realized she couldn't get loose. It was both thrilling and frightening to be completely at Dane's mercy. She bit her lip and took a deep breath, letting it out slowly.

"Ah, nervous, yet still so compliant. You'll get a reward, I promise, but first there's this . . ."

Dane angled his head and his lips tantalized hers in a gentle reminder of how much power he held over her, then he moved down her body, kissing an imaginary path toward her pussy and touching off several tremors as he went. When he reached her throbbing clit, Lydia was all but begging for him to fill her. Dane reared back, grabbed the lubricant and the purple toy and asked, "Do you know what this is?"

"No," she admitted. "And just so you know, you're driving me crazy with this slow seduction."

"Shh, we have all the time in the world, baby. Let me play."

He opened the tube and spread a small amount over the purple toy. "Open your legs for me."

She hesitated, unsure what he was up to. "What are you going to do with that thing?"

He arched a brow. "You aren't supposed to question your dom, Lydia."

"You can spank me, but I still want to know what you're planning."

While he held the toy, he used his free hand to smooth over one thigh. Lydia relaxed a measure, but she wasn't giving in. She wanted to know what he had in mind. He grinned, as if sensing a challenge, and leaned down to place a light kiss to her curls. She opened her thighs a few inches and Dane's eyes sparkled with mischief. His tongue swiped over her clit and Lydia surrendered. She parted her thighs and arched upward, desperate for his special brand of loving. He gave her another slow lick, then pulled her clit into his mouth and sucked it. She screamed his name and closed her eyes.

He swirled his tongue around the little bud and stars burst behind her eyelids. Dane suddenly released her and Lydia opened her eyes, his hot gaze trapping hers. When he cupped her mound in a possessive, yet tender hold, Lydia's heart swelled.

"Your pussy belongs to me," he growled. "Admit it, Lydia."

She shook her head, unwilling to give him so much power. He nuzzled her again and slid his middle finger into her soaked cunt, clear to the third knuckle. He curled his finger upward and pressed against a particularly sensitive spot. She whimpered, helpless to the pleasurable assault.

"Say it, sub."

She couldn't take much more and they both knew it. "Fine, I'm yours! Just please stop torturing me."

He slid another finger inside her and Lydia thought she would die from the pleasure. "My little pussy wants to come, huh?"

"Yes, please," she begged, desperate and aching for him to fill her.

He pulled both fingers free and ordered, "Spread your legs for your master." This time she was quick to comply. Dane flattened his palm against her mound and said, "Don't make the mistake of assuming you can question me. You need to learn to trust me with your body. Your pleasure is my pleasure. I won't hurt you, baby."

"I've never done anything like this, Dane. I don't know what to do."

"Just let me make love to you, little Lydia. In here, in the bedroom, you surrender to me completely. No hesitation or you'll be punished. Do you understand?"

Lydia knew what he was asking. Total submission. The instant she gave it, he would know how much she cared for him, how much he meant to her. Did she dare take that leap?

"Yes," she breathed out.

Dane rose over her, his hands on either side of her head, caging her in. He leaned down and kissed her. It was sweet, gentle and all too fleeting. "Thank you for trusting me."

He moved down her body and parted her thighs. As he knelt between them, his gaze on her pussy, Lydia had to bite her lip against the need to close her legs. As she watched, he picked up the purple toy and smoothed it between her pussy lips, creating a firestorm of need inside her. He slowly slid the tip up and down, teasing her sensitive tissues, then moved downward toward her tight pucker. He swirled the toy around the small opening, lubricating it with each pass, then started to gently push it inside her ass. Lydia stiffened.

"Shh, baby. Relax for me." Dane's tender expression and his deep soothing tone tore away at her fears. The way his gaze soaked her in made her feel special, as if she meant more to him than mere sex.

Lydia took another fortifying breath and let it out slowly, allowing all her reservations to dissipate. Dane hummed his approval and began to press the toy inside her once more. There was a brief moment of discomfort as he pushed beyond the tight ring of muscles surrounding the small entrance, to be quickly replaced by white-hot pleasure. Lydia was thrust back to that delicious moment when it'd been Dane's cock filling her there. Her pussy creamed at the reminder and she opened her legs farther.

Dane rubbed his palm over her pussy, eliciting another series of tremors from her. "Fuck, that's sweet, baby," Dane groaned. "So sweet." As he moved over her, his muscular body pinned hers to the mattress, his arms caging her in. He positioned his cock at her entrance and pushed in an inch. "God, Lydia, you're going to burn me alive with this hot little cunt."

Lydia lifted her hips and he slipped in another inch. She wanted him deep, stretching and filling her, chasing away the cold. She lifted her arms, anxious to touch him, before remembering the handcuffs. "Release me, please, Dane. I want to touch you."

"No. Keep your arms above your head and don't move them again."

She wanted to protest his harsh demand, but he kissed her forehead before her cheeks and lips received special attention. Lydia gave in to the pleasure of the moment. Surrendering, body and soul.

He pushed his cock in a little more, the toy filling her ass added an extra dimension to their loving. He began slowly stroking her hair and smoothing a palm down her arm to her hip where he cupped her bottom and kneaded the plump flesh. She melted, giving them both what they needed in that moment. Dane seemed to sense her submission and began a slow glide inside her pussy, filling her the way she craved. Her body stretched to accommodate his size, and Lydia felt a little pressure from the toy inside her ass but no pain. It was like nothing she'd ever experienced. He thrust hard and her vagina clenched, tightening around him like a fist.

"Damn, you drive me wild. You have the softest pussy in the world, Lydia. So fucking perfect." He pushed forward, hard, and Lydia cried out as sensation after sensation rocked her body. "Mine," he growled.

The single word uttered in Dane's deep voice sent a rush of desire through her womb. With each inward stroke from his cock, Lydia could feel the toy, and it added another level to the pleasure. Her muscles held them both tight. She squeezed, giving Dane a new kind of pleasure.

"Fuck, yeah, baby, do that again," he ground out as he pushed against her hips harder, faster. She complied and he shouted her name, fucking her with wild abandon. She cried out as another orgasm took her to all-new heights. Dane thrust one last time and soared with her. Lydia felt every pulse of his cock as he filled her with his hot come.

Dane collapsed on top of her, both of their bodies damp from exertion. Lydia couldn't move, didn't dare try. Every muscle in her body was sore. It was several seconds before he lifted up. He gently pulled the toy free and tossed it aside, his gaze eating her up. "You make me ache, little Lydia." He brushed her damp hair from her face and kissed her cheek. "Let me stay the night."

She stared up at him, tears filling her eyes. He was her world. Mistake or not, she couldn't deny him. "Don't go," she whispered.

Dane left the bed, then lifted her into his arms, cradling her against his hard chest. "First I'm going to run you a hot bath, then I'm going to give you a massage. Later, if you're a very good sub, I'll show you what else I have in my briefcase."

She shuddered as she imagined what else he could possibly

have in store for them. Her imagination wasn't that good though. "Dane?"

"Yeah, baby?"

"What about the handcuffs?"

He entered her bathroom and flipped on the light. "Soon enough, sub. For now, I like you at my mercy."

The sensual tilt to his lips stole her heart. She couldn't speak for the emotion clogging her throat. There was still so much unsettled, and she hadn't completely forgiven him for deceiving her. Before she could stop herself, Lydia blurted out the one question that had niggled at her since she'd found out Apollo and Dane were one and the same. "Am I the naughty librarian you mentioned at Kinks? Is that what this is for you?"

Dane stopped dead and stared down at her, his gaze filled with red-hot anger. "You think I just want to fuck you? Is that what you've been imagining?"

She hadn't wanted it put so crudely, but she needed to know the truth. Damn it, she deserved the truth. "What else could it be? I've worked for you for two years and you never even hinted at a relationship."

Immediately he set her on her feet. Lydia wobbled and he clutched her shoulders in a gentle but demanding hold, steadying her instantly. "If I only wanted sex, I could get that at Kinks. There are plenty of women who would gladly kneel for me."

An image of some faceless woman on her knees in front of Dane, loving his cock, slammed into her mind. Lydia's palm itched to smack him. "Great," she gritted out, "unlock these handcuffs and go get one of them then!"

"None of them could hold a candle to you," he murmured. The raw need in his chocolate brown gaze tore at her defenses. "You've been a fire in my blood, Lydia. Having you beneath me has been a dream come true. The need to see you without the buttoned-up blouses and the pins in your hair has made it damned hard to keep my distance." He took her face in his hands and smoothed his thumb over her bottom lip. Lydia couldn't seem to catch her breath. "Do you think I threaten to break every woman's door down? I haven't felt this out of control my entire life."

Her mother had tried so desperately to hide behind her own fears and look where that had gotten her. Divorced and alone, cut off from her only child.

Lydia smiled. "I've been half in love with you for a while, I think. I just didn't want to admit it, not even to myself."

He leaned down and covered her mouth with his in a demanding mating of lips. Lydia swayed forward, drifting on a sea of emotion she'd never imagined possible. He lifted a mere inch and whispered, "I want to know everything about you. I could spend weeks getting to know all your little quirks, every sweet little habit. You fascinate me, Lydia. You have from the moment you spilled coffee on yourself that first day."

"Dane," She moaned, emotion clogging her throat.

"This isn't just sex, baby. I'm through with other women and I'll be turning my share of Kinks over to Trent and Mac. This is the real thing for me and I'll die if you kick me out now."

Living a half-life no longer appealed to her, especially not now that she'd tasted heaven in Dane's arms. A woman couldn't go back after that, it simply wasn't possible.

"Stay," she demanded, "please."

A muscle in his jaw jumped. "Be sure, Lydia. I'll consider you mine after this. No more sharing either. Those days are history."

She smiled up at him, beyond pleased to know he wasn't the sharing type. That he was giving up the club made her heart soar. "I don't want anyone else, Dane. Only you. It's always been you."

"God, baby, you blow my mind."

Then something else occurred to her. "I do have one question."

"Anything, Lydia. You can ask me anything."

"The hood. Will you wear it again for me?"

His slow grin was one of pure male sin. "Mmm, you are such a sweet surprise."

Turn Me On

1

"No, damn it, not again!" Roni shouted as her computer froze for the fourth time that morning. It was Saturday afternoon and her one day to get her paperwork done, and what happens? Her computer fizzles out. It'd been happening more frequently. She'd called the computer repair company out once already and the guy had acted as if it were somehow her fault. As if she wanted to waste both their time!

She picked up the phone and hit memory six. It was telling that she had the repair company on speed dial.

"J.C.'s Computer Repair, Lisa speaking. How may I help you?"

"Hi, Lisa, it's Dr. Smart. I'm having that same problem where my monitor freezes. And, yes, I've tried rebooting, but it's not doing any good."

"Hi, Dr. Smart. Let me check who's on call real quick."

"Fine," Roni said as she grabbed her empty mug and went to the break room for a refresher. As she poured her third cup of coffee, Lisa came back on the line.

"Someone will be out within the hour. Will that work?"

"I suppose it'll have to work. Thanks, Lisa."

They ended the call and she went back to her office and stared at her monitor, willing it to work. It was no use. She was stuck waiting for it to be fixed. Again! When her cell phone rang, Roni snatched it up, grateful for the distraction. She checked the number and smiled.

"Hey, Lydia, how're things going with that hot lawyer of yours?" Roni had known Lydia since grade school, but it wasn't until recently that Lydia had gotten serious about a man. She was happy for Lydia. She deserved to be cherished and Dane seemed perfect in the role of lover.

"He's the reason I'm calling. He wants to invite you and Jeannette over for a barbeque next Saturday. Think you can make it?"

"Will it be your place or his?" Since Lydia and Dane had only just started dating there hadn't been time to work out which apartment they'd be keeping and which they would be letting go after the lease was up.

"His. He wants to wow you guys, I think. Win you over."

"After the stunt he pulled? He's got a lot of wowing to do."

"He's apologized a million times. Really, it's all good. Besides, I'm starting to think things happen for a reason."

Roni smiled. It did her heart good to hear her repressed friend so blissfully content. "Heck, if you're happy, I'm happy. He just better treat you right."

"I'm quite happy. I'll be happier if you came to the barbeque."

"Sure, it sounds like fun." Roni heard a knock on her front door and said, "I need to run. The computer repair guy is here. Call me later and let me know what to bring."

"Wait, computer guy? It's broken again?"

Roni gritted her teeth. "Unfortunately. If they don't fix it this time, I'm finding someplace else to handle my computer problems."

"No doubt."

They said their good-byes and Roni slid her chair back and went out front to greet her visitor. The man on the other side of the glass door had her stopping in her tracks though. He was tall, over six feet, with midnight black hair cut a little too long by today's standards. His black T-shirt stretched across a mouthwatering chest and tucked neatly into a pair of well-worn jeans. The bulge between a pair of powerful thighs turned her blood to molten lava.

"Damn, now that's delicious," Roni said in a low tone. As her gaze caught on his, she watched his lips kick up into an ornery grin. It was as if he'd heard her, and although Roni knew that was impossible, she still felt her cheeks heating in embarrassment.

She crossed the waiting room and unlocked the door. Pushing it open a few inches, she said, "J.C.'s Repair?"

He turned, giving her his back. In bold white letters were the words J.C.'S COMPUTER REPAIR. WE'LL HAVE YOUR HARD DRIVE PURRING IN NO TIME.

"I see," she said, suddenly breathless. Purring hell, he'd already fried her circuits and she had yet to find out his name!

"I take it you're closed today?" he said, noting the empty waiting area with a wave of his hand.

"Yeah, I usually do paperwork and finances on Saturdays. But my computer decided to freeze up instead. To be honest, this is the second time it's happened this week. It's getting extremely inconvenient."

"And we certainly wouldn't want you inconvenienced, Dr. Smart. Maybe you should point me to the problem child."

Roni wanted to rail at him, but alienating the man before he had a chance to fix her computer didn't seem smart. She held her tongue and escorted him to her office. Pointing to her flatscreen monitor, Roni said, "I've turned it off and back on three times this morning, but it's not helping."

He moved around her desk and sat in her chair. There was something intensely sexual about seeing the hard-bodied man at her desk. The image of him bending her over the sturdy mahogany as he pounded into her wet pussy flooded her mind. Roni shook the X-rated thought away and asked, "Would you like some coffee? It's still fresh."

"Sure, thanks," he mumbled as he went to work.

A man of few words. Roni shrugged and left him to his geekiness. After pouring the last cup from the glass carafe into a clean mug, Roni brought it back to her office and placed it on the desk. "It's black; will that do?"

"That's fine," he said as he continued pounding the keys.

Roni sat in one of the other chairs and crossed her legs, waiting for him to finish working his magic. Several minutes went by before he rubbed his chin and sat back in his seat. When his gaze moved away from the screen and traveled over her body, awakening her inner slut, Roni had to force herself to stay seated. Jumping the repairman was way too cliché. Right?

"Do you only use this computer for work, Dr. Smart?"

His question surprised her. "Uh, yes. I have a laptop I use for personal matters. The desktop is strictly for client records and to keep track of my business finances, that sort of thing. Why?"

He quirked a brow and tapped a few more keys, before saying, "So, you never go out to the Internet and download videos or images?"

She frowned. Maybe he was hard of hearing. "I just said it's for business. Not pleasure."

"Do you let anyone else use this computer?"

"My assistant has access, but what does that have to do with it freezing up?" Before he could answer, her anger got the better of her. "This has been happening constantly. A tech came out and fixed it and swore it wouldn't happen again. To tell the truth I'm about ready to take my business elsewhere. I simply don't have time for this type of distraction."

"Porn."

"What did you say?" Surely she hadn't heard him right.

"Someone's been downloading porn. That's why your computer keeps freezing up. You've let your virus protection expire and as a result you've been hit with spyware. A lot of it."

"Porn? B-but that's impossible."

He crooked his finger at her. "Come here. Let me show you something."

Roni left the chair and moved around the side of the desk until she stood next to him, his eyes level with her breasts. A few buttons, a little leaning and she could offer him something besides coffee to sip on. The man wasn't here to be mentally molested though.

She cleared her throat and growled, "Okay, I'm here."

His grin wasn't at all professional. "Yes, you are."

She started to chastise him but he turned to her monitor and went back into work mode. "See this?" he pointed to a file she didn't recognize.

She leaned forward, automatically inhaling his clean masculine scent. "What is that?"

He clicked it and her media player popped open and suddenly Roni was watching a video of a woman deep-throating a rather large, hard cock.

Roni gasped. "Oh my God! Turn it off! Turn it off!"

He clicked a button and the player closed. "By your expression I'm guessing it's not you with the porn habit?"

"Of course not!" Roni was no prude, but she wasn't in the habit of watching nasty videos at work either.

"Well, that's just one of many. You have several of those on your hard drive. And those sites are notorious for spyware. You need to find out who's using your computer and put a stop to it. So far it's only been a nuisance, but it could lead to real problems, like a virus that'll wipe out your entire hard drive."

Roni stepped back and crossed her arms over her chest. "It's only me and my assistant, Melissa, and I can't believe she'd do that." She shook her head as she thought of her shy assistant. "No, I won't believe it. There has to be another explanation."

"Maybe it's not Melissa. Maybe it's someone else. There is a way for you to find out, if you're interested."

"How?"

"I can install a motion-sensitive webcam. All you do is hit a few keys when you leave the office and you can catch the horny bugger in his tracks."

Part of her didn't want to know. It was way too creepy to think Melissa could be sitting at her desk getting off on dirty videos. Still, Roni knew she needed to put a stop to it. The idea of someone masturbating while sitting in her black leather chair made her queasy. "You can do this for me?"

"Sure, I can handle it. If you'd rather, I can give you some instructions and you can do it yourself. It's not hard to set up."

Roni went back to the chair across from the desk and sat down. The close proximity was beginning to overwhelm her senses. "I can turn on my computer and use a few of the programs. Beyond that, electronics boggle my mind. No, I'd rather you set it up."

"No problem. I need to pick up a few things, but I can come back later today if you want. That way it'll be in place by Monday. I can update your virus protection then as well."

"Will this be expensive?"

He shrugged and tapped a few more keys on her computer, before he stood. "I'll just charge you for the camera. The virus update is on me. My tech should've talked to you about this when he came out the other day."

Now she felt bad for being such a bitch. She'd assumed the tech they'd sent out was inept. Who would have guessed someone was looking at dirty videos on her work computer? "Thanks, I appreciate it. As it is, I'll be here quite late, so stop back anytime."

"See you in a few then." He stood and Roni followed suit.

As she walked him back to the front door, she realized she didn't know his name. The other tech had worn a name tag, but this dark-haired hunk didn't have one. "I never got your name."

"Jake Cornick."

Roni quickly put two and two together. "You're the J.C. in J.C.'s Computer Repair?"

"Yes, ma'am. None of my other techs wanted to come. I think maybe my other tech was a little embarrassed to have to tell you about the spyware problem."

Heat flooded her cheeks. "They must all think I'm quite the nympho, huh?"

He chuckled. "They're too smart to say anything inappropriate around me. They know I'd fire them for talking about a client that way. But, I suspect there's been . . . talk."

Roni covered her face as humiliation engulfed her. "I'll never be able to face any of them again."

Rough palms covered her hands and slowly pulled them down. When their gazes met, Roni was surprised by the tenderness in his pale green depths. "Don't worry about it. I'll set them straight."

She tugged on her hands until he took the hint and dropped them. Cold emptiness filled her as he stepped back. "Thank you for your help, Mr. Cornick. I really appreciate it."

"Jake," he insisted softly.

"Jake, then," she said, her voice husky with desire. She watched as he reached into his back pocket and pulled out his wallet. When he flipped it open, pulled out a business card and handed it to her, Roni eagerly took it. Their fingers brushed and she swore sparks flew. *Easy girl.*

"See you in a few, Doc."

"Sure," she murmured.

He grinned and opened the door. It was all Roni could do to keep from reaching out and grabbing a handful of his tight, muscular ass.

Damn, the man was delicious. Roni smacked herself out of her lusty haze and went back to her office. As she sat down, she swore she could still smell him. A seductive, woodsy scent that wrapped around her like a warm blanket.

"You're losing it, girl," she muttered to herself. "Get back to work or it'll be a longer night than you planned."

When Roni moved the mouse, her screen blinked on and a new document appeared on the screen with the words, I LOVE POLKA DOTS, DR. SMART. VERY SEXY. SEE YA SOON, JAKE.

Roni's pulse skipped a beat as she glanced down at her pale pink blouse. There it was, her bra with the multicolored little dots clearly visible through the thin silk. "Oh, hell," she groaned.

2

It took Jake a good five minutes to breathe normally again. "Jesus." He swiped a hand over his face and started his Mustang. As he pulled out of the parking lot, he had to readjust his jeans to accommodate the hard cock that had been intent on getting to know the sweet little doctor on a more personal level.

If he'd known what he'd be in for when he'd decided to take the service call, Jake would've been coming around to fix the woman's computer a hell of a lot sooner. He never would've guessed that the Ice Queen, as his techs had dubbed her, would turn out to be a curvy, petite blonde with pouty lips and eyes so blue a man could drown in them.

Dr. Smart had a body made for long hours of loving. Instinctively, he knew they'd fit together perfectly. The flare of her hips and her pretty, heart-shaped ass beckoned a man to get up close and personal. His mind screamed at him to stay away. She was a client and she didn't strike him as the type to play around anyway. A gentleman wouldn't even consider touching her. Good thing he was no gentleman. Hell, it made him hard just thinking of all the dirty little things he wanted to do to her, the pleasure he could give her.

Jake reached between his thighs and stroked his cock through his jeans, the need to take the edge off paramount in his mind. He imagined her naked, her large breasts so gloriously bared, her smoothly rounded hips cushioning him. He'd fit himself between her silky thighs and sink right into paradise. He could almost hear her shout his name. The thought of bringing her to climax nearly had him coming in his jeans.

Christ, she was a dangerous one. A stubborn little spitfire that would have a man begging inside a minute. Jake had never messed around with a client. Hell, he'd never even been tempted. But when Dr. Smart had come around the side of the desk, putting her tantalizing breasts at eye level, Jake had wanted nothing more than to lean forward and suck one of her hard nipples into his mouth, blouse and all.

He smiled when he thought of the note he'd left. Would she change her blouse before he returned? Something told him she was much too headstrong. Embarrassment or no, she'd leave the blouse and the bra on and probably use that sharp tongue of hers to give him a lecture on impropriety. There was something about the woman that made Jake think of whips and chains, though he couldn't say why. She appeared to be the type who liked to have control over her own pleasure. Jake vowed he'd find out, soon. No way would he let this one get away, not without a little taste first.

As he pulled into a space in front of his office a horrible thought struck. Could she be married? Wait, he hadn't seen a ring. A woman like that didn't stay single long though. She'd have a boyfriend or fiancé tucked away somewhere. He could feel his good mood going down the shitter in a hurry. He'd already imagined her naked and beneath him as he pounded into her soft, supple body, but she could very well be off limits.

Jake slammed the door to his car and stalked across the lot to his office. The cool air inside the small building did little to change his mood.

"Hi, Uncle Jake," Lisa greeted him cheerfully. "Did you get Dr. Smart all straightened around?"

"I'm still working on her, er, it," he growled. "I'm still working on it."

"Awesome," Lisa said, totally oblivious to his slip, and went back to texting on her cell phone.

She was his niece, he reminded himself for the thousandth time. Otherwise, he would've fired her long ago. "No texting, Lisa. Put the cell phone away and get back to work."

"Sorry, Uncle Jake," Lisa mumbled before dropping the phone into her purse.

Jake shook his head. He could already see he was going to have to sit her down and give her a stern talking to, otherwise she'd keep riding roughshod over him. He was too soft, that was the problem. Lisa batted her pretty green eyes and he turned to mush. Was it any wonder his brother had such a hard time telling the girl no?

As he entered his private office, Jake headed to the shelf that covered half the left wall. He always kept a few supplies on hand. The webcam he'd purchased a few days ago was about to come in handy.

As he sat down and started filling out an invoice for Lisa to mail to Dr. Smart, one of his newest techs, Jimmy Chalvez, strode in. "You've been working on Dr. Smart's computer?"

"Yep," he replied, not bothering to look up. He was a man on a mission and getting back to the doc was only part of what he had planned.

"Did you tell her about the porn?"

Jake stopped writing and pinned Jimmy with an icy glare.

The smirk on the man's pockmarked face had Jake tensing. "Dr. Smart's computer isn't any of your damn business."

Jimmy paled and stood up straighter. "I only meant—"

"I know what you meant. You wanted to know if Dr. Smart had owned up to the videos. Well, here's a news flash for you, Jimmy. Dr. Smart's hard drive isn't fodder for the damned gossip mill around here."

"Right. Sorry, boss."

Jake ripped the invoice slip off the pad and stood. When he came around the desk, Jimmy backed up a step. "Just so we're crystal clear here. If I catch you or any of the other techs making nasty comments about a client, *any* client, you'll answer to me. Is that plain enough for you?"

"Uh, yeah. Real plain."

"Good," Jake bit out. "Get back to work and leave Dr. Smart to me."

Jimmy bobbed his head and rushed off.

Damn, he was already feeling territorial and he'd only just met the little beauty. What was it about her that made all his protective instincts kick in? Jake hadn't felt such an immediate response to a woman since the day he'd met Sarah.

The thought of his loving wife always made him smile. She'd been his high school sweetheart. They were the couple everyone talked about, perfect for each other and desperately in love. After graduation, Jake had wasted no time asking her to marry him. Their first year together had been rough financially, but it hadn't put a dent on their happiness. They'd spent their nights making love and their days in blissful contentment. Sarah had an energetic presence that made everyone feel better just for being around her. He'd sported a permanent smile that first year. Then the day had come when she'd found out about the breast cancer. His life had spiraled out of control fast. The mastectomy had been too little too late. Within months, he'd been forced to bury his wife, the love of his life. Jake had wanted to die right along with her.

He pushed thoughts of Sarah out of his mind and concentrated on getting back to Dr. Smart. First he planned to find out who was using her computer as their own personal playground, then he'd find out more about the woman who had his head all mixed up and his blood flowing hot and hard in his veins.

Roni had debated changing her shirt. She always kept a few items of clothing at her office for emergencies. In the end she decided it'd be a lot more fun to leave the blouse on. Watching Jake squirm would go a long way toward repairing her confidence. The man had some nerve checking out her breasts to begin with. Admitting to it in writing? Now that was bold. She wasn't sure if she should be turned on by his forwardness or not, but her panties hadn't been dry since she'd spotted the black-haired devil through her front door.

As she finished entering the last of her expenses for the month, Roni hit the save button and pushed her chair away from the desk. She'd been going at it for two hours straight and she'd skipped right over lunch, now it was nearing dinnertime and she was starving. When she entered the break room, she heard a knock on her front door. Her heart sped up as she peeked around the corner and saw Jake standing on the other side of the glass door, his concentration on the box in his hand. She shored up her nerve, all too aware of her see-through blouse, and strode across the room. When he raised his head, their gazes clashed for an instant, then his intense green eyes locked on to her breasts. His grin was slow and sensual and Roni felt her clit throb. Oh, God. This was crazy. She was baiting a tiger, she could feel it. Yet, she couldn't seem to stop herself from throwing down the challenge.

She flipped the lock and opened the door. "Thanks for coming back. I just finished for the day."

"My pleasure," he murmured as he stepped across the threshold. Their bodies brushed and Roni's temperature spiked.

"You, uh, brought the camera?"

He held up a black bag and a square box. "I've got everything you need."

She had a feeling there was more to his words, but she chose to ignore it. Instead she flipped the lock into place and escorted him back to her office. "Explain to me how this works exactly."

When he took up position behind her desk, Roni sighed. He looked entirely too sexy sitting in her chair. He opened the black case and brought out a computer disk. Roni was spellbound by his efficiency.

"First I need to install a program for the webcam. Since you don't want anyone to know it's active, we'll have to run it in the background. So, I'll show you how to use the command prompt."

Already she was lost. "Command prompt?"

He chuckled as he watched the screen. "It's easy. I'll walk you through it. You'll be able to type in a few commands to activate the camera while you're away from your desk. Like I said before, the camera is motion sensitive so if anyone sits down in your chair the camera will turn on and record what they're doing."

Roni thought of her assistant again. At twenty-one, Melissa was sweet and a little shy. She was majoring in psychology and Roni had admired her drive. "I really don't want it to be Melissa."

Jake nodded. "I can understand that." He paused before adding, "Maybe it's the janitorial service."

"Oh, God, I hadn't even considered that. The idea of someone watching those types of videos and . . ." She couldn't quite finish the sentence. It still made her want to replace the chair.

His gaze turned serious. "It's creepy as hell, I know. We'll get it figured out though, no worries."

He was being so sweet even though she'd all but accused his techs of being inept. "Thanks for doing this. I really appreciate it."

"Can I ask you something, Dr. Smart?"

She sat up straighter in the chair, intrigued by his question. "It's Roni," she corrected, "and sure."

"Do you have a significant other, Roni?"

"No, why?" She tilted her head and stared at him curiously. "Were you thinking my boyfriend was helping himself to porn at my office?"

"It wouldn't be the first time."

"I don't even want to know," she mumbled, suddenly feeling shy with the conversation. The odd reaction baffled her. She hadn't felt a bout of shyness since first grade, when Brian the Dork had pulled down her pants at recess.

"There, all set." He positioned the camera on top of the monitor, then stood. "I'm going to need you to come over here so I can show you the commands you'll need to know to activate the camera."

Roni quickly did his bidding. Once she was seated at her desk, a thought struck her. "Won't it seem strange to have a camera in here all of a sudden? What if someone asks me about it?"

He shrugged. "You're a doctor. Tell them you need it for online conferences with your colleagues."

"Yeah, right. I guess I'm not very good at the whole cloak and dagger thing."

He knelt down beside her and Roni had the sudden need to reach out and drag her fingers through his black, silky hair. "Yeah, you'd make a lousy spy," he replied with amusement.

"Good thing I became a psychologist instead then, huh?" She whispered. Oh God, she was nervous and she was never nervous. Damn, he was a virtual stranger and yet he seemed to touch her on a level deeper than any other man she'd ever known.

"Yeah, good thing," he murmured, his gaze never wavered from hers as he pointed to the keyboard. "Type in what I tell you."

Roni turned her attention to the monitor and placed her hands on the keyboard. "Ready." Jake gave her a series of commands, but nothing happened. "Did I do it wrong?"

"No, you did it just right. Now the camera's on and it's recording." He reached out and stroked her cheek, causing Roni to jump. "I had a feeling your skin would feel like satin. I was right." Roni turned her head and his fingers brushed over her lower lip. "I bet you taste like pure sunshine too."

"Jake, we really shouldn't—"

"Shh, it's okay." He pulled his hand away and Roni suddenly wanted it back, touching and caressing. She was surprised at how gentle his large fingers were; she could well imagine how gentle they'd be stroking her to climax.

"Now type in this," Jake said, as he gave her another series of commands.

Roni forced herself to turn back to the monitor, her hands shaking as she tapped the keys. A screen popped up that showed a thumbnail-sized video. "What is that?"

"Our video. Click it, Roni."

Helpless to ignore the sensual tone in his voice, Roni moved the mouse and clicked the video. Their images filled the screen. She watched, mesmerized, as Jake reached out and touched her cheek. The surprise on her face was easy to see, as was the arousal on his. Roni felt her pussy grow damp when his thumb brushed her lip.

"You're beautiful," he growled.

She crossed her arms over her chest and attempted to quell the sexual tension rapidly filling the air. "Actually I look bloated."

"You look good enough to eat," he shot right back. He reached out and hit the escape key, then pointed to the screen. "The next time you type in the commands I gave, hopefully it'll show us our pervert."

Roni was so befuddled she'd already forgotten the damned commands.

"Don't worry, you can write them down and keep them in your purse," he said, as if reading her mind.

"Thanks," she muttered. She felt like such a dolt. He had her coming and going. Well, not exactly coming, but close.

"Buy me dinner and I'll waive the cost of the camera."

She wasn't surprised by his suggestion, but the idea that maybe he did this sort of thing all the time had her withdrawing. "Do all your clients fall for that line?"

He reached out and cupped her chin. "You aren't another in a long line, Roni. I've never dated a client before. You're the first."

She moved back in her seat, forcing him to drop his hand. "We're not dating."

"Yet," he corrected her. His gaze went to her breasts and held. Roni could swear her nipples hardened just for him, as if begging to be licked. Her body's reaction didn't sit well. Roni liked being in control, but Jake made her feel like a runaway train.

"You're much too bold, Jake Cornick."

"Dinner, Dr. Smart. Nothing more." He stood and held out a hand. "What do you have to lose?"

She stared at it a second, before moving the chair back and standing on her own. "You don't have a significant other?"

"I wouldn't be looking at your polka-dotted breasts if I did."

Her face heated and she crossed her arms over said breasts. "Just dinner?"

He held up three fingers and grinned. "Scout's honor."

"You were a Boy Scout, huh?"

He tilted his head to the side. "You sound surprised."

She laughed. "You look more like trouble."

He leaned close and murmured, "Trouble can be fun, sweetheart."

Roni shivered and wondered if she was finally in over her head.

3

After updating her virus protection, Jake gave her his jacket to wear, effectively covering her see-through blouse, and took her to a fast-food restaurant. Jake had insisted that everyone should eat a burger and fries from time to time. He'd winked and said it would be un-American otherwise. She hadn't gone out for hamburgers with a man since high school. Fast food tended to be a solitary event for her. Watching Jake wrap his strong, capable hands around the cheeseburger and take a large bite shouldn't have been a turn on. Jake made it seem sexy as hell. An image of him holding her breast in the same manner and nibbling on her nipple had her squirming in her hard plastic seat.

"You're blushing," he said as he picked up a napkin and wiped his mouth.

"I never blush."

"Do too. You're doing it right now. What's in that pretty little head of yours, Roni?"

"You are," she stated boldly as she swirled a fry in a pool of ketchup. It wasn't her way to play coy with a man.

He chuckled. "You aren't the shy type, are you?"

"Not usually. If I see something I want, I go for it. I see no reason to pretend."

"And do you want me, sweetheart?"

Jake was turning out to be quite a surprise. Without realizing it, he'd stumbled onto her one real desire. To be with a man who didn't feel the need to treat her like fine china. The bet she'd made with Lydia and Jeannette came to mind and she realized this was her chance to make her fantasy a reality. She wanted to get down and dirty with a man. Roni had a feeling Jake could do dirty really well.

"Yes, I want you," she candidly replied.

Jake's expression changed, turned dangerous, his gaze darkening as he pushed his hamburger aside. "You know how to push a man, don't you, Roni?"

She kept swirling the fry in the ketchup and asked, "Are you saying you don't want me?"

He leaned across the table and took the fry out of her hand, then held it out for her. Roni opened her lips and let him feed it to her. He watched in silence until she finished the deep-fried treat. "You want the bald truth, is that it?"

"Please," she whispered, her throat suddenly dry.

"I want to strip you naked, taste every inch of you for about an hour, then fuck that hot little pussy until the sun comes up."

Roni's eyes widened in shock even as liquid heat pooled between her thighs. "And you think I'll go home with you? Just like that?"

"You don't strike me as the type to play games." He paused, then murmured, "Are you afraid, Roni?"

"No, I'm not afraid. Should I be?"

"I'd never hurt you," he promised. "I wouldn't do anything you didn't want."

Trying to act nonchalant, Roni slid her hand across the table and touched his arm. She'd ached to feel his powerful muscles beneath her fingertips from the moment he'd sat at her computer. She stroked upward, teasing them both. When his gaze narrowed, Roni smiled. "Yes, I want you. But first I'd like to know more about you."

"I'll tell you anything you want to know."

Roni drew her hand away and picked up another fry, pointing it at him. "You own your own business. How long?"

"I opened my doors five years ago. It was tough going at first, but I'm doing well enough now that I've been thinking of opening another office up north."

"Do you enjoy being a computer geek?"

He tilted his head to the side. "Do you enjoy being a shrink?"

Roni laughed. "Touché."

He grinned, which had her pulse racing. "I can set my own hours, I don't have a boss breathing down my neck and the money is good. All in all, not too bad. Every job has its drawbacks though."

Roni knew too well. "Do you work long hours?"

"As much as any business owner does, I suppose." He looked over her shoulder, then stood. "Do you like chocolate?"

"It's un-American not to," she replied, using his earlier words.

He winked. "Be right back."

When he walked away, Roni was tempted to turn and watch him move. She stifled the urge and took a sip of her diet cola. She needed to cool down. It was dinner at a fast-food restaurant, nothing more.

"Dessert for two," he said as he set a banana split on the table between them, two spoons sticking out of the vanilla ice cream. "Dig in."

"Two?"

"I'm not eating it all by myself. You're helping."

Roni eyed the hot fudge drizzling down the sides of the rapidly melting dollops with longing. "No, I really can't afford the calories."

His gaze traveled to her chest and back up again. "A few bites of ice cream won't hurt. Trust me."

Roni grabbed the spoon and scooped up a large helping. "Who the hell am I kidding? I can't turn down chocolate!"

He pulled out the other spoon. "That's the spirit."

Roni was mesmerized when a spoonful of whipped cream disappeared between his lips. She wondered what it'd taste like if she slathered him with whipped cream and went to town. Delicious no doubt.

"You really should enjoy the luxuries of life more often, Dr. Smart. It keeps a person sane."

She forced herself to stop visually molesting the man and scooped up another heaping spoonful. She moaned as the sweet dessert hit her tongue. "Yes, I see what you mean."

When they were finished, Roni swiped a napkin over her lips and sat back, totally stuffed. "There really is something special about hot fudge sauce and ice cream."

Jake leaned over the table and pulled her toward him. With their faces only inches apart she could feel his breath on her cheeks. "There's something special about *you*."

Her heartbeat sped up. "You think?"

He nodded. "Mmm, definitely. I bet you taste even better than hot fudge, too," he growled.

"Nothing tastes better than hot fudge. It's impossible."

"How about we go back to my house so I can see for myself?"

He looked her over, his eyes stopping for a heart-pounding few seconds on her heaving breasts where his jacket had parted, before meeting her gaze again.

"You don't even know me," she whispered.

"I know I've never felt so attracted to a woman. Tell me you're feeling this chemistry, too, baby."

Roni couldn't seem to find her breath, she was panting so hard. Her body responded instantly to his seductive words. She wanted to tell him, yes. It would be so easy to yank him to his feet and drag him home where she could be alone with him. But she couldn't seem to form the words. For the first time in her life, Roni was tongue-tied.

"Say something," Jake ordered. "Either tell me to kiss ass or come home with me."

With his face still so close, Roni could see his eyes darken and a muscle in his strong, hard jaw jump. It was time to make the fantasy real. "Yes."

"Yes?"

"I'll come home with you."

"Good answer, sweetheart. Damn good answer."

Jake gritted his teeth as he vied for control over his libido. He was usually content to take it slow with a woman, but with Roni he wanted to fling her over his shoulder and take her away to have his every demand obeyed. That sort of thinking got men into trouble.

He looked down at their dessert. "Done?"

She nodded, then put her spoon on the table and dabbed her lips. Every move she made was delicate and refined. Jake was anything but refined. He couldn't understand why she was giving him the time of day, but he wasn't about to question it. His cock hardened as he imagined her naked in his bed. He wanted to slam his dick into her sweet little cunt until they both begged for mercy. Christ, he was going to have to walk through the crowded restaurant with a boner. He tried to cool himself down by thinking of inane things. Rebuilding a computer, backing up a hard drive. The woman had the power to reduce him to nothing more than a throbbing erection. He should take it slow, romance her a little. Fucking a woman like a wild animal wasn't his way. Usually.

"You're thinking too much, Jake. Why are you overanalyzing this?"

He squinted at her remote tone. "Are you evaluating me, Doc?"

She sat back and frowned at him. "Of course not."

"Yeah, you are."

He stood and went to her. "Come on," he urged as he held her chair, "you can study me while I drive."

She looked at his hand and shook her head. "My car's still at the office."

It was a good area, her car would be safe for the night, but he had a feeling she wanted her own wheels so she could escape come morning. If it made her feel better she could have her car close. Either way it wouldn't matter because he wasn't about to let her slip through his fingers so easily. "We'll pick it up on the way."

His blood pressure soared when she placed her hand in his large palm. She was so small, so delicate. He vowed to remember that later, when he had her naked and beneath him.

Jake tucked her back into his car. When he took off the opposite way they'd come she balked.

"Where are we going? My office is the other way."

"I thought we'd go to the park first. It's still light out and there's something I want to show you."

She was silent so long Jake thought he'd done something wrong. He took his eyes off the road and looked across the seat at her. "What is it?"

"Nothing. You're just . . . you're quite a surprise."

"You think all computer geeks spend their time at the computer, is that it?"

She nibbled at her lower lip and Jake thought he'd never seen anything more adorable. He went back to watching the road. "Have I rendered you speechless, Dr. Smart?"

"Somewhat, yes. And that's a really big deal for me."

Jake could well imagine. Roni wasn't the type to keep her thoughts to herself; she'd proven that when he'd come to her office to fix her computer. He liked that he could surprise her though. "I want you, don't get me wrong, but a quickie isn't at all what I had in mind."

"I should tell you, I don't usually let my dates take control."

He gripped the steering wheel harder and kept his gaze firmly glued to the road. If he looked at her, he'd start touching, and he wouldn't want to stop until he was balls deep inside her hot cunt. "You like to be on top, huh?"

"I have very specific needs, Jake. Can you handle that?"

Oh hell. His cock flexed behind the fly of his jeans. "I can handle it," he gritted out.

"I have a feeling you're going to be in for a surprise."

"Are you trying to tell me that you're really a dude?" he said, hoping to lighten the mood.

She snorted. "Nothing quite so drastic."

"Then what is it?"

"Would you be terribly shocked to know I'm a dominatrix?"

His gaze snared hers. The road, the park, it was all forgotten when she'd uttered that one word. "As in you like to make your men lick your boots and call you mistress?"

"Something like that, yeah."

Jake could well imagine a man on his hands and knees begging her to put him out of his misery. Hell, he was damn near begging himself. He turned his attention back to the road. "Hmm, I see."

"Are you turned off now?"

Jake grinned. She might be a dominatrix, but she was still vulnerable enough to wonder if she appealed to him. "Let me put it this way: My cock hasn't shown any signs of relaxing since you licked hot fudge off your spoon."

"I did not lick it."

"Oh, you licked it. All I could think about was how good that little tongue would feel on my cock."

"I might be persuaded to show you, but you'll have to ask nicely first."

"You're a very bad girl, Roni."

"Do you like bad girls, Jake?"

Her soft voice floated over his body like a caress. "I like you. Good, bad or otherwise. You and I are going to fit like a glove."

"You're willing to submit to me?"

"How about we go with the flow here, sweetheart. No expectations." He turned a corner before asking, "Trust me?"

For a heart-stopping minute Jake worried she would ask to be taken back to her car. He began mentally working on his persuasion technique when she murmured, "Yes, I trust you."

He reached across the middle console and took her hand. "Good girl."

4
_____

"So, what's at the park you want to show me?"

The change in topic wasn't fooling him one damn bit. She was as hungry for sex as he. "It's a secret."

He heard her sigh. "Do you know you can be very annoying at times?"

"My brother has mentioned that a few times."

"You have a brother? Is he older or younger?"

"Spencer is older by five years. He's married and has a daughter, Lisa. She works for me. You've talked to her on the phone."

"Oh yeah, she seems sweet."

"She's a little flighty and I'm constantly wondering how she talked me into giving her the job."

"Because you love her."

He rolled his eyes. "She's got me wrapped around her pinky."

"You're her uncle, of course she has you wrapped. But, be firm too, she needs boundaries."

"I try, then she gives me that look and I cave."

She laughed. "Females learn that look at birth."

"I can believe that." He glanced at her as he turned on the road that would take them to the park. "Do you have any brothers or sisters?"

"I have an older brother, but we don't see each other much. Braden lives out in California."

"Do you miss him?"

"Sometimes. E-mail helps though. We keep in touch as much as we can. He's in real estate so he's always busy."

"A real estate agent and a doctor. Your parents must be proud."

"They are. Neither of them went to college so it was important to them that we get our degree. When I graduated my dad cried. I think he was happier than me."

"I can well imagine. I didn't go to college either."

"How'd you learn computers so well?"

"Figured it out on my own. I guess I sort of have a knack for it."

A few minutes of silence, and then, "I love your car. The pony interior is my favorite."

He gave into the need to glance over at her. She stroked the soft leather with a fingertip. Hell, Jake wanted that little finger on the head of his dick. She wiggled, as if attempting to get more comfortable. The little movement caused her pretty breasts to jiggle a little and he wanted to howl. She'd taken off the jacket when they'd started on the road and Jake had been only too pleased.

To keep from acting the fool by drooling, Jake focused on the road again. "I wouldn't have thought you were old enough to know about pony interior." He winked at her, then murmured, "You a car buff, little girl?"

She smiled, and the small change made her appear younger, and so damn sexy. "Not a car buff. I just love Mustangs. Braden was always buying them and fixing them up. I spent a lot of time helping him. Or rather, pestering him."

"I can't imagine you with grease on your face."

She groaned. "Try head to toe."

He grinned. "The '65 is a beauty." Jake rubbed his hands over the steering wheel in a show of respect. "Even when I was in high school I knew I'd own one someday. I bought it after my wife died."

"Your wife?"

Damn, he hadn't meant to bring up Sarah. "I was married right out of high school. She died a few years ago, breast cancer. Mustangs were her favorite, but we couldn't afford one. After she died, I don't know, I wanted to honor her, I suppose."

"I'm sorry, it must have been difficult for you."

Difficult didn't even begin to cover it, but Jake wasn't about to open that particular box. Not tonight. "It was hard, but you cope."

"One day at a time?"

"Exactly."

"Well, you take very good care of your car. A candy-apple red '65 in such mint condition isn't something you see everyday. It must have cost a pretty penny."

"And worth every one of those pretty pennies too." And then he thought to add, "But there will come a day when I'll part with her. I love her, but time marches on."

"Does it?" She asked as she turned in her seat and watched him with such scrutiny he almost fidgeted like a schoolboy.

He knew they weren't talking about the car anymore. They were talking about Sarah. "A car doesn't keep a man warm at night, Roni. I guess I always knew that once I met the right woman I'd sell her."

"Hmm, no, a car can't keep you warm. But don't you think it's possible to have both the woman and the car?"

She sounded far too serious and that's not what he wanted tonight. He wanted her to relax and enjoy the evening. "Maybe for some it's possible, but not for me. I'm a very focused man. When I have my heart set on something, or someone, I like to give one hundred percent."

"Yes, one hundred percent is good."

He spotted the place he wanted to take her and pulled over to the curb. Jake killed the engine before turning toward Roni. "Giving a woman one hundred percent is the only way I operate, sweetheart."

"Oh," she whispered.

His eyes roamed over her possessively. "We're here."

"Are we?"

Jake leaned toward her and brushed her mouth with his. "Yeah, we are."

Roni licked her lips and pulled back. She looked outside her window, then turned to him with a frown. "You wanted me to see an empty cage and a bunch of trees?"

"Smartass," he murmured. Jake opened the car door, then jogged around to her side to help her out. "I have something better than empty cages and trees."

He took her hand and led her down a dirt path. "I've never been to this park," she said as she looked around. "Usually I go to the one closest to my office. It has great biking trails."

"This place is a little more rustic and there aren't any biking trails."

She shrugged. "It's pretty. I love the outdoors. We used to go camping a lot when I was a kid."

Jake was surprised. The sophisticated woman with her expensive clothes and manicured nails didn't strike him as a nature lover. "You're a constant surprise to me, Dr. Smart."

"You didn't think I'd be the outdoorsy type, did you?"

He held her hand when she tried to pull away. He'd said something wrong, but he wasn't sure what. "You sound disappointed in me."

"I hate when people judge me simply because of my profession. It's annoying to be slipped into the category of china doll."

He pulled her to a stop. She wouldn't look at him, but Jake wouldn't be deterred. "It's not your profession. It's you."

Her head whipped around, her eyes blazing with anger. "Don't make the mistake of thinking I'm some fragile little thing who needs to be coddled. You'll be sorely disappointed."

"I would never think you needed coddling, but you aren't exactly bulging with muscles and tromping around in hiking boots either. You have a delicate way about you. It takes a man a minute or two to see past the surface."

"And what do you see below the surface, Jake? Tell me, I'd really love to know."

"I see a stubborn woman who's strong enough to take charge of her own pleasure. You're polished, but not afraid to get dirty. I see a woman I want to get to know better."

"Then why are we in the woods when we could be in a bed, naked?"

Straight to the point, that was Roni. "Turn around," he softly demanded. She squinted at him, as if suspicious. "You have to turn around if you want to see why I brought you here."

"Fine," she gritted out, then swung on her heel. She stared at the large metal cage before finally letting out a frustrated sigh. "All I see is another empty cage, Jake."

Jake stepped up behind her, letting his body brush hers. He felt her shiver in awareness and it made his blood run hotter. "Look up, on that branch near the top of the cage." He pointed over her shoulder.

He heard her sharp intake of breath and he knew she saw it. "Oh, Jake, it's beautiful."

"It's a red-tailed hawk. She had a broken wing, that's why she's here. Someone found her and brought her here to recover.

She would have died on her own. I don't think she would have been able to hunt for food."

"She looks sad, don't you think? Caged up like that?"

"I'm sure she's a little sad. But they take good care of her here. When she first arrived she was pretty bad off. I don't think they expected her to survive. A hawk doesn't just take food you give her; she hunts for her dinner. It took a lot of work to get her just to eat."

She turned around and Jake was surprised to see a tear slipping down her cheek. "I'm glad they saved her, but shouldn't she have been allowed to die a natural death?"

Unable to keep his hands off her even a moment longer, Jake cupped her cheeks in his palms and swiped away the tear. "I don't know. I'm glad she has a chance to survive though."

"Me too, but she's better now, Jake. Maybe they could release her back into the wild."

"Maybe." Jake didn't like seeing the hurt on Roni's face. "If it was within my power I would open the cage myself and let the bird go free, but even if I could, would it be fair to have saved her, just to let her starve to death now? Or let some other predator pick her off?"

"She survived, even though the odds were against her. It's possible she could fend for herself now."

He wondered. Was the hawk well enough now to survive on her own? "I'll talk to the park officials first thing Monday and see what can be done."

"You would do that?"

He nodded. "It might not help. I'm sure if she could have been set free they would've done it. But it can't hurt to find out more."

She went up on her tiptoes and pressed her lips to his. The kiss was soft and Jake wanted more. He wanted to devour her.

Roni pulled back, her eyes shining bright with emotion. "Thank you," she whispered.

Jake groaned. "How about I get you back to my place where you can thank me properly?"

She grinned. "Yes, good idea."

5

"You're a slob, Dr. Smart."

Roni took in the messy surroundings. Clothes were strewn everywhere, her dresser was a chaotic mishmash of makeup, spray bottles and . . . damn, was that a coffee cup? It was a ridiculous mess. Still, she was glad she'd managed to talk him into coming home with her, instead of the other way around. "It's the way I live, deal with it."

"I bet you say that to all the guys," he whispered as he continued removing her clothing.

Oh, God, they were moving too fast and she knew it. He'd already shucked his clothes and now he was helping Roni out of hers. Roni couldn't seem to put a stop to it. Something about Jake pulled at her. He didn't treat her like she would break. He pushed and demanded and Roni loved it. She'd never let a man take such control. She'd even begun to suspect she was incapable of letting down her defenses long enough to ever have a normal relationship. She'd discovered pretty quickly that going to Kinks afforded her the luxury of being herself. There were no expectations. She could act on her desires and there were no consequences.

As she stood in her bedroom, allowing Jake to undress her as if she were a small child, Roni discovered a new kind of pleasure. When he removed her bra, leaving a pair of white silk panties covering her from his view, Roni was nearly ready to surrender and let Jake run the show.

As he slid the scrap of silk down her legs, Roni suddenly felt a bout of shyness overcome her. When he didn't stand back up to take her to the bed, she frowned. "What are you doing?"

On his knees, his face mere inches from her pussy, he stared up at her. "I'm looking."

Her clit throbbed as she watched him lick his lips. Jake leaned forward and kissed her drenched curls tenderly, forcing her to reach out and clutch his shoulders for support. His talented mouth lingered, licking up and down between her swollen folds. Roni whimpered and dug her fingers into the powerful muscles of his shoulders.

"Oh, God, Jake." Roni didn't know what to do. A storm brewed inside her and she needed to control it. To rein it in. As his arms wrapped around her hips and he cuddled her bottom, Roni tried to wriggle free. She ached to open her thighs, to give him better access. But he was too strong and he wasn't budging.

"Let me play, baby," he cajoled, his voice rough with passion. "I need to savor this hot little cunt for a bit."

Who was she to deny the man? As he sank his tongue in, laving at her, Roni's knees nearly buckled. She would've fallen had he not been holding her in his firm embrace. When his talented mouth found her clitoris, the tremors built inside her by slow degrees. Little ripples moved through her, gaining momentum as he sucked at her clit and licked her pussy.

Roni couldn't take much more of the pleasurable torture. She sank her fingers into his hair and pulled hard enough to gain his attention. His gaze darkened, turned savage, as he pulled back and looked at her. Roni wouldn't be deterred by his feral expression. "Finger-fuck me, Jake," she demanded. "Do it now."

Without warning, Jake released her and stood. She would have fallen on her ass had he not steadied her. When she was about to order him back on his knees, he only slung her around and brought his palm down hard on the sensitive flesh of her ass.

"Ow! That hurt, damn it!"

"Next time we fuck, you can order me to do your bidding," he gritted out. "This time you're mine."

"I told you before I'm a dominatrix," she bit out. "I like to be in control."

He swatted her again on the other cheek. "You got your way when you insisted we come back to your place instead of mine. Now hush and let me play. You'll get your turn."

It wasn't in Roni's nature to hold her tongue. She'd never been good at it. "I'll take my turn now." She tried to turn but his hands gripping her hips were too strong.

"You were doing fine, baby. Why the sudden change?"

"It's not rocket science, Jake. I want to come, it's that simple."

His hot breath against her ear had her pussy creaming. "Let me take you there then. Stop fighting me."

Could she let him have control? She turned and looked at him. "I'll get my chance later?"

He smiled. "I promise, princess."

"Princess?"

He looked her over and groaned. "A pretty, stubborn, blond princess."

She bit her lip and contemplated the merits of giving in to Jake. He wanted to pleasure her in his own way. It wasn't exactly a hardship to let the man take over. "Okay."

Gently, he kissed her lips. "You won't regret it."

When he stepped backward, Roni let her gaze drift over his

muscular chest, then on down to his hard cock. "I know," she murmured.

Jake held Roni's gaze as he slowly lowered himself to his knees in front of her. Her eyes rounded, and there was a fire he hadn't seen in them before. "I want to taste this pretty pussy." She started to protest but in the end stayed silent and let him have his way. Knowing she was willing to relinquish control melted his heart. Instinctively, Jake knew Roni rarely gave a man control.

He licked his lips and stared at the glistening golden curls covering paradise. "You taste like heaven. A slice of sweet honeyed heaven."

Her cheeks bloomed pink and her eyes darkened. The soft light on the bedside table lent to the sensuality of the moment. "Would you like my tongue on your clit, Roni?"

"Yes," she groaned.

Jake leaned in and kissed the little nub. "Say please, pretty baby."

"Please, damn you!"

He chuckled. "Not quite what I had in mind, but it'll do." Jake clutched her thighs and tugged her forward. She moaned his name and it fueled his own raging need. With her body so close, Jake could smell her arousal. Christ, he was starved for her.

"You're so goddamn sexy. Sexy and wet and ready."

"Jake," she muttered, "I'm dying here."

As she held on to his shoulders, sharp nails digging into flesh and muscle, Jake knew he'd never forget this moment as long as he lived.

The need in her quivery voice urged him on. "Put your leg over my shoulder."

She was unsteady but eager as she did as he instructed. The

position put the apex of her thighs directly in his face. It was a major turn on. She looked a little bit awkward and wobbly. Jake cupped her ass and squeezed, then kissed her clit. "I want your juice on my tongue. I'm going to really enjoy licking you dry, Roni."

He spread her open with his thumbs and exposed her hot little cunt. When he leaned in and licked her slit, Jake tasted pure, feminine heat. He ached for more, to drown in her liquid desire. His tongue delved inside her opening as his hands clasped onto her bottom, bringing her closer. Jake was suddenly swept away on a sea of desire as emotions rocked his body and tore at his heart and soul. He sank deeper, his cock throbbing as Roni's inner muscles clenched around him. Her fingers moved to his hair and she pulled him forward, forcing him to bury his head in her wet pussy.

"Your tongue, Jake," she moaned. "I need more of your tongue, please."

He gave in and flicked his tongue over and around her clit, relishing the needy sounds Roni made. Her thighs started to shake and her body began to spasm out of control. Jake tongue-fucked her, sinking in and out of her dewy heat as if starved. Without warning, Roni shuddered and screamed, her juice pouring into his hungry mouth.

He lapped at her several times, eager to swallow every drop of her passion, before he pulled his mouth off her. Roni slumped over him. The feel of her soft curves, leaning on him for support filled him with masculine pride. In this single moment, Roni appeared vulnerable and trusting. It pulled at Jake to see her so open to him. He gently kissed her swollen nub one more time, then pushed her away enough so he could stand. He slipped one arm behind her back and the other behind her knee before lifting her into his arms. After he placed her on the bed, he stepped back. Her quick breathing and heavy-lidded eyes had every one of his possessive instincts kicking in. Damn, she was beautiful. He didn't know what tomorrow would bring, but in that moment he vowed they would be sharing more than a single night together. No way in hell would he be letting her slip through his fingers now that he'd had a taste of sweet heaven.

Roni came out of the pleasurable haze Jake so effortlessly wove around her and peered up at him. He looked edgy and wild. It was a little scary and extremely exciting. She wanted to feel all that untamed strength between her thighs. Some part of her was afraid he was taking too much of her, as if there were more than great sex at stake here. She had a mind to send him home, to put him at arm's length. Luckily, the sane part of her knew better than to let the delicious man out of her sight.

Tomorrow, she'd send him on his merry way.

"You know your way around a woman's body, don't you?" Roni didn't want to think of how he'd managed such skill either.

"Just as I'll bet you know your way around a man's."

Roni laughed. "Maybe. Come closer and we'll see."

A muscle in his jaw jumped. He leaned down and kissed her, hard. As if branding her with his lips. The kiss was urgent and filled with heat. It seared her clear to her soul.

Jake pulled back, his dark hair tousled, his breathing labored. "You won't regret a second you spend with me. I'm going to make you scream, baby." He placed one knee on the bed and moved over the top of her.

When he braced himself on his elbows on either side of her head and delivered little butterfly kisses over her cheeks, Roni blurted out the first words that came to mind. "I think I already regret it."

Jake stopped and pulled back. "What did you say?"

Too late, the words were out, there was no taking them back.

"I figure I must need my head examined for being here with you. We don't even know each other, Jake. I've never had sex on a first date. Ever." It mattered little to her libido, but her head rebelled at this newest stunt.

Jake touched her chin with his index finger. "We may not know each other very well, but there's no way I'll regret this night. I don't sleep around any more than you do, but wild horses couldn't drag my ass away from you right now."

There wasn't a chance for her to reply or even think about his statement as he stood up and wrapped a fist around his cock. He slowly moved his hand up and down, drawing a pearl of moisture to the tip. The man was pure sin. A powerful, broad-shouldered, dark-haired, stunningly bare slice of delicious sin. His cock jutted out, swollen and pulsing, and Roni's mouth watered.

"Touch me."

He was back in command mode, Roni realized. It was in the harsh tone of his voice and his compelling, watchful gaze. Still as a statue, Jake dropped his hands to his sides and waited. It was her move. He clenched and unclenched his fists, the only sign of his agitation. This was a test. Roni suspected Jake was unsure if she would do as told or balk at the notion of submitting to his dominance. Jake liked pushing her past her comfort zone. She understood that now. It aroused her like nothing else. Roni wanted to surrender to him. Had she waited her entire life to find a man strong enough to master her? Maybe. Either way, she was here now and she'd make it good. Who knew what tomorrow might bring?

She rolled to her side and lifted on her elbow before reaching a hand out and touching his stomach. She ached to learn every muscled inch of his body. The ripped abs, the dark sprinkling of hair across his hard chest. Her palm flattened out as she massaged over his bulging muscles and wide ribcage. Her fingers sifted through the springy curls as she touched his left pectoral. Her pussy grew damp, as she imagined sitting on his face while he tongued her.

Jake grabbed her wrist, his blue-green eyes capturing her gaze while he pushed her hand downward.

"You know what I want. Take my cock in your hand."

Testing the waters, Roni held back. "And what if I don't?"

His eyes narrowed and a muscle jumped in his rigid jaw. "Do you like to push me? Does it turn you on to see me lose control, princess?"

"Yes."

One side of his mouth kicked up. "You're a naughty girl."

He released her hand and took a step back, putting a measure of distance between them. "Stand up, then get on all fours in front of me."

Orders? He expected her to obey? Sex games weren't new to her, but usually she did the ordering and the men did the begging.

"You need to know how this works. I never repeat myself, Roni."

Jake's gruff voice traveled along her nerve endings like a forbidden caress. The dark expression made her a little afraid and a lot turned on. As she got up and started to do as he commanded, she was stunned to see him moving to the far corner of the room. He bent and she became pleasantly distracted by his sexy ass. When he turned and started back toward her, Roni noticed his leather belt dangling from his fingers. Her heart sped up and she shook her head. "No way."

Inches away now, Jake angled his head and murmured, "I'm not going to whip you, sweetheart. I'd never hurt you. Maybe you could give me at least a kernel of trust?"

She fidgeted and asked, "Then what are you planning?"

His nostrils flared and his eyes seared her from head to toe, her body coming to glorious life everywhere his gaze touched. "Pleasure," he growled. "Bend over the bed."

Oh God. Could she, of her own volition, accept whatever he had up his sleeve?

For an instant, Jake's implacable mask slipped. "Let me have you."

Roni's mouth went dry and her throat felt tight. Nervous and even a little scared, she turned around and bent at the waist, her bottom facing Jake. A few seconds went by and she was beginning to lose her nerve when she felt the slide of the leather along her cleft. Her pussy creamed as Jake stroked the belt between her swollen folds.

He bent over her body as he slid the warm leather back and forth. "Mmm, my hot little pussy," he whispered into her ear. "So in need of fucking."

"Please, this is torture, Jake."

"Will you get down on your knees now, sweet?"

Roni straightened and turned. Jake clutched the leather belt in his hand as if at war with himself. Without taking her eyes off him, Roni knelt down, then awaited Jake's next erotic command.

"Good. Now, touch yourself."

Reaching between her legs, Roni smoothed her fingers over her clit, her gaze riveted to his heavy erection. The hard, throbbing cock would stretch and fill her.

"Fuck yeah. You look so damn hot," Jake gritted out.

Roni grinned and used her other hand to cup her breast and squeeze. Jake's savage expression had her ready to explode. As she moved her fingers to her nipple, teasing and driving herself higher, she started to smooth two fingers into her tight opening. Jake's hand snaked out and he dug his fingers into her hair. "Enough. I want your mouth. Suck my dick, baby."

When she continued to tease her own body, he tugged a lock of her hair, forcing her to stop.

Roni smiled as her mind whirled with mischievous thoughts. It wouldn't be any fun if he continuously got his way. Time to find out what the man was made of. She rose to her feet and quickly sidestepped him, heading toward the bedroom door. The deep timbre of his voice vibrated down her spine as he called after her.

6

Jake couldn't believe what he was seeing. She was walking away? He could bend metal with the heavy weight of his cock, yet Roni appeared unaffected.

"Where the hell do you think you're going?"

"I'm not in a very cooperative mood."

Damn infuriating woman would be the death of him. "Get your ass back here, Roni. Now!" Jake commanded.

The tone in his voice should have stopped her cold. Grown men scurried when he used that tone. Not Roni. She was baiting him and he knew it.

"If I'm forced to come after you, you'll be punished."

"Sticks and stones, darling," Roni called over her shoulder.

In a few long strides, Jake caught up to her. He swung her around and flipped her over his shoulder, then swatted her ass.

"Neanderthal!"

"Brat," he shot right back as he took her back to the bed and plopped her onto it. Not giving her another chance to escape, Jake held her down with one hand and got on top of her. Straddling her waist, he leaned down and murmured, "I knew it'd be difficult for you to drop the dominatrix thing for a night. Good thing I'm a patient man."

As his lips crashed down on hers, Jake's mind went blank. She so easily lit his body on fire with her addicting flavor. All he wanted was to fill her, push his cock inside her tight heat and stay there for about a century.

He licked her bottom lip and sucked it into his mouth, nibbling the soft flesh. She arched up and moaned, as if ready to plead for him to fuck her. Jake wanted to. Hard. Slow. Both. She would give it to him; he knew it in his marrow.

Before he lost his head entirely, Jake lifted the black belt from the end of the bed and smoothed the warm leather over her wrists. He tickled her a few times before he wrapped the belt securely around both wrists.

He lifted and stared down at the little beauty. Her arms were above her head and she was completely at his mercy. Jake waited for her to protest, but she simply grinned up at him.

"You're a very bad girl. I gave you a specific order and you chose to ignore it."

"Your point is?"

Jake chuckled. Even bound she refused to submit. "That smart mouth will get you into trouble one of these days, princess."

"A big, strong man like you can handle a little backtalk."

He chuckled. "Flattery won't get you out of this."

"What do you propose then?"

He slowly moved down her body until her pussy was level with his mouth. He kissed her swollen clit, then plunged his tongue deep into her silken depths. He closed his eyes and savored the sweet, tangy flavor of her passion. He would crave her hot, exotic taste. When he withdrew and lifted his lips a scant inch, Roni's eager gaze ate him alive.

"A blindfold."

"Jake . . ."

She said his name in warning, but Jake wouldn't be deterred.

He was determined to take Roni to a place she'd never let another lover go. "Will you let me?"

She bit her lip and closed her eyes tight, obviously reluctant. Jake placed another gentle kiss to her pussy before moving back up her body and teasing his way to her firm, round breasts. He nibbled on her berry red nipples, first one then the other, luxuriating in Roni's whimpers and moans at his ministrations.

Jake took his time playing, driving them both mad with lust. As he reached her lips, he groaned, "do this for me, baby. I promise if you don't like it, I'll remove the blindfold."

"Okay." Roni breathed out. "But I swear if you do anything weird I'll knee you in the balls so hard you'll be walking with a permanent limp."

Jake cringed at the vivid image. "Vicious little thing, aren't you?"

"Not vicious, horny."

Jake lifted off the bed and glanced around the room. "Where can I find a scarf in this mess?"

"The top drawer of my dresser."

She trusted him. Roni had never allowed a man to tie her hands and blindfold her, he knew it in his bones. She would be breaking new ground with him. Jake never thought he could feel such tenderness for a woman after Sarah, but something about Roni tugged at heartstrings he'd thought were long severed.

As he moved carefully through the minefield of her bedroom, Jake heard Roni whisper his name. He turned, curious if she'd changed her mind.

"I've never done this before."

The vulnerability in her soft voice went straight to his soul. "I know, baby. It's okay. We're going to take this slow and easy."

Her gaze traveled the length of him and Jake's cock grew another inch as she widened her legs and shifted on the bed. He could see the soft pink folds of her cunt and the tight pucker of her ass. He wanted to fuck her there. Mark every inch of her. He ached to give her a night to remember. A night neither of them would soon forget.

He opened the drawer she'd indicated and pulled out a red silk scarf.

Stepping over to the side of the bed, Jake smiled wickedly as he drifted the colorful silk scarf over Roni's sensitized body. He let the delicate fabric touch the silky skin between her breasts, her ribcage and her concave belly. He stopped there and waited. Roni squirmed, and he knew she was anticipating what the silk would feel like between her thighs, right where she ached most. Instead of continuing his teasing journey, Jake took the red scarf and placed it over Roni's eyes, plunging her into total darkness. He secured it at the back of her head and waited. At once she went rigid, her hands fisting in the blankets above her head.

"Don't, princess," Jake murmured. "It's still just me. I won't hurt you. You know that or I wouldn't be here. Remember?"

"I remember, it's just . . ."

"A little scary because you're completely at my mercy?"

"Yes."

Jake leaned down and touched her lips with his own. It was brief, a barely there caress meant to titillate. "But you and I both know that if you really wanted to escape, you could. The belt is loose around your wrists and you still have that wicked knee you threatened me with."

She smiled and Jake watched the tenseness leave her shoulders and spine. "That's a good girl. Just feel me, Roni."

Rewarding her for her bravery, he drifted his fingers over her pussy, luxuriating in her wet, silken heat. She arched off the bed and moaned deep, driving him wild with her total abandon. He pulled away and Roni let out a tiny whimper. Jake couldn't be swayed. He wanted to see her spread open, screaming his name as he plunged deep. In fact he wanted to tie her legs, too, nice and wide so he'd have plenty of room to play. He didn't think she'd go that far though. At least not yet.

To be sure she wouldn't move unless he commanded it, Jake whispered, "I'll allow your legs to be free. However, if you move them without my permission I'll have to punish you, Roni."

"P-punish me?"

He grinned at the frown creasing her perfectly arched brows. "Yeah," he growled, "I'll be forced to do something like this . . ." Then he bent forward and leisurely licked her swollen folds.

"Oh God."

"You like that?" Jake watched the catlike smile come over her face and he knew she was getting into their little game. Damn, such a willing and open woman, he could easily become captivated.

"I think I can handle your form of punishment."

Roni's husky voice played havoc on his control. Jake took a moment to drink in the delectable sight of her. Her swollen lips parted on a sigh, as if ready for his kiss, and her hands were clenched in tight little fists. Jake carefully moved onto the bed between her thighs. He reached up and pinched one perky nipple. Roni's whimpers were music to his ears.

"From the moment I saw you through the glass door at your office, I wanted to fuck you, princess." She licked her lips and flexed her hands but stayed silent. Jake cupped her other breast and squeezed. "I watched you in that see-through blouse. I swear to God it was all I could do to keep from sucking these pretty tits." Jake leaned down and swiped his tongue over one nipple, then the other, flicking and teasing her until she moaned his name. He lifted his mouth and smoothed his palm upward, until his hand wrapped around the slim column of her neck. "Your sexy ass, so firm and round. It makes a man want to touch and play."

"You're making me insane, Jake."

He licked again at the berry tip, savoring the sweet taste of her. Jake continued suckling on Roni's hardened nipple, gently brushing his tongue back and forth, creating a maelstrom of need inside them both. She arched upward, thrusting her flesh into his voracious mouth. When he gently bit down, Roni moaned and squirmed. Jake took his time, lavishing her other breast with the same attention, savoring the unique flavor of the little hellion.

When he lifted away, Roni's chest rose and fell with her rapid breathing. His cock swelled when he looked at her nipples, glistening wet from his ministrations.

"You're hot and ready for me right now, aren't you?"

She nodded as if too far gone to speak. He smiled, understanding exactly. He licked his lips. "First, if I don't get me a taste of some of that honey I'll surely die, baby." He lowered his head and licked her swollen clit, then farther down to her dewy lips, before finally delving into the slick cream between. Her legs closed a little as if afraid of her own desire. Jake clutched her thighs and held her open. He tasted her tangy flavor on his tongue and knew he'd never sampled anything sweeter. He inhaled her womanly scent before sucking her clit between his teeth and nibbling. Roni's tied hands flew to his head, clutching and grasping handfuls of his hair in stinging desperation for more. When his tongue thrust between her folds, she lost it completely and pushed against his face, undulating as he tongue-fucked her. A few more licks to her clit and she burst wide, screaming and straining against the unyielding hold his hands had on her soft thighs. He stared, mesmerized, as she became lost in the age-old instinct to hold on to the delirious feelings of orgasm for as long as humanly possible.

Jake waited her out, keeping his tongue and lips against her sopping wet cunt while she gained control once again. As Roni collapsed back, the muscles in her thighs going slack as they fell open, her hands dropped back to the bed. Jake lifted and stared down at the tempting picture she presented. She appeared so still, as if nearly asleep already, exhausted from her climax no doubt. When he dipped his finger into her slippery cunt, her body went rigid. He pulled it out and brought the slick digit to her lips, rubbing her lube against them. Jake groaned and leaned down to lick her clean. She whimpered a little, soft precious sounds that tore his control to shreds. She wrapped her arms around his neck, pulling him down on top of her. As her breasts came into contact with his chest, Jake caught himself and stopped.

Rising up, Jake reached over the side of the bed and grabbed his jeans off the floor. Pulling out his wallet, he snatched the condom he'd slipped in earlier. As he leaned back on his haunches, he rolled it on. He lifted a few inches and positioned his cock between her slick folds. When he rubbed up and down, barely touching her clit, Roni bucked, as if intent on taking back control.

"Be still," he growled.

"I can't," she groaned. "Please!"

Jake slipped inside a scarce inch, then moved back out again. Fuck, she was tight. Too tight. He repeated the movement over and over, driving them both crazy with the maddening rhythm.

"Oh, God, more. Fuck me, Jake!"

"Mmm, not just yet, baby. You're little cunt is too perfect. I won't rush this."

"You're the devil," she bit out.

He chuckled. "When you come this time you'll do it all over my dick, won't you, Roni?"

"Not at this rate!"

Jake reached up and squeezed her nipple, then tugged on the little bud.

She bit her lower lip and stayed silent. Jake hooked her legs over his arms and glided his cock slowly inside her wet pussy a few inches. He watched closely as Roni chewed at the already tortured lower lip. He couldn't stand it anymore. He let go of her thighs and leaned down to lick at the wound she'd caused, then slowly rocked his hips back and forth. He controlled every motion, waiting for her tight little cunt to accommodate his size. It wasn't easy, not when he was so desperate to thrust forward. Bury his cock deep. He ached to pound into her, but he wanted only sweet pleasure for Roni. He wanted to hear her cry his name. He needed to be wrapped up in the sexy sounds she made when she reached the peak of satisfaction.

"You're so fucking tight, baby. You feel so damned good hugging my cock." He kissed his way over her face and to her neck, where he found her pulsing vein all but begging to be nibbled on. He bit her gently before licking the little sting away. Roni groaned and began moving her hips, thrusting against his lower body. Jake was bigger and a whole lot stronger; it took little effort to control her.

"This isn't fair, Jake."

"You think I don't want to drive my cock into you right now? If I did, it'd hurt you. You're tight, princess; you need to soften up a bit more for me," he warned.

"It's my pussy and I say it's already softened, damn it."

Jake had to grit his teeth against her appeal, but he wouldn't be swayed. "Slowly this first time, or I could hurt you." To his horror, he saw a tear trickle down her cheek. He kissed it away. "Next time you can get as crazy as you want. Fuck my dick until we're both sore. You can even tie me up if you want. I promise."

She smiled, but it wasn't at all roses and sunshine. "I'm going to enjoy torturing you."

Jake could well imagine. When he resumed his slow glide inside the tight fist of her pussy, his chest swelled as he realized Roni had stopped fighting him. As her inner muscles began to relax, accepting his intimate invasion, Jake braced himself on his arms at either side of her head. Her eyes were hidden behind the red scarf, but her tempting mouth beckoned him. He placed a tender kiss to her lips an instant before thrusting his cock deep, burying himself to the hilt.

"Jake," she cried.

He pulled all the way out, then plunged deep once more. He dipped his head and took her mouth, forcing her lips apart and sucking at her tongue. His control snapped as he fucked her. Hard and fast. Thrusting into her while he licked and played with her lips and tongue. Her lush body trembled beneath him, her hot cunt held his cock like a lover's fist. She belonged to him. The thought of any other man touching her supple curves, hearing her wild cries, pulled a possessive growl from deep within his chest.

Suddenly she bucked against him and screamed his name as another orgasm took hold. Jake spun out of control. He drove into her, grinding his cock deep. With his arms caging her in, keeping her beneath him, he gave his passion free rein. Roni suddenly flexed her inner muscles, dragging a startled curse from him. Three more hard thrusts and he erupted, hot jets of come filling the condom.

He collapsed on top of her, both of them exhausted and sweating. When she wiggled, Jake forced himself to lift his head. Her flushed cheeks and kiss-swollen lips pulled at him. Damn, she was beautiful. So goddamn perfect.

"My arms are starting to ache, Jake."

Jake pulled out of her slick sheath and stood. "Stay still, I'm just going to clean up."

He went to the adjoining bathroom to discard the condom. When he came back, Roni had already managed to free her wrists. He watched her remove the blindfold and sit up. "I thought you were told to stay still," he murmured as he walked toward her.

"I don't do orders well."

He rolled his eyes. "No kidding." As he reached her, she tried to get up, but he was quicker. Within seconds he had her cradled in his arms. "Shower," he explained when she glared at him.

"I'm capable of walking on my own."

"And I'm capable of spanking your cute little ass."

When he entered the bathroom, he placed her on the counter and moved to turn on the water. After he had the temperature just right he moved back to her. She was frowning at him, her arms crossed over her perky breasts.

"What's wrong?"

"You're staying the night?"

He arched a brow. "Did you think I'd fuck you and leave?"

She looked down at the floor. "Well, no, but . . ."

Jake had a feeling Roni wasn't much into sleepovers. Why she kept herself at arm's length with men was a mystery. There wasn't a chance in hell he would let her kick him out now though. He placed his fist beneath her chin and gently forced her to look at him. "I don't do one nighters, Roni. I intend to wake up with you all snuggled against me. I'll make you breakfast in bed. Then maybe if you're a good little princess I'll show you how good a masseur I am."

Her frown disappeared. "Breakfast and a massage both?"

He leaned in and kissed her. "Yeah, baby, both."

"I want an omelet or it's no deal."

He winked and helped her down off the counter. "Omelets are my specialty."

"Then we have a deal," she said, as she stepped into the shower. When he moved in behind her, wrapping his arms around her shoulders to pull her against him, his semi-erect cock pressed against the top of her ass. Damn, he loved her ass. He could so easily imagine fucking the tight passage. And he wouldn't use a fucking condom either. They'd be skin to skin. Christ he was getting hard again.

"Jake?"

"Hmm?"

"Tomorrow night," she said softly, "it's going to be my turn."

Jesus, he'd never live through it.

7

Roni couldn't take her eyes off Jake as he slid his jeans slowly down his muscled thighs and calves. She watched him bend and pull them off, then shove them aside. He hadn't bothered with underwear or a shirt. Now he stood in her kitchen without a stitch of clothing on and Roni suddenly had a craving for male flesh.

"Time for breakfast, sweetheart."

He'd stayed true to his promise of the night before. Roni had slept like the dead snuggled up against Jake. When she'd managed to pry her eyes open it'd been to the sight of Jake setting a tray of food on her nightstand. The omelet had tasted heavenly. The massage afterward had been even better.

She'd only left the bed because she'd wanted to make a pot of coffee, but he'd effectively changed her mind when he'd lifted her to the counter and started to peel the camisole and pajama pants from her body. He'd kissed each patch of skin he exposed until she was completely nude. Now, as she stared at his hard, pulsing cock, Roni couldn't seem to string enough words together to form a sentence. A drop of pre-come appeared at the tip and she caught herself anticipating his salty flavor. She licked her lips.

"Spread those pretty thighs so I can eat."

Roni didn't take her gaze from his erection. "You said I'd get a turn to be in control."

Jake placed both palms beside her body on the counter. He lowered his head and kissed her pussy. "You don't want my tongue here, baby?"

She bobbed her head. Boy, did she ever! "You're supposed to let me have a turn though."

He kissed her belly, then licked her nipple. "Up to you. I can stop if you like."

Roni moved her thighs apart, slowly revealing her wet pussy. The heat in his gaze made her more brazen than normal and she forgot about the fact they were in her kitchen in the bright light of day. All she could see was Jake's powerful body bent over her, ready to make a meal of her.

Once her legs were spread wide, she deliberately teased him by massaging her clit with her finger. God, she was so wet and ready. It wasn't going to take much for her to come.

Roni pulled her fingers away, then leaned back and ordered, "Lick me."

His hands came up to cup her breasts. He squeezed and flicked his thumbs over her nipples, and Roni pushed into his palms.

"Christ, just look at you."

Her entire body revved to life at his sleep-roughened voice and soft touches. "Do you like watching me, Jake?"

"I could watch you touch yourself for hours and not get bored. Hell, I could come watching you finger-fuck yourself."

His candor shocked her. She could be just as bold though. "I'd rather you came while I suck you."

Jake's gaze turned dark with arousal. "I want to come all over your tongue. Will you let me?"

Roni pretended a nonchalance she didn't feel. "Maybe," she hedged. "Eat my pussy and we'll see."

"Damn, you're good at that," he growled.

Roni tilted her head, unsure what he meant. "Good at what?"

"Ordering me around. I've never much cared for aggressive women, but you've shown me the light, sweetheart."

She laughed. "Good, I'm glad."

"Mmm," he murmured as he dipped his head between her thighs and licked her slit.

"Oh, God, that feels good."

"Open yourself more, little princess," Jake demanded. "Show me you want me."

His hot breath against her flesh was all the incentive she needed. She spread her legs wider.

His head lowered, as if helpless to deny himself. Roni watched as Jake touched her smooth slit with his tongue. Powerless against the sensual assault, Roni moaned his name. He captured her thighs in his strong hands and held her open for the invasion of his lips and tongue. He nibbled at her clit and sucked her as if she were a ripe peach. No one had ever taken such time with her before. Jake seemed content to lick her for hours.

He lifted his head and she could see her juices coating his lips. The sight turned her on. "You have such a delicate scent and you taste like heaven. It drives me right over the edge."

Roni couldn't speak. Jake used his fingers to hold her slick, swollen lips open, then licked her again. She felt herself climbing higher, her body as tight as a spring. She began to move against his face, unable to control her own actions. Jake let go of one of her thighs, and continued to ply her with his tongue, swirling and circling her distended clit. He slid two fingers into her opening, then slowly moved them in and out. When he curled his fingers, touching a spot she could swear no man had ever reached, Roni moaned and grabbed on to his head. He finger-fucked her over and over, all the while suckling and teasing her clit. She arched up, pressing more fully against his face, anxious and lost to her own passion.

Jake growled low and buried his face into her wet pussy. He sucked on her clit and thrust his fingers deep once more. Roni slammed against his hungry mouth and exploded, screaming his name.

Jake kept his fingers and mouth on her and inside of her until the very last tremor. He kissed her tenderly, then stood up, his gaze pinning her in place. "Sweet as honey," he murmured.

Roni couldn't move, could barely breathe. He'd destroyed her.

"You're awfully quiet," He said as he touched her cheek. "Did I do something wrong?"

She shook the feeling away and sat up straighter. "No. I'm just . . . savoring."

"Ah, I see." He moved between her thighs and kissed her, the feel of his hard body pressed against her felt so right. Too right. It scared her to feel such a connection with a man so fast. Roni pulled back, forcing him to end the kiss.

She reached between their bodies and wrapped her fingers around his cock. "I believe it's your turn."

His gaze softened as he watched her slide off the counter. "Did I earn my reward?"

She went to her knees and looked up at him. "You did very well. Your mistress is pleased." Without another word, Roni opened her mouth and sucked Jake's cock deep.

"Fuck, girl." Jake groaned and threw his head back.

She took him deeper, then slid his hot length all the way out again. She traced the bulbous head with her tongue and heard him curse. She smiled, enjoying herself. Suddenly, he appeared ready to take back the reins.

"You're a little tease. Suck it for me, princess." He grabbed handfuls of her hair on both sides of her head, and guided her down until her mouth was stuffed full with his girth. His balls pressed against her chin. Roni let her teeth graze him enough to have him cursing and releasing her.

She pulled her mouth off him and said, "That was just a warning. You'd do well to stand there like a good boy."

"Damn hellion."

She laughed at his disgruntled tone but noticed he did indeed do as instructed, his hands fisted at his sides as he waited for her to pleasure him. Roni didn't make him wait long. She licked his balls as a reward for good behavior, drawing a groan from him. Hungry for his male essence, Roni bent her head slightly and sucked him to the back of her throat.

She tongued him and knew he was all but ready to explode. She'd won their little game of tug of war. Of course, she didn't think Jake minded all that much.

She continued to suck on him, licking and teasing then deliberately pressed her naked breasts against his hair-roughened thighs, massaging her aching nipples against his skin. As she swirled her tongue around his heavy length and played with the slit at the very tip, Jake pushed into her mouth so far she nearly gagged. Roni cupped his sac and squeezed. He cursed and took her head between his large palms and fucked her face. Suddenly, he let out a roar and exploded. Roni eagerly swallowed every drop, hungry for his come.

Swiping her tongue over his tip one more time, Roni released his cock and sat back.

Jake reached down and helped her to her feet. "I could get used to mornings like these."

Roni froze. She was letting Jake stroke her hair and he was gazing down at her as if she meant something to him. What was she supposed to say?

"Jake, I—"

Jake dropped his hands and backed up a step. "This is the part where you tell me you aren't interested in a serious relationship, right?"

Why did she suddenly feel so hollow inside? It wasn't like her to fall for a guy so fast. "I'm not saying that exactly. I don't know what to say because I don't know how I feel. Yesterday you were a stranger. You came to fix my computer and now we're standing in my kitchen naked. I don't know where this is supposed to go."

Jake cupped her chin and smoothed his thumb over her bottom lip. "How about if we just let it happen? There's no need to decide anything, sweetheart. I give you my number. You give me yours. We see who caves first."

Roni wasn't sure if she was falling in love or not, but whatever those little butterflies in her stomach were, she sort of liked them. "I think that's a very good idea."

"Don't be surprised if I cave first though. The thought of going more than a day or two without tasting those sweet lips of yours gives me hives."

She laughed and smacked his chest. "You're ridiculous."

"I'm realistic."

Roni bent and picked up his jeans. She handed them over and said, "I do have a suggestion."

He took the jeans and started to put them on. "I'm all ears."

"A friend of mine invited me to a cookout next Saturday. Would you like to go?"

He zipped the jeans and Roni turned to grab her camisole. She was beginning to feel seriously underdressed.

Jake snagged the camisole out of her hands and held it above her head, out of reach. "Would I be going as a friend or as your date?"

She crossed her arms over her chest and glared at him. "How about as my love slave who's in serious need of discipline?"

Jake bobbed his eyebrows. "That'll work."

She laughed. "You're hopeless. Give me back my shirt and go away, I've got things to do."

"Are you sure I couldn't persuade you back into bed instead?"

She glanced down his body and noticed the bulge in his jeans. "Do you ever tire?"

"A pretty blond princess is standing in front of me naked. As it happens that's a sight guaranteed to make my dick really happy."

She propped her hands on her hips and glared at him. "I will use my knee if I have to."

He grimaced and handed her the camisole.

Dressed several minutes later, Roni watched through her living room window as Jake backed out of her driveway. She looked down at the sticky note in her hand. He'd given her his phone number and she'd given him hers. But that wasn't what had her heart nearly beating out of her chest. The crooked heart he'd drawn around the number tore at her defenses. A woman didn't have a leg to stand on around a man like Jake. She held the sticky note to her chest and slumped against the wall.

The ringing of the phone tore Roni out of her romantic haze. When she moved through the kitchen she realized it was clean. "Damn, he did my dishes."

Roni couldn't remember a single time when a man had cleaned and cooked for her. As her gaze snagged on the spot on the counter where Jake had spread her legs and licked her to orgasm, her clit throbbed in awareness. She inhaled and wondered if it were just her imagination or if she really could smell his musky male scent. The phone rang again and Roni grabbed it off the counter.

"Hello?"

"Hey, Roni, it's Lydia. I didn't wake you, did I?"

"No, I was up." God, was she ever. "What's going on?"

"There's a sale at the mall today. Jeannette and I are going. Want to come?"

Normally she loved shopping with her two closest friends.

It was their favorite weekend hobby. Today Roni only wanted to be left alone. She needed to get a handle on her feelings for Jake. Put things into perspective.

"I'm going to skip it this time. I have a lot of housework and bills to work on." Which was nothing short of the truth. "You two have fun."

"Are you sure?"

Lydia sounded worried and Roni hated it. Considering it was the first time Roni had ever opted to clean instead of shop, however, Lydia had good reason to worry. "Yeah, I'm good. If you see anything I might like though, get it for me and I'll pay you back."

"No problem. Talk to you later?"

"Yeah."

They ended the call and Roni looked back down at the wrinkled sticky note. "He just had to go and be all sweet. Damn it."

8

Jake didn't even remember driving to his brother's house, but as he pulled the keys out of the ignition and stared at Spencer under the hood of Lisa's car, he knew he couldn't leave without at least saying hello. When he opened the car door, Spencer stood and turned, his grease-streaked face holding a grimace. Lisa's piece of crap Jeep tended to put Spencer in a foul mood.

Jake walked up the drive and called out a greeting. "Hey, bro. What's wrong with it this time?"

Spencer moved to a workbench and picked up a rag, then swiped it over his face. "Damn thing's burning oil," he gritted out.

"You need to talk her into buying a new car. This thing isn't worth the trouble."

"She thinks the red's cute." He rolled his eyes and tossed the rag on top of a pile of tools. "Stubborn girl."

Speaking of stubborn. "Hey, you got a minute?"

Spencer looked him over. Jake had to force himself to stand still. He still had on last night's clothes and he hadn't shaved. It was obvious as hell he'd been out all night. The grin that came over his brother's face gave him no amount of comfort either.

"I could be persuaded to take a break."

Jake sighed. Hell, he should've known it'd cost him. "What's your price?"

Spencer pointed to the red pile of metal. "Help me fix it and I'll be yours."

Jake cursed. "I'm giving Lisa a raise. Maybe she'll buy a new car."

Spencer laughed and started toward the door leading into the house. "Come on, Tara made a pitcher of tea."

"Mmm, I love her tea. She loads it with sugar."

Spencer pushed into the kitchen and went straight to the refrigerator. "That woman knows how to keep a man happy, that's for sure."

Jake held back the envy that threatened to engulf him every time he thought of how happy Tara made Spencer. Their marriage wasn't perfect, but they were in love and they had Lisa. Jake had thought he'd have that kind of bliss with Sarah. Her death had cheated him. It'd taken him a while to get over the anger and resentment, to realize life went on. Unbidden, an image of Roni slipped into his mind. How she looked that morning when he'd kissed her awake and fed her the omelet he'd whipped up. Her silky blond hair all tousled from sleep, her pretty lips swollen from his kisses. What would it be like to wake up to that every morning?

"Earth to Jake?"

Jake pushed the thought away and took the glass of tea his brother handed him. "Sorry, I'm a little out of it this morning."

"Yeah, I picked right up on that." Spencer pulled out a chair and sat, then pointed to the chair across from him. "Sit down and tell me who put that dreamy look on your face."

Jake pulled out the chair and straddled it. He tossed back half the glass of tea in an attempt to extinguish the blaze raging inside him. He could go to her now. Take her in his arms and kiss her from head to toe. She'd let him too. Roni wasn't an easy lay, but for him, she'd opened up. Like a pretty little tulip in the spring sunshine, she'd bloomed.

"Dr. Roni Smart," he mumbled.

"Smart," Spencer said, frowning. "Isn't that the porn lady?"

Jake slammed his glass on the table. "She's not the porn lady. Hell, she didn't even know about the videos until I showed her. She has someone using her computer as their own personal playground. We're trying to catch the perv."

"So, you're helping the damsel in distress. What's that got to do with your absentminded professor routine this morning?"

"We went to dinner last night and . . ."

"You went home with her? A client?" Spencer thumped his fist against the surface of the table, causing the salt shaker to tumble over. "Damn, Jake, what the hell were you thinking?"

Jake reached over and righted the salt shaker. "It's not like that. She's different." He rubbed a hand over his face, wishing he could put a finger on his feelings for Roni. "She makes me laugh. She drives me right up the wall with her attitude. She's antagonistic and sweet and smart and sexy enough to melt my damn fillings. She makes me crazy. Fuck I just met her!" Spencer watched him, his narrowed gaze assessing. It made Jake crazy when he got that intense, quiet expression. "What? Spit it out."

"I haven't heard you talk like that about a woman since . . . well, ever."

A blast of ice hit him square in the chest and chilled him to the bone. "Don't get any ideas. Roni and I . . . it's not like what Sarah and I had."

"Of course not. Sarah was special, Jake. You were so sweet on her I don't think your feet even touched ground when you were married. But I've not heard you talk about a woman since her death either."

"Christ, I've been with women since Sarah. It's not as if I've lived the life of a monk."

Spencer sat back in his chair, stretching his legs out in front of him. "You've had sex, dumbass. You never once came to me asking for advice about it either."

"That's not why I'm here now." The hair on the back of Jake's neck stood on end as the truth of his brother's words sank in. Damn it, Spencer always did have a way of seeing through the bullshit.

"Yeah, it is," he muttered. "You just met her and yet you have feelings for her. It's scaring you shitless too. I can see it on your face."

Jake wanted to tell him to go to hell. It'd be easier. It wouldn't help his situation, but he'd feel loads better. Spencer was right. Deep down Jake had known the truth nearly from the moment he'd met Roni. She was different than other women. It was like coming out of hibernation. She'd tossed her blond head and looked down her pert nose at him and he'd come alive.

"I should've sent a tech to fix her damn computer."

Spencer laughed. "And take the chance of having some other jerk making time with her?"

The thought of one of his employees touching Roni, kissing her sweet lips, petting her hot little cunt tore a growl of rage from Jake's chest. "No one touches her computer but me," he bit out.

"Figured as much." Spencer stood and took his glass to the sink. After rinsing it and setting it on the counter, he turned and said, "Now, the way I see it, you could sit here floundering around like a trout on a river bank or you could go to her and tell her how you feel."

Jake stood and pushed in his chair. Tara hated when they forgot to push in their chairs. The woman was a neat freak. The image of Roni's messy apartment had him grinning, until Spencer's words reached his brain. "She's not going to leap into my arms, Spencer. This isn't a damn movie. Telling a woman you just met that you have deep feelings for her is bound to send her running for a restraining order."

Spencer yanked the glass out of his hands, rinsed it and placed it next to his own. "I didn't say fall to her feet and start blubbering like a fool. But I know you, Jake. You'll try to give her space. You'll let her make the next move because you won't want to pressure her." He paused and added, "Don't wait for her to make the next move."

Jake stuck his hand in his pocket and drew out the scrap of paper with Roni's number. "She's already invited me to a cookout next weekend."

"And you're content to go all week without a little taste of her? You've got more restraint than me, bro."

Not by a long shot. Jake couldn't imagine going the next twenty-four hours without feeling Roni's sweet curves nestled up close, much less a week. "I could go to her office after work tomorrow. Help her with her perv problem."

Spencer stood up straighter, a gleam of pride in his gaze. "I knew you'd think of something."

Jake shook his head and clutched the phone number in a tight fist. "You don't know Roni. There's something holding her back. I don't think she does relationships."

Spencer moved toward the garage door. "Then you'll just have to change her mind, won't you?"

"Yeah, because the alternative sucks."

"Damn straight. Now, get your head out of your ass and help me fix Lisa's car."

He followed his brother through the door and cringed at the sight that greeted him. "I'll be lucky to make it home by nightfall. How'd I let you talk me into this?"

Spencer picked up a socket, read the size and tossed it back down and continued riffling through his tools. "Think of it this way. When it's fixed, we won't have to worry about Lisa stranded in the middle of nowhere."

"You need to get her out here," Jake said as he glared at the car. "If she sees what a pain in the ass this heap is, she'll change her mind about wanting to keep it."

Spencer cursed. "Now you sound like Tara."

Jake leaned against the fender and crossed his arms over his chest. "Tara's right. You should listen to the woman more often."

Spencer rounded on him. "You're saying I'm too damn soft with Lisa, aren't you?"

Jake let his silence speak for him. Lisa needed a firm hand. That was the bottom line.

"I hope like hell you and Roni get married. When you do I'm going to pray you have a little girl. Then you'll see."

Spencer's head disappeared under the hood, forcing Jake to move to the front of the car if he wanted to be heard. "And what will I see exactly? Besides an indulgent father, that is."

Spencer smiled as he looked over at him. "You'll see that everything you ever thought you knew about life goes out the window when you hear your little girl call you daddy for the first time. It changes a man, Jake."

Jake didn't say anything else. The love on his brother's face said it all.

9

It'd been a long day. Normally Roni enjoyed her work. Helping people slay their inner demons gave her a sense of pride.
She had a purpose in life. By the time she could read and write
she'd known she'd be a doctor. She liked helping people. Today, she'd had to struggle to stay focused. Her mind kept going
back to Jake and the weekend they'd spent together. How could
one man deliver so much pleasure? Her body still tingled in
places she'd forgotten even existed.

The lovers she'd had over the years couldn't hold a candle to
Jake and that just pissed her off. The men at Kinks, the men
who bowed to her commands and gave her their total surrender, were the sorts of men she craved. They cherished her special brand of loving. She could give them what they needed and
vice versa. Like addicts, they ached for that forbidden sexual
gratification that could be had only in a place like Kinks. The
doctor hat came off when she walked through those doors. There
she was mistress and her *pets* enjoyed catering to her. Strong,
virile men who knelt and begged to be spanked. Proud, intelligent, wealthy businessmen, and hard, rough construction work-

ers alike. Their profession didn't matter, not at Kinks. They were all there to be teased, fondled and enjoyed. They used their tongues to clean her boots, while their hands worshiped her body. Their engorged cocks dripped with the need to be touched and stroked by their mistress.

A single evening in Jake's arms and all the nights spent at Kinks seemed shallow and unsatisfying. He'd taken her to places she would've sworn she didn't need, nor want, to go. She'd loved every second of it. After he'd left, she'd spent the rest of her Sunday wondering how one date could rock her world so completely. It'd been a humbling experience for a woman who thought she knew all about pleasures of the flesh.

The little bell on the front door jiggled, signaling she had company. Her last client had already gone though and she'd sent Melissa home for the day. Roni stood and started to go out to the waiting area when Lydia and Jeannette peeked their heads through the doorway.

"You done for the day?" Lydia asked as she crossed the room to stand at the side of her desk.

She was still in her work clothes, Roni noticed. Jeannette held up a large, steaming latte and grinned. "I brought your favorite, vanilla."

Roni hummed in satisfaction and took the proffered drink with relish. She took a sip and moaned. Jeannette made the best lattes ever. "You're a goddess, darling. Thank you." Roni put the cup on the desk. "What're you two up to?"

"Jeanette needs some encouragement."

Roni sat back and crossed her arms over her chest. "Mr. Motorcycle Man I presume?"

Jeanette collapsed into the chair across from her desk, a frown marring her brow. "I can't seem to muster up the courage to speak to him."

"What do you know about this guy?" Lydia asked, as she leaned against Roni's desk.

"Nothing really. He comes in and orders a cup of coffee, black, drinks it and leaves."

"Credit card receipts? Ring?" Roni inserted.

Jeanette shook her head. "He pays in cash and there's no ring."

Good, Roni thought, *at least he isn't married.* "Have you ever caught him checking you out?"

"There were a few times I thought he was staring at my butt, but I can't be sure." Jeanette shrugged. "He was probably thinking I needed to lose a few pounds. Most guys do."

Roni knew Jeanette was self-conscious about her figure. She had a feeling a past lover had something to do with that, which pissed her off. "You're body is perfect the way it is." Roni thought for a second. "Does he sit with his nose in a laptop or a newspaper when he comes in?"

"Nope. Just drinks his coffee, then leaves." Her eyes glazed over. "On his black motorcycle. God, the man is so hot."

Roni and Lydia both laughed. "Well, I think you need to make a move," Roni said. "Nothing overt, just start with saying hi. Maybe introduce yourself as the owner, ask if he's pleased with the service, or something like that."

Jeanette sat up straighter. "You know how I am though. I stutter and stammer and pretty soon I'm making a fool of myself."

"If you don't get over this shyness, he could slip right through your fingers," Lydia said, her voice gentle.

Jeanette started to pick at the hem of her blouse. "I really don't want that."

"Try to think of him as any other customer," Roni said. "The Coffee House is your business and you are in control there. Not him."

Jeanette smiled. "You're right. I'm going to do it. Next time I see him I'll introduce myself. If he's not interested, well, at least I'll have tried."

"Damn straight." Roni said before returning her attention to trying to figure out the command prompt thingy that Jake had shown her. "I'm finished here, just trying to figure out this camera."

"Camera?" Jeanette asked, as she stood and came around the desk to stare at the webcam attached to her monitor. "Why do you have a webcam?"

"Yeah, what's with the webcam?" Lydia said as she moved to stand behind her chair.

"Remember all the problems I've been having with my computer lately?"

"You were having the computer guy out again last we talked. Did he fix it?"

"Yes and no. It seems someone's been using my computer to download Internet porn."

"Oh my God! Are you serious?"

"Yep. that's why the damn thing kept freezing up on me. I had a bunch of spyware on my computer. He cleaned it up and installed the camera so we could catch the person in the act."

"Really? How?"

Roni explained about the camera being motion sensitive, then finally remembered the right commands. She typed them in and pulled up the file containing any images the webcam captured.

"There." Roni pointed to the screen. "See the thumbnail?"

"Yeah," Jeanette said, leaning closer.

"Hopefully it'll show us who's been sitting in my chair while I'm not here. Shit, please don't be Melissa."

Lydia coughed. "You think Melissa is downloading porn on your computer?"

"No, I don't." Roni simply couldn't believe the girl was that devious. "Still, she's the only one with access other than me and the cleaning service."

"It has to be the cleaning service," Jeannette inserted. "Melissa is way too . . ."

"Sweet and naïve?" Roni helpfully supplied.

"Exactly," Jeanette and Lydia said in unison.

That had been her take on it, as well. "There's only one way to find out for sure."

"Click it," Lydia mumbled.

Roni nodded. Moving the mouse until the cursor hovered over the video clip, Roni took a deep breath and hit the button. The video popped up immediately. Next, she hit play. Lydia and Jeanette both gasped when a man appeared on the screen. Man, hell, he was just a teenager! And she knew him, which made it even worse.

All three of them were riveted as the little jerk sat in Roni's chair and started to mess with the things on her desk. At first it seemed he was riffling through her papers, which pissed her off even more, then he leaned back and smiled. His hands went to the fly of jeans.

"Oh my God!" Lydia shouted.

"I think I'm going to be sick," Jeanette muttered and stepped back, her hand going to her stomach.

"I think I'm going to kick someone's ass," Roni growled as she clicked the little X and closed the video. "I know that little weasel."

Lydia's gaze shot wide. "You do?"

Roni stood and paced the room, her anger at the boiling point. "He's the son of the guy who cleans these offices. I've seen him a few times, coming and going. Damn, he must have gotten his hands on his dad's keys and made copies or something."

"I wonder what else he's doing." Jeanette scrunched her brows and sat in one of the chairs across from her desk. "There are several offices in this building. He could be robbing them all blind."

Roni stopped pacing and stared back at Jeanette. "Whatever he's been doing, it stops today. I've got him on video."

"You need to call the police." Lydia pointed to the monitor and said, "Who knows how long he's been at this."

Roni nodded and grabbed the phone off her desk. "First I need to call Jake and let him know his plan worked."

"Jake?"

"The computer guy who installed the webcam." Roni dialed his number. Damn, she didn't even have to look at the little sticky note she'd tucked into her purse. His number had been etched into her brain because she'd stared at it for so long the night before.

Lydia crossed her arms over her chest and grinned. "He's Jake now? Since when?"

Oops. Roni hadn't meant to tell them about Jake just yet. She wasn't even sure what there was to tell. When Jake's voice-mail kicked on, Roni hung up the phone. He hadn't answered. Should she read something into that?

Lydia passed a hand in front of her face and said, "Earth to Roni."

"After Jake fixed my computer and set me up with the webcam, I took him to dinner as a thank you." Okay, so she'd left out the part about letting him blindfold her, tie her hands and spank her ass.

Jeanette and Lydia looked at each other, then back at her. Jeanette tapped the top of the monitor with her finger and said, "A thank you, my butt. We know you better than that, Roni. Spill."

Roni bit her lip as heat stole into her cheeks.

"Oh my God, she's blushing!" Jeanette squealed. "I haven't seen her do that since we were little!"

Lydia sat on the edge of the desk and winked. "Wow. This must be big."

Roni sighed. They were like rabid animals. Okay, maybe not quite that bad, but damn, did they have to know her so well? "If you two must have all the dirty details."

"We must," Lydia said and Jeanette laughed.

Roni rolled her eyes. "Fine. I sort of . . . slept with him."

Both women started asking questions at the same time and Roni went to one of the two chairs across from her desk and dropped into it. "I don't know what I was thinking. He's just so damn sexy. One minute he's making my computer purr like a kitten, the next he's making me purr."

"Good with his hands, was he?" Jeanette said, wagging her eyebrows.

"His hands, mouth, cock. My God, the man knows how to please a woman." Roni's body revved to life at the thought of how well he'd strummed her. He'd taken so much time to play, as if content to spend an eternity licking and petting. Roni had had enough of men who seemed intent on getting to the finish line. Jake had taken the long route and she was ready to do it all again. An addict, that's what she was. And he held the key to her fix in the palm of his large, strong hand.

"Dang, look at her, Jeanette. She has that glassy-eyed look. The one she gets when you bring her one of your homemade brownies."

Jeanette laughed. Roni had heard enough. "I'm not glassy-eyed. It was great sex, but that's all it was." *Liar, liar pants on fire!* Any moment now she expected to be struck by lightning.

Lydia smoothed her hand over her tan skirt but kept her intelligent gaze on her, which made Roni want to squirm like a little kid in the principal's office. "Sounds to me like he was sort of your fantasy guy. The blue-collar worker you craved."

Roni saw an opening to drag her friends past the topic of Jake and she snagged it with both hands. "Exactly. I wanted a guy who wouldn't treat me to a night at the opera. A man who would keep it real. Jake fit the bill perfectly. We went out for hamburgers then did it like rabbits. Which means I've fulfilled my part of the bet."

"A bet, huh? That's all it was? Hot sex with a regular Joe?"

Roni froze. Oh God, she knew that deep tone. Shutting her eyes, Roni sent up a quick prayer. When she stood and turned, her stomach bottomed out. Jake filled the doorway, his dark, furious gaze pinning her in place. His black case clutched in one hand, cell phone in the other. Roni shivered and took an instinctive step back when he moved toward her. How much had he heard? Damn.

"Jake." Her voice shook as she watched him coming toward her. "I didn't know you were coming over."

He wagged his phone in the air. "You tried to call. Dumbass that I am, I was worried. I thought maybe your perv had decided to do something more than jack off to porn." His angry gaze shot to Jeanette and Lydia, then back to her. "Imagine my surprise to find you here talking about slumming it with me."

"It wasn't like that. I didn't mean—"

"That you fucked the help?" He winked and said, "Don't worry, princess, I get it just fine."

"Jake, you misunderstood." The remote tone in his voice had her scrambling to explain. "It wasn't like that, I swear."

"And all for a bet?" he asked, his voice rough. He pushed his cell phone back in the holder attached to his belt. "Fuck it. I should've guessed."

"Guessed what?"

"That there had to be a catch." He bent and spoke into her ear. "A real shame. I was really looking forward to kneeling for you, princess."

Despite the gravity of the situation, Roni's pussy flooded with liquid heat at the image his words evoked. "Damn it, Jake. Will you just listen for a second?"

He stroked her cheek with his fingers. "I think you've said

enough." He turned and stalked out, but not before she saw the hurt etched into the hard planes of his face.

Roni's feet wouldn't move. She ached to run after him, to explain. She needed to set things straight. But her damn feet wouldn't move. Her shoulders began to shake as emotion swamped her. "What have I done?"

Lydia placed her hand at the small of her back. "Sit down, honey."

Jeanette patted her arm. They were both talking softly, trying to soothe her. Roni heard only the anger in Jake's voice. "Oh, God," she moaned as she collapsed into the nearest chair. Lydia handed her a tissue and leaned against the desk, while Jeanette sat in the chair next to her.

"Want to talk about it?" Lydia's voice was gentle.

Roni had the insane urge to laugh. She was supposed to be the one giving advice. "Some psychologist I am. I can't even have a normal relationship without completely screwing it up." She slumped. "I'm such a damn fraud."

"Stop it," Lydia ordered. "You aren't a fraud, merely human. It's okay to be human, Roni. You messed up. We all do."

"I hurt him, Lydia." The raw ache she'd witnessed would forever haunt her. "I'm not sure I can fix this one."

"Yes, you can. You may need to lose the pride though. Can you do that?"

Roni stiffened at Lydia's words. "I'm not that bad. You act as if I've never apologized or humbled myself. I'm not so hardheaded."

Lydia and Jeanette looked at each other, then back at her. Jeanette spoke first. "With Lydia and me, yeah. We couldn't ask for a better friend. But when it comes to men you have a difficult time compromising. You tend to keep them at a distance."

Roni opened her mouth to deny Jeanette's words but stopped when she noticed Lydia biting her lower lip, her brows scrunched in concern. Had she kept men at a distance? Roni tried to think of the last time she'd had a relationship. Something beyond a few nights spent between the sheets. Nothing came to mind. How pathetic was that?

"May I offer a suggestion?"

Roni tossed the soggy tissue in the trash can next to her desk and pushed a hand through her hair. "I'm all ears here, Lydia. Hell, I'm up for about anything at this point."

"Go to him," Lydia urged. "Tell him how you feel. Better yet, show him."

Roni mulled over her friend's words. Did she dare go to Jake? Would he tell her to kiss off? Probably. What other choice did she really have? Wallowing in self-pity wasn't her way. Besides, he'd promised she'd get a chance to be in control and she intended to hold him to it.

Roni stood. "You're right. I'm going to go to him and he's going to listen to me or I'll tie him down and gag him until he does."

Jeanette laughed. "Now that's the Roni we know and love."

Roni went to the phone and dialed the local police department. "First, I have a horny teenager to deal with."

Jake sat in his car at the back of the dark parking lot, watching as a police car arrived along with an old beat-up sedan. A tall, thin man and what appeared to be a scrawny high school kid got out of the car and went into Roni's office, followed by the officer. Jake frowned. She must have caught her perv. Thank God for that at least.

It was a good hour before the police finally came out of the building, the kid in handcuffs, followed by what appeared to be the boy's angry father. Once they were gone, Jake watched as Roni and her friends emerged from the building. He noticed the way the two friends seemed to be surrounding Roni, as if for moral support. When Roni turned, the security light illuminated her face. She'd been crying. His stomach knotted.

He should hate her. Drive off and never look back. Save himself from more pain. But the tears did him in. He had to grip the steering wheel to keep from going to her. He could take her in his arms and hold her tight. They could make love until the sun came up. Yeah, right. That'd be like painting the word pushover on his forehead. She'd put him in his place tonight and what did he do? He sat and watched like some lovesick fool.

Damn it, he needed to make certain she was okay, didn't he? The idea that the perv using her computer might escalate and try something much worse had been on his mind all day. The asshole had been willing to risk a hell of a lot to watch porn videos; what else would he be capable of?

When Jake had seen her number on his cell and realized she'd tried to get hold of him, he'd started thinking the worst. Nothing could've prepared him for the conversation he'd overheard. Roni explaining away their time together, as if it'd meant nothing to her. As if he'd been another in a long line of fucks. He clutched the steering wheel tighter. He wanted to shake her. A bet? She'd wanted to win some damn bet. That's all it'd been to her?

Deep down, Jake knew Roni wasn't so callous. Afraid of intimacy, yes, but coldhearted? Not fucking hardly. Sex was one thing, but when the heart started to get involved the rules changed and the game became a whole lot more intense. Why the fear? *You're deluding yourself, asshole.* Their evening together had been fantastic, but it was over. She didn't give a damn about him.

Jake pushed the key in the ignition and turned. The Mustang came alive with a low rumble. Why had he let himself get close to a woman again? Love led to hurt. Hadn't he already learned that lesson with Sarah?

Some guys never fucking learned.

10

Three days and nothing but voicemail. Roni clutched her stomach as pain tore through her. She stared at the cell phone in her hand, willing it to ring. She'd tried over and over to call Jake. The walls of her apartment seemed to close in around her. She needed air. With no real destination in mind, Roni grabbed her purse and keys off the kitchen table and left the stifling surroundings behind.

She took the elevator to the lobby and kept walking until she was outside. Her car was in the garage, but she didn't feel like driving. Damn it, her chest ached each time she thought of the hurt in Jake's voice. *A real shame. I was really looking forward to kneeling for you, princess.* His words reverberated inside her head over and over. How could she be so cruel after everything they'd shared? He'd been so sweet, so loving. And she'd thrown it in his face.

Fear traveled up her spin as she realized the truth. She loved him. It had been so fast though, and so completely right. It'd scared her. Shit, she was nothing but a coward.

Roni let out a small sound of distress and wrapped both her

hands around her abdomen as a sense of dread filled her. What if she never saw him again? Never heard his sexy laugh, never saw his ornery grin. His sweet touches had been more powerful than anything she'd ever experienced at Kinks. God, when she thought of all the time she'd spent at that club. So many nights. She'd thought all she really needed was some good hard sex. A nice way to take the edge off. Well, she wouldn't be going back. She needed more than a willing body now. She needed Jake.

Why had she cheapened their time together? To save face in front of Lydia and Jeanette? Hardly. It'd been out of self-preservation. As she strode down the dark quiet street, she admitted the truth. Jake had stolen her heart and the knowledge had pushed her to protect herself.

Roni reached a little street café and went inside. Even though it was summer, a chill swept through her. She sat at a table, shivering, when a waitress hustled over to her. Roni ordered a cup of coffee, but the only thing she really wanted was to be left alone. After the bouncy blond brought it to her and took herself off to handle the other customers, Roni pulled her cell phone out and tried Jake once more. She slumped when it went to voicemail.

Go to him, a little voice inside her insisted. As she stared at her phone, a plan began to form. She couldn't go back and undo that moment in time where everything had come crashing down around her. What was done, was done. But maybe she could go about repairing at least some of the damage her careless words had caused.

Finding out where Jake lived had been a simple matter of wheedling it out of his niece, Lisa. Roni had called his shop on the pretense of returning the webcam. Lisa had insisted Roni keep it, but she'd pretended to let slip that she was interested in Jake. Lisa had been only too happy to play matchmaker.

It was Friday and she wasn't waiting another second to have

it out with him. Roni shored up her nerve, opened the car door and stepped out. As she smoothed her hand over her hair and walked up the sidewalk to the front door, she wondered for the hundredth time what Jake would think of the clothes she'd chosen.

He'd seen her in a conservative skirt and blouse and he'd seen her in nothing at all. He'd never seen her as Mistress Roni. She looked down at herself and bit her lip. The skin-tight, shiny black PVC pants and high heels weren't overly wild, but the matching scooped-neck vest with the sexy little zippers over each breast definitely screamed *come and get me!* She was intensely grateful it was dark out. Waiting until eight at night had definitely been the right decision.

Taking a deep breath, Roni pushed the doorbell and waited. When no one answered, she started to ring again. Suddenly the door opened and Jake stood on the other side of the glass storm door. The loose-fitting, low-slung jeans and bare chest sent a lick of fire over the inside of Roni's thighs. Damn, the man was tasty. Hunger for a heaping helping of Jake's delicious body nearly overrode her fear of rejection.

Nearly.

As his silvery gaze traveled down her body, Roni's pussy responded with liquid heat. She bit her lower lip and watched as a muscle in Jake's jaw jumped, his gaze zeroing in on her mouth. He still looked angry, but she couldn't miss the bulge in his jeans. He wanted her. It went a long way to salvaging her self-esteem.

Without saying a word, he pushed the storm door toward her and moved back to let her enter.

Her heart leapt as she stepped over the threshold. She glanced around and noticed one glaring difference between her apartment and his house. His was neat. From the floor-to-ceiling cherrywood bookshelf to the polished coffee table, everything seemed to have a place. The big blue couch and matching chair looked soft and inviting, but she wasn't there to admire his furnishings.

Roni turned on her heel and found Jake watching her from across the room. He hadn't moved away from the door, an obvious sign that she wasn't welcome to stay. With his arms crossed over his bare chest and his feet braced apart, it seemed as if he were ready to do battle.

She put her black bag on the coffee table and placed her hand on her hip. "We need to talk."

"I thought when I didn't return your calls all week you'd get the hint."

"Fine, you don't want to talk; you can at least listen."

Jake dropped his arms and moved closer. "So, talk. I have things to do."

The ice in his voice cut her to the bone, but she'd come this far and she wasn't going to back down now. "I'm sorry for what I said," she muttered, unable to contain the quiver in her voice. "It's true that Lydia, Jeannette and I made a bet. We wanted to try and make our . . . fantasies come true."

"And your fantasy was to be with a real guy. A blue-collar man," he ground out. "Yeah, I got that part, princess."

She stiffened her spine and barreled on. "When you asked me out, I didn't agree because of the bet. I admit, it crossed my mind, but that's not why I slept with you, Jake."

"Then why, Roni?" He moved closer. Only a few inches of tan carpet separated them. "Help me understand your reasoning here, because I'm clueless. I know we just met. I never expected declarations of love from you, for Christ's sake, but I deserved better than to be treated like nothing more than a good fuck."

"I know." Roni placed her palm on his cheek. He flinched, but didn't move away. Hope bloomed. "I got scared when they started asking me about you. I didn't want to explore my feelings, at least not then. It was too soon. I only wanted to get them to drop it."

Jake cupped her face in both hands and stepped closer. His hard body brushed her curves. Roni's libido leaped to life. "Your friends aren't here now, baby," he growled. "Give me something. Either you care and you want to see where this thing between us will lead, or you don't. The truth now; no more bullshit."

"I care," she cried out. "It scares the crap out of me, but I care about you, Jake."

He smoothed his thumb over her bottom lip and Roni closed her eyes for a few seconds, relishing the bare stroke. God, she'd missed him. It'd been a hellish week.

"Why the fear, princess? Talk to me."

It hadn't been the way she'd envisioned. She'd expected him to slam the door in her face. Instead, he was giving her a second chance. One she didn't think she deserved but would take anyway.

Pointing to the couch, Roni asked, "Mind if I sit down?"

Jake dropped his hands and shrugged. Roni walked around the coffee table and sat on one end of the couch. It didn't escape her notice when he chose to stay standing.

"I grew up in a very loving home. My parents have always been head over heels in love with each other and they spoiled Braden and me. Most families have at least one skeleton in their closet, but not ours. We were the average American family. Still are. My parents still go on romantic vacations together and they still hold hands and cuddle while they watch the nightly news."

"They sound pretty great. What's the catch?"

Roni shook her head. "That's just it, there is no catch. Seeing how in love they are can be inspirational, but it can also cause you to set some pretty lofty goals for yourself. I wanted nothing less than what they had. Dad is totally devoted to Mom. He still looks at her as if she's the most beautiful woman that ever lived. I guess I decided that if I couldn't have that same kind of affection from a man, then I didn't want any. Sex is nice, but beyond that I've never met a guy who fit all my qualifications."

"And you didn't want to settle for second best," Jake quietly surmised.

"Right," she whispered as their gazes locked. "Then you came along and rocked my world."

Jake stepped around the coffee table and sat on the polished cherrywood surface, directly in front of her. His legs caged her in. "This week has really sucked. I've missed you, baby."

Tears filled her eyes. "I thought you hated me."

He stroked a finger down her cheek. "I was pissed at you, and a little scared if I'm being honest."

Roni swiped a tear away and frowned. "Scared?"

"After my wife died I decided love hurt too damn much. It wasn't worth the pain. I vowed never to go through it again."

Roni could so easily see the love Jake still had for his wife. Some part of her worried she'd never be able to hold a candle to the woman. "I'm sorry, Jake. She must have been very special."

He nodded. "She was, but life goes on, Roni. It's time for me to let the past go and take a chance." He paused, before adding, "So, do I meet Dr. Smart's qualifications?"

Heat filled Roni's cheeks. "It would seem I'll need more time to properly assess the situation before I can give an accurate answer to that question."

He tilted his head to one side. "And you think you deserve more time with me, huh?"

Butterflies flitted around in her stomach. Would he send her home after all? "Probably not," she answered honestly. "You should kick me out on my butt. I'd rather you didn't though."

"Kicking you out is no longer an option," he murmured.

"What would you like to do then, Jake?"

"I'd like to make love to you, princess." He leaned close and kissed her. His lips caressed hers in a touch so light she wasn't sure she hadn't dreamed it. "I'd like to be the man who takes you to the barbeque tomorrow," he murmured, as he kissed his way over her chin to her neck. "I want to be the guy who proves to you that sex is hell of a lot more enjoyable when you're with someone you love."

"Love?" she squeaked. No one had said anything about love.

He sat back, a mischievous gleam in his eyes. "Eventually. For now, how about we start with a few dates."

"Dates," she repeated. "Okay, I can do dates."

Jake looked down at her chest and her nipples hardened beneath the black vest. "And now that we have that settled, how about you tell me what this hot little outfit is all about?"

Ah, the outfit. "You promised I'd get a chance to be in control. Remember?" Damn, her voice shook and that wasn't how Mistress Roni played. Then again, her heart had never been involved before either.

He reached out and smoothed his knuckles back and forth over the zippers across her breasts. It took an incredible amount of willpower not to lean into his touch.

"Mmm," he whispered, "so I did."

"D-does that mean you'll let me?"

Jake slowly pulled his hand back. With quick efficiency he scooted the coffee table to one side of the room before going to his knees in front of her. His powerful thighs spread wide and his impressive erection filled out the well-worn jeans. He winked and lowered his head. "As you wish, Mistress."

Roni's temperature spiked as she stared at Jake. His head was appropriately lowered and his arms were behind his back. Total surrender. Her clit throbbed. Slowly, Roni came to her feet and walked to the coffee table where she'd placed her black bag earlier. She reached down and slid the zipper back, and pulled out the riding crop she had tucked inside. When she came back to Jake, she was pleased to note he hadn't looked up. He had to be curious, but his gaze stayed obediently on the floor.

"I like you on your knees, Jake. It turns me on." Roni waited to see if he'd reply, but he stayed silent. The only indication that he'd heard her was in the flexing of his biceps. "You show remarkable restraint, pet. If I didn't know better I'd think you'd done this before."

"Permission to speak, Mistress."

Roni could barely contain her gasp of surprise. She'd expected this particular game to be new for Jake, but his submissive pose and words told a different story. Jealousy stole through her at the thought of Jake submitting to other women before her. As unfair as it was, she didn't like the idea that she wouldn't be his first mistress. "Permission granted," she said, unable to contain the bite in her voice.

"I've done some Internet research this week. I wanted to be properly prepared for you."

Her heart soared. So he hadn't done this before. This would be his first time submitting to a woman. Roni's pussy creamed at the thought of giving him his first taste of pleasure at the hands of a dominatrix.

"You've pleased me well, pet. I think you deserve a treat for your hard work." Roni placed the riding crop beneath Jake's chin and forced his gaze to hers. Flames of desire licked over her breasts and pussy. His hot, savage gaze ate her alive. Roni had to swallow and take several breaths before she could speak without trembling. "Unzip my tits."

Jake grinned. Slowly reaching up with both hands, he pulled the zippers back, revealing the swollen orbs. Her nipples tingled when his fingertips accidentally brushed across them.

"Good boy. Now, pull them out and suck my nipples."

"My pleasure, Mistress." He growled low as one large hand slid inside the opening he'd created and tugged. Once her breast was framed by the shiny black material, he did the same with the other. Roni moaned as cool air brushed her nipples. She kept her gaze on him as he leaned forward and licked. She cupped the back of his head, aching and ready for him already.

"I didn't say lick. Suck it like you were told, pet," she demanded in an attempt to keep to the erotic game they were playing.

Jake hummed, then opened his mouth and sucked her nipple into his hot, wet mouth. Roni grabbed a handful of his hair and held him to her, loathe to let him go anytime soon. His tongue stroked the hard bud and her clit throbbed, as if begging for his touch. As he moved to the other breast, suckling hard, arrows of sensation ripped through her.

"Oh, God, that feels so good," she moaned.

"Damn, I missed you," Jake whispered a second before he gently bit down, nibbling on her as if she were a luscious dessert.

"Stop," she demanded and tugged on a fistful of his rich, dark hair. The little sting forced Jake to remove his mouth.

When he sat back on his haunches and looked up at her, Roni nearly caved. Christ, even on his knees he had a commanding presence. He didn't have to speak—Roni could feel his need to take over. He wanted her and forcing him to go at her pace was pushing him to the limits of his restraint.

"Stand and undress, pet." Within seconds Jake was nude, his huge cock pulsing with the need for release. A pearl of moisture glistened at the tip and Roni couldn't resist the invitation to lick it off. She closed the distance between them, lowered her head over his erection and swiped her tongue once around the bulbous head before sucking it into her mouth. The warm sticky liquid coated her voracious tongue. Jake's harsh groan forced her to pull back. His hands fisted at his sides as his gaze pinned her in place. Roni knew their game had only just begun.

11

Jake couldn't take his eyes off her. It wasn't just the clothes, though those were hot as hell; it was the way she moved. An exquisite self-confident woman taking command of her man. It intoxicated him. He'd never understood female domination and he hadn't been lying when he'd told her aggressive women did nothing for him. Submitting held little appeal, but Roni had changed him. Besides, letting her lead meant he was free to enjoy.

"Would you like to know a secret, pet?"

"Yes," he groaned, all too aware of how close he was to coming. The round swells of her tits were mere inches away. He could close the gap and have her hard little nipple in his mouth so easily. Jake stayed still and tamped down the urge to take over.

She smoothed a palm over one hip before venturing to the juncture between. As her fingers passed over the pussy she had yet to reveal, Jake's mouth watered. A trickle of sweat traveled down his spine as he waited for her to speak.

She stepped forward and whispered. "I had these pants custom made."

Jake didn't give a damn about the pants, but he couldn't say that without ruining their little game. "Yeah?"

Roni smiled as her gaze traveled down his body. When she reached out and wrapped her fingers around his cock and squeezed, Jake cursed.

"Mmm, you're beautiful. This cock belongs to me, doesn't it, pet?"

"Yes, Mistress," Jake growled. "But if you squeeze it one more time I'm going to come all over your pretty fingers."

Roni laughed and released him. "I'd be very upset if you decided to come before I had a chance to play."

Jake started to speak but remembered he wasn't supposed to and held his tongue. As Roni started to move toward the couch, Jake stepped forward.

Roni held her hand in the air. "I didn't give you permission to move."

Jake froze. Fuck, she was good at sounding bitchy. It took him a full ten seconds before he could form a reply. "Yes, Mistress."

Roni arched a brow, then took a seat on the couch. Jake licked his lips as she spread her thighs wide. His eyes narrowed as he noticed a series of snaps over the seam of her crotch.

"Do you like my pants?"

"I'd like you better out of them . . . Mistress."

Roni extended a hand toward him. "Come over here and unsnap them for me."

Jake didn't need to be told twice. Within a few strides, he stood in front of her. Roni's cheeks turned pink as he bent at the waist and ran his hand over the smooth, shiny material covering her pussy. As he popped the first snap Roni shuddered beneath his touch.

"You drive a man to the edge, princess," he admitted, his voice hoarse with desire. "I can't seem to muster an ounce of control around you."

Roni ran her hand over his abs and hummed her approval. "I like you out of control, Jake."

He undid another snap, then another, revealing soft, bare skin. There weren't any panties blocking his view. "Christ, you're so fucking sexy."

"Unsnap them all, pet, then taste me."

At her gentle command, Jake dropped to his knees. "My pleasure, Mistress."

He spent little time unfastening the remaining snaps. As he pushed the material wide, Jake's cock flexed, his balls drawing up tight. Not only weren't there any panties, but she'd also waxed. He let one finger stroke the baby-soft skin he'd exposed. "I like this. Such a lovely cunt."

"I hoped you'd be pleased."

"You did this for me." He made it a statement, but she nodded in confirmation anyway. Knowing she'd wanted to please him had his chest swelling with possessiveness. Her legs were spread open, her hands at her sides, nails digging into the couch cushion. Jake inhaled her luscious scent.

"The sweetest nectar," he growled as his head descended.

He kissed the soft bare flesh first, needing to show her how much he adored his pretty present. She whimpered and clutched his head between her palms. Jake slipped his hands beneath her ass and held her still for the invasion of his tongue.

He swirled his tongue over and around the little knot before dipping inside her tight, hot passage. The instant her sweet cream hit his taste buds Jake forgot about their little game. She invaded his senses, slipped inside his soul.

Jake licked her slit, entranced by her uninhibited response. "I want you needing me, Roni," he whispered against her hot, wet flesh. "Only me."

"I do need you. This week has been pure hell, Jake."

Jake heard the catch in her voice and it did him in. "Have

you touched yourself, baby? Did you use your fingers to take the edge off?"

"No. I only wanted you."

Her candid reply forced something primitive and savage to well up inside Jake. "You have me, princess."

Jake spread her legs wider and tasted her pussy. He kissed the tip of her swollen and sensitive clit, thrilling at the way her body began to move against his mouth. As he parted her with his fingers and sank his tongue deep inside her opening, Roni thrust against his face. He knew she was close. He nibbled on her clit, teasing the sensitive bundle of nerves. The sudden burning thought of another man touching and licking Roni tore a growl from his throat. Jake had never been a jealous man, but he knew if any other man dared to take Roni from him he would have gladly gone for his throat.

The need to claim and mark rode him until he found himself moving away from her pussy. He used both hands to grasp the shiny black material of her pants and yanked. The material gave way, exposing the satiny curve of one hip and thigh.

"Jake," she whimpered.

"Mine," he said, answering her unspoken question. He put his mouth on her inner thigh, licking and suckling until a small purplish mark appeared.

"As long as I get to do the same," she said, her voice husky with arousal.

An image of Roni's blond head between his thighs, nibbling and teasing, sprang to mind. He grinned. "Not a problem, princess."

Jake began sliding his tongue in and out of her, slowly, building her pleasure by small degrees. He used his thumb to stroke over her clit, teasing and playing. All too quickly Roni screamed and buried her fingers in his hair, anchoring him to her as she rode out her climax.

Several seconds later her hands fell away and Jake stood.

Unable to hold back, he wrapped a fist around his cock and squeezed. Roni's eyes were closed and her lips were parted as she attempted to drag air into her lungs. Jake reached down and cupped her chin. With her gaze once again holding his captive, Jake said, "I need you."

Roni smiled and stood. As skillfully as a stripper, she bent and pulled off the high heels and peeled away the black plastic clothes, revealing smooth womanly curves. Her seductive movements shredded the last thread of Jake's control. He pumped his cock, captivated by the tilt of her lips as she padded leisurely toward him. Unable to wait for her to start issuing demands, Jake bent and picked her up, cradling her in his arms.

"Bedroom," he growled as he headed out of the room.

Roni laughed and wrapped her arms around his neck. "Jake, you're supposed to let your mistress control the show, remember?"

Jake didn't feel like smiling. He was too far gone already. As he moved along the dark hall to his bedroom, he said, "My mistress can order me around later, after I've gotten my dick inside her for a few good hours first."

She hugged him tighter. The gentle swells of her tits fueled his need to push his cock deep inside her cunt and stay there for about a decade.

"I'll spank you later for your disobedience you know," she warned.

"Deal," he whispered against her hair.

As he entered the bedroom, the moonlight streaming through the window allowed him to see the bed. He crossed the room and placed her in the center before turning on the lamp on the nightstand. He stood back and took in his fill of her. The black comforter emphasized the golden halo of her hair and smooth ivory skin. Her bare pussy drew him like a moth to flame. Jake leaned forward and kissed the smooth flesh. "Mmm, my pretty little princess."

"Jake, I need you so badly."

Her breathless voice, so filled with eagerness, drove him crazy. "I've ached for you all week," he admitted. "Each time you called I was a click away from answering."

Hurt filled her gaze. "Why didn't you?"

"At first I was pissed at you, but then the hurt took over. I didn't think I could hurt for a woman again, Roni." It was nothing short of the truth. It hadn't been a comfortable realization to know how easily she affected him.

"And now?"

He sat on the edge of the bed and cupped her breast. "I was prepared to come to you. I'd planned to wait until tomorrow morning. I was going to make you breakfast."

She frowned. "But when I came here you were so angry."

"I'm still pissed about the bet." He pinched her nipple, rewarded by her gasp of surprise. "My pride took a hit with that little remark, but I'm not about to let my pride ruin everything."

She cupped his cheek. "A reasonable, forgiving man. I'm not sure I deserve you."

Jake reached over and opened the drawer on his end table. He took out a condom and handed it to her. "Show me how deserving you are, princess. Roll the condom on, *after* you lick my cock like a juicy popsicle."

Roni turned to her side and patted his thigh. "Stand up for me."

Her expression, centered completely on his dick, seemed to have the same effect as a lick from her soft, wet tongue. Jake held back the need to pounce on top of her, finesse be damned, and instead got to his feet. "Okay, I'm up."

Roni stared at him for another few seconds, which felt more like an eternity. After ripping the foil open with quick efficiency, she moved to a kneeling position on the mattress and tucked a lock of hair behind her ear. As she took him into the palms of both her hands, Roni looked up at him with a siren's smile curving her sweet lips, then dipped her head and slipped his entire length into her mouth and sucked.

Jake let out a hoarse cry of pleasure-filled shock and grabbed fistfuls of Roni's heavy fall of hair, preventing her retreat. She wrapped her arms around his hips and dug her fingers into his buttocks as she swirled her tongue over and around the bulbous head of his penis.

Jake lost all semblance of control when she moaned and used one talented hand on his balls, fondling and caressing just the way he liked it. He was close, too fucking close. Suddenly she slid her lips off him, releasing his dick with an audible pop. Jake's legs shook with the effort to keep from stepping forward and fucking the hot haven of her mouth. When gentle fingers deftly rolled the condom down his pulsing shaft, he cursed.

Roni sat back and smiled up him. The naughty smile and the way she licked her lips had sweat gathering on his brow.

"Is that the way you like it, Jake?"

The little witch knew he liked it a whole hell of a lot. "Jesus, baby, I'm so turned on here I can barely remember my own fucking name." He grabbed her hips and turned her to face away from him. When she tried to wiggle out of his grasp, he held her tighter. "Be still," he softly commanded. When she relaxed, he pushed at her upper back, urging her to put her face against the mattress. Now her ass stuck up in the air, facing him.

"Such a juicy little butt. I want to fuck it, princess."

Roni moaned and spread her legs wide. It was all the encouragement he needed. He put one knee on the bed, then the other, until his cock and balls were wedged between her buttocks. Jake nudged her, forcing her thighs wider still. Roni's legs trembled, the nervous reaction revving him up the way nothing else could. He leaned over and opened the drawer on his nightstand. Jake took out a tube of lubricant and uncapped it before squirting some of the gel onto his index and middle fingers.

"Tell me, princess, has a man ever taken this little ass before?"

Before she could speak, Jake swirled his fingers around her anus, once, twice, then he pushed them inside. Roni groaned and clutched the comforter tighter. "One tried. I . . . didn't like it, Jake."

Jake had to grit his teeth against the fear in her voice. "Easy, little baby, slow and easy."

To prove she had nothing to fear from him, he pulled his fingers out and only pushed his middle finger in. With little effort, Jake slid past the tight ring of muscles protecting her anus. His other hand moved beneath her body to caress her clit. Roni moaned his name and pressed backward. Jake slipped his finger in another inch, until finally he was buried to the last knuckle inside Roni's tight ass.

"Christ, you make me nuts. I want to pound this ass, princess."

"That feels so good. Oh, God, Jake."

Jake pulled his finger free and added a second, stretching the sensitive tissues. He pumped in and out, teasing her at first, before moving faster, harder. He finger-fucked her tightest hole and plied her clit at the same time. She moved her hips, forcing his fingers deeper than before, and Jake cursed.

"Mmm, you want it harder now, baby? You want my dick filling this little hole?"

Roni shook her head and pressed her face into the mattress, as if unable to give into her own forbidden needs.

With his other hand, Jake took her clit between his finger and thumb, then squeezed hard enough to coax a moan from her. She moved against his hand as he pumped the little bud.

"Who am I, Roni?" Jake growled. "Tell me." He needed to hear her acceptance. He'd never had a desire to gain a woman's complete trust. Something about Roni tugged at the animal in him. He suspected she'd always push him to his limits.

"Please, just fuck me, Jake."

It would be so easy to slip his dick inside her, to give them both what they craved. Instead, he pulled his fingers out, pleased by Roni's tiny whimpers. He bent over her body, caging her in, and nipped her earlobe. "Am I yours, Roni? Do I belong to you?"

She dropped her head to the bed as if in defeat. "Yes!" she screamed.

He kissed the side of her neck and murmured, "Then you belong to me. This isn't dirty or bad. It's not painful either, not when a man knows what he's doing. It's just a different way for me to love you, princess."

She sighed, her body going pliant beneath his. "I do trust you, Jake," she whispered.

Jake's heart soared. "Good girl." He kissed the top of her head and lifted away.

Grabbing the tube of lubricant again, he squeezed a small amount of its contents onto his cock this time. He smoothed it around, completely coating the condom. "Next time, no condom," he growled. Pressing the blunt head against her tight, pink pucker, he pushed forward, barely breaching her entrance. Jake clutched her hips in one hand and buried his dick another inch inside the tight passage. He bit back a curse as she clenched her inner muscles, hugging his dick like a soft fist. It took every ounce of strength he possessed to keep from shoving forward.

"Ease up, princess," he commanded.

As he held her still, Roni let loose a needy little sound. The yearning turned his heart to mush and he gave her another thick inch of his cock. In the same instant, he took his right hand from her hip and flicked her clitoris. He watched her back arch, her hands clutching the black comforter as she became lost in the delicious sensations. With no warning she screamed his name and pushed against him as her climax took hold. He pressed the pad of his thumb against her clit and massaged. Roni shouted out her pleasure. It was music to Jake's ears.

He clutched her hip and snarled, "All of me."

"Yes!"

Jake thrust forward, burying his hard length deep inside Roni's tight ass, her muscles sucking him in.

"Christ, princess," he swore. The pleasure-pain of her body's clutch was the sweetest torment.

"Jake, fuck me," she cried.

Unable to deny either of them in that moment, Jake smoothed his palm over her ass cheek, then swatted the smooth flesh. Roni moaned and he did it again, then again, turning her flesh a pretty shade of pink. "You like it, don't you? You like when I get rough."

"Yes," she admitted in a voice so low Jake had to strain to hear.

Jake began a gentle rhythm with his hips, fucking her, building the pace until his balls slapped against her pussy.

"Mmm, this is my little ass," he ground out.

She neither denied nor confirmed his claim, only pushed against him, joining in the rhythm of their erotic dance. Soon his cock swelled and his balls drew up tight. One more thrust and he was there, erupting inside her, hot fluid filling the condom.

She collapsed on the bed and Jake would've landed on top of her had he not been so aware of her small, fragile form. Bracing himself on one arm beside her body, he leaned over her and brushed the sweat-soaked hair off her cheek. "No woman has ever made me lose control the way you do."

She was silent for a moment and Jake took the time to place a tender kiss to her cheek.

"What about Sarah? Didn't she make you lose control?"

Jake was so fascinated by the glistening skin beneath his lips he nearly missed her question. When the words, and the fear behind them sank in, Jake stilled. He slipped his cock free of her tight opening, then sat back on his haunches and stared down at the little blond beauty. Damn, she was sexy. As Jake let his gaze travel over the toned thighs, luscious ass and nipped-in waist, he could well understand a man's need to create poems about the female form. As gently as possible, he grasped her waist and turned her to her back. Their gazes clashed.

"Sarah and I loved each other. She still holds a piece of my heart." When Roni tried to look away, Jake cupped her chin and admitted something he hadn't even told his brother. "But it was different than what you and I have, Roni. It wasn't wild and out of control. I didn't ache to possess her the way I do you." He leaned down and kissed her swollen lips. "And I sure as hell never called her mistress either."

Roni stiffened. Terror filled Jake when it seemed she was trying to put some emotional distance between them. As her slender arms came around his neck, he let out a harsh breath of relief. She pulled him down for a kiss and his chest swelled. Jake lowered until he covered her smaller body with his own much larger frame and kissed her back. His tongue dipped inside her mouth, Roni shuddered and held him tighter. He trailed kisses down her chin, teased and nibbled at the exquisite line of her throat. He licked a fiery path farther until he zeroed in on the soft skin between her breasts. He tasted her there, hungry all over again. When she grasped his hair and pulled, Jake chuckled and stopped.

"We need to shower," she whispered.

"Yeah," he murmured as he kissed first one breast, then the other. "Afterward you can show me what else you have in that big black bag of tricks you brought."

"What makes you think I have more toys?"

He winked and moved off the bed. "Because you're a very naughty girl, princess."

Roni's hot gaze traveled over his chest to his abdomen. She

stopped and stared at him there, before moving farther south. When she looked at his cock and grinned, Jake started to get a little concerned. *Just what* did *she have in that bag?* She shoved herself to a sitting position and reached out a hand. He took it and helped her to her feet.

"Are you sure you can handle it, pet?"

He arched a brow and crossed his arms over his chest. "Should I be worried?"

"Now that all depends on how obedient you can be, doesn't it?"

Jake bent at the knees and picked her up, holding her against his chest as he started toward the bathroom. "You have a mean streak in you, princess, but you aren't a dominatrix."

"What makes you say that?"

"According to my research, and I had a lot of time this week to research, you're a switch. Someone who likes to both submit and dominate."

"You're right, but you're the first man I've ever submitted to."

Jake stopped in midstride and stared down at the woman in his arms. "And I'll be the last," he murmured before kissing her once more. As she melted against him, peace stole through him. Yeah, this is what he'd ached for all week.

"Jake?"

"Hmm?" he mumbled as he walked into the bathroom and placed her on the counter, then turned and flipped on the light.

"That bird you showed me. The hawk. Did you call the park ranger?"

He nodded, hating to have to tell her something that was sure to upset her. "They can't let the bird go. She's healed, but she can't fly."

She slumped and crossed her arms over her middle. "I see. Thanks for asking."

Jake went to her and wrapped his arms around her shoulders, holding her close. "I'm sorry, baby."

"It's okay. Maybe we could visit her again though."

"Of course. We can go over there tomorrow, after the barbeque."

She pushed at his chest and he relaxed his hold enough to see her looking up at him. "I forgot to tell you. They caught the guy using my computer. Or the kid rather. He's the son of one of the janitors. He's only sixteen, but he's been breaking into some of the other offices, stealing money and office supplies. When some pretty expensive stuff went missing, one of the business owners decided to set up a hidden camera. They caught him stealing a few thousand dollars worth of office equipment. He's in quite a bit of trouble."

Jake kissed the top of her head. "I'm damn relieved it's over."

Roni smiled and wrapped her arms around his neck. "Me too."

"Now," he growled, "back to us."

She snuggled closer and sighed. "Yeah, back to us."

"First I'm going to wash every inch of this hot little body," he promised, "then I'm going to let you use me."

"Mmm, I can't wait."

He winked. "Me either, princess."

Jake stepped out of her arms, then turned to adjust the shower. When he stepped inside and held out his hand, Roni slid off the counter and came toward him, a wicked gleam in her eyes. Jake knew if he lived to be a hundred years old that look would still drive him wild.

Tasty Treats

1

When the chimes over the door jangled, Jeanette's gaze darted to the front, anticipating the arrival of Mr. Motorcycle Man. Disappointment rocketed through her when a couple of teenage girls pushed through the door instead, giggling while they texted. *I'm pathetic.* Every morning the hunk came into her café, sat at the same table, and drank the same thing, and yet she couldn't bring herself to even ask his name.

Cory, the new waitress she'd hired a few weeks ago, went over to take the girls' orders and Jeanette went back to writing checks. She loved her coffee shop. When her Aunt Rhonda had died and left her a sizable inheritance, Jeanette had been dumbfounded. She hadn't gotten to know her reclusive aunt well and she'd felt terrible. She couldn't imagine why, of all people, her aunt had chosen her as the beneficiary.

The idea to open her own little café had sprouted when she'd talked to Roni and Lydia. They'd encouraged her to put her baking skills to good use. As she looked around The Coffee House, a spurt of pride shot through her. She'd taken her time deciding how to decorate. From the very beginning she'd known that it would need to have a trendy art deco feel, but she also wanted to use the small space. She had a few corners set up as conversation areas. Situated in one corner was an old, rust-colored love seat and matching chair she'd found at a garage sale. In another corner stood a bookshelf, filled with everything from poetry to romance to English mysteries. A pair of wingback chairs and a little round walnut table between them made for the perfect spot to relax and enjoy a good book with your coffee. A mishmash of tables and chairs were scattered throughout the main area. She'd hung paintings by local artists on the walls and added Wi-Fi, because really, what would a coffee shop be without it? The look she'd envisioned had come together brilliantly.

As the place started to fill up, Jeanette let out a contented sigh. She loved Mondays. It was her busiest day of the week. Everyone needed the extra boost to get through the day. The door chimes sounded again, signaling another customer. She tried not to look, but her eyes seemed to have a will all their own.

Jeanette stopped writing and peeked at the front door. Her heart sped up. Motorcycle Man's large body filled the doorway. He was staring straight at her. As his lips tilted up in a half grin, Jeanette's temperature spiked. God, the man was hot.

His dark, wavy hair curled up at the ends and made her want to reach out and play. The hard line of his jaw seemed to sport a permanent five o'clock shadow. Today's T-shirt was heather grey. It stretched over a hard chest and impressive six-pack abs. Jeanette had a distinct notion she could bounce a quarter off those abs. The faded jeans cupped his sex in the most scrumptious way. Jeanette imagined peeling them down his thighs. She'd want to take her time, reveal all that smooth, hard flesh by small degrees. As her gaze took in the scarred black biker boots, she noticed them move. She looked back up and realized he was striding toward her.

Jeanette straightened in the stool and forced herself to look at his face. His eyes narrowed as he closed the distance between them. In all the time he'd been coming to her café for coffee, she'd never spoken to him. She'd always ached to be the one to serve him, but she wasn't a waitress nor was she that daring. In her heart, she knew any attempt at conversation would be disastrous anyway. She'd end up tripping over her words, or worse, getting clumsy like she usually got around handsome men.

He came to stand in front of her until only a few feet separated them. As he planted his hand on the counter and leaned in, Jeanette's mouth went dry.

"You," he growled.

"W-what?"

He looked down her body until his gaze snagged on her chest, and he licked his lips. "I want you to serve me."

God, did she ever want to serve him. Jeanette squashed the wayward thought and stiffened her spine. "I'm not a waitress. Cory can—"

"No. I want you, not Cory, or I'll take my business elsewhere."

Her heart beat so hard she thought surely the man could hear it. "Elsewhere?"

He stood to his full height and crossed his arms over the muscular chest she'd been admiring for the last six months. "There are other coffee shops."

And never see him again? Not a chance. She moved off the stool and smiled up at him. "I'll be glad to serve you."

"Hunter," he inserted as he stepped aside to let her move around him.

Jeanette stopped and looked up at him. *Jeez. Just how tall is he?* Definitely over six feet. She felt positively tiny in comparison. Wait, he'd said hunter. He wanted to tell her he hunted? Maybe she'd heard wrong. "I'm sorry, what did you say?"

He pointed to his chest. "My name's Hunter Trace."

"Oh." She laughed. "I'm sorry. I thought . . . never mind." She brought him to his usual table and waited for him to sit. "Your usual this morning, Mr. Trace?"

"Yes, and please call me Hunter. And you are?"

"Jeanette Williams."

"I'm pleased to finally make your acquaintance, Jeanette."

He smiled finally and Jeanette stood there, just basking in the glow. His smooth, deep voice caressed all her erogenous zones. Too late she realized she hadn't moved to place his order.

"I-I'll just go get your coffee."

"Hurry back," he murmured.

It took every ounce of her meager self-control not to fall into his lap and beg him to take her right there in the middle of The Coffee House.

Watching the coffee shop owner walk had become one of Hunter's favorite pastimes. Her jean skirt and loose-fitting yellow blouse couldn't even begin to be sexy, but Jeanette had curves, enough that she bounced a little when she moved. It mattered little what she wore, Hunter still loved watching that teasing jiggle.

Not for the first time, he imagined her naked, her ass raised up for him to pet and fuck. He couldn't understand his fascination with the pretty brunette. She avoided him like the plague and he still came back for more.

When she moved behind the counter to get his coffee, he sat back and smiled. She'd been trying to foist him off on one of her employees, but he wouldn't have it. It was time they finally met. Time he made his move. As she poured his usual decaf into a mug, he nearly groaned though. Damn, he liked coffee, but he sure as hell didn't love it. He'd had more coffee in the last six months than his entire life.

Jeanette picked up the steaming cup and came toward him. She blushed a little when she noticed him staring. Yeah, he liked coffee, but he didn't have a craving for it the way he did one elusive brunette.

She placed a napkin on the table and the mug on top of it. "Was there anything else I can get for you?"

What a loaded question. Fuck, if she only had a clue what he wanted from her she'd run screaming. Hunter made a point to look around the near-empty café before saying, "How about some company? You don't appear too busy at the moment."

The pink in her cheeks turned a deeper shade. Hunter had a sudden urge to stroke her. With his tongue. He ached to find out for himself if her skin was as deliciously soft as it appeared. He squelched the need and forced himself to relax back against the seat.

"I am sorry, but I do have to get back to work." She smiled and played with the hem of her blouse. "Running this place keeps me hopping."

"I can understand, but surely you can spare a few minutes for a paying customer." He winked, hoping he didn't sound pushy. He had a feeling if he used too much force, the shy coffee shop owner would run in the opposite direction. That wasn't at all what he wanted.

Jeanette bit her lower lip and stared at him a few seconds. When she frowned, Hunter wondered how long it'd been since a man had taken the time to flirt with the woman. Finally the frown disappeared, leaving a brilliant smile in its wake. Hunter knew if he could bask in that smile for a few hours he'd feel like he could conquer the world.

"I can take a few minutes, I suppose." As she slid a chair out and sat, Hunter wanted to shout in triumph.

"So, how long have you had this place?" Not that he cared much. He just wanted to hear her talk some more. She had a soft, husky voice. A bedroom voice. He wanted to hear that voice shouting his name as he licked her to climax.

Jeanette crossed her legs and adjusted her skirt, the ponytail in her hair bobbing a little with each move she made. "For a year and a half. Most people hate their jobs, but I'm lucky enough to do something I love."

"You run a good business. In the few months I've been coming in I've noticed an increase in customers."

"Thanks. I know coffee shops are a dime a dozen, but it's my hope that when you mix quality with friendly service word gets around."

He pointed at the large menu hanging behind the counter. "I'm ashamed to admit I've never eaten here. Guess I'm not big on Danishes."

"Ah, but I do more than Danishes. In fact you really should try my double-chocolate brownies. You'll change your mind."

He chuckled. "Not that you're bragging or anything, right?"

Her chin lifted. "It's not bragging if it's the truth."

Hunter folded his hands on the table and leaned forward. "I don't know. Brownies don't do much for me."

"Double-chocolate," she stated, as if he hadn't heard her correctly the first time. "Everyone loves double-chocolate."

"How about I come back at closing time?" He let his voice drop to a whisper. "You can show me what I've been missing."

Her gaze drifted to his lips and stayed there. "You're hitting on me," she murmured. Her tongue swiped at her lower lip and Hunter's cock flexed in his jeans.

Mmm, lick it, baby. "Yeah, I am," he growled.

"I-I don't even know you."

Hunter noticed her stutter. She'd done the same thing when she'd introduced herself. The telltale sign of nerves. He thought it adorable as hell. He also thought her hard nipples pushing against the flimsy blouse were adorable. Damn, he wanted to eat her up.

"We can fix that little dilemma tonight." A really shitty thought struck. "Unless you have a date?"

She shook her head. "I'm not seeing anyone right now."

Thank God. "Me either." He wrapped his hands around the warm coffee mug and lifted it to his lips. While he drank, Jeanette sat quietly and watched. He liked the way her eyes went drowsy as he sipped the hot liquid. Licking his lips, Hunter lowered the mug and asked, "So, are you going to educate me on the magnificent aspects of double-chocolate brownies or am I doomed to forever be in the dark?"

She tapped her fingers on the tabletop. "You know, you could just order one now."

"And miss the tutorial?" He shook his head and grinned. "No way, sweetheart."

"I really shouldn't," she whispered.

Hunter reached across the table and touched the back of her knuckles with his index finger. He couldn't help himself, he had to know if her skin was as satiny as he'd imagined. Unfortunately, he only managed a single stroke before she jerked her hand away.

"You're pretty bold, Mr. Trace."

He laughed and crossed his arms over his chest. "I've been coming here for six months, Jeanette. If I were bold I would've asked you out that first morning I came in and saw you trying to fill in for that waitress who quit with no notice."

"Renee," she stated, clearly bemused. "How did you know about that?"

"I'm observant. I tend to notice things others don't." Hunter didn't want to talk about himself, he wanted to get to know her.

If she had half her mind on work, she would never relax enough to let him in. "Now, about that brownie." Hunter let the statement hang in the air between them, content to let her decide in her own time. It wouldn't be any good if she only agreed because she'd felt coerced.

"I suppose it wouldn't hurt."

Her answer, so quietly spoken, had his blood running hot. As she stood, Hunter did the same. "When should I be here?"

"Closing time is eight thirty. I'll have some things to finish up, but if you don't mind waiting you can come then."

Hunter pulled out his wallet and prepared to pay for the coffee. "No problem. I can admire the view while I wait."

"View?"

He handed her a few bills, then leaned close to her ear and whispered, "You, sweetheart."

"Oh," she breathed out.

As Hunter walked away, leaving her standing in the middle of the café, three more customers came in. When he glanced back, he noticed Jeanette hadn't moved to greet them. One of her waitresses ran over to her, drawing her attention. The primitive beast in Hunter wanted to sweep her into his arms and take her to the backroom. He could kiss those full, pouty lips and slide the buttons on her blouse free of their holes, then suck on her erect nipples. Give them both something to think about while they were at work the rest of the day.

Instead Hunter never broke stride until he reached his motor-cycle. As he slung one leg over the seat and slid onto the soft black leather, he groaned at the erection pumping hard behind the fly of his jeans. Strapping the helmet on, Hunter allowed his mind to pull up an image of Jeanette's pretty brown eyes so full of wonder and desire. She had the look of a woman on the verge of discovering her own passion. As if she were ready to embrace that side of herself she'd kept hidden from the world.

Maybe she simply needed the right person to aid her in her little erotic journey. Hunter vowed to be that man. Her sweet innocence had lured him, but what would she be like once he moved past that layer, when he reached the sensual woman beneath? He had a sneaking suspicion she'd surprise the hell out of them both.

2

Jeanette dropped another mug and cursed. Thankfully this one didn't break.

"That's the third time you've done that. What the hell's up with you today?"

Dean, her busboy-slash-dishwasher-slash-gopher, wasn't one to mince words. Still, Jeanette wasn't about to tell the nineteen-year-old college student that she had a crush on one Hunter Trace.

"I've just had a lot on my mind." She paused, then added, "And you shouldn't cuss."

"I'm a big boy now, *Mom.*"

His sarcasm had her grinning. "You still shouldn't cuss."

He flicked water at her and winked. Jeanette swiped her hand down her blouse and pointed her finger at Dean's chest. "You get water all over my blouse and there will be consequences."

"You always work too hard, Jeanette," he said, his voice suddenly soft with concern. "Why not let me handle the rest of these. Isn't that why you pay me?"

Jeanette rolled her eyes at the familiar argument. Dean was a steady worker, but she knew the job she'd foisted on him was too much for one person. Not for the first time she wished she could hire more help. It just wasn't in the budget. Yet, she reminded herself.

"I'm not leaving you in the lurch, Dean, so forget it."

"Fine, but if you drop another mug, I'm telling the owner."

She pretended to shiver in fear. "Ooh, I heard she's a real witch."

"She can be a pretty tough cookie. Trust me, you don't want to mess with her."

"I'll try and be more careful then." She winked. "Thanks for the warning."

"No problem."

They went back to rinsing off the dishes and adding them to the others in the dishwasher. After the last dish was placed on the rack, Dean poured the soap in the well and shoved the door shut. Jeanette dried her hands on a dishtowel and glanced at her watch—for the thousandth time. Ten minutes. Hunter would be there in ten minutes. Oh God, what if he didn't show? Even more frightening, what if he did?

"Are you distracted because of that motorcycle dude you had coffee with this morning?"

Jeanette jerked her head up to see Dean watching her intently. "What did you say?"

"Cory said you had coffee with some hottie this morning. She was going all gaga over the guy."

Jeanette glared at him. "I didn't have coffee with him."

Dean arched a brow at her. "So there wasn't a motorcycle dude in here this morning?"

Jeanette blushed. Damn, did everyone have to know her business? "Well, yes, but I didn't exactly have coffee with him."

"Then what exactly did you do?"

Dean's attitude pricked her temper. He tended to do the big-brother thing with her way too much, even though she was the older of the two and he wasn't even her brother. "That's none of your business. And Cory shouldn't be gossiping."

Dean shrugged and leaned against the counter. "Cory always gossips, but I've never known you to flirt with a customer."

Damn, had she been that obvious? "Who said anything about flirting?"

Dean picked up a dishtowel and started twirling it around. "All I know is what Cory told me. She said you were flirting with this motorcycle dude and he was hitting on you big time."

Jeanette's body heated at the memory. Who knew mousy Jeanette could gain the attention of a man like Hunter? She still wondered if he'd been playing her. If he didn't show tonight, she'd have her answer. She sent up a quick prayer that he'd show.

Dean flicked the towel at her. It grazed her hip and the slight sting caused her to jump back. "Stop that or I'm taking back that raise I gave you last month."

"You went all glassy-eyed for a second there. I was just trying to get you back on the conversation."

"This conversation is over." Jeanette turned and started toward the office.

Dean jogged up beside her. "So, did you two set up a date or something?"

Jeanette swiped at her brown hair and sighed. "You're way too preoccupied by my social calendar. Go home and call that co-ed you were going on and on about last night."

Dean moved in front of her and pushed her office door open, then waited for her to enter before he shuffled in behind her. "Turns out she has a boyfriend. Besides I've got my eyes on someone else."

Jeanette moved around her desk and sat in the old, worn-out brown leather chair. She resisted the urge to pull her purse out of the bottom drawer and use the little mirror she kept tucked inside to check her makeup. It'd been a long day, her ponytail was probably a wreck and she'd probably sweated most of her makeup off hours ago.

Dean plopped into the chair across from her and stretched out his long, lean legs. "So, give it up. Are you going out with the dude or what?"

"If it will get you to go home, yes. He's coming here tonight."

Dean sat up and leaned forward, his interest obviously piqued. "Damn, really? When?"

Jeanette checked her watch again. "He should be here"—the chimes on the front door jangled, signaling a new arrival—"now." She'd left the front door unlatched for him, otherwise she'd have locked up after the last customer.

Dean shot out of his seat and went to the office door. Before she could blink, he'd already made his way halfway across the kitchen. Jeanette sprinted after him. "Where do you think you're going?"

"I want to meet him."

His arrogant tone grated on her nerves. "You have no business meeting my dates, Dean. This is going too far."

"I just want to see if he's as fabulous as Cory says he is."

Before she could protest further, he'd pushed through the doors leading to the dining area. Jeanette took a deep breath and followed. She spotted Hunter sitting on a stool at the counter. When he looked up and noticed her striding toward him, his lips kicked up at one corner. It was the sexiest grin she'd ever seen. As Dean moved up next to her, Hunter's smile disappeared.

"Am I interrupting something?"

His deep baritone gave her goose bumps. "Hunter, I'm sorry to keep you waiting." She glared at Dean. "Dean is an employee. He was just leaving."

To her surprise, Dean held out his hand. Hunter took it and

the two men seemed to have a silent exchange. "Pleased to meet you, Hunter," Dean said as he released the much larger man and stepped back.

"Same here." Hunter glanced at her and winked. "Your boss promised to give me a few lessons tonight."

Dean shoved his hands in the pockets of his jeans. "Lessons?"

Jeanette spoke up, knowing Dean's mind had gone straight to the gutter. "He made the mistake of telling me he doesn't care for brownies. I aim to change his mind."

Dean licked his lips. "You're in for a treat then. Jeanette's brownies are out of this world. They aren't even brownies. They're like a slice of heaven or something."

Hunter laughed. The sound seemed to travel straight to her clit. Good lord, she was getting turned on and they hadn't even done anything. What if he went home after the brownie? She'd never be able to sleep for thinking of the delicious man.

"Well, I'm not convinced," Hunter said as his intense gaze traveled over her body. "I'm going to need proof."

"And on that note, I'm out of here." Dean turned to her. "I'm only a phone call away if you need anything, okay?"

Jeanette rolled her eyes at his proprietary tone. "Okay, *Dad*," she said, remembering the way he'd called her "mom" earlier.

Dean flicked her nose. "Don't make me ground you, young lady."

She laughed and shooed him away. "Get. You have homework to do, I'm sure." When he only stood there staring at her, she gentled her tone. "I'll be fine, Dean."

Dean glanced once more at Hunter, his gaze lingering for a moment, then he nodded and headed toward the swinging kitchen doors. When he disappeared through them she shook her head. Such a good kid. He'd make some lucky woman a fine husband one day.

"He's protective of you."

Hunter's words drew her back around. He watched her in

that quiet, predatory way. Like a man looked at a woman he wanted to sleep with. It both heated her blood and terrified her. She didn't know how to deal with a man like Hunter. Her previous lovers had been the mild-mannered, *let's make love in the dark* types. She had a feeling Hunter would insist on having the light on. A series of images zipped through her mind. Hunter naked. Hunter spread out on her bed, ready to be pleasured by her.

Forcing a stop to the mini X-rated movie, Jeanette said, "Dean's a good kid. I think he sees me as this passive older lady who needs to be handled with kid gloves."

Hunter stood and came toward her. "And are you?"

Jeanette smoothed her hand down her blouse in an attempt to give her hands something to do. She wished she were bold enough to place them on Hunter's chest instead. Yeah, right.

"Passive? Yes, I suppose I am. I'm not quick to temper and I'd much rather logically work through a situation and find a solution than let my anger get the best of me. But I'm tougher than I look. I don't need to be coddled."

He cupped her cheek and leaned forward. "I can see how a man would feel the need to pamper you though. Would it surprise you to know that I'm extremely attracted to you, Jeanette?"

Could it be true or was she about to wake up from a really good dream? His warm, rough palm felt very real to her though. If she were dreaming she hoped she'd forgotten to set the alarm. "You are?"

"Yes. Very much."

"I-I'm attracted to you too." Damn, she hated when she stuttered. She took a second to calm her jumpy nerves before admitting, "I have been for quite a while."

"That's good, baby," he growled. "But I need to warn you, I'm not very good at moving slow. You'll have to tell me if I'm going too fast. Can you do that?"

His fingers had begun to stroke and Jeanette knew without a

doubt she wanted that stroke farther south. "I can do that," she whispered, her voice hoarse with desire.

"Mmm, good girl." He dropped his hand and stepped back.

Jeanette ached to wrap her arms around his neck and kiss him. Just once she wished she were more like Roni. Self-confident, smart, comfortable around the opposite sex. For whatever reason God hadn't seen fit to give her those particular qualities.

Hunter took her hand in his and entwined their fingers, then turned in the direction of the kitchen. "Now, how about you give me that brownie you promised. I've been dying for a taste all day."

Jeanette smiled. Ah, food, an area she knew well. "I guarantee you're going to love it."

Hunter brought her hand to his lips and kissed the back of her knuckles. "I'm a very lucky man."

"You are? Why?"

"A lovely woman who enjoys baking. Men have gone to war to possess such a creature."

Jeanette wanted to laugh off the outrageous compliment, but how long had it been since a man had taken the time to flirt with her? She had Hunter's full attention tonight and she intended to do everything in her power to keep it.

3

Hunter whistled low as he entered the kitchen and took in the gleaming stainless steel surfaces.

"What?"

"The health inspector must love you, huh?" Every counter shone, the white tile floor was spotless and everything seemed to be tucked away as neat as a pin. It was clear she took pride in her work. Hunter understood that quality well. His respect for her grew.

She turned to pull a plate out from a cupboard. "I admit, they never have much to say when they're here."

When she pointed to a little rickety table situated along one wall, Hunter said, "I thought you had some work to finish up. Don't let me interrupt. I can wait."

Jeanette went to a large refrigerator and brought out a can of whipped cream. Hunter had ideas for that whipped cream, and not one of them included a brownie.

Jeanette flipped her long ponytail behind her shoulder. "It's okay, I finished early."

"Good, I have your full attention then." She nodded and

quickly looked back at the brownie, as if his words embarrassed her. Damn, he'd never seen a woman so timid around men. Still, he liked knowing he'd have her all to himself for the rest of the evening. Maybe he could get her over some of the skittish behavior.

Hunter sat in one of the metal chairs. It wobbled a little and he stiffened. "Uh, is this thing going to hold me?"

Jeanette turned, a frown marring her brow. "I hope so."

He chuckled. "Not very reassuring."

She pointed the knife she'd grabbed out of a drawer in his direction. "If it breaks, are you going to sue me?"

He eyed the knife carefully, then took in the teasing gleam in her eyes. She was playing with him, getting comfortable in his presence. A surge of male pride shot through him at the notion that maybe he was seeing a side to the pretty brunette other men weren't privy to. Maybe he was deluding himself, but Jeanette didn't strike him as the type to play with just any man.

Remembering her question, Hunter murmured, "I wouldn't dream of suing you, sweetheart. Money isn't what I want from you anyway."

Jeanette bit her lip as her gaze traveled over his torso. "Uh, okay."

As she went back to cutting a slice of the double-chocolate brownie, Hunter noticed there weren't two plates on the counter, only one. "Aren't you eating?"

"No, I'm really not hungry."

Not an option, he thought to himself. He wanted to watch her lick the whipped cream and nibble on the chocolate treat. No way would he be denied that erotic show. "I'm not eating alone," he stated.

Jeanette took out a spoon and brought the chocolaty treat to the table. "You'll change your mind once you taste it."

Hunter laughed. "Pretty confident, aren't you?"

Jeanette pulled out the other chair and sat down. The distance bugged him. He wanted her closer. In his lap would be better. He wanted to touch her, watch her eyes take on that warm espresso shade he'd witnessed earlier that morning. Patience, he reminded himself. He didn't want to spook her by moving too fast.

"About baking I'm very confident," She rested her chin in her palm. "I've been doing it ever since I could remember."

Hunter could so easily picture her as a little girl, brown hair in pigtails while she helped her mother in the kitchen. He cocked his head to the side. "Were you the little urchin getting flour everywhere while you helped Mom bake cookies?"

Jeanette's cheeks turned pink, causing his hand to itch. With so little effort he could reach out and stroke the warm, soft skin. Hell, he wanted to spend hours caressing her.

"Yep, that pretty much describes me," Jeanette said, her expression thoughtful. "My parents live in Arizona now. They wanted a drier climate."

"Do you see each other often?"

Jeanette nodded. "We always get together for holidays."

"Do you have any brothers or sisters?"

"No. It would've been pretty lonely if not for Roni and Lydia."

Hunter quirked an eyebrow. "Roni and Lydia?"

Jeanette pointed to the brownie. "Eat and I'll tell you about them."

He liked to hear that commanding tone in her voice. It made him curious whether he could get her to use it more often, maybe in bed. "That's blackmail," he said, as he became aware of how easily she had him wrapped around her little finger and didn't even know it.

She crossed her arms over her breasts, inadvertently drawing his attention to the soft mounds. A few delicate buttons and a little lace, that's all that kept him away from creamy perfection. *Easy, boy.*

"Do you want to know about my friends or not?"

Friends, right. Damn, he couldn't seem to keep his head out of his pants for five frigging minutes. Hunter picked up the spoon and scooped up some of the brownie and whipped cream combination, then brought the spoon to Jeanette's lips. "Help me eat it."

"You want to feed me?"

"Yes. Now open those lovely lips, sweetness."

Jeanette dropped her arms and leaned forward. She opened her mouth and Hunter slid the spoon over her tongue. As she closed her lips around the sweet morsel, Hunter's cock throbbed and hardened. An image of her on her knees sucking his dick sprang to mind. He wondered if she could take all of him. Suck him down her throat. If not he could sure let her practice on him. He was all about practice.

Slowly pulling the spoon from between her plump lips, he watched in heated fascination as her tongue dipped out and took in a drop of cream. He wondered if she were trying to drive him crazy or if it was purely an accident.

"Watching you is making me damned hungry," he admitted, his voice rough with arousal.

"Then maybe you should taste the brownie, Hunter," she murmured.

He dropped the spoon and reached across the white laminate tabletop. Taking her face in his palms, he growled, "Fuck the brownie. I want you."

"I-I don't know about this."

The pulse beating erratically in her neck begged to be nibbled on. "Yes, you do," he whispered. "You never would've let me come back after hours if you didn't already know."

Jeanette closed her eyes tight. A few seconds passed before she opened them again. "I won't lie. I do want you, Hunter. I'm just not sure I can do this."

His cock sat up and cheered at her rushed admission. "What

can't you do, sweetheart? Let me please you? That's all I want. That's all I've wanted for the last six months."

"But this is so fast. I've never had casual sex. I need you to know that right now. It's not that I'm against it, but I'm not the type to just . . . to just—"

"Fuck and then part ways?" he helpfully supplied.

"Yes!" she screamed, her breathing more rapid now.

Fueled by the fire in Jeanette's eyes, Hunter stroked his thumb over her lower lip. Soft as satin and just plump enough to bite and tease. He had to grit his teeth against the little whimper she emitted. "Who said I want that?"

Her hands came up to grasp onto his forearms. "You mean you don't?"

"I'm not interesting in a quickie at your little café, sweetheart. I'm not going to just take off on my motorcycle after I get you up against the wall either. I'm going to want a lot more of you than that."

"You want more than one night?"

"Six months, Jeanette. I've got six months to make up for here."

"What do you mean?"

"For the last six months I've been imagining fucking you." It was crude, but he needed her to understand what she would be getting herself into. "Sixty different ways, baby, and even then I'm going to want more." He leaned close and kissed her, a light peck to her lips meant to entice. "So, this is a really good time to tell me to go to hell. I'll leave and I won't bother you again. It's your choice."

Her choice? Send the man home or take him on. Could she handle him? The answer to that question was an unequivocal no, but sending him home seemed like a really stupid thing to do too. Hadn't she been dying to make love to the hunky man? She'd even allowed herself to be suckered into the bet with

Lydia and Roni because she'd wanted him so badly. The sad truth is, if Hunter hadn't come on to her she'd still be trying to figure out how to ask him out.

The decision made, Jeanette stared into eyes so dark they were nearly black and replied, "I really don't want you to go to hell."

Hunter dropped his hands and stood up so fast the chair fell backward. "Stay right there. I'll be back in second."

Jogging across the kitchen, Hunter shoved through the kitchen door. A few seconds later, he reappeared. "The front door was still unlocked," he explained, moving to stand in front of her. "We wouldn't want any interruptions."

"Oh, of course," she mumbled. He'd locked them in. A shiver of excitement skittered over her.

Staring up at him, Jeanette suddenly felt very small, which was a rarity. Usually the size of her butt alone made her feel rather awkward. Hunter's large, muscular biceps and powerful build practically dwarfed her and did little to ease her jumpy nerves. When he leaned down and grasped onto her waist, then lifted her out of the chair as if she weighed no more than a child, Jeanette squealed and grabbed onto his shoulders.

"What are you doing?"

He sat her gently on the table and answered, "I'm eating my brownie."

The rough, dark tone traveled straight to all of Jeanette's erogenous zones, setting off several fires along the way. How could a voice be so stimulating? "Your brownie?"

"Mmm, yeah. First, I'm going to take your blouse off."

Proving he meant what he said, Hunter tenderly fingered one pearl button before popping it free of its hole. Another soon followed. Jeanette could barely breathe as he made his way down the front of her blouse.

With the last button undone, he said, "Then I'm going to unhook your bra and get a good look at your pretty tits."

Pushing the blouse down her shoulders, Hunter exposed her upper body. The silky white lace bra Jeanette had chosen that morning barely covered her. Somewhere in her mind, she knew the impropriety of what they were doing. As he flicked the front hook on her bra, revealing her swollen mounds, Jeanette forgot about all the reasons why she shouldn't be fooling around in her café after hours.

He cupped both round orbs in his palms and squeezed. "Fuck, you're more than a mouthful, aren't you, sweetheart?" He flicked his thumb back and forth, eliciting a moan from deep in her throat. "Christ, baby, I could suck these fat nipples for hours."

"Hunter," she pleaded, needing to feel his mouth on her aching flesh more than she needed her next breath.

"Shh, it's okay," he murmured as he leaned down and placed a kiss to each of her breasts. "Do you want to know what I'm going to do with that brownie you gave me, Jeanette?"

"W-what?" Damn it, she hated when she stuttered. It only happened during high-stress situations or if she was very anxious. Anxious, hell. Try eager, turned on, wet and throbbing. Yeah, that about summed it up.

"I plan to spoon up some of that brownie you're so proud of and I'm going to slather it all over these succulent nipples. Then I'm going to have my dessert."

Hunter picked up the spoon and scooped up a portion of the brownie and rapidly melting whipped cream, then ordered, "Lift your breast for me."

Jeanette cupped her breast and lifted. "Like this?"

"Yeah, like that. Now don't move." He used the fingers of his free hand to pinch off a corner of the brownie, then carefully placed it on her nipple.

Jeanette had serious doubts about Hunter's plan when it appeared the brownie was about to drop onto the table. "I don't think this is going to work."

Hunter grinned. "Trust me, baby." He used his thumb to spread the brownie around until he'd coated her nipple with chocolate and cream. "Mmm, now that's a tasty treat," he whispered a second before dipping his head.

His firm lips closed over her flesh, tearing away any doubts she harbored about using her body as a living spoon. He flicked her nipple with his tongue, taking his time to savor the sweet confection. Grabbing on to the table for support, Jeanette arched forward. Hunter took his time, savoring and licking away every last crumb before lifting his head.

His eyes were half closed, pure male satisfaction in the rough angles and planes of his face. "You were right. This really is the best brownie I've ever had."

Jeanette said the first thing that came to mind. "Maybe you should have a little more. You know, so you can be sure."

Hunter planted his hands on either side of her body, then leaned over her, effectively caging her in. "I really love the way you think, sweetness."

4

Hunter took his time, pinching off another corner of the brownie and spreading it over Jeanette's other tempting nipple. "I should eat all my desserts like this."

"It might be difficult to fit into your clothes if you do."

"Don't worry, I already figured out a way to work off the extra calories."

He cupped her tit and brought it to his mouth, then started to lick her clean. With her gaze soaking him in, Hunter bit her nipple. Jeanette cried out his name and clutched on to his head. Unable to help himself, he swiped his tongue over the other turgid peak, then suckled. Jeanette shuddered and tunneled her fingers in his hair. He swirled his tongue around the puffy areola before sucking as much as he could into his mouth.

"Oh God, yes," she breathed out. "That feels . . . that feels so good."

He pulled back and stared at her. "Take your hair down," he commanded as he stepped back away from the table. He yanked the hem of his shirt out of the waistband and pulled it over his head. Tossing it aside, he went to work unbuttoning and unzipping his jeans. When Jeanette lifted her fingers to her hair, Hunter stopped, riveted to the sight she presented. As she pulled the elastic band free, then shook her head, Hunter's cock throbbed. Shiny strands the color of mocha fluttered down her back, nearly hitting the table. In the brightly lit room, her hands now clutching the edge of the table, Hunter thought she looked too damn young for what he had in mind. A tempting little innocent and he had no goddamn business touching her. The hell if he could bring himself to stop though.

She'd been in his sights for too long; walking away was not a fucking option. It didn't much matter that she had the look of a woman who'd barely been touched. He didn't want to think about all the women he'd been with before Jeanette. For now, the sweet coffee shop owner was all that mattered, and he'd be damned if he didn't make the most of every moment he had with her.

Hunter closed the few inches between them and cupped her cheek, her desire visible in her expression. His gut clenched. "I've wanted you for too long, baby. I have a lot of wicked ideas for you. And it's going to be pure hell going slow, but I want this to last. I need to savor you."

She slid a hand over his chest, sifting her fingers through his chest hair before moving down his ribcage. When she came to his abdomen and stopped, Hunter nearly snarled in protest. He ached to feel her slender hand wrapped around his cock, squeezing and driving him insane.

"I'm not the most experienced woman, Hunter, but I want you. You gave me a choice, remember? I could've let you walk away. I didn't."

"I'm very happy with your choice," he whispered.

"I do have one request though."

"A request?"

"Yes. I want to lick the brownie off you, too. Will you let me?"

If any other woman had asked a question like that, Hunter would've known she was playing the innocent card to the hilt. But this was Jeanette and she didn't seem to know how to titillate a man. Her softly spoken question had his cock swelling painfully. As it was he'd be lucky not to come the instant her tongue touched the head of his dick.

Hunter leaned forward and kissed her, letting his tongue drift over her lower lip. Damn, he loved her mouth. His preoccupation with it was rivaled only by his fascination with her ass. "I think I can accommodate that request," he said against her lips, "but you'll have to get undressed first. I wouldn't want you to ruin that pretty skirt."

When she bit her lip and looked away, Hunter knew he'd said something wrong. "What did I say, sweets?"

Jeanette picked at an imaginary speck on her skirt and crossed her legs at the ankles, as if suddenly uncomfortable. "My body isn't . . . I'm not model-thin."

Hunter couldn't have been more shocked if she'd thrown ice water on him. "You think you're fat?"

She quirked her brow at him. "I'm shaped like a pear. Trust me, I should know."

"Horseshit."

"What?"

"You heard me," he chastised. "I've been salivating over your ass for months."

Jeanette's eyes widened. "You have?"

Hunter clutched her waist and lifted her off the table. He went to his knees in front of her, clutching her hips to keep her from retreating. "I haven't seen you completely naked, baby, but I've undressed you about a hundred times in my mind. None of my thoughts had anything to do with pears either." He drifted his hands under her skirt and slid them upward. He didn't stop until he had them filled with her soft womanly curves, covered by what felt like satin and lace. "Take the skirt off," he softly commanded. "Let me worship this sweet ass."

Jeanette didn't speak as her fingers went to the zipper at her side. She slid it down, then popped the button free. Hunter did the rest. Grasping at the material, he tugged until he was eye level with a pair of sexy white panties. As the skirt pooled at her feet, he ordered, "Step out of it."

Clutching on to his shoulders for support, Jeanette lifted one foot, then the other. Hunter sat back on his haunches and stared right at paradise.

He smoothed his palms over lush, creamy hips, a nipped-in waist and full round tits. As he pinched both puffy nipples, Jeanette's fingers dug into his shoulders, the little sting barely dragging him out of his lusty haze.

Hunter captured her warm, brown gaze with his own. "I don't see a pear when I look at you. I see a sweet, tempting woman. Sexy and as soft as silk. I want to run my tongue over every inch of you."

"No one has ever talked to me like you do," she admitted, her chest rising and falling with her rapid breaths.

"Maybe you weren't dating the right men then."

"I wish you would've asked me to serve you six months ago."

"Me too, baby." He ran his hand down her side and trapped her hip in a firm hold. He squeezed. "Christ, I could so easily bruise you. I don't want to hurt you, baby, but right now I'm finding it really tough to keep from dragging you to the floor and driving my cock into this hot little body."

Jeanette covered her face in her hands. "Oh, God, what am I doing? I've never done anything this irresponsible. If I caught my employees doing something like this I'd fire them."

Hunter placed his hands over hers, then tugged them away. He ran his lips over her knuckles and murmured, "Haven't you ever wanted to be a little naughty, sweetness? Break a few rules?"

"Yes, but wanting and doing isn't at all the same."

"True, but we're only going to play a little, I promise." He bobbed his eyebrows and said, "Besides, I'm saving the main event for when I get you in my bed."

Jeanette smoothed her hands over his chest, the touch so faint Hunter wondered if she even realized she was doing it. "What are you planning to do to me?"

Unable to deny himself any longer, Hunter leaned forward and kissed the soft skin of her belly. "You'll have to wait and see."

Jeanette gently swatted him. "You're a tease."

Cupping her lace covered mound, he bit out, "I'm horny and I need a taste of this." Without warning he grasped the corners of the delicate lace and yanked. The material easily gave way beneath his strength. He tossed the now ruined panties aside and took in the beautiful bounty he'd uncovered. Soft, brown, neatly trimmed curls protected what he knew would taste like pure honey.

"Spread your legs, sweetness; let me have the rest of my dessert."

"I can't come standing up, Hunter. I've never been able to."

"Do you trust me?"

"Yes, but—"

"Then spread your legs. Let me do the rest."

Jeanette bit her lip, doubt clouding her expression as she moved her feet apart a few inches.

"More," Hunter ordered, pleased when she quickly obeyed. "Good girl. Now hold on to me."

When she grabbed on to his shoulders, he let his gaze soak in the sight of the glistening pink lips of her sex and the swollen clit he craved so badly. Wasting no time, Hunter clutched her hips and leaned forward. A quick swipe of his tongue over wet pink flesh told Hunter what he'd already suspected from the beginning. Her sweet, tangy flavor would definitely be addicting.

"Mmm, strawberries and cream. My favorite."

Allowing one of his hands free rein, Hunter drifted his palm over her hip before using his fingers to stroke her wet folds open. He held her gaze and sank one finger deep.

Arching her neck and throwing her head back, she shouted "Yes! Oh God, please, Hunter!"

Her pleading spurred him on. With her breasts swaying back and forth in her struggle for completion and her fingers digging into the muscles of his shoulder, Hunter leaned in and licked her sweet little clit as he finger-fucked her.

"That feels so . . . oh, damn," she groaned.

Her wild cries were music to his ears. The clutch of her tight cunt as her juices soaked his finger drove his body into a frenzy of lust. He pulled his finger out, then seized her clit between his index finger and thumb and rolled the swollen nub. He pinched and caressed, then sank his finger even deeper than before.

Wrapping his arm around her hips to steady her, Hunter placed his lips against her clit and kissed the swollen and sensitive bit of flesh. A primitive growl reverberated inside his chest at the way her body began to move against his face. Pulling his finger free, he used two of them to part her swollen pussy lips. Hunter sank his tongue deep into her hot opening. Jeanette thrust against him so hard he nearly fell backward.

Christ, she was in a bad way. When had she last had an orgasm? The unexpected burning thought of another man touching her had him nearly snarling. Hunter knew it was irrational; he'd only just met the little beauty. He wasn't sure what to make of his feelings toward this one woman.

Aching to have her juices pouring into his mouth, Hunter began sliding his tongue in and out of her, slowly, building her pleasure by small degrees. He used his thumb to stroke over her soft clitoris. Licking and nibbling, he plied her flesh until suddenly she screamed his name. Her fingernails bit into his flesh as she anchored him to her and rode out a wild and glorious climax.

After her little tremors subsided, Hunter dipped his finger into her pussy, then brought it to his mouth and sucked it clean. "Fucking perfect," he murmured, then pressed a gentle kiss to her mound. When he lifted his head, he made sure to keep his hold on her hips.

Perspiration caused her flesh to glisten. Her head was thrown back, eyes closed, as she attempted to gain her equilibrium. A burst of male satisfaction shot through Hunter as he watched his little butterfly come alive.

"Still think you can't come standing?"

5

―――――――

"You've convinced me," Jeanette said between pants.

Never once had she come so hard that she'd nearly blacked out, yet Hunter had managed to give her that very thing the first time out of the gate. By sheer will—Hunter's—she'd managed to stay on her feet too. If his powerful arm hadn't been wrapped around her so tightly she would have fallen flat on her butt. Not the way to impress a man.

He carefully released her and stood. "I'm glad." Then he pulled her into his arms and claimed her mouth.

His lips were hard, his tongue pushing its way in. Jeanette wrapped her arms around his neck and sank into his embrace. Hunter dropped kisses over her chin to her neck, where he angled his head and teased the sensitive skin with his lips. He grabbed handfuls of her hair and skimmed his tongue up and down her flesh, directly over her vein. As he gently bit down, Jeanette's pussy pulsed and swelled all over again. She closed her eyes and gave herself over to the delicious man. His mouth moved farther south, sliding over the swells of her breasts. When he lapped at first one nipple then the other, her pussy flooded with liquid heat.

"You're so goddamn hot. Your sweet, round tits make my mouth water, baby."

"Y-you're a little overdressed, Hunter," Jeanette whispered, eager to see if he was all she'd imagined he'd be. Seeing his drool-worthy chest was pure heaven, but it wasn't enough. She wanted all of him.

He mumbled something against her flesh before he let his teeth graze her nipple. Arrows of pleasure zipped across her nerve endings. She arched against him, his stubbled cheek creating just the right amount of stimulation to pull another whimper from her. As he cupped her other breast, flicking his thumb over the hard bud, a hunger like never before blocked out all rational thought.

Jeanette pushed out of his arms and said the first words that came to mind. "I need to feel you sinking deep, Hunter. Please, stop teasing me."

He cupped her face in his hands. "I'm teasing us both, sweetheart. When we make love it'll be explosive."

She eyed his undone jeans. "You have to remove your pants first."

He chuckled. "I need to get you home first."

Jeanette pouted and crossed her arms over her breasts. "Uh-uh. I want a taste. It's only fair, you know."

Hunter's smile disappeared, replaced by a look so hot she felt singed. "I always play fair, sweetness."

His hands went to his fly, snaring Jeanette's attention. Deft fingers slid the zipper down. He tugged the material, revealing a pair of tight black boxer-briefs and strong, tan thighs. She gasped at the impressive length and width of his cock barely hidden by cotton, so much larger than she'd expected. As he leaned down to unlace his boots, then shoved them off his feet and stood, Jeanette had to remind herself to breathe. Without a moment's hesitation he removed both the jeans and the boxers until he stood in her kitchen fully naked. The thickly veined erection jutted away from his body, a pearl of moisture beaded on the purplish head. The feral expression on his face sent butterflies flitting inside her stomach.

He held out his hand and Jeanette took it without hesitation. "Use that pretty mouth to take me to paradise, baby."

A bout of shyness should have been suffocating her right about then, but all Jeanette felt was the white-hot stroke of desire. Succumbing to the need riding her, Jeanette slowly sank to her knees in front of Hunter, the fingers of her left hand still entwined with his. She looked up his body until their gazes clashed.

"Suck, Jeanette," he softly ordered.

She tried to pull her hand away, aching to touch his smooth, hard flesh, but he only tightened his grip. "No. Just your mouth."

Jeanette didn't care for that answer so she brought her other hand up instead, wrapping it around his cock. "I want to touch you," she explained, her need to feel warm satin over hard steel overriding her usual fears.

Hunter leaned down and placed his own hand over hers. "Later for that, I promise. Right now, I want those pretty lips wrapped tight around my dick."

The devilish bad-boy look Hunter seemed born with was aided by the disheveled midnight black hair and dark mysterious eyes. Mesmerized by him, Jeanette slowly released the hold she had on his cock. Hunter took advantage and grasped both her wrists in one large fist then held them above her head, stretching her upper body taut. Completely at his mercy. Her pussy creamed as she realized the submissive picture she presented.

"You like this, don't you?"

Her cheeks heated, embarrassed all of a sudden. "What do you mean?"

"Me," he growled, "taking charge."

Jeanette licked her lips and stared at his cock, unable to meet his gaze.

Hunter tugged her arms, gaining her attention. "You're on your knees for me, Jeanette," he whispered, as if unwilling to let her hide from her own forbidden cravings. "I'm in complete control and it turns you on. I bet if I touched your cunt right now, I'd find you wetter than hell, wouldn't I?"

"Yes," she blurted out, unable to save face by acting blasé.

Tenderness filled Hunter's expression, softening the harsh planes of his face. He leaned down and pressed his lips to the top of her head. "It's okay, baby. I won't hurt you."

"I know. I trust you, Hunter." It was nothing less than the truth. It was a strange feeling to trust so quickly, so easily. There was just something about the man. He might look sinfully delicious, but he was one of the good guys, she could feel it in her bones.

Without wasting another second, Jeanette leaned forward and licked him from balls to tip.

"Christ, yes," he said in a desire-roughened voice. "Like that, baby."

Jeanette licked once more, then angled her head and took Hunter's cock into her mouth, as deep as she could go without gagging. She hollowed her cheeks and sucked hard on his engorged flesh.

"Mmm, fuck. You like that cock, don't you?"

The last layer of her shyness fell away, and for the first time Jeanette let herself free to explore. Swirling her tongue over and around the bulbous head of his shaft, she tasted the sticky fluid of his arousal. Hunter groaned and pulled her arms a little higher, stretching her. The grip he had on her wrists was unyielding, but not so tight as to be painful. Pleasure spiked anew at the realization that Hunter had total control over her. Her pussy wept with need. She slipped his cock from between her lips and licked down the underside to his balls, before sucking one soft orb into her mouth.

"Jesus, baby, enough," Hunter demanded. "I can't take much more."

He used his other hand to cup her chin, trying and failing to pull her off him. Jeanette wasn't through; she needed just one more taste of his addictive male essence. Releasing his balls, she licked the throbbing, swollen head, moaning as the salty precome hit her tongue. His delicious width caused her to imagine him sliding into her pussy, filling her. She clenched her thighs together as the visual made her clit throb. Encouraged by the guttural sounds he made, Jeanette teased the slit in the head, then took him in farther, suckling gently. Suddenly he released her hands.

"No more," he groaned.

Jeanette let him slide out from between her lips. He grasped her around the waist and lifted her to her feet. Their gazes clashed.

"Come home with me."

Jeanette nodded. Denying him would be akin to shooting herself in the foot. And she wasn't much into pain.

"Will you ride with me?"

Her eyes shot wide at the question. "On your motorcycle?"

"Yes. I'll bring you back to your car tomorrow morning."

She'd dreamed of riding on his bike with him, her arms wrapped around his hard body, hugging him tight as Hunter maneuvered the streets with absolute confidence. Unfortunately, reality intruded. "I need to open tomorrow morning. It'll be early."

Hunter shrugged. "I don't need much sleep. Never have."

Did she dare? "Yes, I'll ride with you." The sudden decision set her heart racing.

The grin he gave her was enough to curl any woman's toes. "Get dressed," he groaned, "you're in for a treat."

"I thought I just had my treat," she replied, as she eyed his still extremely large erection.

"Naughty, naughty girl." Then, before she could respond, Hunter turned her until she was facing away from him and swatted her on the ass. Not so hard as to sting, but enough to surprise.

"Hey! What was that for?"

"I've been dying to do that since the first day I came in." He massaged the spot he'd spanked and she heard him groan. "You're ass is so damn pretty, but it's going to look even prettier all pink from the spanking I plan to give you."

A frisson of fear stole through her. "I've never done anything like that, Hunter. I'm not sure that's something I'll enjoy."

Hunter hugged her to him, his cock pressing against the upper curve of her bottom. "Nothing but pleasure, Jeanette. We'll experiment a little. If you don't like it, we'll try something else, okay?"

She liked the sound of that. "I've never done much in the way of experimenting."

"Then let me be your teacher, sweetness," he said into her ear. "I won't disappoint you."

"By all means teach me, Hunter," Jeanette whispered, putting herself in his very capable hands.

"My pleasure, baby."

6

"Here, put my helmet on. I want you safe." Hunter slid the hard protective covering over Jeanette's head, her brown hair hanging down past her shoulders. He wrapped the strap beneath her chin and made sure it was tight.

"What are you going to wear?"

"I'll be fine." He grabbed his leather jacket from the lock box and slung it over her shoulders. "The coat isn't just for warmth, it's protection too."

She pushed her arms in, but the cuffs hung down past her fingertips. Hunter had to roll the sleeves up three times to get them to fit right. He zipped it up and noticed her grinning. "What?"

"I feel ridiculous."

Hunter kissed her on the tip of her nose and murmured, "But you look adorable."

Her soft laugh flooded his senses. He liked when she let herself go, forgot the shyness. Like when she'd licked his cock and nearly drove him right over the edge. She hadn't been the least bit shy then either.

Hunter slung his leg over the leather seat, and took hold of the handlebars. "Climb on, sweetness."

She looked down at herself and frowned. "Um, I didn't allow for the skirt. This might not work, Hunter."

"It'll be fine, just make sure the material is wrapped around your legs, then lift your leg over."

Jeanette pulled the material up and bunched it between her thighs, then stepped onto the footpad and boosted herself up and over. When she slid onto the seat behind him and wiggled around to get more comfortable, he went rigid. Christ, even through all the layers of clothing, Hunter could swear he felt her hot pussy pressing against his ass. Maybe it was just his lust-filled brain. Either way, concentrating on the road was going to be a bitch.

He looked back and checked her skirt, making sure none of the material hung down. Satisfied she had it all tucked around her, he asked, "Ready?"

"As I'll ever be."

He winked. "Don't be nervous. I'm not a daredevil and my house is just a few streets from here."

"I'm not nervous."

He quirked a brow at the bold-faced lie and she caved. "Okay, I'm a little nervous. I've never been on a motorcycle before."

"I've been riding since I was a teenager. My uncle used to take me out on his. When I was old enough to earn my own money, I saved up and bought my first bike. An old piece of crap, but still, I loved that thing."

"I've never dated a guy who rode."

"I bet you've never given head in the kitchen of your café either. I guess it's a night of firsts."

She laughed and smacked him on the back. "You're bad."

He only grinned back at her before turning the key. The engine roared to life immediately. "Hold on tight, sweetness," he called over his shoulder.

When he felt her arms slide tentatively around his middle, Hunter took hold of both her hands and tugged until she was snug against him. Ah yeah, that was more like it. "Ready?"

"Yep," she yelled back.

Hunter revved the engine and maneuvered out of the lit parking lot and onto the dark city street. By the time they'd driven half a mile, Jeanette's grip on him had loosened and he could feel her cheek against his back. Something about the sweet, vulnerable way she held on to him, so trusting, as if she had nothing to fear, melted the ice around his heart.

Hunter wasn't sure where this thing between them would lead. Relationships hadn't been a big priority. In fact, he usually went for a few days with a woman, then he happily moved on. He'd never messed with a woman who didn't know the score. He offered a good time between the sheets, not tender emotions. Pretty words and sweet promises wasn't his style.

Jeanette was different though. He wanted more than sex from her. He wanted to see her smile again. To see her blush for him. He ached to watch her go all soft when he paid her compliments. Her innocence, he assured himself. It had pulled at him like a dog to a bone. Surely there wasn't more to it than that.

Still, the idea of bringing her back to her café in the morning and never seeing her again had his gut in knots. A few hours in his bed weren't going to suffice. Hunter was smart enough to admit the truth. Little Jeanette had gone to his head. No way in hell was he anywhere close to being ready to walk away. In fact, for the first time in his life, the notion of spending time out of bed with a woman didn't have him immediately growing wings on his feet. Fuck. Sex he was good at, but romancing a woman? Now that was foreign territory.

He turned onto the cul-de-sac where he lived, anticipation a low hum inside him. She'd be in his bed soon, naked and his to pleasure. He'd obsessed over Jeanette. Not like a sick perverted type of obsession, but still, she'd been in his thoughts for months. The only reason he'd held back so long was because it'd become clear to him that she had *good girl* stamped all over her. He had no business screwing around with her. In the end, he'd caved, knowing she'd be a fire in his blood until he finally had a taste of her. He hadn't figured on becoming addicted.

As he slowed and drove the cycle up his driveway, Jeanette stiffened behind him. He turned his head and called over his shoulder, "Open the compartment behind you, sweetheart. There's a garage door remote in there."

Jeanette wiggled around, inadvertently driving him crazy with the feel of her crotch pressed against his ass. She pulled the black remote out and asked, "Is this it?"

"Yeah, thanks," he said, his voice rough. If he didn't get his dick inside her soon, his balls were going to explode. Not a happy thought.

Hunter pushed the button and the garage door slid upward. He drove slowly forward before shutting off the engine. After he pushed the remote again, closing them in, he turned and whispered, "We're here."

Jeanette nodded, then used his shoulders for leverage, hoisting herself off the seat and onto the cement floor. Hunter flipped the kickstand out and stepped off the bike.

Jeanette's eyes darted around, looking everywhere but at him. He took her chin and coaxed her to face him. "Second thoughts?" Christ, he sure as hell hoped not. His hand would be a poor substitute tonight. His dick was way past ready to feel the tight fist of her pussy.

"No, just nervous."

He let himself breathe. Leaning down, Hunter kissed her, then whispered against her lips, "I'm going to make you forget all about your worries. Only sweet pleasure tonight, baby."

Jeanette's eyes turned drowsy and her lips tipped up at one corner. "I probably shouldn't even be here, but I'm glad I am."

"I'm glad too." Hunter took off her helmet and placed it on the seat, then led her by the hand and escorted her to the door leading into the kitchen. He flipped the light on and looked over at her. "Home sweet home."

"Wow, your kitchen is huge!" she said as she unzipped his leather jacket and placed it on the coat tree next to the door. "I could really have a lot of fun in here."

Hunter looked around the room with pride. Green granite counter tops, cherrywood cabinets and a refrigerator big enough to hold several Thanksgiving dinners. No doubt about it, his kitchen was a thing of joy. "I'm not big on cooking, but on the rare occasions I like to do it up right."

"You can definitely do it right with a kitchen like this," she said, as she walked around, touching surfaces and humming her approval. She popped open the door on the wine cooler and pulled out a drawer. "You like wine, don't you?"

"I like a lot of things." He moved toward her. "For instance, there's this sexy coffee shop owner I've had my eye on."

Jeanette pushed the drawer back in and closed the glass door before backing up a step. Her pretty grin lit up the room. "What if she's not into you?"

Hunter let his gaze travel over her upper body, noting the way her nipples hardened for him. Slowly, as if stalking prey, he cornered her between the stove and the dishwasher. "I have proof she's very into me," he growled.

"Oh, really?"

"Mmm," he murmured as he planted one hand on the counter beside her and let the other slide over the top swell of one breast, then down over the hard bud tempting him beyond reason. "For instance, if she wasn't ready to be fucked, then I doubt her nipples would be so hard."

"M-maybe she's cold."

Her unsteady voice was a testament to how excited their little game made her. "I don't know, she feels pretty warm to me. In fact, I'd say she's downright hot."

"You would?"

He nodded. "The hottest thing I've seen in a long time."

She placed her palm against his chest. "Before we go any further I have a confession to make."

Hunter froze. "A confession?" Fuck, that didn't sound good.

"Remember those two friends I mentioned earlier?"

"Roni and Lydia."

"You remember their names?"

He stepped back and crossed his arms over his chest. "I never forget names."

"I see. Anyway, I sort of . . . made a bet with them. And it has to do with you."

He'd expected her to tell him she was secretly engaged or something equally as horrifying, but a bet? "I don't think I'm following you here, Jeanette. We just met today."

She played with the hem of her blouse, something he noticed she did whenever she was nervous. "But I've been attracted to you for a long time. I've just been too afraid to approach you."

She'd had the hots for him? Why hadn't he noticed? He shook the thought away and said, "Okay, but what does any of this have to do with a bet you made with your girlfriends?"

"We bet on who could make their fantasy come true first."

"And I'm your fantasy," he surmised. Damn, now they were getting somewhere.

"Yes. I'm so sorry!" She stepped forward, closing the small space between them. "Do you feel terribly objectified?"

He chuckled. "Baby, men like being the object of women's fantasies." He thought for a second then asked, "So, in this bet, what do you have to do to win exactly?"

"I have to sleep with Mr. Motorcycle Man," she blurted out.

His lips twitched. "Motorcycle Man?"

Her cheeks turned pink. "Well, at the time I didn't know your name."

Hunter cupped her face in his hands and kissed her forehead. "How about we go see if we can win that bet, shall we?"

7

Jeanette allowed Hunter to lead her into his bedroom. Much like the kitchen, no expense was spared. When he turned a little dial next to the door, soft light filled the room. A vaulted ceiling with two skylights made the room seem much larger than it really was. A pair of French doors opened to a balcony. The beautiful canopied, king-sized bed covered in a burgundy satin comforter made Jeanette keenly aware that Hunter liked his comforts. The light pine wood had gorgeous diamond-shaped carvings on the headboard and footboard. An overstuffed burgundy chair sat next to a large bay window, and a huge entertainment center took up nearly the entire wall across from the bed. She turned to where Hunter leaned against the doorjamb, his arms crossed over his chest.

"Just what do you do for a living?"

Hunter stood and came toward her. "I'm an author."

"Judging by your house, you must be a best-seller. What do you write?"

"Thrillers," he said, as he moved to sit on the edge of the bed.

Jeanette walked around the room, curious about the man who'd held her interest for so long. She spied a framed photo on his nightstand and picked it up. An older man stood next to Hunter, their arms over each other as Hunter held up a hard-back book with the name Grayson Rivers on the cover. Oh my God, she knew that name! She had a few of his books on her shelf at home. He really was a best-seller. The older man resembled Hunter, his smile shining with pride and love.

She turned toward him and held up the photo. "Is this your father?"

A flicker of something passed over his face, before he shuttered it and moved to sit on the edge of the bed. "No, my Uncle Raymond. Remember I mentioned the uncle who taught me to ride?" She nodded. "He taught me a lot of things. He practically raised me."

"I see." She carefully placed the frame back on the top of the dresser and moved away. "He must be very special."

"He was. He had a heart attack shortly after that photo was taken. I still miss him."

Drawn by the emotion in his gaze, Jeanette stepped closer. His musky male scent filled her senses. "He sounds pretty wonderful. What about your parents?"

He stiffened. "I never knew my dad. My mom passed away six years ago. She'd been in a car accident but walked away without any injuries. A few days after the crash she started having headaches. I talked her into going to the hospital to get checked out. She went downhill really fast. She slipped into a coma. It wasn't long before Uncle Raymond and I were burying her."

"Oh, Hunter," Jeanette said, emotion clogging her throat. "I'm so sorry."

Without warning Hunter grabbed her arm and pulled until she fell into his lap. "I don't want to talk about my mom and uncle," he whispered against her ear. "I'd much rather help you win that bet."

Even with all they'd done together already, she still found herself blushing at the reminder of the bet. "I can't believe I told you about that."

"I'm glad you did." He flicked her nose. "I wouldn't have been pleased if you'd kept it from me. I enjoy being the object of your fantasies, baby, but I don't want to be kept in the dark."

"That makes sense."

"Since we're on the subject," he said as his hand skated up her thigh only to disappear beneath her skirt. "What did you fantasize about exactly?"

He nudged her thighs apart and his fingers moved in small circles over her clitoris. Her panties had been ruined and she'd been forced to go commando. Jeanette could barely concentrate on the conversation as he began to pinch her clit and stroke her sensitive pussy lips. "You want details?"

Hunter slid his middle finger inside her wet heat, humming his approval when she moaned and spread her thighs wider. "A lot of details."

Her clit was teased as he plunged his finger in and out. "I-I thought men didn't like to talk in bed," she managed around a whimper.

While Hunter continued to ply her swollen bud, his other hand went to work on the buttons of her blouse. "That doesn't pertain to fantasy talk. Tell me what you want from me, sweetness."

Jeanette's breathing turned rapid, her temperature spiking as Hunter undid the last button of her blouse. "I'm not very imaginative, but there was one fantasy . . ." Her words trailed off as he pushed his hand inside her bra and cupped her breast.

"Go on," he murmured. "Tell me your naughty little secrets, sweetheart."

Attempting to form sentences wasn't easy with Hunter's fingers teasing her beyond reason. "I have this one fantasy where we masturbate together." She took a deep breath before continuing. "We're sitting across from each other, not touching, you're watching me as I play with my pussy. You're stroking your cock."

Hunter nibbled her earlobe and slipped two fingers into her tight passage. "I like your fantasy very much, baby, but how about we modify it just a touch."

"Hunter, you're driving me crazy," she moaned.

He pulled his fingers free, then sank them deep once more, finger-fucking her. "My cock wants to feel this hot little cunt, Jeanette. I'm so close to coming in my jeans right now it's not even funny."

"Then stop playing and take off your clothes," she begged, shameless in her passion.

Hunter cursed and removed his fingers, then placed them against her lips. "Suck them," he ordered.

Helpless to deny either of them in that moment, Jeanette opened her mouth. Hunter slid his fingers over her tongue and she closed her lips, sucking the digits clean.

Hunter's arm tightened around her. "Damn, that's sexy. Such a sweet little baby."

Jeanette moved on his lap, sliding back and forth over his hard cock as her tongue flicked back and forth over his fingers. But the feel of his heavy cock and powerful thighs beneath her bottom was simply too much temptation. She whimpered.

Hunter slid his arm beneath her legs and lifted her off his lap and onto the bed beside him. "Clothes," he explained as he started to push her shirt off. She clutched his T-shirt and tugged upward, revealing the smooth, hard abs and powerful chest she'd admired earlier. Within seconds they were naked, Hunter towering over her. "Have you ever let a lover videotape you?"

Her eyes shot wide. "No. No way." The mere thought of

the wide expanse of her backside being on camera was like a dash of ice water.

Hunter's gaze narrowed. "Is this about the pear thing you mentioned earlier?"

"Yes." She bit out, her stomach churning just thinking about it. "I definitely don't want to see my butt on tape."

Hunter planted his hands on the bed beside her hips, fire in his eyes. "I thought I made it clear your ass is perfect the way it is."

"You did, but—"

"Why do you think I've been itching to play with it for the last six months?"

She glared at him. "You must need glasses, Hunter, that's all I can think."

"I don't need glasses to know I want to fuck that hot little butt of yours. To spank it until your flesh tingles. I want to fill your tight little asshole with my come, Jeanette. It's all I can think about."

Her clit throbbed as the taboo images filled her mind. "Anal sex?"

"Christ, yeah." His deep voice fueled the fire building in her soul. "First, I want to watch you masturbate like you talked about, but I want to do it behind a video camera. Is that so scary, baby?"

Not the way he put it. Suddenly she wondered how far she could push Hunter. Could she, the shy wallflower, drive a man like Hunter wild with lust simply by playing to his camera? "As long as I can stay on my back," she finally relented. "And we have to destroy the tape afterward."

One eyebrow kicked up. "Destroy it?"

She nodded, firm on this one point. "It would be appalling if it ended up in the wrong hands."

His head snapped back as if she'd slapped him. "You think I'm going to put it up on the Internet?"

She lifted her hand to his chest, flattening her palm over his left pectoral, directly over his heart. "No, of course not," she said softly, "but it still pays to be careful."

He nodded. "So, we destroy the tape after we watch it. I can live with that."

She dropped her hand and closed her eyes tight against the horror of what she'd just agreed to. "I can't believe I'm doing this."

"Jeanette, look at me." His quiet, gentle tone had her doing his bidding. When their gazes locked, he said, "It's just me here, baby. Let yourself go. Leave all those fears for another day. Tonight it's just you and me. If at any time you feel uncomfortable and want to stop, we'll stop."

"Promise?"

He leaned down and pressed his lips to hers. "You have my word," he murmured.

"Okay."

"That's my girl," he praised.

Strong hands caressed her thighs, the carnal expression spreading across Hunter's face fueling her bravado. She reached out and wrapped her fingers around his cock, then squeezed the hot, hard flesh. The lopsided grin he shot her way went clear to her toes. His mouth skimmed below her ear, touching off another little jolt of electricity inside her.

As he stroked the curls covering her mound, Jeanette began to plead in earnest. "Hunter, please."

He pulled his hand away and straightened. "Show time, sweetness."

"Oh, God," she groaned.

8

He could be inside her within seconds. Feeding the hunger and finally satisfying the cravings he'd had for so long. Hunter couldn't explain why he'd decided to combine Jeanette's hot little fantasy with one of his own. When a little voice in his head called him a liar, he faced the truth. Yeah, he knew damn well why he'd chosen to play rather than pounce. He didn't just want to satisfy an ache with Jeanette. He could do that with any woman. This was the voluptuous creature who'd captured his attention without even having been aware of it. No, a quick fuck wouldn't do. He wanted to watch the sweet, curvy woman blossom. To succumb to her own feverish needs.

She'd trusted him enough to come home with him, a veritable stranger, but touching her own soft pussy, teasing herself into a frenzy while he watched? It would be the ultimate form of surrender. With her mind and body wrapped up in hot, liquid pleasure, a woman was at her most vulnerable. Defenses were shattered. Nothing but raw feeling.

The real problem would be keeping his hands off her. Letting her pet the little cunt he so badly ached to bury his dick in was going to be sheer torture.

Hunter pushed the record button on the side of the camcorder he'd retrieved from a drawer in his entertainment cabinet. "Touch yourself, Jeanette."

Leaning against the dresser, he held the camera in front of his face, watching through the viewfinder. His pretty coffee shop owner lay on his bed, legs pressed tightly together, hair spread out all over the dark red comforter. Her skin like cream, lush and soft, seemed frighteningly delicate. He reminded himself for the thousandth time to be gentle with her when he finally managed to bury his cock inside her. He couldn't let his savage instinct take over. He'd need to maintain control or risk hurting her. The thought that he could cause Jeanette even an ounce of pain took his ardor down a few notches.

Her hands clutched the comforter at her sides, her breathing choppy. Nervous tension filled the room. Hunter wrapped a fist around his cock and growled, "Look at me, sweetness."

Jeanette's pretty brown gaze shot to his, then quickly traveled a course down his body to land on the hand he had on his dick. "Do you see how hard I am? How badly I want you?" She licked her lips and nodded. Hunter moved his hand up and down, a slow massage, giving her the fantasy she craved. "We're going to make that fantasy come true, baby. Drive me wild. Show me that pretty body all hot and flush with arousal."

Jeanette bit her lip. When her right hand released the comforter, Hunter sucked in a breath, anticipating what would come next. She slid her hand over her flat belly first, then moved upward to her breast. As she cupped the soft orb, Hunter cursed, his hand on his cock tightening. A delicate finger flicked and toyed with the nipple he'd sucked earlier, making his mouth water for another taste. Suddenly her other hand came up to cover her pussy, her legs spreading open a few inches.

"More," he demanded, unable to stand the slow pace she'd set for them. "Show me."

"More?"

Hunter's hand tightened on the camera as he zoomed in on the swollen, pink lips of Jeanette's sex. "Open for me. Tempt your Motorcycle Man, baby."

Jeanette's eyes were at half-mast as she watched him stroke his cock. Slowly, as if deliberately teasing him, she moved her legs wide and massaged her fingers over her clit a few times before dipping two fingers into the slick entrance. Hunter squeezed his cock tighter before giving into the need to pump. Once, twice, then he forced himself to stop. Too close. Fuck, just watching her tentatively touch herself took him to the very edge. A few more pumps from his fist and he'd be shooting his load all over the damn carpet.

It was an exercise in control to stand across the room, watching. So easily he could drop the camera and go to her, he could stroke that smooth female flesh himself, play to his heart's content. In an effort to maintain control, he fisted his hand at his side and kept hold of the camera.

A sexy smile curved Jeanette's pretty mouth. "Do you like what you see, Hunter?"

His hand on the camera clenched, his leg muscles flexing with the urge to take her rough, the need to prove how good it would be between them nearly too strong to ignore. His dick was like granite, he was so fucking hard. Just a few steps and he could slide it between Jeanette's succulent pussy lips. Again he had to remind himself to go slow. Rough would come later. Right now he needed to see more of that confident smile.

As she touched the pad of her thumb to her clit, Hunter licked his lips and knew a momentary pang of jealousy. That sweet little bud should be in his mouth right now.

Without conscious thought, he stepped away from the dresser.

Hunter didn't stop moving until he was standing at the end of the bed, looking up the length of Jeanette's beautiful body. She rewarded him with a shy smile, as if knowing her little show was pushing him beyond reason. She slid her fingers in and out of her tight heat, and toyed with the little bundle of nerves, her moans filling the room. He drank in the sight of her as her breathing increased, her shyness slipping slowly away until all that remained was a gorgeous seductress.

"So pretty," he murmured as he leaned down and pinched her nipple.

When she arched off the bed and buried her fingers deeper, Hunter groaned. Her hips moved back and forth in a rhythm that had his cock dripping with pre-come. As she cupped her free hand over one round breast, plucked and tugged at her own nipple, Hunter's control snapped. He dropped the camera on the bed and leaned down. Jeanette's eyes widened, fingers stilled.

Planting both hands on either side of her head, he snarled, "You win. I'm putty in your hands, sweetness."

He touched the inside of her thigh, smoothing his hand toward the tempting wet center he ached to sink into. The staccato of Hunter's heartbeat nearly drowned out all else.

"Hunter, I want to watch you touch your cock a little more." The throaty purr in her voice tore down shields he'd thought impenetrable around his heart.

Hunter kissed her. "The show's over," he whispered against the satin of her lips. "I need to feel your body hugging my cock."

"Just once more? Pretty please?"

Yeah, like a man could say no to such a plea. "Fuck, you really like watching, huh?"

"I like watching you. You're so big, so hard. It's exciting to see your fist wrapped so tight around your cock."

"Your wish is my command, sweetness." Hunter crawled onto the bed and sat back on his haunches, then wrapped a tight fist around his heavy length. He pumped, slowly, up and down, intrigued when Jeanette's eyes grew dark with passion. Her lips parted and her small pink tongue darted out, licking, as if imagining his taste. He watched the movement, sensing that tentative stroke on his cock.

"Is this what you like?" he asked. Jeanette's eager nod sent a jolt of possessive heat through his body. He swiped his thumb over the pre-come at the bulbous tip, then brought it to her lips. "Lick it, pretty baby."

She never hesitated. Jeanette wrapped her hand around his, holding his finger still, then her tongue darted out and licked the sticky fluid. Hunter lost it. Her soft tongue. Her wild little whimpers. It was all too damn much.

"Come for me now. I can't wait much longer to have you."

Jeanette flicked a finger over her clit once before pinching the little bit of flesh. Riveted to the carnal display, Hunter gripped her thighs and spread her wider until he could see all of her. Wet, swollen lips and the tight pucker of her anus. Damn, what a view. First he was going to fill her cunt with the width of his cock. She would be tight. If he didn't go insane from the pleasure of it, he planned to take her from behind, fuck the hot little ass he'd dreamed about.

Two slim fingers dipped inside her cunt, once, twice, only to slip free and toy with the little bundle of nerves all over again.

Hunter absorbed the sounds of her hoarse cries and whimpers. Suddenly she threw her head back and bucked off the bed, wildly, screaming his name over and over again as she came. Watching Jeanette take her own pleasure would forever be etched into his heart and soul.

Not giving her a chance to come down from the high, Hunter reached over and pulled out a drawer on his nightstand. He grabbed the box of condoms he kept there and tore at it. Jeanette's eyes darted open. Snaring her gaze with his own, Hunter ripped open the foil packet and rolled the condom down his cock.

Poised at the entrance, he held himself still, mesmerized by Jeanette's tender, innocent gaze eating him up. When her hands moved to wrap around his forearms, the fine-boned fingers tore through his lust-driven brain as nothing else could.

He cupped her cheek and murmured, "You've been in my head for months, but I'm not going to hurt you, baby."

Jeanette released his arms to press a palm on his chest, her fingers curling in his chest hair. "I've been hungry for you, Hunter. I haven't been with anyone since you started to come to my coffee shop. I only wanted you."

The quietly whispered admission pleased him, too damn much, but it was the heat and emotion behind them that made mincemeat of his heart. Hell, if she had any idea how easily she could crush him. For a loner like him, it wasn't a pleasant thought.

He pushed in an inch, effectively disintegrating all thought. "We can't have you hungry, now can we, sweetness?"

"No, we can't."

9

The head of Hunter's cock stretched her tender tissues, but he took his time, as if afraid she'd break if he pushed too hard. Jeanette needed to tell him she wouldn't break.

She wrapped her legs around his hips and nudged him to move faster. "Hunter, you're killing me."

He leaned over her, a muscle in his jaw jumping wildly with the control he continued to maintain. "You're so goddamn tight, little love. Too fast and I could hurt you."

"I'm not so fragile, please," she pleaded, beyond ready to be filled by her dark, mysterious lover.

She couldn't look away from the tender affection so clear in his expression. There was a darkness in Hunter, a savage predator, but he seemed intent on keeping that side of his nature chained. As if she were too delicate to handle the intensity of his passion. The man was an inferno and yet his gentle touch gave nothing of that away. He quite simply fascinated her.

When he took her face in his hands and held her still for his kiss, her insides fluttered. He bit her lower lip, the pleasure-pain zipping straight to her clitoris. As he coaxed her lips apart, their tongues playing, Jeanette wrapped her arms around his head and held him tight, loathe to ever let him go.

He pulled back a fraction and growled, "You drive me right out of my mind, baby. No woman has ever tied me in knots the way you do."

Jeanette didn't know how to respond to such a declaration. It was as if she were on a high wire with no net to break her fall. "It's never been like this for me either," she confessed.

He slipped in another inch, his voice dropping to a dark whisper. "Like what?"

Jeanette's thoughts scattered at the feel of his hard length pressing ever closer to where she needed him so desperately. Realizing he'd spoken, she managed a breathy, "Huh?"

He pulled out all the way, then slid back in. Still it wasn't enough. She needed to feel the wild man lurking just below the surface. Jeanette moaned, aching and restless.

Hunter skimmed his hand over her hip, then farther north to cup and squeeze her breast. The delicious torture took her to a new level.

"You've never been like what?" he asked, his voice a harsh sound in the quiet room.

Jeanette managed to focus finally. "I've never gone home with a man so quickly."

The look he gave at her confession singed her. "This is unique for me too, sweetness."

When he dipped his head and kissed her nipple, then licked the sensitive tip, she arched upward, anxious to feel his lips wrapping around her, taking her to heaven.

"Open yourself more," he ordered. "Show me you want this. Show me you want *me*."

His hot breath against her flesh was all the incentive she needed. She spread her legs wider, then pushed against his hips, forcing him in another inch.

"Fuck, baby," he groaned. He lifted to his hands and without warning thrust forward, burying deep the full length of his large, hard cock.

She gasped as inner muscles burned and stretched to accommodate the intimate invasion.

Hunter stilled, his gaze boring into hers. "Too much?"

"No, it's . . ." She couldn't find the words to express the sensations bombarding her. His cock touched places inside her body she was sure no man had ever reached.

"Damn, you feel incredible," he uttered as he pulled all the way out only to thrust forward again.

One large, calloused palm swept over her nipples, and she arched upward, seeking more of his rough caresses. When he smoothed his way down her ribcage and belly to play with her tiny bud, she flew apart.

"Hunter!"

"Yeah, baby," he snarled, "come for me again." He thrust harder, holding on to her hips as he plunged deep.

Jeanette came, starbursts filling her vision as Hunter took her over that invisible edge once again.

"Goddamn, even through the condom I can feel you bathing my cock with that sweet cream," he growled. Muscles pumped and sweat glistened off his chest and abs. His thrusts turned faster, harder. Suddenly he flung his head back and shouted her name as he reached his own climactic finish. Jeanette wrapped her arms and legs around him, holding him to her in a tight embrace.

When he collapsed on top of her, most of his weight on his arms beside her body, peace stole through her. She never wanted the moment to end. She never wanted to let him go. How would she survive when he rode off on his motorcycle?

Warm, gentle fingers coasted over her hip, bringing her awake in an instant. As her eyelashes fluttered open, her gaze collided with Hunter's. "Did I fall asleep?"

He lay propped up on his elbow on his side, staring down at her. His sensual grin melted her bones. "Yep. I wore you out."

No kidding. She'd never felt so sated her entire life. "What time is it?"

His hand continued sliding over her skin beneath the black throw blanket. He'd covered them and she hadn't even been aware of it. "You've only been out about an hour. It's midnight."

She started to get up, but he only held her down with his palm against her stomach. "Going somewhere, sweetness?"

"I should probably get moving. I do need to clean the kitchen before my morning waitress gets there. And I'd like to go home and get a shower beforehand."

Hunter shook his head. "No. I'm not letting you go just yet. We still have plenty of time."

He pressed his body against her side, letting her feel the hard length of his cock. "My lord, don't you ever get tired?"

He chuckled. "I've had an hour to recover, baby. More than enough time."

"I don't know if I can take more." He cupped her pussy. As if he'd flipped a switch, her clit swelled and throbbed. "Okay, so maybe I can."

He leaned down and kissed her. "I promised you wouldn't have to show your cute ass on the camcorder."

Her temperature spiked at the mention of the video she'd allowed him to take of her. "Yes, and I appreciate that."

"But the camera is off, baby, and I've been dying to play with that particular part of your anatomy."

"What are you asking?"

"Will you get up on all fours for me, sweetness?"

"So you can do what?"

"Pet. Spank. Fuck."

"Hunter." His name was a breathless plea on her lips.

"I've been very good, Jeanette," he coaxed. "Give me my pretty treat."

Her blood raced, her body wild with anticipation. Dare she? Taking a deep breath, Jeanette obeyed his sensual command. "Like this?" she asked, as she got up on all fours next to Hunter.

"Perfect," he growled. Moving behind her, now on his knees, Hunter stroked the seam between her buttocks. "You're so perfect. This ass has had me practically salivating. Did you know that?"

"N-no." Her voice shook with both trepidation and excitment. She'd never been comfortable with the size of her backside. She'd always felt so out of proportion. One boyfriend had even prompted her to go on a diet, stating she'd be prettier if she'd only lose a few pounds.

"I've never obsessed over one particular body part before you." He smoothed both hands over her hips and growled, "I hate that other men are thinking the same dirty thoughts as me when they watch you walk. It makes me want to fuck you here, to mark you as mine."

She turned her head to look at him. "Men don't look at me like that, Hunter."

He kissed her nose and smiled. "Yes, they do," he whispered as his palm massaged little circles over her flesh. "And I've wanted to pound them for staring, but I didn't have the right then."

Without realizing, Jeanette had parted her legs, giving him better access to places no man had ever touched. "And now?"

"And now things are different, sweetness," he simply stated.

His finger drifted back and forth over her puckered opening. A moan erupted from deep within Jeanette. Though she'd never had a man in such a forbidden way, the thought of Hunter there didn't scare her. In fact, her pussy creamed just thinking about Hunter's cock pushing inside her, claiming her as he'd said.

He leaned over her and kissed the base of her spine. "Would you like me to fill this little ass, baby?"

"Hunter, please . . . I don't know."

"Yes, you do," he urged as his finger penetrated her. A mere inch, but it was enough to cause her to clench in fear.

"Easy, little love, let me in."

Jeanette forced herself to relax. When she did Hunter buried his finger deep inside her anus. She shuddered and pushed against him. The single digit moved in and out, fucking her with slow, careful precision.

As Jeanette started to think she could take no more of his teasing, one of Hunter's big, warm hands connected with her upraised bottom. The erotic sting tore a scream from her lips.

He quickly soothed the area he'd swatted with a kiss. "Do I stop?"

Jeanette couldn't think past the pleasurable haze covering her mind. When Hunter pulled his finger all the way out she whimpered. "Please," she managed around the pounding in her head.

"Please, what? Please continue?"

"Yes!"

"Fuck, you're a delight. Such a sweet delight."

His finger slipped inside her once again, while the fingers of his other hand caressed her clit. Jeanette writhed and moved in time to his strokes. When she squeezed her bottom, Hunter growled.

"Such sweet torture. I'm going to love fucking this cute little butt."

His finger penetrated deeper, the fingers torturing her little nubbin suddenly disappearing. The only warning she got was the rush of air before his hand came down harder than before on her ass. He swatted one cheek, then the other, his finger moving in and out, pumping faster. Her skin burned, her body alive with sensation. Every heated touch took her higher. Three more swats, then he began massaging the ache he'd created.

"Two fingers now, sweetness. I need to prepare this virgin ass for my dick."

As a second finger joined the first, barriers dropped away. Jeanette went wild. She gyrated against Hunter, begging him and aching for everything he had to give.

"Play with your clit, baby. Take the edge off."

Jeanette reached down and took her clit between her finger and thumb, pumping and driving herself mad. Suddenly Hunter cursed and leaned down, then bit her hip.

Jeanette's climax came from somewhere deep inside. She screamed hard and loud, her back arching as her body flew apart. Everything she thought she knew about sexual pleasure seemed to pale in the wake of what she'd just experienced.

Hunter's rough voice just barely broke through the quagmire of her mind. "I want this ass," he hissed, then he moved his fingers out of her and cupped her dripping mound. "Look at me, little love."

She tured her head, already limp and sweating from her orgasm. When she saw the intensity, the insane yearning etched into Hunter's not-so-perfect features, her body went from sated to hungry in a heartbeat.

As she watched, Hunter squirted lubricant over his sheathed cock. She hadn't even been aware he'd grabbed a condom, much less lube. When the heavy weight of his erection entered her bottom, inner muscles clenched. Fear had her attempting to close her legs, panicked and scared.

"Hunter," she cried out, her body tensing further.

He pulled out instantly and caressed her buttocks. "Shh, it's okay. There's no rush, sweetness."

Jeanette relaxed, relieved by the soothing tone. Hunter appeared as if he had all the time in the world. He kissed her shoulder and she rocked against him. His tongue flicked over a sensitive spot behind her ear and her panic disappeared.

10

Hunter stared down at Jeanette on all fours in the center of the rumpled bed. The low lighting turned her alabaster skin into a creamy latte. Her luscious body and plump bottom were mere inches away from his eager fingers and cock. The sight had him nearly whimpering like a greedy pup.

"You're a feast for my starving libido, Jeanette."

She turned her head to speak, flipping her long hair, the color of milk chocolate, over one shoulder.

"You've been with other women, Hunter," she said, her voice small and unsure. "Probably a lot of them more exciting and prettier."

"I don't deny I've been with other women, but none could compare to you," he told her as candidly as he knew how. "All I want is you. All I need is this." And then he touched the soft curve of her ass. The sleek skin, softer than any silk he'd touched. "So round and firm and kissable," he murmured. *And so far away from my mouth.*

On his knees between her legs, Hunter leaned down and licked one smooth cheek. The startled sound Jeanette emitted urged him on. Already Hunter recognized her sounds. The needy little whimpers and anxious groans were for his ears alone.

He touched the cleft of her ass and stroked her intimately. "Only desire at my hands, never pain, sweetness."

She didn't speak, but her body told him all that he needed. She trusted him. It was the type of confidence he hadn't expected from a woman he'd met only hours ago, but he treasured it nonetheless.

Hunter caressed Jeanette's collarbone and shoulders, then moved to massage her long, elegant neck. Damn, so delicate and vulnerable. His teeth ached to nibble on the velvety-soft skin.

As he skated his palms down her arms to her wrists, he could feel the wild pulse beating there. "You're excited, aren't you, baby?"

"Y-yes."

"And a little scared?"

"A little."

Hunter tsked. "Sweet baby. No fear with me, remember?"

She nodded and Hunter traveled his fingers down her back, taking care to massage each vertebra until he felt the stiffness leave her body altogether. With Jeanette relaxed finally, he leaned down to place small kisses to the base of her spine and over her upraised ass.

He then smoothed his fingertips over her lower back, and growled, "Does this feel good?"

"Mmm, don't make me talk right now." She dropped her head to the comforter and moaned, "Oh my, that feels so incredible. You are one talented man, Hunter."

He smiled, cocky and turned on all at once.

He let his fingers drift over the small indentations above her bottom before saying, "You are being such a good little girl, sweetness."

Mindful of her fears, Hunter squirted more lube onto his fingers, then slid them between her ass cheeks. He stroked the tight, pink pucker over and over again, making certain she would experience nothing but raw pleasure when he entered her.

"You're going to kill me when I get my dick in here, baby." The need to fill her with his cock began to ride him hard. "It's going to be so fucking warm and tight."

"Oh God, Hunter."

His body was on fire and his dick was aching for release. He couldn't wait another second. Gently, he separated the round globes of her backside and touched the head of his cock to her entrance. He slipped inside, barely breaching her entrance. It was such sweet torture to hold back from thrusting deep. Fucking her hard and fast, the way his body so desperately craved.

"Hunter," she cried out.

Her quivery voice, so full of heat, nearly pushed him beyond reason. She thrust backward, as if eager for more. Hunter gave her another inch, pushing past the tight ring of muscles protecting the most secret part of her body.

"Christ, baby," he groaned. "You feel so damn good."

Another inch more and Jeanette went wild beneath him, thrusting her hips backward, taking control of their lovemaking in such a way that both surprised and pleased him. Her body bowed and Hunter had to clutch her hips to keep from sliding in too far too fast.

"Gently, little love," he commanded in a tone that brooked no argument. He refused to hurt her—despite the way his primal instincts kept battering at him to fill her completely.

Holding her firmly by the hips to keep her body still for his slow invasion, Hunter heard Jeanette let loose a needy little plea. The yearning, delicate sound turned his heart to mush. He gave her another heated inch of hard flesh, unable to deny either of them in that moment. In the same instant, he took his right hand from her hip and toyed with the tender little bundle of nerves of her clitoris. He flicked and pinched. Without warning Jeanette moaned and pushed against him as her orgasm took her.

"Now," he snarled. "Do you want all of me inside this pretty little ass?"

"Yes, damn it!"

A rumbling growl escaped him at her feral response. He buried his cock deep, and inner muscles clamped around him, holding him in a grip so exquisite any move at all would set him off. Jeanette's body went rigid, her ass clenching tighter. Hunter bit back a curse. Her body's clutch took him to another level of pleasure, where pleasure mingled with pain. Raw and untamed.

"Ease up, little love," he managed in a tortured voice.

"I-I can't," she cried.

Her hands were above her head, clutching fistfuls of the red blanket. He stroked her sweat-soaked hair away from her face, then covered her body with his own much larger frame, folding himself around her protectively. He kissed her upturned cheek. The tension in her shoulders and spine eased a fraction. Hunter sent up a silent prayer.

"That's the way. Let me in, sweetness," he whispered against the shell of her ear. Hunter bit the smooth line of her neck and received a moan as a reward. He licked and suckled at the tempting vein before beginning a leisurely rhythm with his hips, building the pace until soon his hot flesh slapped against hers.

"Mine," he gritted out, unable to hold back the declaration any longer.

Jeanette didn't speak. As she pushed against him, joining in the rhythm of their beautiful dance, Hunter's mind splintered and broke apart, pleasure swamping him. He reached beneath their bodies and rolled her swollen clit. Soon her shouts filled the room. His cock swelled, balls drawing up tight. He flung his head back, slamming his hips against her once more, and came, hot jets filling the condom. He wished like hell he could fill her hot little ass instead, see his come dripping out of the tight, pink hole. In that moment Hunter had never hated condoms more.

Sweating and breathing as if he'd run a marathon, their bodies sticking together, Hunter's arms tightened around her. When Jeanette wiggled against him, he sighed and pushed away. As she turned over, a peculiar expression passed over her face, causing him to wonder at her train of thought. Was she beginning to regret what they'd done?

"You're amazing, Hunter."

Nope, no regrets. "You're pretty amazing yourself, sweetness."

She blushed. Even after everything they'd done, she still shied away from his compliments. "Thank you."

He touched his lips to hers, enjoying the sweet, strawberries-and-cream flavor of her. "You just screamed and came beneath me and yet you're still so polite," he wondered aloud. "I'll treasure the sight of you in that moment, little love."

That look came across her face again, so fleeting he wasn't sure he hadn't imagined it. "I should be going. It's getting late."

There was something in her voice, but Hunter couldn't quite put his finger on what. Determined not to dwell, he moved off the bed and reached out a hand. "Come, we'll shower together."

She took his hand and he helped her off the bed. When she grabbed for the black throw blanket, Hunter scowled. "What are you doing?"

"Covering up."

He tugged her away from the bed. "No. I like looking at you. Besides, I've already touched, licked and fucked every delectable inch of you. I think it's safe to ditch the shyness."

She glared at him. "Do you have to spell it out like that?"

He nudged her into the bathroom and turned on the light. "You didn't mind my dirty mouth when we were in bed."

"Well, we're not in bed now."

Hunter leaned down and kissed her. He'd never been that big on kissing but he couldn't seem to keep his lips off Jeanette. As he went to the shower, turned the knobs, and tested the water, he noticed Jeanette start to get a little antsy. He moved to discreetly dispose of the condom, then stepped into the tub and wagged his eyebrows. "Come on, sweetness, time to wash all those pretty curves."

When she stepped under the hot spray and closed her eyes, as if savoring the moment, Hunter moved, inexorably drawn by the wet, sensual woman. He let his hand wrap around the nape of her neck, directly over the little bruise he'd given her when he'd suckled and bit her. Jeanette's eyes darted open.

"What is it?"

His gaze shot to hers. "You have a bruise here." He stroked the spot with his finger.

Her hand flew to her neck. "A hickey?"

Water cascaded down her breasts and Hunter had to swallow back the need to go to his knees and worship her with his tongue and mouth. "Yeah, sorry."

She squinted up at him. "You don't sound sorry."

Hunter shrugged, his hand tightening before he forced himself to release her. "Fuck it, I'm not sorry. I'm glad you have my mark on you."

Jeanette looked him over. "You don't have my mark. That doesn't seem fair."

He angled his head, exposing the side of his neck. "I'm all yours, sweetness."

Jeanette took a step forward, pressing her breasts against his chest. Hunter wrapped an arm around her middle and pulled her in tight. She licked her lips and stood on her tiptoes. He couldn't take his eyes off her. She was the picture of seductive beauty.

At the first touch of her tongue, Hunter went rigid. "Suck, pretty baby," he urged.

Jeanette hummed against his skin, the vibration traveling straight to his cock. Her tongue swiped over him once more before she pressed her lips to his wet flesh and sucked. Teeth scraped over his pulse. Hunter let loose a vicious string of curses. Several torturous seconds later, she released him and stepped back, a pleased smile on her face. "There, now we're even."

"Yeah." The sound of blood rushing through his veins had obliterated his ability to think. How could one small woman so effortlessly drive him to his knees? He couldn't get used to his reaction to Jeanette. Lust was too shallow a word to describe the way he felt. A best-selling author and yet he couldn't put his own feelings into words.

Later for that, he decided. Right now he had a sexy, slippery female to lather up.

Hunter drove his motorcycle into the abandoned parking lot, Jeanette's small, stiff body behind him. She'd barely said two words after they'd showered. As he pulled up to the back door of her coffee shop, next to a little silver two door and shut off the engine, Hunter helped her off.

She unstrapped the helmet and handed it to him, then began to smooth the wrinkles out of her skirt. Hunter frowned. She wouldn't meet his gaze and it was beginning to piss him off.

"Thank you for . . . everything," she said, her voice soft, uncertain. "I had a wonderful time."

Thank you? Hunter hooked the helmet over the handlebars then flipped the kickstand down and stood. He closed the gap between them. "Talk to me, Jeanette. Did I do something wrong?" Unable to stand the distance, he wrapped his arms around her shoulders and pulled her in close. Damn, she fit him perfectly. It felt so fucking right to have her in his arms. Tension seeped out of him when Jeanette's slim arms slid around his neck. So easy and comfortable, as if they'd embraced like this a hundred times.

"Was it the anal sex? Did I hurt you, sweetness?" He held his breath, afraid he'd been too rough and hadn't realized it.

She shook her head and buried her nose into his T-shirt. He

held her tighter, unwilling to let her go until he got to the bottom of what had her so pensive all of a sudden. "Talk to me, baby. You're worrying me."

After what seemed an eternity, Jeanette pulled back and stared up at him, eyes brimming with tears. "I-I don't want this night to end."

His brow kicked up. "That's what's got you so quiet?" She nodded. Relief poured into his soul. "Baby, I told you from the start this wasn't a one-shot deal for me. I want to see you again. After work later, if you aren't busy."

"You really do? You're not just saying that?"

"I'm not stringing you along here, Jeanette. I want to spend time with you. Get to know you."

One corner of her lips kicked up. "We sort of skipped that part, didn't we?"

He chuckled. "Yeah, but I'm not sorry."

"Me either." Her gaze filled with tenderness.

Hunter patted her on the bottom before releasing her. "Come on, let's get your kitchen cleaned up so you can get a few hours of sleep tonight."

"You're staying to help?"

Hunter had no intention of leaving her alone at the café. It was a good neighborhood, but bad shit could happen anywhere. Still, he figured he'd keep that part to himself. "If I recall correctly, eating brownies and whipped cream off your hot little body was all my idea. So, yes, I'm staying to help."

She laughed and the soft, lilting sound went clear to his heart. "I wasn't exactly protesting, Hunter."

"No, you weren't," he whispered. He cupped the back of her head and held her still for his kiss. The instant his lips touched hers, his cock jerked. She moved against him and Hunter's kiss turned possessive, untamed. His lips forced hers open and his tongue delved deep. His fingers clutched her hair tighter before he traveled farther south. When he reached the bruise on her neck, he licked the little mark. Hearing Jeanette moan his name and hold on tighter brought him back to the here and now.

Hunter pulled back and released her hair. "If we don't stop this, we're going to get arrested for public indecency."

Jeanette laughed. "I wouldn't mind."

"Minx," he growled. Hunter forced himself to step away from her. "Come on, sweetness, we've got work to do." He entwined their fingers and started toward the back entrance, his mind already teaming with ideas for the night to come.

11

"You didn't answer either of our calls last night and that's not like you. So, spill. Where were you last night?"

Roni and Lydia had come into The Coffee Shop right before closing. They'd parked themselves at the counter and Jeanette knew they were going to pump her for details the instant she closed. They hadn't disappointed her. How much was she supposed to tell them? That she'd slept with Hunter? That he was coming for her tonight to do more of the same? Her feelings were so mixed up she didn't know which way was up.

Roni whistled low. "Oh, boy, you slept with Mr. Motorcycle Man, didn't you?"

Her face heated. "What makes you say that?"

"You turned red, dork," Roni said.

Jeanette slumped against the counter. "His name is Hunter Trace and I came so many times I lost count."

Roni and Lydia both cheered. Jeanette waited for them to finish before adding, "And now I think I'm in love with him."

The cheers stopped. When they were both silent for so long,

Jeanette said, "Well, don't just sit there! Help me figure this out!"

Lydia blinked as if she'd been staring at a strobe light. "Was this, like, your third date with the guy or something?"

They knew her too well. Sleeping around had never been her style. Usually she had to be in a relationship at least a month before heading to the bedroom.

"No. I met him yesterday. He came back after hours and before I knew it we were headed to his house. I rode his motorcycle." She groaned as she recalled what else she'd done. "And I let him videotape me."

Lydia's eyes bulged out. "Damn, really?"

"Really. And I forgot to have him erase the tape. What if he doesn't come back tonight like he promised? What if—" Suddenly Jeanette couldn't breathe and her face felt hot. Too hot.

Roni cursed. "I think she's about to hyperventilate. Lydia, get her a glass of water." Roni came around the counter and patted her on the back. "Breathe, Jeanette. Take several deep breaths, in and out."

Jeanette listened to the soothing tone of her friend's words. In and out, she reminded herself. After she had herself under control, she grabbed the glass of water Lydia had retrieved for her and took several sips. She set the glass on the counter. "Thanks," she muttered, feeling like the biggest fool.

"No problem. Now, tell us more about this guy," Lydia said. "What does he do for a living?"

"He's a best-selling author." She told them Hunter's pen name and Lydia squealed.

"I love his books! I have all of them on my keeper shelf."

"I know, some of them are mine."

"Oh, right. I need to get those back to you, huh?"

Jeanette shrugged. "Whatever. The thing is, Hunter and I didn't really get around to chatting about his career. The most I can tell you is that he's sexy as hell and likes to spend hours in bed." No way could she tell them what they'd done with the brownie and whipped cream. Every time she looked at the little table and the spot where he'd licked her to climax, her panties grew damp.

"So, you two got hot and heavy. If he promised to come back tonight, then what's the problem?"

"I'm so afraid he won't show. Why can't I learn to have great sex without getting my heart all tangled up?"

"Honey, you aren't built that way. You were close to marrying Richard, remember?"

"Richard Feltzer, and no, I wasn't close to marrying him. We dated longer than the others, that's all. I never contemplated marriage. He was too much of a stuffed shirt." She still remembered the way he'd climb on top of her to have sex. A few thrusts later and he'd be snoring into his pillow.

"Okay, but what makes Hunter different?"

"He's so sweet, so incredibly gentle. Attentive, too, as if he wants to know everything about me. But he has this rough side. Oh my God, it's so hot when he gets all wild and dominating."

Roni and Lydia looked at each other; both women wore twin grins. "Wild and dominating, huh? I like the sound of this guy." Roni paused, then asked, "So, you don't think he's coming back like he promised?"

Jeanette bit her lip. "He seemed so sincere." She glanced at the clock on the wall. "He said he'd be here at closing time. That was fifteen minutes ago." She still recalled the text message he'd sent her earlier. I MISS YOU, SWEETNESS. AND I'M HUNGRY FOR MY STRAWBERRIES AND CREAM. SEE YOU TONIGHT, HUNTER.

"Maybe he just got held up or something," Lydia said, her voice soft with concern. "He'll be here, sweetie, you'll see."

At that moment, Dean emerged from the kitchen. "Hey, pretty ladies."

Jeanette pretended to scowl at him. "Dean, I thought I told you not to flirt with my friends."

He winked at her. "But they're so hot."

"And they have really big strong boyfriends who would kick your butt if they saw the way you were looking at them."

He laughed. "Ooh, I'm shaking." He grabbed a to-go cup and filled it with his favorite, café mocha with an extra shot of espresso. "If you're done lecturing me, I'm taking off for the night."

"Fine, but don't forget to do that calculus homework," she reminded him.

He stuck his tongue out at her as he backed his way through the kitchen doors. "Don't worry, Mom, I'm on it."

Jeanette rolled her eyes and laughed. "Delinquent."

After he was gone, Lydia said, "He's such a charmer."

Jeanette agreed. "Just don't tell him that. He's much too cocky as it is."

"So, back to your multiorgasm-giving lover," Roni said, her eyes alight with mischief.

Jeanette started to say something when the chimes over the door jangled. All three of them looked over to see a tall, thin man wearing a heavy blue hoodie striding through. His hands were in his pockets, his eyes on the floor.

"I'm sorry, but we're closed." Jeanette had only left the door unlocked for Hunter.

The man pulled his hand out of his pocket as his eyes lifted. Jeanette paled. There was no mistaking the gun in his hand or the crazed expression on his face. "I'm not here for your damn coffee." He pointed the gun at the cash register and shouted. "I want your fucking money, bitch!"

Roni started to shift, but the movement caught the robber's attention. He swung his arm around until the gun was mere inches from her face. "Move and I blow your head off!"

Fear for her friends galvanized Jeanette into action. "You can have the money. Please, just don't hurt us."

"Then get it. I don't have all night!"

"The register has been emptied already. It's in the back, in my office."

"If you're fucking with me, I'll kill you."

"I'm not, I swear."

"Fine. Let's all take a little trip to the back."

Together, they moved through the swinging kitchen doors, the gunman at their back. Jeanette could feel the barrel pressed into her back. Her legs shook by the time she reached her office. Jeanette walked around the side of the desk, as she looked up, her gaze connected with the robber's wild blue eyes. "The money bag is in my drawer. I'm just going to reach into my pocket to retrieve the key."

"Fine, just fucking hurry!"

She reached into the pocket of her slacks and pulled out her keys. Her fingers shook so bad it took three tries to get the drawer unlocked. When she pulled out the money bag and held it out, the robber snatched it out of her hand and shoved it into the pocket of his hoodie. "Now give me the keys!"

Suddenly a dark figure appeared in the doorway. Jeanette's fear ratcheted up several notches as she watched Hunter place a finger against his lips in a bid for her silence. Jeanette started to hand the keys over. As the robber lowered the gun to grab them from her, Hunter sprang into action. He jumped onto the man's back and wrestled the gun away. The robber cursed and struggled, but his thin frame couldn't match Hunter's muscular build. Within seconds Hunter had the man pinned to the hard, tile floor, his hands behind his back.

Jeanette tore around the desk and shouted to her friends, "Call 911!"

Roni dug into the pocket of her blazer, pulled out her cell phone and started dialing. Lydia and Jeanette hugged, both speaking at the same time. "Are you okay?"

The man kicked and writhed, cursing a blue streak. Hunter pulled his arms harder. The robber, who'd just minutes before threatened to kill them all, started wailing.

"Keep it up, asshole, and I'll hogtie you," Hunter gritted out.

"The police are on their way," Roni said, her voice shaking with fear.

"Sweetness, why don't you three ladies head out to the front and wait for the cops. I've got dumbass here under control."

Jeanette didn't want to leave him there alone with the guy, subdued or not. When she heard sirens off in the distance, relief poured through her. "Go, baby," he urged. "He's not going anywhere, I promise."

"Come on, Jeanette," Roni said. "He's right, we should go wait for the police."

Jeanette sent up a silent prayer before leaving the office, Roni and Lydia hugging her close.

Hours passed before the whole ordeal finally ended. All of them had to give statements and the paperwork seemed to take forever. When Dane and Jake arrived at the police station to collect Roni and Lydia, Jeanette's composure shattered. As they all gathered at her car, tears filled Jeanette's eyes. Her two best friends in the world could've been killed and she would've been helpless to stop it.

"Oh, God." Her voice shook. "I was so afraid he was going to shoot us."

Hunter hugged her close, his voice filled with tenderness when he said, "I know, little love, but it's over now."

Roni patted her on the back with a trembling hand. "I can't believe how brave you were, sweetie. I nearly wet myself back there."

Jeanette swiped the tears out of her eyes. "Brave? I shook

like a leaf when he pulled that gun out." She held out her hand, palm down. "I'm still a mess."

"It didn't show though," Roni said. "You stayed in control; that's the important thing."

"Roni's right. You were a rock, honey," Lydia said from beneath Dane's arm. Jeanette noticed he hadn't let her friend leave his side since he'd arrived.

Jeanette looked up at Hunter. "I'm just glad you showed up when you did."

"Me too. Hell, I think I lost ten years of my life when I saw that asshole holding that gun to your face."

"I'm surprised the bells over the door didn't alert him though," Jake said as he pulled Roni into his side.

"Heck, *I* didn't even hear the bells," Jeanette admitted. "I think my adrenaline was pumping too hard."

"It's my guess he's a junkie in need of a fix. Your coffee shop was probably just convenient," Dane said as he rubbed Lydia's arm soothingly.

"That reminds me," Hunter growled, frowning down at her. "No more leaving the door unlocked after hours."

Hunter's protective attitude surprised her. Warmth chased away some of the fear that had assailed her since seeing the gun coming out of the pocket of the hoodie. "I didn't want you to be locked out. Besides, I wasn't alone."

"Yeah, well, I'll knock next time. And maybe you should consider an alarm system too." He dipped his head and kissed her. It was fleeting and tender and her heart skipped a beat. Jeanette smiled as she realized what he'd said. Next time, which meant he planned to stick around.

"Okay," she murmured, unable to resist the gorgeous man.

"Well, I'm beat," Roni said as she wrapped her arms around Jake's middle. "It's been a long night."

Lydia sighed. "No doubt." She came over for a hug and soon

the three of them were holding each other in a trembling embrace as they said their good-byes. "Call us tomorrow." Lydia winked. "We still have things to talk about. Remember, sweetie?"

Jeanette nodded, knowing they would want an update on her relationship with Hunter. As Hunter started to open the car door for her, a stray thought struck. "You called me sweetie," she said to Lydia. "Why does everyone always call me sweetie?"

Lydia laughed. "Because you always smell like caramel."

"No, it's vanilla," Roni corrected her.

Hunter ran his hand down her ponytail and shook his head. "Nope, you're both wrong. It's strawberries and cream."

Jeanette laughed. "One of the perks from owning a coffee shop, I suppose."

Hunter opened her car door and said, "Come on, sweetness, it's time to get you home."

Jeanette nodded. Once they were in the car, Hunter behind the wheel, she remembered he'd been nearly half an hour late for their date. "So, where were you tonight? I was expecting you at eight thirty."

Hunter reached over the middle console and took her hand, entwining their fingers. "It's a surprise," he whispered.

Jeanette's blood pressure spiked. "For me?"

He grinned. "Of course, for you. Who else?"

Her curiosity piqued now, she asked, "And are you giving me this surprise tonight?"

He nodded as he pulled onto the street leading back to her café. He'd left his motorcycle there when they'd had to go to the station to write up their statements. Jeanette's fatigue vanished. Her mind whirled as she imagined what he could possibly surprise her with when they'd only just met.

He drove into the parking lot and Jeanette's stomach fluttered when she spotted Hunter's shiny black-and-chrome cycle illuminated by the security lights. It was a powerful, well-built machine. Like its owner.

He parked next to the bike and turned off the engine. "Come on, I left it in the restaurant."

"You did?" How'd she possibly miss it?

"You were a bit distracted, sweetness," he said as if reading her mind.

She shuddered at the reminder. Hunter got out of the car and jogged around to her side and helped her out. He took her hand again. He did that a lot, she noticed, and she liked it. They walked to the front door and he handed her the keys. She let them in and Hunter leaned down. "Close your eyes, little love," he whispered against her ear. Jeanette let her eyes drift shut, her heart doing cartwheels.

He walked her forward when she grabbed onto his arm. "Hunter, you're driving me crazy."

"Almost there," he said, his hot breath fanning the flames of her mounting passion.

He maneuvered them around something, a table most likely, and Jeanette gripped his forearm tighter. "Where are we going?"

"Ah, there we go," he said, tugging them to a stop. "Now, open your eyes."

Jeanette opened her eyes. There, sitting on the table where they'd shared their first conversation, sat a sparkly red helmet. Wrapped around the back of one chair was a smaller version of Hunter's black leather jacket. Small enough for a woman. Jeanette picked up the helmet, then ran her fingers over the soft leather collar on the jacket. Her gaze shot to his. "Hunter?"

"It's for you," he explained, a hint of vulnerability in his expression. "So you'll have your own gear when we ride." Hunter reached out and turned the helmet. On the back, written in fancy white script, were the words LITTLE LOVE.

Jeanette's vision blurred. "Hunter, it's beautiful." She placed the helmet carefully on the table and went up on her tiptoes. "Thank you," she whispered as she pressed her lips to his.

Hunter groaned. His arms came around her, hugging her

tight as he deepened the kiss. He licked her lower lip and growled, "Baby?"

His rough voice had her pussy creaming. "Hmm?" she said, having a hard time focusing on the conversation with his scent filling her nostrils and his soft, firm lips a breath away.

"Can we please go back to my place now? I really want to talk about those fantasies of yours some more."

Jeanette pushed her fingers through his thick, dark hair and said, "I can tell you about this one fantasy I have. There's a blindfold . . . and a feather."

Hunter's gaze darkened as his hands skimmed down her back to cup her bottom. "You want me to blindfold you?"

"The blindfold isn't for me."

He stiffened against her. "Uh, sweetheart, I think it might be more fun if we—"

She placed two fingers against his lips, silencing him immediately. "You got your way with the camera, which we forgot to erase, by the way. It's my turn."

Hunter squeezed her buttocks, his cock a hard length between them. "You are so fucking hot."

In that instant Jeanette no longer felt like a pear-shaped wall-flower. She was a beautiful, curvy woman. "So you'll let me?"

Hunter kissed the tip of her nose. "Anything you want, sweetness. I'm yours."

Jeanette smiled. "Let's go for a ride, Motorcycle Man."

"Hell yeah," he growled.

Epilogue

Lydia looked out Dane's front window at the three tall, shirtless hunks standing in the driveway. They were drinking beer and oohing and aahing over Hunter's motorcycle. She laughed when Dane smoothed his hand over the chrome for the umpteenth time. "I've never seen Dane stroke something quite so much. Look at him. He's half in love with that thing. I think I'm jealous."

Roni snorted. "I wouldn't be at all surprised if Jake kissed it. He loves anything with pretty paint and a great engine."

Jeanette licked icing off her fork and said, "Hunter wants to buy me a motorcycle, but I don't know if I'm ready for that yet. I sort of like riding with him."

Roni's eyes bulged. "Damn, I'm still trying to get used to seeing you with that leather jacket and red helmet."

"This strawberry cake is heavenly, Jeanette," Lydia said as she took another bite of the sweet confection. "No one bakes like you."

"Thanks. Hunter likes it when I cook. He says I smell

yummy." She covered her mouth to stifle a laugh. "God, the man is insatiable."

"It's been a month since the bet," Lydia blurted out, as she put her fork down and stared at her two best friends sitting at the counter next to her. "So, who won?"

"That's a good question."

The comment came from the other side of the room. Dane stood there, his tan muscular chest and black swim trunks sending her libido into overdrive. The man had a body to rival the gods. His hot gaze ate her up. Lydia's stomach did a little flip, knowing what that look meant. When Jake and Hunter stepped into the room behind him, both grinning, Lydia knew they were in for trouble.

"Girl talk, fellas," Roni inserted. "Go back to admiring Hunter's sexy machine."

Jake crossed the room and took Roni into his arms. "I don't think I like you talking about Hunter's *machine*, princess."

"I'm with Dane," Hunter said, a mischievous grin on his face. He came over and pulled Jeanette out of her chair, then sat down with her perched on his lap before he continued. "I'm real curious who won that bet."

"Well, I fulfilled my fantasy first," Lydia said, "so I should win."

"No way, girlfriend. Your fantasy was a stranger. Dane wasn't technically a stranger." Roni smiled up at Jake and said, "that makes me the winner."

"Wait just a second," Jeanette piped in. Lydia watched her friend's cheeks turn pink when everyone looked over at her. "I fulfilled my fantasy, too."

Lydia crossed her arms and grinned. "You're right. But technically Roni filled her fantasy first, which means I have some help cleaning Roni's car."

Jeanette frowned as Roni tapped a finger against her lips. "And I'm going to expect it to shine, ladies."

Jake tugged a lock of Roni's hair. "Then again, maybe you should be disqualified, princess, considering you didn't come clean about the bet beforehand."

"I thought you were on my side," Roni grumbled.

"Always," Jake whispered, as he stroked a finger over Roni's lower lip.

"Come on, sweetness," Hunter said, kissing the tip of Jeanette's nose. "It's time for you to get into that red swimsuit I've been ogling. I want to see you all *wet*."

Jeanette smacked his chest. "Behave."

"Great idea," Dane growled, his lips kicking up at the corners. "I'm dying to see you in that little pink thing you bought last weekend. You've been teasing me with it all week."

Lydia stood. Jeanette and Roni followed suit. "I'll wear the pink two-piece, but you have to make me a promise first."

Dane narrowed his eyes and crossed his arms over his chest. "What do you want?"

"You have to help us clean Roni's car."

Dane cupped her chin, his voice dropping to a low whisper. "I'm going to expect payment then."

Lydia had a sudden visual of herself tied to Dane's bed. Her blood turned to molten lava. "That sounds fair," she said, her voice husky.

He leaned down and kissed her. It was much too quick and left her wanting. "Go on," he ordered, "before I forget we have company."

Lydia forced her feet to move. Out of the corner of her eye she saw Hunter petting Jeanette's bottom and Jake stroking Roni's hair. Once the three of them were in the guestroom, closed off from the men, Lydia leaned against the door and let out a breath.

"I don't care what anyone says," Roni said, as she threw her satchel onto the bed. "That bet was the smartest damn thing we've ever done."

Lydia looked over at Jeanette. They both grinned. When Lydia picked up the pink bathing suit, excitement raced through her veins and a sense of freedom washed over her. Knowing how Dane would react when he saw her wearing it sent a warm shiver down her spine. "Oh yeah, I'm definitely glad we made that bet."

Turn the page for a sizzling sample from

YES, MASTER . . .

Featuring three scorching stories by
Tawny Taylor, Anne Rainey, and Vonna Harper.

An Aphrodisia trade paperback on sale now!

1

"You want the truth?" Ruby shouted into the phone. "Because you have a small dick! There, feel better?"

Ruby cringed at the angry tone on the other end of the line. They'd dated for close to two months and Ruby still wasn't sure why she'd let it go on as long as she had. Bryan, like all the other men before him, just didn't light her fire. She was starting to wonder if there was something seriously wrong with her when she looked forward to having alone time with her vibrator more than she did a flesh-and-blood man.

As Bryan went from angry to downright mean, spewing out nasty things about her body, her job, even her mother, for crying out loud, Ruby pulled the phone away from her ear and clicked the END button. She placed the phone on the railing and let out a sigh of relief.

As she stood on the deck of her two-story home in the burbs and looked out at her freshly cut lawn, Ruby took a mental tally of the number of relationships she'd ended in a similar fashion. Okay, it wasn't a big number, thank God for that. Still, it made her wonder if she'd ever find a man capable of satisfying her. Hell, it wasn't as if her expectations were over the top. A nice guy with a good job would be welcome. A decent-sized cock and a cute smile would be a plus. Preferably someone who wasn't living in his mother's basement. So, why was it so hard to find Mister Satisfaction Guaranteed?

Pondering that ever-present question, Ruby lifted her glass and swirled the dark red liquid before taking a sip. It was good. Slightly pricey, but when she'd purchased it she thought it was going to be worth the money. It was Friday night and Bryan was supposed to be there celebrating with her. She'd finally landed the job as director of operations. It was a big deal, and yet she stood on her deck in the dark, alone. She should've taken her friend Carol up on her offer to hit a few nightclubs. Dancing and loud music would've at least taken her mind off her orgasm-starved body.

The sound of splashing water caught her attention, and Ruby looked to her right. Her neighbor, Drake South, and his latest sex kitten, had apparently decided to go for an evening swim in his pool. She rolled her eyes as the woman's naked breasts bobbed in the water. "Fake," she muttered as she watched the pair of lovers. When Drake caught the woman around the waist and pulled her up against his hard, wet chest, Ruby froze. Whoa, was he naked as well? It was too dark out and the water hindered her view of the lower half of his body.

Ruby had often wondered about the dark-haired hottie with the scruffy facial hair and the lightning bolt tattoo that traveled down his right bicep. He was big and muscular, not an inch of fat on him thanks to his landscaping business. His tanned body could make a nun drool. The harsh features of his face could never be considered handsome, but there was something primitive about Drake. Something rough and wild. It appealed to her on a level she generally chose to keep hidden.

Unfortunately, Drake lived life on the edge, and Ruby had always steered a wide path around him. She'd seen his type.

Her own father had been an adrenaline junky. He'd never taken life seriously. His need for adventure had eventually killed him. Ruby could still remember that moment as if it were yesterday. It'd been a perfect summer day. A nice breeze, warm sun shining down. She'd been twelve years old and already more of an adult that her father. She'd heard her parents arguing that morning right before her dad had stormed out of the house. He'd sworn to be home in time for supper. Only he'd never returned. Ruby had learned later that her father had died in a skydiving accident. Ruby's heart still ached when she thought of the sadness in her mother's eyes. The knowledge that it all could've been prevented had her dad stayed home that day. It still made Ruby angry enough to see red. Her father's drive for that next big thrill had been the only thing on his mind that day.

Ruby was the exact opposite of her dad. She prided herself on her well-ordered life. She had goals and was determined to meet them. She liked men who were responsible and stable. To Ruby, common sense was more attractive than empty promises. The Drake Souths of the world had no place in her world.

So, why was she watching him kiss a petite blonde as if it were his last day on earth?

Just then Drake's gaze lifted, and suddenly Ruby was caught in his snare. All the blood left her face. She froze in place, unable to look away from the heat in his eyes. Unable to do the right thing and go inside, giving the lovers a measure of privacy. Ruby clutched the deck railing and watched the erotic display playing out in the pool next door. When Drake lifted his head and his lips curved upward, Ruby's heart nearly stopped beating. Oh crap, he knew she was watching! Her pussy flooded with liquid warmth and her nipples pebbled. *Go inside. Simply turn around and walk away.*

Ruby didn't move. Could barely think as Drake lifted the woman to the edge of the pool and sat her down on the hard cement. As his head descended between her thighs, Ruby's own clit throbbed and her panties grew damp with arousal. "Ah hell, this is so freaking wrong," she mumbled as she let her hand travel downward to the hem of her black skirt. As she lifted the material and touched the soaked, silk panties beneath, the muscles in Ruby's legs quivered. At that moment, the blonde's legs widened and she let out a loud moan.

"Ah, screw it," Ruby said to herself. It wasn't the celebration she'd anticipated, but a live show was better than her vibrator, any day of the week.

Ruby was clearly out of her mind. "Do the right thing," she quietly scolded her inner bad girl. "Go inside and give the pair of lovers their privacy." The demand didn't do a bit of good, though. Instead, the fire sweeping over her raged wildly out of control. "Oh God, I'm going to hell," she whispered as she watched Drake, her neighbor, use his mouth and hands to pleasure his petite, blonde date.

The woman wrapped herself around Drake's large, muscular frame and moaned.

A niggling of jealousy crept over Ruby as she quickly took a step backward, slipping deeper into the shadows of her deck to keep from being seen. Drake titled his head back, his gaze unerringly seeking hers in the darkness and a forbidden thrill ran through her.

"He can't see me now." Ruby's breath caught in her throat. "Surely, he can't see me."

Ruby cupped her mound through the dampness of her panties and watched as Drake clutched the woman's hip in one hand, holding her firm while he smoothed his other hand up and down her bare, wet back. As his head once again descended between the blond woman's thighs, Ruby massaged and kneaded, running her fingers in little circles over her clit. In her mind, she imagined it was Drake's hands on her body. *His* fingers teasing and playing.

As she slid the silky material aside and touched the slick and swollen folds of her pussy, Ruby heard someone moan. Her eyes shot wide, wondering for a moment if the sound had come from her. When she saw Drake cover the other woman's mouth with a palm, Ruby relaxed once more.

"What the hell am I doing?" she muttered, even as she slipped a finger inside her overheated pussy. Her gaze took in the erotic sight next door and a rush of moisture trickled down her thighs. Drake mumbled something, but Ruby couldn't make out what. The woman spread her legs wider and arched her back. Ruby thrust her middle finger deep and her legs quivered. As the blonde pressed her pelvis into Drake's face, Ruby's heart raced. What would it be like to have Drake's undivided attention like that? To be on the receiving end of all that untamed male hunger? She suspected he would easily have her begging for him with the slightest effort. There was just something about Drake. It was part of the reason Ruby had steered clear of him. From the moment he'd moved in next door earlier last year, Ruby knew she wasn't cut out to handle him. He was too intense, too extreme for her tastes. She preferred a man she could keep at arm's length. Drake struck her as the type who wouldn't be content unless he was snug and warm under a woman's skin.

Suddenly Drake lifted his head, tilting it sideways, and once more Ruby could swear the heat of his gaze was scorching a path over her body. It was impossible, of course, she was too well hidden with her back pressed against the siding. A large walnut tree provided a decent amount of cover too. Between the distance, the tree, and the darkness, she knew he couldn't see her.

When Ruby slipped a single wet finger in and out of her slick opening, teasing gently, she flattened her other hand against the cool wall behind her, desperate for the support. She closed her eyes and an image of Drake filled her mind. Suddenly she pictured him thrusting his long, talented fingers in and out of her, stroking her to a fever pitch. She could almost feel the brush of his body against her sensitive nipples. Each erotic image brought forth a moan and Ruby had to clamp her lips closed tight to contain the eager sounds.

She used her thumb to flick her clit and a cry tore free. Ruby thrust two fingers deep, but it wasn't enough. She needed more. She wiggled a third finger inside her, and the snug fit caused her to widen her stance. She pumped hard and fast. Her husky groans turned sharp with desire. Ruby coasted her other hand down her body and fondled her distended clitoris. At once, Ruby flung her head back and burst wide open. Her juices soaked her fingers and her pussy clenched and unclenched, making her ache to feel the heavy weight of Drake's hard cock. It would feel good; she knew it in her bones. Drake would fill her. He wouldn't be like Bryan, content with a quickie in the dark. Drake would take her all night long. Fuck her until she couldn't stand up.

As her body relaxed, her pussy softening, Ruby pulled free and opened her eyes. The pool was empty, Drake and the woman gone. Ruby sighed and stepped away from the wall, feeling more alone than ever. "I need a man," she muttered. Once more, Drake's sexy smile slid into her mind. The way he'd stared at her just moments ago. Her fingers itched to touch his big, powerful body. Ruby's heartbeat sped up and she cursed. Why had she watched? She'd tortured herself and now she would never get the man out of her head. "It's going to be a long, lonely night." She turned and headed back inside. Another glass of wine, that was what she needed. It'd relax her and maybe, just maybe put her to sleep.

As she tugged on the sliding glass door, a sound from behind her caught her attention and she froze. *Please don't be Drake.* Ruby turned. "Bryan?" She frowned when she saw him stagger.

Was he drunk? Fear skittered up her spine. "What are you doing here?"

"Y-you hung up on me, Ruby."

Oh, he was definitely drunk. And pissed, judging by the ugly glare. His white-knuckled fists weren't giving her a warm cozy feeling either.

Wow, could her evening get any worse?

2

Drake watched Skylar back her little red coupe out of his driveway. After she was gone, he closed and locked his front door and shoved a hand over his face in disgust. "I'm fucking insane," he gritted out. Why else would he tell a hot blonde who was willing to do anything and everything he asked of her to leave before he could even get her to the bedroom? "I'm certifiable." Skylar had been more than willing to play with him the rest of the night. He could be satisfied fifty ways to Sunday instead of standing in the middle of his living room with his dick as hard as granite in a pair of soaking wet swim trunks.

Too worked up to sleep, Drake went upstairs and changed into a pair of old, worn jeans and a black tank. A few minutes later he headed into the kitchen and grabbed a beer from the fridge. That's when he knew the truth. Ruby was to blame for his hard-on. He popped the top and took a long drink, then slammed the longneck bottle onto the countertop. Ruby had been standing on her deck earlier. Watching. Drake had felt those baby blues of hers on him.

He smiled when he thought of how she'd hidden deeper in

the shadows, thinking she couldn't be seen. But Drake had known she was there. He could feel her. Unfortunately, the knowledge that she wasn't the one naked and in the pool with him had put a real crimp in his Friday night plans. It'd taken him all of ten seconds to realize that Skylar was nothing more than a substitute. He even knew why he'd chosen her from all the other women at the club tonight. "She was Ruby's exact opposite," he muttered. Short, petite, and blonde. Skylar had big brown eyes that weren't anything like Ruby's deep blue pools. The two women couldn't be more different. No doubt about it, Skylar was cute and eager, but she wasn't Ruby. Only his red-headed neighbor's voluptuous body would satisfy the ever-present ache that Drake had been living with for the last several months. The problem was, Ruby avoided him like the damn plague, and he was getting good and tired of it.

If he smiled at her, she frowned. If he said hello, she mumbled under her breath and stuck her nose in the air. Like a queen addressing a lowly peasant. Shit. No way in hell was he going to get a wink of sleep tonight.

He'd never get any peace of mind. Not until he had the snooty woman in his bed. Drake crossed the room and opened the back door. He wondered if she was still up. When Drake stepped out onto his deck and looked toward her house, his hopes plummeted. No movement at all.

Their houses were close enough together that if it were daytime he'd be able to see the dirt on Ruby's white siding. He'd noticed the almost totally unobstructed view of her entire backyard the moment he'd moved in. He'd been impressed with her well-groomed lawn and the flower beds she clearly took great pride in. He'd yet to spot a single weed anywhere. Last week she'd purchased a new patio set. When she seemed to have trouble putting it together, Drake had offered to help, seeing it as a chance to get to know her better. Then her asshole boyfriend had shown up and screwed with his plans. The pale little dweeb with his perfectly manicured nails and neatly pressed shirt had struggled for hours putting together the swing, making Drake wonder what the hell she ever saw in the guy.

The woman had the sort of curves a man drooled over, but she wasn't just a pretty face. She was smart and independent and ambitious as hell, judging by her work schedule. So why was she with the dweeb? He'd cursed and gotten nasty with her, and she'd put up with it. Drake groaned and rubbed at the sweat beginning to bead on his forehead. Midnight and still hot as blazes. August in Ohio sucked.

He closed his eyes and thought back over the one time he'd gotten more than a quick glimpse of Ruby's pretty curves. A little over two weeks ago, Drake had been lucky enough to catch the little beauty sunbathing. He'd spotted her through his kitchen window as she'd sprawled out on her lounger wearing the cutest little black bikini he'd ever seen. He'd stood there, unable to move, staring at her. Her round, lush bottom beckoned him to walk right over to her and grab a handful. Hell, even now Drake remembered the little white drops of sunscreen she'd dribbled on her skin. Drake couldn't figure out why she'd bothered to lie out to begin with. Ruby didn't have a tan. Her skin was way too fair, and probably too delicate. She'd burn to a crisp. Still, he'd sure as hell imagined how delicious all that creamy skin of hers would taste against his tongue. He wanted to lick every inch of her body just to find out if she tasted as good as she looked. Drake had enjoyed the view that day, but he'd vowed to stop torturing himself with fantasies of taking her to his bed. Which was why he'd brought Skylar home.

"Great plan, dumbass," he muttered as he stood alone in the dark, aching for a woman who didn't even know he existed.

He needed a cold shower. As he turned to head back in, movement from next door caught his eye. Someone came around the side of Ruby's house and stepped onto the deck. It wasn't Ruby. And judging by the way the person staggered, Drake would bet money that they also weren't sober. Suddenly Ruby came out of the shadows of the deck and Drake wondered if maybe she was meeting a man on the sly. Drake couldn't make out who the person was in the dark, but the larger frame definitely resembled a man.

When the guy stepped onto the deck and grabbed hold of Ruby's arm, Drake stiffened. She jerked away and started for the house, but the guy was faster as he grabbed Ruby around the waist, pulling her to a stop.

"What the fuck?" Drake muttered as he sprinted across his deck and hit the grass running. When Ruby yelped, Drake saw red. He'd break the bastard's hand if he hurt her.

"Bryan, I thought I made myself perfectly clear on the phone," Drake heard Ruby say. "You and I are through. You can't just pop up here in the middle of the night, as if you have the right."

Drake slowed as he reached the steps leading up to the deck, and listened as Bryan tried to talk his way back into Ruby's bed.

"Ah, you don't mean that, sweetie."

"Yes, I do," she bit out. "And don't call me sweetie. I'm not your *sweetie*."

Ruby was clearly pissed, and Bryan was drunk as shit. Drake had just about heard enough. He rushed up the steps as Bryan grabbed Ruby by the arms and tugged her up against him.

"Let go of me!" she yelled as she tried to wrench herself free.

Drake knew she was angry by the tone of voice, but it was the fear in her eyes that spurred him into action. He took hold of Bryan by the back of the collar and yanked him backward. "You heard the lady, Bryan," Drake bit out. "Get lost."

Ruby's gaze widened as she looked over at him. Unless he missed his guess, there was a huge dose of relief in those blue eyes too.

"Who the hell are you?"

Drake about gagged at the amount of alcohol on the guy's breath. "Do us all a favor, buddy, and shut the fuck up." He looked over at Ruby. "Do you want him to stay?"

She rubbed her upper arms and shook her head. "Definitely not."

Drake nodded. "Then you might want to call the law. I'm not sure it's a good idea for Bryan to get behind the wheel right now."

"Oh, of course!" She turned and ran for the back door.

"Fuck you," Bryan spit out. "I'm not going anywhere."

After Ruby was safely inside the house, Drake wrapped a hand around Bryan's wrist and squeezed. "Lay a hand on her again and I'll break it." Drake tightened his grip for emphasis. "We clear?"

"I wasn't going to hurt her," Bryan sputtered as he tried to pull free.

Christ, was he going to start crying? Drake had zero patience for drunks and even less for a man who would hurt a woman.

"You blew it with her. Time to move on." Drake dragged Bryan to the nearest chair and shoved him into it. He heard a siren off in the distance. "And Bryan?"

"Huh?"

"Don't come back," Drake warned.

The next hour was spent talking to the cops. Bryan mostly cried. Ruby barely looked at either of them. The few times that her gaze had strayed his way, a blush stole into her cheeks and she'd quickly glance away. Drake thought he knew why too, but he wanted to hear her say it.

Once they were alone, Ruby escorted him into the kitchen and offered to brew a pot of coffee. It was the olive branch Drake had hoped for, and he wasn't about to turn it down.

Once they were seated at her round, oak table, each of them nursing a hot cup of coffee, Drake found himself at a loss for words. Ruby was so quiet, and Drake was beginning to worry that maybe Bryan had meant more to her than he'd initially realized.

"Did you love him?" Drake asked, needing to know what he was up against before he moved any further on his campaign to get the woman in his bed.

Ruby's gaze shot to his. "Who? Bryan?" Drake nodded. "God, no. I'm not sure why it took me two months to break it off with him, to be honest."

"Then why so quiet?" Drake thought of the way she'd rubbed at her upper arms earlier and he frowned. "Did he hurt you when he grabbed you out on the deck?"

She shrugged and ran her left hand over her right arm. "Not really. I'll have a bruise probably, but I bruise easily."

Drake got up and came around the table. He crouched in front of her and took her arm in his, rubbing over the spot Bryan had grabbed. "That little shit," he ground out. "I should've hit him."

One corner of Ruby's lips kicked up. "No, then Bryan could've said you assaulted him or something. This way he gets to spend the night in a jail cell and you get to sleep in your cozy bed."

He grinned and went back to the chair he'd vacated. "You do have a point there."

"I'm sorry you had to deal with all this." He watched her look toward the other end of the kitchen. "God, it's one in the morning, you must be exhausted."

Drake shrugged. "I couldn't really sleep anyway."

Ruby's cheeks turned red and Drake knew immediately that she was thinking about the little interlude in the pool. "Oh, I, uh, I see."

Drake smiled. "What about you?"

"Me?"

"You're up later than usual, aren't you?"

"Oh, well, sort of. I was celebrating."

"Celebrating?" She'd been alone, hadn't she? What sort of celebration was that?

She nodded. "I got a promotion at work. One I've worked really hard for. It was a big night for me."

And yet she'd spent the evening alone. "Then Bryan had to go and ruin it, huh?"

She swirled a finger around the rim of her cup and Drake wished like hell that finger was playing with his cock instead. He tamped down on his overeager sex drive. A woody wasn't a good way to start off things with a woman as classy as Ruby.

"I was supposed to be celebrating with him actually."

Drake frowned, not liking the idea of her celebrating anything with Bryan. Or any other man, for that matter. "Then why were you home alone tonight?"

Her nose wrinkled. "I said some not-so-nice things to him when I broke it off with him on the phone earlier."

He chuckled and leaned closer. "Now this I've got to hear."

She shook her head. "No, you don't. It was rather crude."

"Now I definitely need to know."

"Well, I sort of told him he had a small—"

Drake held up a hand to stop her, not needing to hear the rest. "Ouch, no wonder the guy was wasted."

She snickered and slapped a hand over her mouth. "Oh God, I'm a horrible person."

"Hell, you ask me, he deserved it."

"No," she rushed to say. "He isn't really that bad. He and I just didn't click, that's all."

"So, you never got to celebrate."

She shook her head. "Not really."

Drake stood and carried his cup to the sink. He poured most of the contents down the drain, having only managed a few drinks. All his concentration had been on Ruby. When Drake turned, he caught her staring at him. She bit her lower lip, and Drake imagined what it'd be like to have the right to tug the plump flesh free of her teeth and lick the little sore she was creating there. *Quit stalling. It's now or never.* "How about you and I celebrate together then?"

Her gaze widened. "Huh?"

"I can pick you up tomorrow around noon. There's a little place that serves the best ice cream known to man." He crossed his arms over his chest and leaned against the counter. "Are you in?"

Ruby was quiet a moment, her gaze eating him up from head to toe. Finally she stood and crossed the room. This close, Drake could see the way her full breasts filled out the flimsy blouse she wore. Drake's mouth watered for a nibble. "Is this a date?" she asked, a frown marring her pretty features.

Damn, the woman was skittish. Drake crossed the little bit of linoleum separating them and cupped her chin in his palm, needing the connection. He was desperate to touch her. Every inch of her. "I'd like it to be, yes," he answered.

She shook her head. "I'm not sure that's a good idea."

Drake shrugged, uncaring if it was the smart thing to do or not. All he could think about was spending more time with her. "What do you have to lose?" he asked, hoping logic would sway her to his way of thinking.

She took a deep breath and let it out slowly before replying, "When you put it like that, how can I say no?"

"Exactly," Drake murmured. He suddenly felt as if he'd won the lottery. He dropped his hand, but before he left there was one other little matter to tend to. He leaned close and whispered against the shell of her ear, "I saw you tonight, by the way." Ruby gasped, telling him in a heartbeat that she knew exactly what he was referring to. Before she could attempt to recover, Drake growled, "It was naughty of you to watch, Ruby." He stepped back and their gazes connected. "Good thing I like naughty."

"Drake, I—"

"I'll pick you up tomorrow at noon," he said, halting her rushed explanation. "It's supposed to be a hot one, so you might want to wear shorts."

She nodded. "Yes," she replied in a shaky, quiet voice. "Okay."

"Sleep tight," he murmured, leaving her standing in the kitchen and staring at him as if she wasn't quite sure what to do with him. On the other hand, Drake knew exactly what he wanted to do to her.

As he reentered his own house, a shot of adrenaline sped through his system. Tomorrow he would take Ruby to lunch, but if the gods were at all kind, it'd be her delectable body he'd get to feast on afterward. "About friggin' time too." He'd ached for the woman long enough. It was high time to bring a few of his X-rated thoughts to life.